Praise for The Binding

"A gritty, hopeful narrative with emotionally rich characters. reminiscent of Margaret Atwood's classic, The Handmaid's Tale…"

Kirkus Reviews, Our Verdict: Get it

"Humming with urgency, *The Binding* carves a cleft into not just the imagination, but North American history and its evasive possibilities. Fraught with emotion and the layers of hurt laid down over generations, *The Binding* leaves the reader clutching a fragment of tentative hope in a world radically changed--and radically the same."

Marisca Pichette, Bram Stoker Nominated author of Every Dark Cloud

The Binding is a spellbinding story of a future world that is as full of danger and futility as it is of compassion and hope. Caldwell creates a fascinating alternate history populated with strong characters who are driven by their joint and separate visions to create a better world.

Libby Gill, Award-winning author of Malibu Summer

A gripping story set in a world that might have been, and a world that could yet be, rich with detail and rife with incident. Deft character work and intriguing worldbuilding grounds this suspenseful, political, and ultimately bittersweet story about identity, loss, and doing what it takes to survive. A rousing read.

Khan Wong, Lambda Literary Award Finalist, author of
The Circus Infinite and Down in the Sea of Angels

"In this nuanced portrayal of a continent split by an alternate history and a society ravaged by greed, *The Binding* takes the reader on a journey from hopelessness to hope, from alienation to community, and from loss to love. The ideas will challenge your mind while the characters capture your heart.

Jennifer Sherman Roberts, Amazon best-selling author of
The Village Healer's Book of Cures

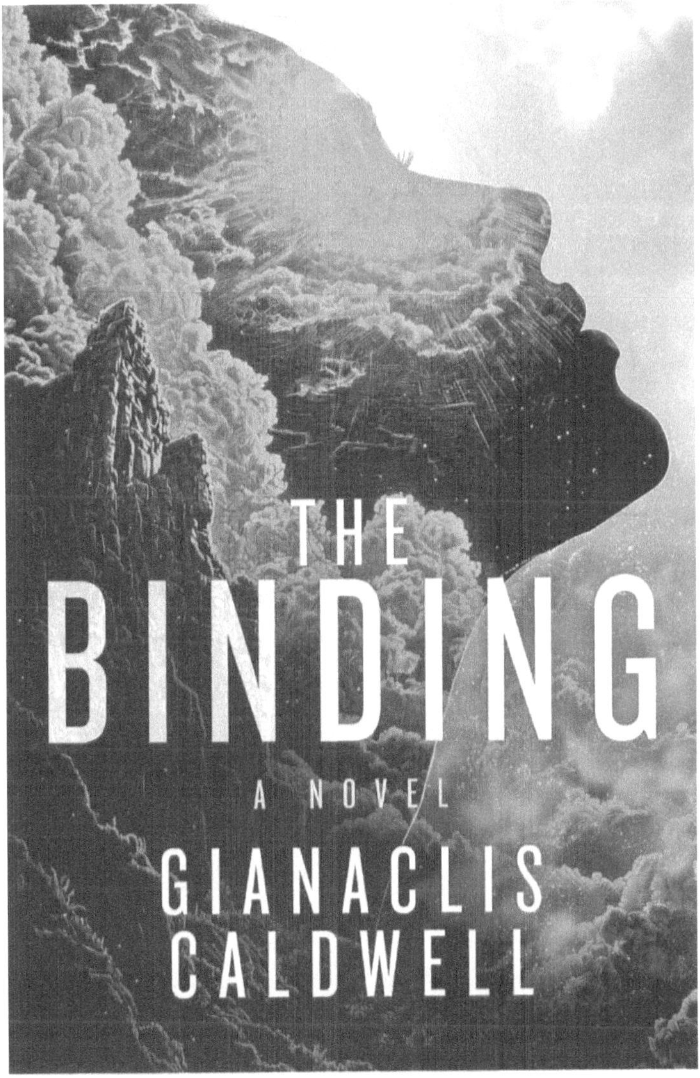

THE BINDING

A NOVEL

GIANACLIS CALDWELL

Grants Pass, Oregon

Cover design by Stuart Bache
Editorial by Kenneth Zink
Interior Design Gianaclis Caldwell

Library of Congress Cataloguing-in-Publication Data available

ISBN 978-0-9861907-2-8
eISBN 978-0-9861907-1-1
Audio ISBN 978-0-9861907-3-5

GC
Grants Pass, Oregon
gianacliscaldwell.com

For my dear mother and my friend Kara. You were both always there for me. I wish you were here now.

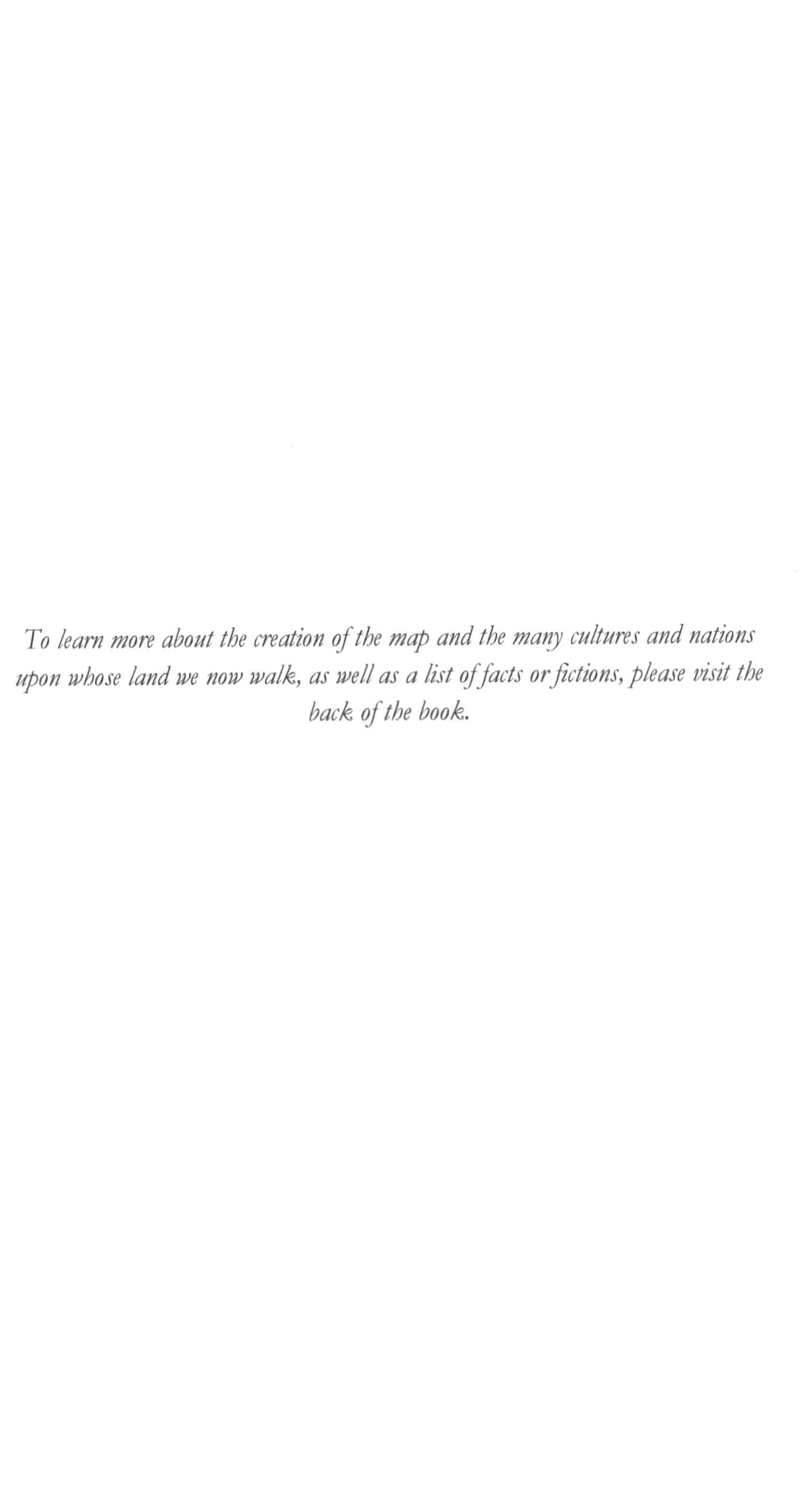

To learn more about the creation of the map and the many cultures and nations upon whose land we now walk, as well as a list of facts or fictions, please visit the back of the book.

The Royal Proclamation of 1763

"That Lands beyond the Heads or Sources of any of the Rivers which fall into the Atlantic Ocean from the West and North West, or upon any Lands whatever, which, not having been ceded to or purchased by Us as aforesaid, are reserved to the said Indians, or any of them."

Given at Our Court at Saint James,
the Seventh Day of October, One thousand seven hundred and sixty-three,
in the Third Year of Our Reign
George III
God Save the King

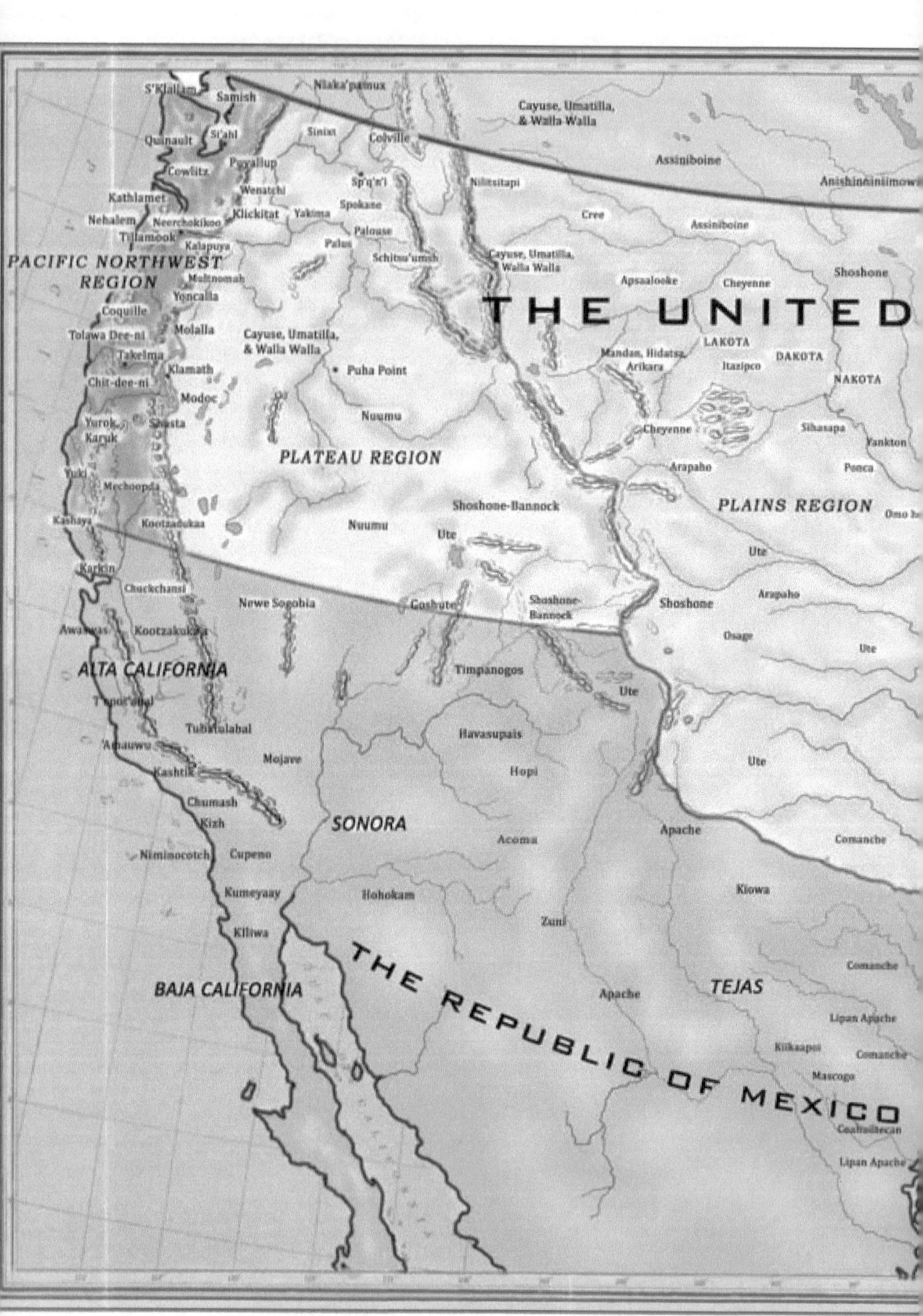

S'Klallam
Samish
Nlaka'pamux
Cayuse, Umatilla, & Walla Walla
Assiniboine
Anishinhiniimowi
Quinault
Si'ahl
Sinixt
Colville
Assiniboine
Cowlitz
Puyallup
Sp'q'n'i
Nilitsitapi
Cree
Kathlamet
Wenatchi
Spokane
Nehalem
Neerchokikoo
Klickitat
Yakima
Klamath
Palouse
Tillamook
Palus
Cayuse, Umatilla, Walla Walla
Apsaalooke
Cheyenne
Shoshone
Kalapuya
Schitsu'umsh
PACIFIC NORTHWEST REGION
Multnomah
THE UNITED
Yoncalla
Coquille
LAKOTA
Tolawa Dee-ni
Molalla
Cayuse, Umatilla, & Walla Walla
Mandan, Hidatsa, Arikara
DAKOTA
Takelma
Klamath
Puha Point
Itazipco
NAKOTA
Chit-dee-ni
Modoc
Yurok
Shasta
Nuumu
Cheyenne
Sihasapa
Yankton
Karuk
PLATEAU REGION
Arapaho
Ponca
Yuki
Mechoopda
Shoshone-Bannock
PLAINS REGION
Omo ha
Kashaya
Kootzadukaa
Nuumu
Ute
Ute
Karkin
Goshute
Shoshone-Bannock
Shoshone
Arapaho
Chuckchansi
Newe Sogobia
Osage
Ute
Awaswas
Kootzakukwa
ALTA CALIFORNIA
Timpanogos
Ute
Trupor'etjal
Ute
Tubatulabal
Havasupais
'Amauwu
Mojave
Hopi
Kashtik
Ute
Chumash
SONORA
Kizh
Apache
Comanche
Niminocotch
Cupeno
Acoma
Kumeyaay
Hohokam
Kiowa
Kiliwa
Zuni
BAJA CALIFORNIA
THE REPUBLIC OF MEXICO
TEJAS
Comanche
Apache
Lipan Apache
Kiikaapoi
Comanche
Mascogo
Coahuiltecan
Lipan Apache

KANATA
WEST
Metis
Cree
Anishinaabe
Anishinabewaki
Chippewas
Mississauga
Mohawk
Houlton
Bangor
Lewiston
Rockland
Concord
Portland
ewakanton
Menomomoinies
Wyandot
Haudenosaunee
Springfield
Boston
Sacs & Foxes
Odowa
Petun
Albany
Hartford Providence
Wahpeton
Sauk
Onodowaga
Ioway
Millioki
Winnebagoes
Miamis
Shikaakwa
Erie
Osage
Allentown
New York
Trenton
Potawatomi
The Great Swamp
Lenape City
Philadelphia
NORTHERN WOODLANDS
REGION
Kickapoos
Great Gathering SS
Shelter Rocks
Enclave
Denton
Ihwero
Chalagawtha
Washington
Niuachi
Patawotomi
Kickapoo
Myaamia
Werowocomoco
Sauk &
Fox
Tutelo
Lynchburg
Richmond
Otoe-Missouria
Shawnee
Cherokee
Niuachi
Yuchi
Raleigh
awakoni
Osage
Shawandasea
Tula
Choto
Waccamaw
Sitiki
Enclave
Morgantown
Fayetteville
Kaskaskia
Koasati
Charlotte
Wilmington
Ogaxpa
Yuchi
Miccosukee
Greenville
Columbia
Chickasaw
Chickasaw
Coosa Enclave
Charleston
SOUTHERN WOODLANDS
REGION
Muskogee
Coosa City
Yamacee
Caddo
Chickasaw
Hitchi
Guale
Port Tomochichi
Choctaw
Muscogee
SEMINOLA
Natchez
Alabama
Hitchi
Muskogee
Choctaw
Pensacola
Natchitoches
Chatot
Timucua
Coushatta
Avoyel Koroa
Pascagoula
Apalachee
Opelousan
Acolapissu
Atakapa
Chawasha
Akokisa
Chitimacha
Seminole
Houma
Tocobaga
GULF OF MEXICO
Mayaimi
Mascogo
ATLANTIC STATES OF AMERICA

Part I
Deceptions

Beyond the Great Sunrise Water, there lived a people who had iron, and those dirty and unnatural things, who seethed with diseases, who fought to death over the names of their gods! They had so crowded and befouled their own island that they fled from it, because excrement and carrion were up to their knees.
They came to our island.

Tenskwatawa, the Prophet (1775-1836) Shawnee,
brother of Tecumseh

1
Ruby Roth

Bound

She will come to think of her youth as a time when she believed that just the right question would unlock the secrets of her past. So many mysteries, so many questions. They hang unanswered, links in an unseen chain growing heavier with time.

On this dark morning in the May of her twenty-third year, the only question Ruby is asking is will she make it to work on time?

A clock sits on a shelf in the boxy room of the run-down motor lodge where she lives with her grandmother. It ticks. The numbers glare.

Ruby struggles into the rough fabric of her hatchery boilersuit and drags the long brass zipper to her throat. Like the clock, like her conscript ID, like the boilersuit, everything is pale blue. Conscript-class blue. CC blue.

It's a color she knows used to be that of the sky.

A moan comes from the pile of old quilts hiding her grandmother's wisp of a frame.

The numbers on the clock flip. *Late, late, you're going to be late.*

Ruby steps quick and soft across the fraying floor of the second-story flat. Another groan rises from the quilts. The blankets lift and rustle; the squares of faded patchwork shift and slip to one side. It's a quilt her gram sewed a long time ago. A shock of urgency shoots through Ruby; she's been waiting, waiting for her grandmother to rally, to be willing to answer a few more questions. But what if it's too late? What if she'll never learn the origins of the piecemeal squares? Is that fading pea-green bit of wool maybe from a coat that belonged to her long-dead father? And what about the single square, the only one of its kind, the one where if you pry open the stitched seam spreads a gash of deep pink? Ruby's always been sure it once made up a section of skirt or dress or blouse from the mother of whom no one will speak.

Her gram's moan slides up to a wail. It's a hammer inside Ruby's head. Pounding, pounding, hard and true down to the lowest reaches of her gut. And just for a moment, Ruby forgets. Just for a moment, she lets down her guard, lets her grandmother's pain reach out and bind her to the agony in the old woman's body.

Gram's voice comes wobbly and frail, but still somehow cuts through the air like the slash of a willow switch. "You're doing it. Ain't ya, girl?"

Ruby drops her hands to her sides. Tries to rip away from the connection with will alone.

"Using the binding, even after all these years. Girl, ain't I done enough to teach ya right?"

Fast comes the memory of the willow switch on Ruby's legs, her back, her bottom, each blow landing like punctuation, Gram's words cutting deep: "The binding is bad. The binding hurts everyone around you." Standing here now, a grown woman working to keep what's left of her family together, Ruby feels like a child again—as if Gram is rising from her pallet, trying one more time to beat the binding from the girl she got stuck raising.

A scream sticks in the back of Ruby's throat. She wants to shout at the old woman, *I do try! I do. The last thing I want is to feel the pain of others.* Instead, she bites her tongue until blood tips it with the distraction of copper and iron.

"Hold on, Gram, I'm getting your pills." Her voice is flat, anger deflating her of compassion. But another woman's words slip into the compressed space:

It is pain, Ruby. It is pain which sharpens your grandmother's burden. Your own burden, dear one, is to forgive her.

Sister O: the wise woman from the West, as Ruby thinks of her. As old as Gram, but you'd never know it. Now, the woman's advice fills her.

She grabs the pill bottle and a chipped mug, then goes to the table holding their big filtering unit. Suddenly, her empty stomach spasms. Did she forget to take the unit to the community spigot last night? Her memory of the evening before is blank. But a trickle of clear water threads into the cup, a burp of air chugs inside the chamber, and her gut unknots. As the mug fills, she rests a hand on the polished whorls of the table's tightly joined boards. It's perfect, this thing, except one small square bit, about midway, where the seams holding the pieces have come apart, just a little. Ruby often finds herself drawn to this one broken piece. It entrances her, this proof of imperfection.

"Hurry now, I need my pills. Need 'em bad." Gram tries to rise to a sit, her yellowed eyes wide with the effort. It's her liver, the McComb Corp docs told Ruby. Doomed, they said, from an early age—from growing up in the years *before*, back when everyone thought chlorine tabs and boiling was enough.

"I have them. Hold on, Gram." Kneeling beside her, Ruby tips the bottle. The last two pills tumble from the upturned container. A wave of fatigue crashes over her; she'll have to stop in town after her long shift. But she takes a deep breath and reminds herself that going to the Outreach for medicine will at least mean seeing Sister O, the Elohi monastic who, in some ways, has been another grandmother to her.

She's torn from this moment of pleasure by the sound of an engine outside the old motor lodge. Lifting the corner of the ragged curtain over their single window, Ruby sees a dark pickup crouching there. A waft of exhaust trails up in the dim light of the coming dawn.

Her grandmother shuffles and groans beneath the quilts. She mutters, to herself perhaps, but Ruby cringes at the words. "Damn girl. Damn curse. Stop. Don't let it get you."

There's a clack from the wall. Numbers flip. *Late. Late. Late.*

Before Gram grew sick, Ruby was never late, not once in the six years since she began fulfilling her life-contract. But now it's the reason their cupboards are almost empty. It's the reason her stomach almost constantly growls in hungry protest. A second violation in less than a month might mean something worse than withheld food vouchers.

Gritting her teeth, she finishes settling Gram for the day. Just as Ruby's ready to leave, a whimper slips up through the floorboards from the flat below. Her insides wilt. A sadness, for the cry comes from the young boy below, who's as close to a little brother as can be. He's dreaming something, something bad.

Pulse racing, she grabs her satchelpack and hurries from the flat. The pickup is gone, but a sense of something being not as it should hangs dense in the morning air.

At the lower level, Ruby's heart tugs her to a halt. Just a few doors away are Harold Sr. and his boy, Little Harold. Every part of her yearns to check in, to hold the growing boy to her, to do something to keep him safe. But then above, a door slams. Ruby jumps, slings the satchelpack over her shoulder, and runs for the omnibus stop.

She's rounding the last corner of the quarter-mile stretch between the old motor lodge and the stop, her lungs burning, legs aching, when she sees twin brake lights through the carpet of fog. For a moment, her body floods with relief. The omnibus is still there. She's going to make it.

But then the lights dim and her only chance of getting to her shift on time, of avoiding the punishment that will come, accelerates away.

Colin Tate

For a moment, Ruby is frozen in place. She feels nothing, but there's no comfort in that. Her heart begs her to turn around. To go back and wash Gram's quilts, tend the bedsores on the woman's bony hips, even, maybe, spend time with Little Harold. The price of not showing up would tower over simply being late. She'd risk being turned out, of being set adrift, of being made worse than the lowest caste in the country. No, moving away from those she loves is her only real choice. Denton's three miles away, and the hatchery another two north of that. If she hurries, there's a chance she might make it to the transfer station in time for a different omnibus to the hatchery: still late, but at least not absent. So, she sets out, her footfalls sounding oddly soft in the dark morning, like it's just a casual stroll.

A touch flutters gentle ghost fingers on her shoulder. She turns, squints into the dark. But there's nothing there. For a moment, she thinks she hears a whisper, the voice soft and sweet and sounding a bit like Little Harold. Like HJ, as he's so recently insisted she call him.

Something's happening to the boy, something beyond just growing up. Ruby's felt a change in him and the growing anxiety of Harold Sr. Just two nights ago she was out back of the motor lodge, pushing their rubbish into the big burn pit, when Harold Sr. joined her.

After a moment, with Ruby moving more slowly, certain the older man was trying to muster the courage to speak, he said, "Ruby, there's somethin' I been meaning to tell you." Harold was using a long rake, the tines worn almost to nubs, to push some burnt ends of waste further into the thick mess. A wave of smoke plumed up at the disturbance. Ruby was glad for the distraction, relieved for an excuse to not meet the man's eyes.

"It's 'bout my boy," he said. Ruby's heart seemed to skip a beat. Here in the Atlantic States, bad things happen to good people, little kids especially. Getting older didn't mean one got used to it.

"He all right, Harold?"

"Oh sure, he fine, body-wise. Boy's growing and starting to scare me with how soon he's gonna be, well, you know." He cleared his throat. "Of working age." Harold Sr. was a plainspoken man, but the last three words were drowned with dark meaning.

"You see, here's what I think. He been dreaming a lot. Not just the usual though. A whole nother thing. Maybe akin to what you got? You know, that *thing* you do?"

Ruby thinks of this now as she's running toward a place she doesn't want to be. Harold Jr.'s having dreams. Dreams that sometimes come true, so his daddy says. Then another thought comes to her, a way to make something positive of this day: Maybe Sister O at the Outreach will know what Ruby should do. Ruby can help both HJ and his daddy. It's been something she's been trying to do since even before Little Harold was born, but guilt, she's learned, is about as hard to lose as the micro-ID in her arm.

Twenty minutes later, the eastern sky is a smutty yellow, the rising sun doing its best to burn through the ever-present wall of haze sitting over the Eastern Shore. Sweat stings her eyes as she jogs past another old motor lodge, a cousin of the one they live in, with a crumbling brick façade and peeling white columns at the corners. Just past that sits a rambling structure that used to be a self-storage facility. Like the motor lodges, all are now McComb Corp conscript housing.

She's over halfway to Denton, panting and coated in sticky sweat, when from behind comes the low rumble of an engine. Her mind jumps to the pickup from earlier, and her heart leaps to her throat. Her steps turn stiff as she fights the urge to run or dive behind a curtain of kudzu draping some forgotten relic from before.

The growling grind of tires against tarmac slows to a crawl behind her. A knot bunches in her throat and it's hard to breathe, but she doesn't turn. The engine thrums. The car pulls alongside. The knot loosens a little when she sees it's not the pickup from earlier, but the fact it's a McComb Corp micromulti isn't good either.

The window slithers down, and Ruby's stomach sinks. Colin Tate, the hatchery assistant manager, sits there in a suit, silvery gray with the kind of sheen that looks like corp class, but the lime-green ID badge of a free-worker hangs around his neck. One arm rests on the steering wheel, the other on the edge of the door. He smiles, flashing polished white teeth, too evenly spaced, out of place in the gray morning. Out of place grinning at her.

"Ruby Roth. Looks like you're about to get lucky."

She forces herself to nod and keeps walking.

"What I'm saying is get in. I'll give you a lift. Don't want you being late again, now do we?"

Ruby swallows. A grimy, slippery fist grabs at her insides, gives them a twist.

"Come on. Don't make me give you an order." He laughs the kind of laugh that doesn't invite a smile. "Get in."

For a moment, Ruby does nothing but keep walking. She's never expected much from life as a conscript. But just now, with her boss sitting there in his shiny suit, she feels a bit more of her free will fall away, like it's being whittled down to something others can shape to their own needs. It burns, this bending, sets sparks and flames through her in a way that almost makes her feel like she can set fire to this whole place.

But she quenches the urge, nods, and gets in.

The Ride

The cluttered details of the Eastern Shore slip past, clarifying and sharpening as the sun pushes up. In the micromulti, it only takes a few minutes to reach the outskirts of Denton. Here, on the western edge, a shantytown of the adrift sprawls over vacant lots and the nubs of old foundation walls. It overflows with folks who've been turned out, shunned, and now live with only the meagerest of what can be scratched up or begged. The shantytown sprawls out, a giant patchwork of undulating canvas, slabs of rusty roofing, and reclaimed cardboard stitched tight. Every day it gets a bit bigger, a bit more like a kind of living thing. There's a sour odor that seeps through the micromulti's closed windows. The smell knots Ruby's stomach, but she's grateful, for it helps distract her from the sadness spilling from the place. Passing the town is like a lesson from Gram. Ruby can almost hear her saying, "See girl, the binding, it does nothin' but bring pain. Your daddy, he let the feelings of others take him over, lead him by the nose like he some kind of dumb beast. It's that what got him killed. Didn't do nothin' but hurt me—you too, it gets down to it. You think you the only one hurtin' when you bind to others' feelin's? Well, that ain't so."

Colin Tate lifts a kerchief to his nose. Ruby catches the scent of flowers. Lilies, she thinks. "Someone," he says, "should do something about these leeches. Just look at what they're doing to this place." His words puff out the dainty fabric of the kerchief. He glances over, catches her staring. "Don't give me that look. You think I'm the same as back then? Everyone changes, Roth. Everyone can be someone better."

Ruby puts her eyes back on the passing landscape. Change. He's right of course, but she doubts he's changed in the ways she has. He's the one climbing the ladder from free-worker up. She wonders how many backs he's put his feet on to get there.

The car slows near the far edge of the shantytown. Ruby tries not to stare at two Shepherd officers stalking the fringe of tents, slapping their zap-crooks on their open palms. Without warning, they pounce on a tattered-looking man, legs sticking from his lean-to and partly blocking the sidewalk. Ruby closes her eyes quickly, but it's too late. Electricity burns through her legs like fire as the Shepherds bring their zap-crooks down on the poor man. She grits her teeth with such force, she's certain a tooth will crack. But the tactic works, and like a tide creeping out, the agony of the poor man fades from her body and mind.

A few minutes later, they're through Denton, heading north toward the hatchery. At last, Ruby settles into the cushiony comfort of the passenger seat and rubs her jaw. Glancing again to the side, she takes in Colin Tate's profile. Waves of brown hair pushed behind his ears, cowlicks lifting from his haughty forehead. He still looks like the Colin she knew when she was young. The Colin Tate she once mistook as a friend.

They've just crossed a small bridge over one of the Choptank River's myriad tributaries. Though it's choking with debris and shiny with oil-slick water, it holds fond memories for Ruby, having hunted and foraged out this way when she was young. Now, those years seem impossibly long ago. She wonders if the Colin Tate sitting here recollects anything of that time. And with that, her memories turn rancid. There is so much she wishes she could, if not go back and do it differently, at least forget, let the weight of her wrongs sink into the muck of the backwaters, be forever buried.

"You know, Roth," Colin says, startling Ruby, "you're the kind of worker that's got a future—if you know where to look, that is." They've reached the hatchery, and he pulls into the worker entrance. "We all can't make it to the top, of course." His voice has a puffed-up sound to it, making Ruby picture a tom turkey strutting before something shiny, impressed with its own reflection. "But there's still room for reasonable ambition, even at your level. Capeesh?"

There's a long pause. A bubble of something pushes into Ruby's throat, and she finds herself muffling an urge to laugh. But it bursts and fades when he adds, "I remember how good you can be at getting what you want. We made a good team, back then, back before you got all high-and-mighty. We could again."

Ruby knows she should feel relief at arriving before the clock runs out, but acid slips to the back of her mouth. A good team. His words dredge up the things she wants to remain buried. How can he remember the same things so differently? They'd never been a team. She'd just been stupid, letting him lead her into mischief for the sake of humiliating others.

Saliva and bile pool in her mouth. It's all she can do to not spit on Tate's shiny shoes. What would it be like to just once react, to not have to always think about the consequences? Instead, she swallows.

Colin laughs again. It's a low chuckle this time. One she's heard before. "I want you to keep what I said in mind… in the days to come… should the situation arise." Then his voice pitches up. "Well, I got you here on time. Look at that, will you? The omnibus you missed is just pulling in. Guess you owe me now."

The New Shepherd

Ruby fumbles with the door latch, flings it open, and almost falls out. Once her feet are firm on the tarmac, she moves away from the micromulti, trying to walk with a nonchalance she doesn't feel.

"Don't forget what I said, Roth." She hears his chuckle as the vehicle pulls away. As soon as it's out of sight, Ruby lets her hands fall to her knees, bends forward, and sucks in air. When she stands, her eyes catch a patch of dark blue in the carpark. She blinks. But it's still there. A Reo pickup of midnight blue. Her skin prickles with recognition.

Then her well-trained feet pull her into line with the other blue-suited conscripts flowing into the building. Each holds their right forearm extended, boilersuit sleeve cuffed to the elbow, exposing a small scar beneath which a micro-ID hides. A Shepherd stands at the entrance as usual. Ruby keeps her eyes lowered and shuffles forward with the others of her class. Today's Shepherd officer is new. He stands with his feet wide, forearms crossed, wearing the standard-issue uniform of the Shepherds: a deep matte black uniform with bloodred piping running arteries around the edges. At his hip, like all domestic enforcement specialists, hangs the wicked curve of a zap-crook. His name badge says, *Downs, B.* Ruby sneaks a look at his face: strong chin and nose, sharp cheekbones, pale blond hair. He looks up and locks eyes with her. In the moment before she jerks her gaze away, she gets an unsettling feeling of familiarity. And there's a whole nother thing, as if even if she tried to use the binding, nothing would happen. He's a blank of emotions, a wall of stone.

"Arm," Downs, B says. Ruby feels his eyes sliding over her.

She clenches her jaw and places her bare forearm under the BrandScan's eye. A flash of red, then blinking green.

"Proceed, Ruby Roth." The Shepherd's voice is high-pitched, and she's almost certain she's heard this man's voice before. Long ago. Maybe.

Inside the hatchery, the day shift scurries into place, early arrivals scrambling to the end of the long black conveyor belt that's already slapping and snapping along. The best spots are at the end, where healthy chicks that have passed inspection tumble into waiting crates. Once filled, workers slide the container onto a second belt, where it's whisked off to shipping, then stacked, loaded, and transported to one of the McComb grow farms. Ruby slips into one of the last slots at the beginning just as the carts of hatch trays begin arriving from the big incubation room. She tries to disconnect, to not think, to not feel. She goes to work, sorting the newly hatched chicks, their little bodies littered with bits of shell sticky with wet membrane. Her gloved hands close around any weak and malformed hatchlings and do what she's expected to do.

A floor supervisor makes the rounds, a radio crackling at her shoulder. The Shepherds don't bother patrolling inside. If they're needed, they'll soon enough know.

The first tray of chicks seems vigorous and ready to face their short future as one of the biggest moneymaking products of the Delmarva Peninsula. A slim part of Ruby thinks maybe this will be a special day. But it doesn't last. As time flies by with no chance to even look up, the muffled peeps from the kill bin at her side grow louder. She despises the way her black-clad hands toss the little bodies aside like their lives don't matter. Sometimes, most of the time, she tries to pretend those gloved hands belong to someone else.

Nine long hours later, including the one break to eat the corp-provided bowl of Cham stew while the National Show blares propaganda from a giant screen, the shift-change klaxon again sounds. Eyes watering with tears of relief, Ruby stretches her aching back and rubs her sore jaw, then follows the other workers into the locker rooms. For the first time since this morning, she allows herself to think about her visit to the Elohi Outreach. It feels again as if she can breathe and stop trying to stay afloat, like a life raft is drifting at last within reach.

The Elohi Outreach

Ruby takes the omnibus back to Denton and arrives to find a raggedy marching huddle of protesters in front of the building that used to be, back before, a fabric store. Most of them hold a placard at half-mast as they march in a circle. Some are in the lime-green boilersuits of the free-worker class or personal clothes, their lime-green IDs swinging with each step. But a few wear CC blue. It confounds her, the reasons these people gather. Surely she's watched the very same broadcasts on the McComb lunchroom radiovision as they have. The National Show is, after all, the only station the corps play for the workers. Everyone has to listen as Chairman Powell, or one of the other national board members, rails on about how much he cares for the hardworking citizens, how the work shortage is a direct result of oppression from the West. But just how people swallow this as truth makes no sense to her.

Now, their stares follow Ruby as she heads for the door, their judgement both repellent and magnetic, as if they hate her, but also want her to join them. As she steps through the entryway, she passes the banner whose words she knows by heart.

The Elohi Order: Serving others to ease and prevent suffering.

When she was old enough to read, Sister O had answered Ruby's question about the banner. "Oh, yes, dear one. It means we Elohi monastics strive to treat suffering when it is manifest—present—but also, and even more important, we hope to prevent such suffering through education and opportunities."

Ruby had puzzled over this for a few moments. "You mean like the books here that show us better ways of doing things?"

Sister O nodded. "But ultimately, we want to change the hunger of the species from one of greed to gratitude, for it is seeking and desire that are truly the rootstock of all suffering."

Now, as she steps past the evidence of such suffering in the people outside, a sense of something she can only think of as "home" almost smooths away the ragged edge of the day. A small bell chimes as the door swings in. Brother Q's head appears from behind the shelves of one of the aisles.

"Well, hello!" Brother Q is much younger than the other two monastics, Sister O and Sister M. Unlike the women, Brother Q arrived only a year ago, showing up right about the same time Gram got sick. Like the other monastics from the West, he's dressed in the colors of the Elohi Order: a reddish-brown headwrap, a matching long-sleeved shirt with brass buttons up the front, and long, loose-fitting trousers. His eyes are a startling green, reminding Ruby of the kelp she saw washed up on the banks of the Chesapeake during her one visit to the mouth of the Choptank. But there's something beyond the color that has, from their first meeting, unsettled her. Like the new Shepherd, Downs, Brother Q seems to hold a barrier over his emotions. But unlike the Shepherd, the monastic lets something through, something warm and caring and safe. But in turn, he seems to see into, and even through, Ruby.

"Greetings, Ruby." Sister M pops up from the treatment area along the far wall, where the monastics offer the vaccinations, supplements, medications, and treatments allowed by the ASA. About Ruby's height, only the top of Sister M's head is visible. Ruby smiles, then looks back at the front doors to the protest scene outside.

"Do you think it's all right to bother Sister O?" Ruby stands on the other side of the display as she asks Brother Q, pushing up on the balls of her feet and trying to force herself to hold his gaze.

"Of course. Go on in, Ruby Roth." She feels a blush. The sound of her name coming from his mouth sends strength into her tired muscles. It does something completely opposite from when Colin or the Shepherds say her name. She can't put a word to it, only that she feels, maybe for the first time that day, like a real person.

"Thank you," she says, and walks past the shelves of free books the Outreach stocks. There are thick and thin volumes on things like growing food in depleted soils, composting for rich earth, restoring waterways, and the like. But there are also volumes which Ruby, despite knowing she should focus on what helps her survive, what helps keep her gram and the Harolds safe and fed, finds herself drawn, as always, to: adventures, mysteries, and true tales of the West. She used to read to herself, to Little Harold, even to Gram. Just brushing her fingertips across the spines of these volumes leaves her longing for the past, at least some parts of it.

In the back room, Ruby finds Sister O sitting at a small worktable. The older woman's ample chest almost wedges her in place, so snug is the chair lodged between the table and a shelf behind her. The work surface is covered with a forest of medication bottles, a board, a knife, a scoop. Sister O's eyes are bright, a watery blue behind thick, round black-rimmed glasses. The last remnants of Ruby's unease from the day fade upon meeting the woman's eyes.

"Hello dear, what a treat to see you." Crinkles web out from the corners of her smiling eyes. "As you can see"—she waves her gaze at the table— "I'm filling the orders for the week. I have your grandmother's here; I expect she's running low?"

Ruby nods, relief filling her, for she'd imagined things like the Outreach being out of the drug, or Sister O not having time to fill the request.

"You need any help?"

Sister O laughs, pushes up her glasses. "Always, my dear, always. Many hands, as they say back home."

Ruby pulls out a chair and sinks into it. It's the first time she's sat, other than on the hard bench seat of the omnibus, since wolfing down the insipid slop at lunch.

They work for some minutes in quiet; the chuff and chime of pills sliding and slipping into bottles takes on a kind of rhythm. Somehow, it doesn't feel like time wasted. As she tips a scoopful of medication that will secretly help someone ailing into its bottle, Ruby feels a sense of fighting back. It's a secret, a different kind of protest, this quiet activity in a closed room, but that doesn't mean it's not real.

Ruby's about to mention Harold Sr.'s concerns about Little Harold and his dreams when the door opens. Brother Q leans in. "I hate to interrupt, but a trio of Shepherds are *dispersing* the protestors. Probably nothing to worry about, but…" His green eyes sweep the table top and then pin on Ruby.

Her mind whirls. What if the monastics are caught providing these unsanctioned medicines? And what if Ruby gets caught not just helping, but taking some? She shoves her chair back, almost tipping it to the floor.

"It will be alright, Ruby," Sister O says as Brother Q closes the door. "Take a breath, dear. Let's get your order sorted." She taps a capped bottle. Their usual order. But then Sister O lifts her hand and taps another, almost the same, but dark amber rather than clear. When she looks up at Ruby, her blue eyes radiate a tender sadness. Ruby feels it immediately. Her knees weaken, and she braces her hands on the chair back. At least, she thinks, here in the presence of the monastics, especially Sister O, there's no need to hide when the binding strikes.

Sister O gives her a smile that balances somehow between sympathy and encouragement. Once, long ago, Ruby asked the monastic if there was a drug she could take to cure her of the binding's curse. There hadn't been, and not only that, but Sister O had tried to convince Ruby that what she feels is not a curse, but a gift—a thing in the West the people revere and nurture.

"I want you to take this too," she says, and pushes the dark-colored bottle slowly across the table.

"What is it?" Ruby reaches her fingers toward it, but stops a hair's breadth away. Something makes her not want to touch the smokey amber glass.

"An option. An option used by many people in the West—when the time is right. Taken in small doses, it is a wonderful sedative and pain balm, but taken in its whole form, it is a way for your grandmother to end her suffering—when, and if, she chooses."

Bile rises in Ruby's throat. "Oh, no, I couldn't do that. I couldn't let her do that. It's not right." She forces herself to swallow the acid pooling there.

"Does your grandmother still have her wits? Is she able to understand if you explain this to her?"

Ruby nods yes, then shakes her head no. "I don't think I…"

"Would you like me to visit her in your stead?" Sister O lays her veined, strong hand over Ruby's small one. Her rings click on Ruby's knuckles.

A bang comes from outside. A shout and raised voices flow into the Outreach store.

Ruby's heart pounds in her throat. "Can I think about it? Can I… Can I…?" Ruby points to the back door. Sister O presses the two bottles into Ruby's hands.

"Of course, dear child." She rises. Her cheeks lift into little round apples, and her wide mouth curves upward. "Of course, dear." With a touch to Ruby's shoulder, Sister O sends Ruby out the back entrance.

The Notice

Ruby makes it back to the old motor lodge after dark. Her steps lag, the implication of the tiny bottle of pills a heavy weight in her satchelpack. Her head throbs. She feels strung together with faulty parts, like some of the old cars the free-workers drive with wire and string holding busted bonnets and doors in place. Even the lure of Little Harold's, HJ's, flat fails to distract her. Her calloused hand loops around the doorknob before she sees it: the color of bad news. A dandelion-yellow sheet of paper peeks from the mail slot.

For a moment, Ruby's sure it's just the dimly lit landing, or perhaps her exhaustion making her see yellow where there is none. She tugs on the extended corner. It's not an illusion. The sheet slithers from the mail slot and into her unwilling hand. As if she needed confirmation, the McComb brand logo, a ridiculously happy-looking white rooster, is emblazoned at the top center.

There'd only ever been one other bright yellow notice received at flat 23. A year earlier, when Gram grew too sick to even do token work for the corp. Now, looking at this one, Ruby understands. Last year's notice degraded their status from family to single-worker. She'd thought that status would be enough: she is young, she is strong, she is a good worker. But then Chairman Powell's nasally voice slips into her mind: work shortages, housing shortages, a reconsideration of the very infrastructure of the Great Classification that had, two generations earlier, guaranteed housing and jobs and provisions for each worker who signed up.

She unfolds the sunny yellow paper.

EVICTION. The words are bold, in capital letters, lest she mistake the tone of the note.

Ruby's chest forgets how to pump air in and out of her lungs. Every bit of reserve she has left melts away. She stares for what feels like a lifetime. Then, she blinks hard and forces herself to read the rest.

Notice to all workers residing at McComb Housing Unit No. 48 on Coast Highway. Due to a housing shortage, a new eviction policy is being enacted. All flats are now designated as suitable for family units only. Couples with children will have top priority, young pairs second, single parents with children third, and older work-age couples fourth. New arrangements are being made to house the elderly in consolidated facilities to provide better care and render younger workers able to optimize the terms of their conscription contracts. McComb Human Resources Department of Housing.

Better care.

Optimize the terms.

New arrangements.

That's when her knees give way, and Ruby Roth crumples to the scuffed planks just outside the only home she's ever known.

2
Kaileh Clearwater Lewis

The Border Guard

S everal hundred miles north of Denton, Maryland, and just west of the Appalachian Mountains border, known formally as the Proclamation Line, another woman struggles to loosen the clench of her jaw. She barely notices the tourists as she pushes through the crowd toward the ever-changing hologram at the center of the cavernous room. In her chest, her burdened heart seems to take on more weight, and her body arches in a slight curve away from the display. But still, she moves toward it, caught in the gravitational pull of the shimmering, morphing exhibit.

She reaches the front just as the hologram resets its display. It begins at the time when the North American continent was a green-and-gold swath flanked by oceans of blue. Tiny dots show villages, seasonal camps, cities, earthworks, and massive herds of bison. Then, in the sneaking way of a virus, 1492 arrives, almost unnoticed at first, as the People naively attempt coexistence. They feed these starving newcomers, so pale, so unskilled. They teach them of maize, of tobacco, of the ample bounty before them. The virus takes hold.

She stares at the hologram. Her eyes sting and burn and threaten a dropping of her guard. She squeezes them shut, but not for long. It's critical to *see* it, to take in the devastation, the fall of the Eastern Woodlands, the decimation of the buffalo, the spread of disease, the near extinction of the People in every corner of the continent.

But it's not real.

It's what could have, most certainly *would have*, happened.

It's what could still happen.

Officer Kaileh Clearwater Lewis feels this certainty flood her veins, oxygen to her hemoglobin, nourishment to her body. Fortification of her purpose as a Warrior.

A low cough at her side steals her from her focus. Irritation flushes her cheeks at being caught off guard. She wipes the emotion away and looks at the man who's somehow managed to slip close without her noticing.

At last. Her wait is over.

He keeps his lowered gaze on the hologram. "Profound, is it not? This reminder of how close the Europeans came to destroying everything."

"Indeed," she answers, and shifts her left arm closer to the tall man. His own hand inches toward hers, and with barely a touch of skin, she passes him the folded slip of paper. "Thank you for helping me."

He nods again, then whispers, "I admired your mother's work. Consider this my thanks. I will see if I can help. Now, friend, enjoy the rest of our collection here." He walks away, swallowed, moments later, by the black maw of a hallway leading back to the main Warrior Archives, housed in the same massive building as the hologram and other displays comprising the Pontiac Victory Center.

She undoes the clasp holding back her long hair, smooths it with her hands, yanks everything tight, and rebinds her thick black horsetail. *Someday*, she thinks, *I will chop it all off.*

"Excuse me?" says a woman with a guttural accent from some European country Kaileh has no interest in identifying.

Her eyes catch another movement: a stocky man wearing a bright red docents' sash identical to her own stands waving on the other side of the hologram. Her friend and fellow Warrior, Mateo Vazquez.

"Excuse me," the foreign woman says a little louder, a tart irritation in her voice. "You are a guide, are you not?" Kaileh catches a whiff of smoked meat and something sour on the woman's breath. A tiny smudge of yellow mars her puffy jawline.

Mateo, still standing on the other side of the hologram, smirks. She almost, just almost, sends the foreign tourist to him. But she can imagine the ribbing he'd give her later. So instead, she looks around, making sure none of the permanent staff are within hearing range, then turns to the woman, plasters on her most apologetic look, and says, *"Páanx t'umúuxi. Bée túu."*

"Beh… do? I sorry," the mustard-splattered woman fumbles. "I thinking… well mind not… and, uh, have a good day." The tourist's voice rises with every word, as if a language barrier equates with deafness. But, as usual, Kaileh's reply works. The woman looks around, spots another docent, and heads that way. And it wasn't exactly a lie. She is hungry, in any language.

Who was that? Mateo signs, not yet within conversation range. His square hands dance the words, somehow conveying curiosity. Her spine stiffens. Did he see her pass the note to the archivist? No, no, and if he did, would it matter?

She signs, *You ready for break?* Her stomach rumbles.

Always, Mateo signs, and rubs his surprisingly flat belly. As he makes his way around the display, Kaileh glances again at the hologram. The animation has once more reached 1620. Slowly at first, then with greater speed and moving east to west, the centuries-old forests are butchered, turned into the aggressive masts of ships, devoured by furnaces smelting iron into weapons and deep-sod plows, filleted for sprawling cities along the Atlantic coast. Then, as the hovering calendar of years reaches the mid-1760s, there's a flash, a reminder of the moment United West historians agree it all changed. The rest, the unspooling destruction of the continent shimmering before her, thank the gods, never happened.

Mateo, in his Warrior service uniform the color of wet putty, is closer now, pushing gently through the crowd. If Kaileh doesn't stare, but lets her eyes drift just to the side, he looks, for a luxurious moment, like her big brother.

"Pardon me?" a feminine voice with a strong English accent says. The hair on Kaileh's arms rises. She grits her teeth at the accent, doesn't turn, and readies her usual statement in her culture's native tongue, Takelma. Or she can just assume a purposeful air and walk away to matters that are more pressing.

A male voice now, a clearing of the throat. "Um, hum, miss, we were wondering where the… water closet might be?" After a beat, she sighs, mentally bowing to the docents' sash striped across her own putty-tan uniform.

Before her stand two adults with a small child bridging them. The little boy squirms in a way that only the recently toilet-trained are wont to do. The woman, his mother, Kaileh guesses, bites her lip. The man's head is tipped forward, all business, his eyes earnest. The child, a small boy with a shag of auburn hair, looks up, scrunches his face, and wiggles his nose in unspoken words Kaileh immediately understands. He doesn't just have to urinate: he's bored. A brisk whoosh of air escapes her. The Takelma words on her tongue melt away.

She remembers her own visit here as a child, her first time at the Pontiac Victory Center—long before the hologram was installed. She was in her ninth year and her brother Tareq, so much older, or so it seemed, in his fifteenth. The visit seemed to last for days. Their parents guided them to each exhibit, read the panels, put their own polish of wisdom on the artifacts and reminders of the People's history. Tareq, as usual, devoured every fact and prompt while Kaileh squirmed and kept asking if they were almost done.

"Momma, I really gotta pee!" the little boy whines, clutching at his crotch, the final signal of impending disaster. A grin tempts Kaileh's lips. She gives in and she lets herself smile.

"Apologies, my mind was elsewhere." She directs the family to the nearest washroom, tells them to enjoy their visit, and watches as they usher their small one to the facility. The boy looks briefly over his shoulder, wrinkles his nose, and sticks out his tongue.

Something else in her cracks, just a little bit, and before she can stop herself, her own tongue extends. She waggles it at the boy.

The boy's shoulders lift in a quivering giggle she cannot hear.

The Talk

"Hey." Mateo's smooth voice, his strong hand a weight on her shoulder, brings her back. "You got a few minutes? I'm ready for a break and we should talk."

"All right." Maybe he did see her pass the note. Maybe she should tell Mateo about her plan. But hasn't she already gotten him in enough trouble? Her mind works to find some way to deflect his inquiry as she leads the way to the wide balcony overlooking the speartip of land where the Pontiac Victory Center sits in Lenape, the capital city of the Northern Woodlands Region. Next week their administrative leave ends, and the two will return to the Shelter Rocks enclave from where they were exiled. None of it was her friend's fault. Only his lack of not stepping in, of not stopping Kaileh from what she'd done, led to his implication.

"Officer Kaileh," Commander Tao said during the administrative counselling session just prior to their exile. "As much as the cur deserved it, you can't take their punishment into your own hands. Am I understood?" Kaileh nodded. No one held any love for the Atlantic couriers, or *curs*, who, for the right price, ferried illegals across the border. Nothing and no one but protocol blamed Kaileh for losing her temper on the one who'd let a baby drown while the profiteering cur tried to escape east.

"And regarding your and Officer Mateo's leave of absence," Commander Tao continued, "use it as a time of reflection. Take a break, enjoy Lenape City." She bore her eyes into Kaileh as she added, "And get your head together." And Kaileh *has* enjoyed the city; it's the perfect opportunity for her to stop waiting for answers about Tareq's death. Somewhere in the Archives are her brother's files. And, perhaps, answers.

She finds seats and turns two chairs to face the river view while Mateo makes coffees from the self-serve cafe. The early-summer air washes over her, warm and heavy with the promise of coming humidity. The watery scent of the river mixes with the sweet smell of flowers, the brisk, grassy scent of young stalks of corn, just a few inches high, growing in the demonstration garden. On one side of the sprawling patio flows the Allegheny River. On the other, behind a green wall of trees, the Monongahela. Not many meters downstream, the two rivers join to form the mighty Ohi-yo. The scene is enhanced by the high viewpoint of the building, elevated to survive the seasonal floods. A level down lie the remains of the fortified earth walls of Fort Duquesne, the stronghold built by the French and later renamed Fort Pitt by the English in the 1700s. Before. When this area was claimed by the colonists and named

Pennsylvania. But, that was before the Proclamation, before the People won the first and second Border Wars.

Just as her mind loops back to the past that could have been, a tiny swarm of trabajadoras hums past her head, on their way to who knows what sort of micro maintenance, from touching up the photovoltaic paint on the building to plucking and destroying harmful insects from the patio and roof gardens.

"I added an extra shot," Mateo says, setting down two mugs and watching, with pride, she thinks, the Mexican-made tek fly past. The weather, warm already, does not deter Kaileh from craving the hot, bitter liquid. Mateo's teeth flash in the big smile that so easily lights his face. For a second, she's sure there's something else, an artifact of the deep longing she can never fully gift back.

"Tuuwuù'k^h," she answers in Takelma.

"De nada," Mateo says, not in the language of his family's original indigenous culture but in Spanish. Kaileh wonders if she'll ever *not* resent the fact of colonial languages—English in the United West, French in Kanata, and Spanish in Mexico—having become the everyday tongue of the People. Luckily, most citizens also learn one of the hundreds of original languages. Just thinking about it brings her mother's scolding voice to Kaileh's ears. *You need to practice more, my daughter.* Of course, Bennu is right, but that doesn't mean Kaileh has to agree.

She stares at Mateo as he sets his keitai down on the table beside his coffee. She could have made her Archive inquiry through him. He has an uncle or aunt or cousin or friend or something who works at the Southern Regional Archives farther south. But whether from not wanting him to know or something else, she instead reached out to a stranger, leaned on her mother's reputation for a favor.

"So," Mateo says, plunking his keitai down on the table beside his coffee, "what do you think of the news?"

Kaileh frowns, tries to scratch up a memory of what the rot Mateo is hinting at. She glances at his keitai lying face down beside his plate. Oh, she understands their value: they are portals to knowledge, communication devices, a portable office. Even now, her own keitai sits in the pocket on the side of her britches. But she's not carrying it by choice. They are required to keep them near. But... over the last few days, ever since she decided to take the investigation of Tareq's death into her own hands, she might begrudgingly admit there is some point to the gadgets.

Just as she opens her mouth to admit ignorance of what Mateo hints at, a vibration makes her jump. "Rot," she says. "Hold on a second." She rises, pulls her keitai from her pocket, and looks at the number. Her pulse ticks up. So fast. She didn't expect to hear something this soon. Her finger lifts. She glances at Mateo, turns away. If she answers now, she'll have to walk away, which will only make him more curious. But if she doesn't connect, will the archivist leave a script message that she can read in private? It was early, too soon really to get excited, but this could be the break, the news, the fish she's been casting for.

As her finger hovers, paralyzed by indecisiveness, the keitai goes silent. Her jaw aches, and she loosens the vise of her bite, wiggles the joint.

"Who was it? Is your mother…?" Mateo's heavy dark brows knit together. She knows she can lie, say it was Rosalia, her mother's live-in caregiver; it would excuse so much. But his look of concern loosens her own pain. She would never do that to him, never choose to hurt Mateo's gentle spirit.

Not for the first time she thinks, *Why? Why can't I feel what he does? Why can't I love this man who would be so good for me?* They've known each other since he became an exchange officer. They've been friends for most of those years. Lovers twice. Even before Tareq died Kaileh knew she could never become Mateo's lifemate. But she couldn't explain, even to herself, why.

"No. Um, wrong number." She pauses, loosens her jaw. "You see? This is exactly why these utensils are a problem, Mateo. How do you stand the constant input?" Even as she asks him, Mateo is glancing at his own keitai.

"What? Sorry," he says, but looks up at her with an impish grin.

"Akh!" She cuffs him on the shoulder, but in reality, she's grateful. Grateful for the reminder of the sweet devil in her brother Tareq. What she'd give to be teased or tricked by him now.

"I'm serious," she says.

"Like I keep saying, Kai, there's good and bad to all things. For example, *having* our keitais with us let us know immediately about the big change next week."

Her mind spins for a response that might both hide her ignorance and defend her stand, but nothing comes.

"Aw," he grins, "you don't know yet, do you?" Then the impishness falls from his expression, and his brows dip again. "It's mixed news actually, and I wanted to make sure you were doing all right with it." He pats her chair. "Better sit down."

The Reassignment

"If you're about to tell me I still have to visit my spirit healer when we get back, I already know." Her reaction-and-response therapy was an ongoing treatment—a punishment in her mind. No amount of docent service would get her out of that.

"Aw, no. You really don't know, do you?" The rising pitch of his voice makes Kaileh stop. There's something he doesn't want to be the one to say.

Her stomach does a small roll. "No, what is it? Go ahead, just pitch it to me."

"Well, you, me, and a couple of others are headed south. For training. In the new task force. For the Intra-Continental Enforcement thing. ICE." He pauses like he's waiting for her to say, *Oh, right, I remember now.*

"I know about the task force, but I didn't know that we… I mean, when did…?"

She pulls out her keitai, sees again the missed call from her contact at the Archives. A little icon blinks, a script waits. When they arrived in Lenape City, when she had the idea to at last pursue her doubts about how her brother died, she paid attention to little else.

"But that's so soon." Almost without noticing, her hand lifts to the stab of pain in her right mandible.

"I know, but it's rather exciting, right? It will be the first joint operation between the United West and the Atlantic States."

Kaileh snorts, waits for him to laugh. But her friend's face remains serious.

"I know," Mateo says. "Don't look at me like that. We all agree the ASA government is a joke. Still, it might be an opportunity to learn more about the problems of the East."

She nods and shakes her head in succession. "Yes, yes. You're right. But I don't have your… your interest, I guess, in spending precious energy studying them. That's not our, that's not *my* job." *My job*, she doesn't say aloud, *is to keep the Atlantics behind the Proclamation Line, clear and simple*. Somewhere from her training the Sun Tzu decree of knowing your enemy rises in objection. She makes her own decree: *I know all I need to do my job*.

"I understand, sure, but the Atlantic people, what drives them west is their government."

"No," she says. "Well yes, but their government is a result of them: of who they are as a culture—if you can even call it that."

As she says this, she again hears her mother's voice, her tone one of frustrating patience. "Daughter, no matter our losses, the Atlantics—the working classes, in particular—are to be pitied. To be helped. To be understood."

"Our losses, Mother? Maybe Daddy would still be here if he hadn't pitied them so much." Her father, a healer, had served in Healers-Across-the-Line, contracting some sort of blood poisoning that had ultimately taken his life. "And what about your son? What about Tareq?" The words out, Kaileh recoiled at her mother's expression, at the crumpled pain there, something more than a sibling and child could ever fully grasp.

Despite the tainted smell coming from an assignment linked with the Atlantic States, part of her knows this is a promotion of sorts, and after what she did, after she once again let her temper rule her heart, she was worried Commander Tao wouldn't allow her back out on patrol—much less consider her for a promotion.

Then it hits her. She'll be leaving not just Shelter Rocks but the proximity to the Northern Woodlands capital, Lenape City. Leaving her contact at the Archives. But will it even matter? In her pocket, her keitai with its unopened script feels as heavy as a brick. Could he really have found out anything that quickly? And what is she hoping to find?

Everything about her brother's death has an official explanation. He was on patrol with Onas Steeprock. They became separated. Tree poachers fatally shot him, shot Steeprock as he came upon the scene, and then somehow, and for no good reason, stole Tareq's body, took it back across the border.

From the beginning, it never seemed quite right, never fully plausible. Something isn't right about the story. It's like a dead thing buried in a too-shallow grave: it stinks.

She feels Mateo's expression change before she meets his eye. "You all right?" he asks.

"Yes, sorry, yes." She looks into her friend's compassionate brown eyes. "It's been a year, you know? A year this month."

He cups his hand over hers. "I know. I feel his loss, too. Nothing like you, but still. Tareq was a good friend. A very good friend." His hand stays on hers. Thick calluses buff against her knuckles. It's somehow both annoying and calming.

Mateo clears his throat. "If you didn't know about the relocation, I guess you don't know where…? Right. Well, I'm not sure how you'll feel about this." He squirms on the seat, tips back the tiny espresso cup, made all the more miniature by his big hand, and swallows the last bit. "But next week we're leaving the Northern Woodlands and heading south. South to Waccamaw."

She pulls her hand from beneath his, fights the urge to cover her mouth. Her pulse beats a rapid staccato in her ears. *Waccamaw.* Where Tareq was stationed when he died. Where she went only a year ago to pick up his tiny bundle of personal belongings. It surprises her, this response. And just how is it that Mateo seems to have anticipated her reaction? She scowls at him, this man who sometimes knows her better than she knows herself.

But then a new thought: what if this is a good thing? If the archivist here finds nothing, or only part of the answer, this trip south could, if she rises to the occasion, be the thing that will crack open the nut of the case. Searching the Archives at Lenape is one thing, but returning to the place where it all happened might open other opportunities.

She bites her lip and lowers her hand, lets it rest atop Mateo's. He gives her a puzzled look, and his thick eyebrows lift.

"It's all right. I think this will be a good thing," she says. "Yes, definitely a good thing." She will make certain of it.

3
Ruby

The Dream Girl

The morning after receiving the eviction notice, the flat seems both more dismal and, though it makes little sense to Ruby, a precious thing. She always knew things would change when her grandmother died. But not before, and surely not eviction. And what about her grandmother? She pictures the McComb Human Services micromulti pulling up to the motor lodge, bundling Gram in the tattered quilts, and tossing her into the back as if her physical weight defines her value. It's not right. It's not fair. After all these years, after all the promises of their life-contracts.

Drowning. That's what this feels like to Ruby. Like she's underwater, her feet tangled in trash, the surface just out of reach. Her head floats. A dark ring closes in around her vision. Something Brother Q said not long after he arrived at the Outreach comes back to her. *If you feel like you can no longer swim, try putting your feet down.* At the time, she hadn't understood. Brother Q was strange back then, like he wasn't quite sure how he'd gotten to Denton.

But now, as she begins to breathe normally again, it gives her an idea. Colin Tate. She'll go to his office. Maybe he has changed. Maybe his hint at her potential isn't as sleazy as she first thought. Yes, she'll go there. She'll make her case. The thought brings her heart to her throat, but then she remembers: today is her one day of the week when she does not have to go to the hatchery. If she waits just one day, what could it hurt? She finishes caring for Gram, still sleeping from her earlier dose of pills, and marches down to flat 13.

An hour later HJ throws open the door when she again knocks. "I got my tools and stuff with me, Roobs. I'm all ready for some mudlarking!" Little Harold says when he throws open the door of the Harolds' lower level flat an hour later. The delight sparkling in the boy's brown eyes almost erases her anxiety about facing Tate the following day.

After a quick walk to the omnibus stop, they're aboard and heading to Denton. The boy, almost as tall as Ruby now, pats his satchelpack, a tattery green thing passed down from his dad. His shoulders wiggle and squirm, partly from the bumping and rocking of the omnibus and partly because that's what an eleven-year-old boy does when he's too happy to hold it in.

"Maybe you'll get lucky, Little Harold. Maybe you'll find something *really* valuable." He tips his dark head of short cropped hair to her, chews on her words, nods all solemn and thoughtful like.

"I sure am hoping so. That'd be the best."

The omnibus follows the same route Ruby takes to work, but in the hazy light of day, it feels a world apart. The transport is mostly empty: a couple of" " McComb conscripts in CC-blue boilersuits, heads bent as if dozing; a few free-workers, lime-green IDs around their necks; and three girls sitting in the back, a year or two younger than Ruby. Their presence during work hours, their carefree posture, their shared laughs, mark them separate from the free-worker class. She glances back, recognizes two as daughters of Shepherd officers working the Denton streets. Something makes her lower her eyes to her lap. She lays a hand on HJ's bouncing knee beside her.

The omnibus slows as they reach the shantytown. The road has narrowed with the growing bulk of the settlement.

Ruby jumps when HJ grabs her arm. "I see her!" His voice fills the omnibus. A man sitting in the seat in front of them turns, scowls. The girls in the back seats laugh a mean snicker. Ruby cringes when she hears them whisper words like "baby" and "freak," but HJ doesn't seem to notice. His palm slaps the glass. "There. There she is!"

Ruby lifts her head. The closed windows don't keep out the sour smell of the place, but it's the sight of the hunched, impoverished people that threatens to bind her.

"Can you see her, Roobs?" HJ tugs on her arm. Ruby takes a deep breath, focuses on the distracting smell, and leans to the window. How would Little Harold, HJ, know someone living here? But then she flinches. This, this horrible place may soon be where she too will huddle.

"Who do you see, Lit—HJ?" A tattered, greasy-haired couple hunkers at the side of the road, arched over a small pile of belongings. A few feet in, a trio of men squat on the ground, poking bent pieces of wire into smoking coals. To one side, a woman with lank brown hair, knotted and sticking to her forehead, is trying to hang clothes on a makeshift line attached to a hovel of rags and bits of metal. The line, loaded now with damp rags that must be her clothes, falls as soon as the woman turns. As she bends down to try again, exhaustion spreads into Ruby's arms, and she feels suddenly terribly old and hopeless.

HJ's voice parts the fog in Ruby's brain. "The girl, right back there, see, by the side of the road?" He's pointing and tapping, but they're passing the far edge of the camp. He gives a puff of frustration and plops back down.

Ya gotta not let it in.

Ruby squeezes her eyes shut, works to break the connection. Then she does something she knows her gram would cuff her for: Ruby tries to link, instead, to the boy. To use his disappointment as a sorce of distraction. It's easy and safe to sense the boy's feelings, safe and somehow pure, even when he's sad or frustrated.

"How do you know her?" Ruby asks, her curiosity piqued by her secret sharing of the boy's deflation at her not seeing the girl.

He turns his round, brown eyes up to her. "I dreamed her," he says with such pride, Ruby can't help but smile. But then, she remembers. He *dreamed her.* The dreams Harold told her about; the dreams that worry HJ's father so. The dreams she never asked Sister O about.

The omnibus thunks into a pothole. Ruby looks up. They're pulling into Denton. From the seats at the rear, the trio of girls whisper and giggle. A buzzing tingles Ruby's skin, so like the feeling of a zap-crook just before it connects, she almost flinches away. She risks a glance back, sees one of them staring at her, a hateful glint in her dark eyes. It's then that Ruby knows: this won't be the last she sees of them.

Mudlarking on the Choptank

The omnibus station is less than a mile from the spot on the Choptank River where Ruby likes to take HJ to mudlark. It's usually a safe enough walk, but she has taken her usual precautions. A small pig sticker nestles in a sheath strapped to the small of her back. Its weight, its bulk, adds just the right feeling of safe.

"You still want to go down to the river?" Ruby asks, knowing the answer.

"You bet I do!" The growing resemblance of the young boy to his father suddenly takes her breath away. How can HJ be already at the cusp of becoming a young man?

She was there when he was born, when Gram wrapped his slick little body, the color of a fresh bruise, in a towel, and tried to get his momma to put him to breast. And Ruby was there the next morning when the only two people left in flat 13 were Harold Sr. and the squalling baby boy. At the time, Ruby never thought much about where, or why, his momma went. Gram told her later, when Ruby finally asked, that she just packed a bag and walked out. "She weren't from here" was her grandmother's cryptic explanation. Later, Ruby would overhear their neighbor Ms. Simpson saying, "Surprising it lasted as long as it did, her being from Balt-i-more and all."

Now, HJ's sweet enthusiasm puts a smile on her lips. How is it that he can be so accepting? Ruby, for her part, finds it hard not to hate a mother who would leave of her own will. Maybe it's better to be like her, Ruby, left with a mystery of what happened to her mother.

HJ's satchelpack clanks with his collection of wares and mudlarking tools: a tiny shovel, a brush, a magnifier. He'll use the opportunity to try to salvage something of value from the riverbank. Lately, it's been slim pickings as more of the adrift spend their hours mudlarking the old refuse piles and grimy shores.

As if HJ can not only dream the things that were yet to come, but also read minds, he says, "I sure hope there's gonna be something left. Roobs, you think that new corp is combing the banks too?"

"I doubt it, buddy. Refudyne is sticking to those big ol' landfills. There's plenty of them, and filled with all sorts of treasures dumped from the big cities like Washington and Baltimore." Like everything of value, though, sooner or later a big corp takes it over, makes the real money.

They reach the shore, and leaping over and sidestepping, HJ makes his way through the scrub and refuse, the sort nobody wants, to the water's edge. There he digs a palm-sized elliptical stone from between the shreds of old plastic bags and sand. Then, looking first over his shoulder to make sure he's got Ruby's attention, he angles his body, pulls back his arm, and lets it fly. The stone skips four slaps across a pool of brackish water. For a moment, Ruby is plunged into another memory of throwing stones, not at water, but at a person. But then she's back, clapping her hands at HJ's innocent throw. The boy spins in a gleeful circle, trots up the bank, and grabs Ruby's fingers with his small, strong, sweaty hand.

Her heart swells. She laughs and squeezes back. "I used to be able to do that, make a rock do pretty much whatever I wanted."

"Want me to dig you out one too, Roobs?" He starts to pull from her, but she holds on tighter.

"Nah, it would be wasted, buddy, trust me. Besides, I'd rather watch you." HJ gives her a funny look, like he can't imagine being too old to not want to play.

Soon, HJ switches to the earnest work of salvage. He has a knack for it. Despite the ambitions of others, the boy always manages to uncover something of value. Ruby paces the shore, on alert for brigands with no qualms about taking a child's treasures. Things have changed. Before Ruby began fulfilling her life-contract to McComb—or later to whatever corp she might be traded or sold to—things seemed in some kind of equilibrium. The conscripts were poor, sure, but they'd seemed aligned, protective even of their own. She remembers older cons, and even the occasional free, helping children, not robbing them.

Was it when Chairman Powell was voted in that things changed? The thought startles her. She sounds to herself, suddenly, like an actual grown-up. Not that there is anything their class, grown-ups or otherwise, can do about it. She feels, though, a growing awareness of something she can only think of as layers. Layers of society, layers of complications, layers of deceit, coating a life until it hides away who you used to be.

"Hey sweetheart." A male voice shakes her back to the moment.

Ruby spins to see a well-dressed free-worker, or maybe a corp-class, leaning against a post some feet away. His hair is dark, slicked back with care and expensive vanity products. He's holding a slip of paper in his hand. Even from this distance, Ruby sees, almost smells, the smoothness of his skin. She knows the thing in his hand is not a grocery list or innocent note, but a McComb Corp store voucher—the thing that, for her class, is as good as money.

"Not interested, mister." She tries to keep her voice casual, but fails to hide a tremor as her imagination fast-forwards to the worst. She's not afraid for herself. But for Little Harold? Her body stiffens.

Please stay back, HJ, please, she thinks with all her heart. And to her shock, he looks up. He stands. The binding shares his sudden fear, the bunching of his muscles to come toward her. But he doesn't, and the man doesn't seem to see him. Her body relaxes some. She lifts her right hand to the small of her back, slowly, subtly working her fingers to the knife nestled there.

"Come on, baby, bet you'd clean up just fine. Slip of a thing like you, why you're practically still a little girl, aren't you now?" He waves the note. "This here, this is probably what you get in a month. That boy over there, that your little brother? Well, I just bet he'd be grateful for a bit of candy."

She knows she could kill this slime of a human. It would be no harder than killing a full-grown wild pig. This man, his type, the tusks are all in their head. But Ruby knows of predators. She's been one.

But—and here she risks a glance at HJ—if she kills this man, or even cuts him, just a little, she'll lose HJ. Or rather, he'll lose her. Even the smallest offense will have McComb trading her to Refudyne or Energy Corp or who knows who, or where.

The man takes a couple of easy steps toward her, stretching his arms back behind him like he's warming up. He scans the area; no matter what upper-class caste he's from, the Shepherds don't take kindly to the mishandling of corp property. But no one, not even the usual couple of adrift folks that show up at the river during the day, is here now. They are alone.

Maybe, just maybe, she could hide the body—if it comes to that. But HJ. Would he be so traumatized that he'd be harmed forever? His dreams. His own version of the binding, perhaps. She doesn't want to risk adding to his burden.

The man is only ten feet from her now. His head tips to the side, his eyes scanning her, a small, wicked smile sitting at the corners of his mouth.

He thinks he has her. He thinks this will be easy.

"I told you, I'm not interested." She closes her hand around the handle of the blade. The steel is short and sharp. Meant more for severing the bulging veins and arteries of a pig's neck than for piercing the rib cage and reaching the heart. Still…

If she lets him catch a glimpse of it, he could have her arrested. He takes another step. One hand goes to his belt.

Her bladder feels suddenly full. All she can think of is what could happen to Little Harold. Should she go with this creep to get him away from the boy?

Then, before she can act, there's a sudden soft thunk. The man's body crumples and drops. A smooth, elliptical stone falls with him. Before Ruby can process what has happened, HJ walks up. A stunned silence engulfs them.

"Did you…?"

"Yup," HJ says.

Ruby feels a laugh and tears welling at the same time. Before she can say anything, HJ pipes, "Well, guess he'll never know what hit him."

"Oh HJ," is all Ruby can say in response. Her mind flip-flops, her eyes scanning the shore. If they were seen… if they are caught… She pictures all the worst and it would all be because of her.

"We'd better skedaddle, Roobs, don't you think?"

Ruby can't speak, but nods and hurries up the bank. At the access road, she looks back, expecting to see one of two things: the man's body sprawled on the shore or him standing, moving toward them. But instead, the weeds and trash look as before. On the omnibus home, they're both quiet. HJ didn't even beg for a few minutes in town to set out a display of his wares. In her head, Ruby scolds the boy for his foolish bravado. He, they, got lucky. If the man had only been dazed, or even if the stone had sailed cleanly past his head, they might not be riding the transport home. They might, instead, be in a dark cell at a Shepherd station. She finds herself shivering despite the stifling heat of the omnibus.

HJ stares out the window as they pass the shantytown, but says nothing. Ruby leans her head back, closes her eyes, and tries to wipe the man's face, his voice, from her mind. She must doze, for his face shifts, becomes Colin's, and then someone else's, a shape in the shadow, only the sound of hoarse breathing letting her know it's a living thing.

She starts awake. HJ's wide brown eyes narrow at her, and she almost asks him about his own dreams. But her mind won't leave the bank of the river. She's never been threatened like that, in the bright of day, so close to town, so close to other people. Is that what being adrift will be like? A constant state of danger? Surrounded by despair and suffering?

It's then that she knows she cannot let that happen. She'll go to see Colin. She'll convince him, somehow, that she should stay in flat 23.

The Face in the Shadows

The next morning, she wakes eager to confront Tate. To her relief, Gram, as the day before, seems more peaceful, dozing, tiny snores rattling in her chest. As Ruby zips up her boilersuit, her mind intent on convincing Tate, she hears an engine. Once again, the dark blue Reo pickup appears in the gloom outside the motor lodge. Dread fills her. She can't know, but she does, that it's here for her. But who? And why? And maybe it's her mood, her determination to void the eviction notice, for looking at the pickup makes something in her snap. Without another thought, she slides the sheathed pig sticker into the tall side pocket of the boilersuit leg and flies out the door. She's down the stairs and to the road in moments, her bare feet numb to the scuffs and scrapes she'll later have to tend. She's almost at the driver's window of the pickup when the engine roars and the vehicle tears away, sending gravel in a spray behind it. As in her dream, the face is in shadow, and even more confusing to her is the lack of connection. Usually, no matter how hard she tries not to let the binding link her to another, she feels something.

During her shift, whispers travel along the line of roundups and beatings. One of the incubator room staff, David, a man Ruby's age whom she's known since she started work, tells her a darker tale that day at lunch.

"I got a cousin over Burrsville, works at the grow farm out thatta way," David says between bites of Cham stew. His voice is low and breathy, his eyes shifting back and forth like he's checking to see if they're being watched. "Well, she has a friend whose man couldn't take it anymore. They had a bit of money, seeing as how they're free-workers. Low, don'tcha know, but still, free. They take it out from whatever rock or mattress they was hiding it under and paid some courier fella to carry 'em across the border into…" He looks to each side. "… the West. But they get caught, see?"

Part of Ruby wants to dismiss what David is saying. It's an unspoken truth that folks regularly attempt the crossing. But the news reports say they're always caught. They're always punished. They always face horrible consequences.

"Well, after they was caught," David continues, "you'd of expected 'em to be sent to harder labor, right? Or made conscripts or something. But the Shepherds actually put 'em on display smack in the middle of the town. Placed signs around 'em saying how they ain't patriots, how they stole from the other workers, how they done made it harder on everyone what used to be their neighbors." David shakes his head, looks around again. "Them folks as was their ol' neighbors gets all worked up, and over the days, the pair of 'em gets stoned, actually stoned by their own people." His voice trembles and grows thick. "One eye out for the woman, broken ribs and such, but the man…" He glances around. "They done killed him."

Ruby's stomach twists. The gray stew sloshing in her belly threatens to come up. "It's barbaric, like something from the Middle Ages."

David's eyes open wide, and he tips his head to one side. "Look around us, Ruby. Where you think we're livin' now?"

It makes no sense to Ruby. According to the upper folks, there isn't enough work for all the working class. And the adrift are another problem. A burden to society, according to the bosses and the news and the country's board of directors. Yet their numbers continue to grow. Wouldn't it be easier, better even, to let people flee? But she suspects it's not about that. It's about control, about making examples of those that disrespect that control.

By the end of her shift, Ruby's resolve to talk to Colin Tate is still there, but drained of vigor. She feels like one of the little yellow chicks she condemns to the kill bin. Still, she slips past the locker room door and into the corridor of offices. It's not a place workers go—unless they're in serious trouble. It's quieter than she expected, and for a moment, she thinks this is a good sign, that it will mean they can have a conversation in relative private, but when she gets to the door marked *Colin Tate, Assistant Manager*, it's locked, the window dark.

"Can I help you, hon?" a woman's voice says in the kind of tone you use when you find someone where they're not supposed to be.

"Um, I was looking for… for Mr. Tate?"

"Was you now? Well, that there's going to be a problem. He's out of town, see. Won't be back for a couple of weeks. Better get on back to your part of the building now."

With a mixture of relief and exhausted frustration, Ruby does just that.

The Delay

May slides into June, and the sweltering heat and closeness of summer presses down on the Eastern Shore. Neither Tate nor the pickup have returned, but it's small comfort. Every day, Ruby fears a visit from Human Services, ready to haul her gram away. The dark bottle of pills sitting high on a shelf tries to get Ruby's attention. But she finds reasons to ignore it, to not tell her grandmother of its existence.

Then, only days into June, Ruby arrives back at the flat to find the old woman halfway across the floor. She's lying on her side, panting, nightshirt up around her chest. Ruby stills her gasp; how did this happen? Not just finding her gram on the floor, but the dramatic decline of her grandmother's body, now revealed before her? The woman's rib cage is a ripple of bones. The hollow of her belly like a bowl. Her flaccid yellow-tinged skin lies in folds and wrinkles, yet still, she looks so terribly thin.

"Oh, Gram, what'd you try to do?" Ruby forces the words into slow, patient shapes. But her body rebels. The binding agony shoots into her, radiates from her belly like an exploding star.

"Had to go." Gram's face is stretched with exhaustion, but the half slits of her eyes peer sharply at Ruby from beneath the drooping lids. Ruby darts her gaze away, does her best to hide the thing the old woman is, even in her last days, searching for.

Ruby blows air through clenched teeth. "Where, Gram? Where'd you have to go?"

"Toilet."

"Didn't Missus Simpson come help you earlier?" Both Harold Sr. and their neighbor, Agnes Simpson, help out during the day, taking Gram to the night bucket, making sure she drinks water, tries to eat, and takes her pills.

"Did." Gram's voice seems weaker, the tone less of defiance than despair. Ruby wonders, for the first time, what, or if, the old woman thinks about death. Well, not about death, but about *dying*. But she dares not ask.

As Gram tries to push up on one quaking arm, Ruby slips her hands into the deep hollows of the woman's armpits and slides her toward the kitchenette, intending to prop her against the cabinet while she tries to put things to right. With slow, dragging steps, they cross the floor. Gram moans. "Ooooh! Ooooh!" Her face knots and twists. Her agony blows on the fire already scorching inside Ruby. The pain is sharp, but Ruby feels an odd numbness.

It comes to her suddenly: they've reached a fork in the road. Two paths diverge. On one sits the dark amber bottle of pills. On the other, the McComb old folks' home. But both destinations repulse her; each leads to a place Ruby doesn't want to think about.

But still, Ruby cannot make herself talk to her gram, to show her the pills, tell her what Sister O said: of how she can take away the pain. Forever.

Then, as if Gram, too, has the binding and reads her mind, she says, "Ruby. I cain't go on like this. I just cain't."

Hot tears spring to Ruby's eyes. Her body flags, and she slips down the cupboard and sits beside the woman who raised her, the woman who worked to keep Ruby safe, to make her strong, to protect her, not just from the binding, but from all the ills of the world. Plump tears roll down her cheeks, and for once, she does nothing to hide them, nothing to scour away the proof of feeling too much. She owes everything to this wisp of a woman who's lost so much. First, her husband during the civil war of the 1990s, just before the Great Classification. And later her sons: first a baby boy whose name Ruby was never told, then finally Nicholas, just entering the prime of his life.

The old woman turns her gaze on Ruby. Her dry lips part as if words are struggling to break free. Ruby jumps up, wipes her eyes, and gets a pillow from the bed, tucks it gently behind her gram's bony shoulders. Then she sits back down, this time in front of the old woman, so she doesn't have to move. She can feel something building, something important. Something she must take in.

"Honey," Gram begins, and this word, its rarity, stops Ruby's breath. "Honey, I got some things I needs to tell you. It's time. Time I tell you about your mother."

A Fork in the Road

The next morning, the world looks different. It's not just the fact of it being again her day off, but that her past, or part of it, has been a lie.

Now, as she goes about her morning chores, she replays everything.

"Girl, I ain't told you the whole story, won't now," her grandmother wheezed as they sat on the kitchen floor. Ruby held her breath.

"Your daddy's first mistake was loving the wrong woman." Just hearing her gram say "your daddy" softened Ruby's heart. Her daddy. She knew so little of the man and woman who gave her life, the taboo of their story being her first remembered lesson.

"His second mistake," Gram said, "was thinking he could have her." There, leaning against the cupboards, exhausted and soiled, her rib cage moved in and out in little bursts. It was hard to picture this was the same woman Ruby, for most of her life, had feared.

"Them Shepherds, the crooks, they caught 'em at the border, you know that? Took him. Took the tiny babe that was you. No reason to take the woman. She belong on the other side anyways." Gram's head dropped to her chest. Ruby stared at the thick vein in Gram's neck, the artery pulsing beneath it, all galloping and racing toward the end. The old woman stayed like that for some time, and just when Ruby was sure she'd dozed off and was about to lift her back to the pallet, Gram roused.

"When the crooks brought you back here, I knew he dead. But her, that woman, no. No reason they'd'uv hurt her, would'uv started a war." Ruby clung to every word, waited, hoping for more, wanting to ask a thousand different things.

Ruby's mind roiled with the things said and implied. It was as though she'd flushed out a warren of plump rabbits, all scattering in a different direction, Ruby not knowing which one to chase.

A moment later, while Ruby held her breath in pale hope, Gram said, "What're ya waiting for? Get me back to bed, girl."

The next morning her grandmother seems worse; not with pain, but as if the confession of the evening before drew something essential from her. She blinks at Ruby as she accepts her usual dose of pain medication. Her eyes have dimmed, the spark of yesterday, the fire Ruby had seen all her life, so obviously dying.

Ruby settles in to sit beside her. It feels as if it could be the last time. But after only a few minutes, her gram's eyes open wide. She turns her head to Ruby and stares for so long, Ruby thinks she's sleeping with her eyes open.

But then she speaks. "You go on now, girl. You carry that boy down below us, and you get on. Livin' is for the livin'. Oh, don'tcha look at me like that. I'm not fixin' to leave just yet. But get on. Let me rest."

The voice is both that of her gram and not, some essential part of the old woman already departed. At first Ruby shakes her head no, but then she sees the spark. It's still there. Just dimmed. The woman narrows her eyes at her granddaughter. With a sigh, Ruby does as she's been told.

A lunch packed and HJ in tow, they catch the Omnibus into Denton. HJ's satchelpack rattles with wares and treasures he's collected. A tattered dark blue blanket is tucked under one arm. He says the dark blue sets off his finds nicely. Usually, the idea of bartering for the odd low-value voucher, or even a bit of real coin, animates the boy. But today he rides beside Ruby, quiet, shrunken almost.

"What's up, buddy?" she asks a few minutes into the ride.

He squirms for a minute, hugging the blanket to him. At last, he says, "I keep seeing *it*, Roobs. Seeing *her*. Seeing *them*."

They're nearing the shantytown. A heavy yoke slides over her neck. The right words do not find her. For what can she say to him?

Without warning, the omnibus lurches to a stop. They're at the edge of the shantytown. Something makes Ruby stand. Through the wide front window of the transport, she sees the dark shapes of two Shepherds blocking the road. They stalk back and forth along the line of tents, zap-crooks slapping their open palms. The predatory energy coming from them vibrates through Ruby. Her stomach lurches, and she covers her mouth with her hand. Stop it. *Stop it. Stop it*, she yells silently to herself.

Her head throbs, her body tenses. HJ's trying to pull her back onto the seat. She lets herself fall onto the tattered cushion. Harold Jr. looks at her with eyes both old and wise.

"It's starting, Roobs. You can't stop it."

A shiver spiders up her spine. "What do you mean, HJ?"

He doesn't answer, but says, "But she's safe for now." She feels his hand, the scrape of calluses already roughening his young skin. A bit of his calm travels into Ruby, and before she can think of what to say, the omnibus pulls around the violence and accelerates the last distance to the station.

Trying to put both the boy's words and the incident from her mind, Ruby leads HJ to a safe-looking corner not far from the station. As if nothing out of the ordinary just happened, HJ spreads the blue blanket and lays out his wares. For her part, though, Ruby can't shake the feeling of something being amiss; it's not just the incident or the boy's words, it's a whole nother thing. Something she somehow knows has not yet happened.

Townsfolk pass by, most without seeming to see them. A few give sympathetic nods. One or two stop to look at HJ's goods: metal and glass buttons, a few pieces of cutlery, a glass bottle without a stopper, and one kitchen knife with the tip like a snub nose. Only two follow through and exchange coins or vouchers for a trinket or two. Perhaps they buy out of pity, rather than need, but it doesn't much matter. The pleasure bubbling from HJ makes Ruby almost forget her earlier sense of danger.

It's a pretty day for the Eastern Shore. The sky isn't as gritty brown as usual, and a light breeze whispers from the east. Ruby breathes it in, imagining it's tinged with salt and aromas from across the ocean. She pictures the winds now wisping past them, traveling on west—to freedom. Could these winds even, just perhaps, reach the woman who is her mother? Would they lift a strand of hair and lay it gently back on a face that maybe looks something like Ruby? Or—

Suddenly HJ grabs her arm. Ruby returns to the moment, her heart choking her throat. She's certain it will be the man from the riverbank, come back to punish them for all of their trespasses. But instead, she sees three figures crossing the street. Three figures she'd almost forgotten. They saunter toward HJ and Ruby. The young women from the omnibus of the week before move with long strides and wide, wicked smiles. Something flicks beside one of the girls: a baseball bat clutched at her leg. The girl at the front, square of shoulder, with short, stocky legs, lets a long piece of ridged metal slide from her cuff into her hand.

This Ruby did not plan on. The most resistance they'd ever met was from a free-worker merchant driving them off.

Ruby's hand lifts to the small of her back, seeking the reassuring knob of her concealed pig sticker. But it's not there. Her heart drops.

"Pack up. Quick," she hisses. The girls have paused a few feet away. A short one with pale straw hair and a prominent chin—one of the Shepherds' daughters, Ruby's pretty sure—looks up and down the street. Ruby keeps her eyes locked on the leader as HJ pulls the corners of the blanket together, clattering all his goods into one bundle, and shoves them into his satchelpack. As he hoists it to his back, Ruby guides him behind her.

"Hi there," the head girl chirps. Her smile makes Ruby think of the jaws of a rat snake unhinging to swallow a mouse. The girl lets the piece of metal, rebar, Ruby sees now, drop a little more into her hand. The handle end is wrapped with tape and cloth. Something about that shoots dread into Ruby. This is something they do, something they've planned, something they've practiced. Ruby forces her focus into the periphery, looking for anyone, even a disgruntled shop owner, that might dissuade the girls.

"Whatcha got in your pack, little boy? Something fancy? Something I might like?" Her snort makes it clear that anything that has touched the boy's hands is below her.

HJ starts to answer, but Ruby interrupts. "He's only got a bunch of junk. Worthless to you." She doesn't add, *But you know that, don't you?* Then, from the corner of her eye, she sees movement.

"HJ, go," she says, nudging her head toward what she hopes to be help. She expects the boy to argue, to assert more of his growing independence, but he backs away a few steps, then turns and marches off.

The two girls in the back snicker. "Baby!" one of them calls out. "Run home to your mommy—'less she's busy with a *customer*, that is." The girl laughs and thrusts her pelvis in and out, making a grunting moaning sound.

"Oh Sarah, you're so bad!" the lead girl giggles. The others follow her lead, their own snickers hitting like a handful of thrown gravel.

Ruby suddenly doesn't care what happens to her. She'll lose HJ to the conscript system soon enough anyway, even if she does find a way to not be evicted, to keep her flat—and her small bit of freedom.

Keeping her hand behind her, but clenching the muscles of her arm as if getting a firm grip on a hidden weapon, she steps forward. An icy peace comes over her. She smiles, keeping her eyes cold, ready, willing to lose everything. The girls hesitate. Their expressions freeze. Ruby takes another step. She looks at the lead girl's soft belly, her unblemished face, the smooth hand that grips the padded handle of her makeshift weapon. Ruby's fingers stiffen. It won't take a knife to mar this girl, to leave her with a scar she'll forever regret.

She's a single lunge from the leader now. The other girls shift back and forth on their feet. Ruby feels their urge to flee like the pull of a magnet on metal. She wonders, just vaguely, what it's like to have friends. She almost laughs at an odd thought: if she was born free, would she be the fourth in this little gang? Then, picturing it, she lets part of the laugh escape.

Immediately, the two girls in the back step away. The vulgar girl, Sarah, says, "Come on, Matty, we… we're going to be late. For that thing."

The lead girl, Matty, Ruby supposes, slides her teeth over her top lip. Her eyes narrow, weighing the risk. With a snarl, she begins to retract the makeshift weapon into her sleeve. Ruby catches a glimpse of something marring the pale flesh of Matty's forearm. A handprint of red-purple bruises. The girl cannot hide her wince as the rebar slides past the marks.

Ruby feels her nerve falter, but can't hold back her tongue. "Yeah, Matty, go on. Get on to that *thing*."

Matty stops, swings back toward Ruby, but a klaxon sounds from a half block up. They all turn. A Shepherd cruiser is creeping toward them.

The dark-haired girl hisses, "Matty, it's your old man. Come on."

Matty's face crumbles. Hatred, fear, and humiliation vibrate from her.

Ruby steps back from the scene, slouches her back, assumes a humble, innocent stance, but doesn't linger. Up the street, she sees HJ, not far from the corner. As she makes her way toward him, head down, she hears the raised, pleading voice of the girl Matty. She hears the cruiser's door, the sound of a hand meeting skin, the high-pitched cry of pain.

It's then that Ruby realizes that to be a female, even from the free-class, is to be forever bound.

The Price

She and HJ are back near the omnibus station when it happens. Ruby looks over her shoulder one more time to make sure they aren't being followed. A held breath escapes her. There's no sight of the girls or the Shepherd. Just as she feels, once again, that she and the boy have narrowly escaped a terrible danger, her body slams into someone in front of her. She looks up. And into the smug face of Colin Tate.

Colin Tate. She was so ready to face him, but now and here everything's as muddled and cluttered in her mind as the banks of the Choptank. He's close. The scent of lily both sweet and nauseating.

They were friends once, or so she'd thought. It's a time, a version of herself, she's tried with all her might to forget. So many things were different back then. There was school, for all of them, cons and frees attending the same place, even sharing the same classrooms. Not like now, when by age fourteen conscript kids are moved to trade schools. A ruse, Sister O told her, for what most of the world considers abusive child labor. School is where she met Colin. He was a year ahead of her, although the same age. She cringes, remembering how easily she, a loner and mostly invisible, succumbed to the mere fact of being noticed.

Other kids, even cons she knew from the motor lodge back then, either ignored her or made fun of things like her handsewn clothes, the lunches she brought of foraged and hunted food, and the snares and traps and net she kept in her satchelpack. But Colin, who moved from another local school to theirs when she was twelve, seemed at first to study her like an odd specimen of animal life. Later, he took an interest, or so it seemed, in her foraging skills. By the time she saw through the glamor of this attention, it was too late.

She lifts her eyes to him now. Even with her small stature, she doesn't have to tip her neck far. She thought she was prepared to see him, ready with her speech about all the reasons she should stay in her flat. She'd offer her help, for didn't he hint at something she could do for him in the micromulti that day when she was late?

But then, from the corner of her eye, she sees Harold Jr. Has she been his friend, his teacher, his part-time mother as a way of making amends for what she did to his father? A thing Colin led her to do?

It happened after school one day when a brisk early frost reminded them all that winter was coming. She headed out after class, determined to check a rabbit snare she'd laid the day before near signs of a thriving warren. The thought of a hot stew floating with bits of meat that were not Cham, of a soft hide to turn into liners for gloves, had been on her mind, not becoming part of a prank.

"Stay back with us, Ruby," young Colin said.

"Can't. Got stuff to do."

"Aw, come on. We've got something fun planned. Come on, you're one of us now."

One of us. She'd never been one of anything except her tiny, broken family packed into flat 23 of the tired old motor lodge. But that family counted on her.

"I've got stuff needs doing," she said again, her voice a little less certain.

"Aw, come on, it won't take long. I'm sure you'll still have time for whatever *needs doing.*" She hadn't noticed, at that moment, the sarcastic way he'd repeated her words. When had he changed? Or had it always been there, she later wondered?

Then, and she'll always remember this, her stomach rumbled so loud, and so long, that Colin laughed. "You know what? You do this and tomorrow I'll give you my lunch. Heck, I'll bring doubles of everything."

Her mouth watered. Colin's mom was the envy of all, or rather, her packed lunches were. They were well-off free-workers, able to afford things like chocolate and sugar and even soft-ground flour. In that moment, Ruby's hunger won out. There'd be time to check the snare, she told herself. Time to harvest a rabbit too.

She nodded. "All right."

"Great," he said. "Here's what I want you to do…"

Thirty minutes later, she, along with Colin and his cohorts, were hiding behind a rubbish bin out back of the school, stifling their laughter. They watched as Harold, the new janitor at the school and not yet Ruby's neighbor, peeked from the door of the male-workers locker room entrance. Even though he tried to hide his body, the group could see he wore only a towel wrapped around his slender waist.

"All right now," he called out, "you kids done had your fun. Lemme have my clothes back and we'll forget all about this." His voice was strong in volume only. Was that the first time Ruby had felt the binding to a near stranger? Embarrassment and shame and another kind of fear flowed from the poor man into her. Then, without staying to find out if he'd find a new boilersuit after Ruby had sneaked in and hidden his while he showered, Ruby ran away. She can't look at Harold Sr. to this day without feeling all that again. She thinks telling him the truth would expunge not all the guilt, but a part of it. But this, like telling her gram about the amber bottle of pills, she can't bring herself to do.

Now, here she is again. But it's not just for a free lunch, a real sandwich, a piece of chocolate cake, it's for shelter, for life.

She takes a deep breath, tries to keep a quiver from her voice. "I've been wanting to talk to you. Mr. Tate," she adds quickly.

"That so? Welp, this is good timing then."

His smile spreads, just like back then. "Heard about your little predicament." He says the word with exaggerated syllables. "Oh, and let me add…" He makes a sad face. "Your poor granny. So sad about that. She's your only family, isn't that right?"

A lump forms in Ruby's throat, as if all the words of her long-rehearsed speech about her productivity at the hatchery and value to McComb and how not moving her out and another family in would save them money are lodged there.

When she says nothing, Colin's eyes narrow; a conspiratorial glint twinkles in the green flecks of his hazel eyes. Eyes too much like her own. "Ah, let me guess, you need me to help you?"

It's all she can do to not tear herself from his superior gaze and storm away. But HJ is still there in her peripheral vision, still reminding her of what she has to lose beside her pride. She swallows hard. "Um, yes. I was wondering—"

"Come on, let's talk. I might just have a way we can help each other."

He puts a hand on her shoulder and leads her around the corner of the grocery. Ruby flicks her eyes to HJ, sends him a "stay there" look, and is relieved when the boy seems to understand. This isn't like the man at the river or the girls with their makeshift weapons. It's not what Tate could do to her that makes her nervous, it's what he'll want her to do.

As they round the corner, a blast of hot fetid air funnels up the alley. There's a metallic crash and clatter from farther down. A yelp as a feral dog is kicked away from the rubbish bins by a McComb worker. But otherwise, the alley is empty, no one around to witness whatever low she is about to consider.

"So, I've got this plan, you see," Tate says. "If you do this, I'll make sure you're not kicked to the curb. Capeesh?"

So, she listens. She listens to the price of her safety and her independence, to just what selling another bit of her soul might be worth.

4
Kaileh

The Briefing

Kaileh and Mateo return to the Shelter Rocks enclave knowing they won't be there for long. Kaileh, for her part, has herded herself into a corner of acceptance, regarding both the new assignment and the relocation to the place where Tareq was murdered. She holds tight to the small piece of information she's learned from the archivist. To others the information may not seem like much, at least on the surface of things. But to Kaileh, it seems like a trail of footprints scratched in the leaf litter: the place Tareq was killed, where the forest soaked up the blood of his heart's final beats, is a good kilometer from where he and his partner, Onas Steeprock, were supposed to be. Everyone, let me have your attention," Commander Tao calls over the clatter of dishes and buzz of conversation in the dining hall where first meal is winding down. Kaileh scrapes the remnants of her food into the compost bin, washes her plate, and sets it back on the rack. She takes a deep breath, puts on her best "I'm ready for anything" expression, and heads to an empty chair between Mateo and Lena, another Shelter Rocks officer selected for the task force. Only a few officers are leaving Shelter Rocks for Waccamaw, but the room is filled with everyone not currently out on patrol.

Tao stands, a patient, urgent smile on her face, as chairs are turned to face the front of the room. The commander is a slight, sturdy woman in her fifties: a competent, enigmatic person who, for reasons Kaileh can't pinpoint, unsettles her. It's as if she's met a long-admired mentor, anxious about how she'll be judged—and, of course, thanks to her own actions, she has been.

To one side and slightly back from Tao sits the person soon to be Kaileh, Mateo, and Lena's new leader: Commander Toma Briento. Sitting just ahead of her is the Lappite Detention Center guard, Jakob. His pale brown hair and bush of thick beard block part of her view.

The room quiets, and Tao speaks. "Wonderful. I have the honor of introducing to all of you an old friend and, for some of you, your new leader: Commander Toma Briento. Toma was my first unit commander when I graduated from Warrior Academy. I have the utmost respect for xem, as I am sure you soon will. Xe will brief you on ICE and answer any questions."

Tao turns to Briento, shakes xyr hand, and steps to the side. Of medium height with the muscular build and slightly pudgy belly that makes Kaileh think of a former lacrosse player, Briento steps to the front and flashes a warm, toothy grin that seems both confident and somehow playful. Then xe does something that creates within her a feeling of kinship: xe shakes the electronic clipboard in xyr hand as if it were the old-fashioned kind, with papers flapping for emphasis. Someone, she thinks, should program the e-utensil to simulate a fluttering noise.

Xe clears xyr throat, giving the c-board another shake. "Thank you, Commander Tao. It is always a pleasure to see you. And now, I have the honor of stealing away some of your finest officers."

Finest? Kaileh thinks, and can't resist glancing at Tao, who, to Kaileh's surprise, is looking right at her. Tao gives a small smile and—*was that a wink?*—looks back at Briento, who is again speaking.

"Those who know me might find my appointment to this political assignment rather surprising. It is no secret the distaste I hold for all things political. But I have a personal interest in this operation. Full disclosure, friends, my lifemate is an International Assembly of Nations human rights worker. He was recently held captive by a small group of hostile protesters in the Atlantic States." Briento holds up a hand to the sympathetic intakes of breath and worried shifting in seats. "Not to worry, he has been subsequently freed and returned, bringing with him firsthand reports of disturbing information." Murmurs thread through the room, sounds of concern and dismay filling the space. Briento lets them play out, a patient expression about xyr mouth.

"I will not delve into the machinations that occur at the top levels of our nation, but suffice it to say, when our Silvers gathered to hear the ASA's demands, requests, and posturing"—here xe makes finger quotes—"they listened, and have settled on a multifaceted approach. Part of this is creating this task force—the Intra-Continental Enforcement Office, ICE. For those of you who are sticklers about grammar, I apologize for the loss of the letter 'O' at the end of the acronym."

Polite laughs come from around Kaileh. She raises her hand. Briento nods.

"Commander, if I understand what you are saying and implying, we're to work *alongside* ASA *officers*? Side by side with, with these *Shepherds*? And we'll be patrolling the West in search of undocumented Atlantics? Is this essentially a way of stalling, of creating a buffer of time for our operations?"

Mateo elbows her. "Well, isn't it?" she hisses.

"To answer your equally astute and blunt question," Briento says, "yes. It might be a facet of this operation. Time might be the thing allowing us to evacuate the many aid workers and inspectors still in-country."

Kaileh's hand itches to shoot back up. To press further. But Briento goes on. "However, I am counting on your—on *all* of you"—xe gives her a look that makes her sit on her hand—"being professionals. In short, you will perform these jobs to your best ability, despite this unsavory partnership. You are all trackers here, and that's what you will be doing, just with one of the—"

"Enemy?" someone says. Kaileh snorts, feels a hint of irritation she didn't say it first.

"Other side," Briento corrects, but not unkindly.

Briento and Tao answer more questions and an hour later, right on schedule, Briento dismisses the group. "I will see you in Waccamaw in two days."

A flurry of relief and conflict tumble around inside Kaileh. Only two days to consider the information provided by the archivist. It could mean nothing. The trail will likely lead to a simple administrative misunderstanding, something easily explained. But every time she rolls the concept around and tastes the subtle nature of it, she's certain there's something else. But its exact nature eludes her. She makes her way from the room, trying to slip away without talking to anyone, craving solitude and, hopefully, clarity of mind.

She's almost to the door when a shoulder bumps hers, pivoting her slightly toward the other person. Kaileh blinks, tries to get her head back into the moment.

"Officer Kaileh," the Lappite Jakob says. Why does the way he says her name, the very way he talks, irritate her so? Her mother says she's always been this way, finding the tiniest piece of sand in an otherwise clean set of bedding.

She works to loosen the clench of her jaw. "Uh, yes?" This man is a coworker, a friend of the West through service, nothing more. But no matter what her head says, something makes her want to jump away, like she's just heard the rattle of an unseen snake.

Jakob tips his head, now capped with his broad-brimmed black hat, and continues to look down at her. Kaileh's tall, 180 centimeters. It's not for many people that she must look up. And she does not now. Instead, she keeps her gaze somewhere near his chest, takes out her keitai, cringing inwardly at turning to the e-utensil for rescue, and says, "You'll have to excuse me." And, in the way of the guilty, she embellishes. "I have a script, a very important one, I need to reply to."

Feeling his gaze on her back and knowing her steps, her way of walking from the room, are somehow giving away her lie, she leaves him standing there.

Tareq's Record

The afternoon before they leave Shelter Rocks to travel south to Waccamaw, Kaileh finishes packing her bag, then studies the small space that has been her quarters for two years. One year earlier, she packed the same leather bag and also headed south. A somber, tragic journey to retrieve her brother's few belongings. This time will be different, she tells herself. She'll make sure of it.

She pulls out her small bound notebook and looks again at the archivist's script transcribed from her keitai. *It may mean nothing, but satellite surveillance of the team of Steeprock and Clearwater-Lewis indicates they "strayed" from their assigned patrol route for the day. At this point, it's all I was able to find. Be well.*

But then a second script arrived, days after the first. The archivist, on his own instigation, had looked into Onas Steeprock. What he found wasn't much, but she's certain it means something. Oddly, Steeprock's birth records are missing from his files.

It sends a tingle through her, this odd discrepancy. It may not seem like much, but something tells Kaileh it's the ripple beneath which a big fish hides.

She lowers herself to the floor of her tiny domicile and attempts the meditation pose and breathing that Nibaa, her spirit healer, taught her. But ten futile minutes later, she sighs, rises, puts on her boots, and leaves the building. There's time for one last hike to her favorite place.

The Border Wars Memorial earthwork is perched on a tall hillock with a long, gentle view of the eastern continental divide to one side, the Allegheny Plateau, and the slouching hulk of Nemesis Peak to the west. Below, the Little Yok-i-gay-nee River snakes through the small valley, collecting the water of Gap Creek and others and shepherding it to the Monongahela.

As Kaileh walks the winding path of Memorial Mound, rising ever higher, she tries to see it anew, knowing it may be her last visit for some time. The earthwork is unique from other nearby mounds, like Headwaters Burial Mound near Lenape City, where her parents took she and Tareq during their long-ago visit. Memorial Mound was built for reflection and contemplation; the only ancestors interred inside are the intangible artifacts of sentiment.

As always, upon reaching the apex, she removes her boots and sinks bare feet into the soft grasses and native plants growing across the gentle expanse. A breeze, floral, grassy, and laden with pollen, fills her lungs. Nearby, a bronze plaque nests in the plants. She's read it once. A brief acknowledgment of the English King George III and his Proclamation of 1763, the very thing that, in later world courts, justified—and sustained— their expulsion of the settlers from the west. Kaileh likes that the engraved plate sits low to the ground, its credit to the British king all but obscured by the living earth.

She raises her arms like wings, closes her eyes, and turns in a slow circle. The diminishing warmth of the sun low on the western horizon and the whispering of the tree canopy on the eastern side of the knoll caress her senses, calm her like no enclosed meditation in her room can. Beneath her feet, she feels the centuries, millennia even, of history and culture the earthwork represents—and the throb in the east of the broken land.

Kaileh recalls her family's visit to Headwaters Mound. They went just after their visit to the Pontiac Victory Center. It seemed a lifetime ago, and in some ways, she supposes, it was. They walked up the long slope of the earthwork as a bonded unit, Kaileh happy to be outdoors, her parents probably even happier not to be watching their children like clucking hens. She bounded ahead, determined to be the first to the top. Tareq lagged, his dark curls, so like their father's, flagging forward, his head down, likely distracted by some botanical/entomological/geological thing that would have bored her as much as being dragged through a museum did.

Her eyes squeeze shut, trying to wring something new from the memory. It was a time when the concept of losing all her family, in one way or another, was impossible to imagine. She's on the other side of that reality now. Her father's not coming back, her brother neither. And her mother will be next. She feels cocooned by the memory—not in a comforting way, but as if she's bound tightly, unable to free herself from the sad, solitary life that is now hers.

When she opens her eyes, she's facing south. A few hundred miles away lies Waccamaw. There's a tug, a pull, like an invisible wire, the clear strand of a fishing line hooked into her. And she knows she'll follow it. Let it reel her inexorably toward whatever she can learn of her brother.

Even if it only brings more pain.

5
Ruby

Caught in the Corner

Ruby and HJ ride the omnibus back from their failed day in Denton. The boy, along with Ruby, seems to know it is their last time trying to mudlark or hawk the finds—at least with the same innocence and assumptions of the past. Ruby feels chased. It's not just the crime she's agreed to be a part of for Colin Tate, it's like she's barely keeping ahead of a pack of feral dogs snapping at her heels. She senses an end, as if some crucial gear working inside her is about to seize up and fail.

HJ is quiet, but presses his face to the window as they pass the shantytown. He's made sure they're sitting on the same side where, just a week earlier, he grew excited about seeing the mysterious girl. Ruby's so distracted by what Colin has asked of her that she almost doesn't sense the thundering oppression of the community of adrift. It isn't until the omnibus klaxon gives a shrill blast and the vehicle lurches to an abrupt stop that she fully reenters the moment. It takes an effort to lift her head, as if what she's considering doing for Colin, the dangers in town, her dying grandmother, all of it, are heavy stones lodging inside her skull.

In the road ahead, two men in tattered rags struggle against each other, a large, rough piece of metal clutched between them. As they turn, Ruby sees the metal sheet is the bonnet from a long-abandoned car. Shreds of kudzu vine from wherever they found the treasure dangle. The men radiate a desperate need, as if owning the piece of scrap is a matter of life or death. She swallows when she realizes that of course it is. Of course. And she could be in that same situation soon. Terror washes over her, then guilt for thinking more of her own future than that of the poor adrift outside.

"There she is!" HJ bounces on his seat, points to the side of the bus where a young girl, maybe his age, perches on an overturned bucket near a faded green tent. She sits hunched, intent on what she's doing. A long stick is clutched in one hand and she appears to be drawing something in the dusty earth before her. HJ vibrates beside Ruby. He taps the window. The girl lifts her head and scans the omnibus. Her eyes lock on Ruby's with a gaze both old and young, like she's seen too much. HJ waves. The girl hesitates, then raises an arm that's nearly as thin as the stick she's drawing with, her fingers fluttering back. Her light brown hair is short and choppy. Ruby tries to read something in the girl's gesture. Does she know HJ? Maybe he's waved at her before. Certainly, he hasn't visited the camp? The thought makes Ruby feel sick. Harold Sr. wouldn't survive if something happened to his boy.

Ruby might not either.

To her relief, the road clears and the omnibus pulls away. There's a moment of silence and then HJ touches Ruby's arm. "I wanna…" He pauses, then corrects himself. "I *want to* give her some of my ol' toys, Roobs. Some food, too."

Ruby studies his small hand clutching her own ropy muscles. "That's sweet of you, buddy." And for just a moment, she tries to think of a way to help him accomplish it. But the Shepherds beating the adrift, men nearing fisticuffs over a scrap of metal, and the other unseen dangers are too much. What would happen if she and HJ walked into the camp bearing food and toys?

But then her cheeks flush with shame. They're just people, people who've been dealt a worse hand than even she. But children walking into such despair and desperation? The young can so easily be made the victim. She should know.

Back in school, after the sad prank on poor Harold Sr., Ruby did her best to stay away from Colin and his group. But it didn't last. One day, only weeks later, she was halfway back to the motor lodge walking one of her favorite foraging routes. It seemed like a good day, a lucky day. She had a rabbit dangling from one hand and a basket of early strawberries in the other. Then she stopped short. Her mood reversed. She'd forgotten her homework. Irritated, she turned and trotted back to school, arriving just in time to see Colin and another boy from his gang talking to a girl Ruby didn't personally know, but recognized from a grade or two below. At first, Ruby thought they were tricking her into doing something mean like they had with Ruby. She paused at the corner of the building, then almost went on, but froze when she saw the girl was crying. She had stringy brown hair and wore a dingy dress of faded plaid. Her name came to Ruby then: Liza.

It was then that Ruby knew the boys were up to far worse than stealing clothes from a poor janitor. Ruby's feet grew roots. Even though they attended the same school, she held no illusions about the difference of class. Colin might be the same age as her, but different rules applied; his freedom included not only more opportunities now, but fewer consequences for stepping out of line. In horror, she watched as Colin clutched the girl by the shoulders, holding her still while the other boy snaked his hand between Liza's skinny, struggling legs. Her crying turned to a wail. The boys laughed. It was the kind of cackle that had nothing to do with humor.

Anger shot through Ruby. For one blink of a moment, the consequences of intervention flashed before her: as a conscript class, could Colin, son of a high free-worker, have her turned out of school? Or worse? But then the boys laughed their rough, lusty sound again and she stopped thinking. She didn't notice herself drop the rabbit and basket. She didn't notice herself picking up the rocks. But her intent and body merged as she took two long steps from behind the wall, focused on her target, and sent the stone flying. It skipped off the round head of the boy doing the dirty work. He screamed, raised his hand to the back of his skull, and spun around. Dark red blood seeped over between the fingers pressed above his ear. It was the color of rubies, she remembers thinking with deep satisfaction.

"Leave her alone!" She leaned down, grabbing two more dusty rocks.

Colin called out, "Come on, Roth, this is none of your business." It was the way he said it, like it was just some vegetables they were stealing that pushed her over the edge.

She threw the other stone, aiming for Colin. But he was still behind the sobbing Liza. She stared at Ruby with big, pleading eyes. The rock whizzed just past the already bloodied head of the other boy. He looked once at Colin, then at Ruby before he ran away.

Abandoned, Colin's expression changed.

Ruby tossed her last stone, a nice elliptical one, back and forth in her hands. She didn't care. She didn't care if she killed him. Or so she told herself.

Luckily, she didn't have to. Colin dropped his hands from Liza and held them out, palms toward Ruby. "Hey now, that's enough." His gaze suddenly dropped to Ruby's side. His eyes sprang wide.

She looked down and saw her hunting knife in her other hand—a short child's version of the ones she'd later have, but still a working blade. It was the one, in fact, she'd dispatched the rabbit with. A bit of blood and fur still clung there. It was this evidence, she'd later think, that was the final persuasion.

"Go home, Liza," Ruby said, a new confidence in her voice. "It'll be all right." Of this she wasn't certain, but something in Colin's expression told her he would not be telling on Ruby. He wouldn't be sharing this incident with his dear mommy.

Liza took two shaking steps and sent Ruby a look of gratitude she's never forgotten, before breaking into a run.

It was dangerous enough back then. It's worse now.

So, to sweet HJ she says, "It's good to care, buddy, but it's not safe." She shakes her head. "I'm sorry, but it's not going to happen, all right?" He nods, but there's something in the set of his shoulders, in the hard-as-nails tension from him that, if she were more present, she would realize is defiance.

Bud Downs

Ruby does her best to go on as normal. Over the next two days, Gram seems to fade, yet somehow endure, like a fog that lingers despite a rising sun. It's both a marvel and a horror how her heart seems determined to continue. Ruby does her best to be present, to, despite soaking in the woman's pain and despair, appreciate these last moments.

Colin told her to be ready to do her part in his plan. Not when. Not where. He claimed it's minor; hardly even a crime, he said. Just some papers that need *freeing* from inside a locked building. "Petty" was another term he'd used. A petty crime. Still, she's certain it's not so minor that if she, a conscript is caught, punishment will be overlooked.

Each morning at the hatchery check-in, the Shepherd Downs studies her like he's appraising a new car, or maybe a fancy menu. The intensity of it burns and freezes at the same time. At first, she thinks she's imagining it all, then, on a morning about five days after her encounter with Colin Tate, something shifts. She's at the BrandScan, the green light flashes, but Downs doesn't give the command to proceed. She wonders if she should go on in. Behind her another worker clears his throat. Uncertain, Ruby at last lifts her eyes. The same sense of familiarity rushes into her, like she knows him from some other life, but she looks in Downs's gold-flecked eyes and sees something change, a hardening: he's done appraising and shopping. He's made a choice.

Ruby takes a sudden step back, slamming into the man in line behind her.

"Watch where ya going!"

"I'm sorry," Ruby says, and runs toward the entrance. She feels Downs watching her, two hot coals burning into her back. Ruby spends her entire shift feeling the heat of his stare as if he's still there, as if his gaze is still on her. So, she's not surprised later, when her shift is done, to find Downs waiting.

She steps from the worker exit desperate to get back to the motor lodge. It's not just the unsettled feeling of Downs's attention, it's another prickling sense: something bad has happened at home. Maybe Gram has again fallen, or tipped over her water, or needs more pain medication, or what if Mrs. Simpson didn't show up for her afternoon visit?

Then Downs steps from around a corner, a dark shape where none should be. Ruby freezes, her fists clench, then loosen, dropping her take-home ration of Cherky bars. They fall to the tarmac in a soft, unnoticed clatter.

"Roth," he says in that slightly too-high-pitched voice. "I'd, uh, like a moment of your time."

It's hot out, the humidity coating her with tackiness, but still, cold sweat trickles between her shoulder blades. Her thigh muscles bunch, wanting to run. But cons don't run from Shepherds, unless they crave the zap-crook. Ruby bites her cheek, says nothing. Downs nods, motions for her to step over to the side of the building.

No no no, Ruby thinks. No.

Downs pulls a red-and-white smallcigar pack from his front pocket. Ruby catches the brand name, Marlburg, the "Pride of Maryland Smokes."

"Ya want one?" He holds the packet out.

Before she can stop herself, words stumble out. "I don't smoke." Then she thinks, *Stupid!* Anyone in their right mind would say yes. She could take it to give to someone else. Or sell. Anything but risking offense. "Um, thanks, though." Part of her wonders if she should stop resisting the binding, reach out instead and see if it can be put to use. But the thought makes her shiver, like she'd be opening a door holding back an unseen presence and would find she's released a monster. Still, even without trying, Downs radiates a blank space where feelings should be. It's like with Brother Q, but not, as if the two reasons, the two men, even, are East and West.

Downs taps out a smallcig, lights it, draws in deep. The end glows red, then dims. Ruby waits. After another long moment, he blows the fragrant blue smoke downward, his top lip a hood over the small circle of his mouth. "You don't remember me then."

She feels lost, like she's taken a wrong turn and has suddenly noticed she's not where she thought she was. Her tongue is tied in knots. Who's to say that doesn't push that wrong turn one step farther and take her over a cliff?

"I'm sorry..." she finally manages.

He nods, takes another long pull, then drops the half-smoked smallcig to the ground, grinds it with the heavy heel of his boot in a slow, solid arc. "Guess it don't matter."

Before she can process or even think what to say, Downs walks away.

Ruby watches him go; a long exhale blows from her lips. She almost turns for the omnibus just pulling in to the hatchery, but then stops. Downs is climbing into his personal vehicle, which is, of course, no surprise. But it's the color, the familiarity of it that sends ice to her veins. He slams the door of the dark blue Reo pickup and drives away.

All the way home, Ruby tries to put it together. Has it been Downs all these early mornings? But why? Why? Why? Why? It makes no sense. And his cryptic implication of knowing her from the past? Her mind is a confusion of clutter, like a net of debris and weeds and refuse pulled from the river, nothing worth saving, but everything too entangled to be rid of.

Ruby arrives back at the motor lodge feeling like she's barely keeping ahead of a pack of feral dogs. It's only when her hand touches the doorknob that she comes back into the moment. A tingle vibrates up through her arm like a warning shock. With her breath held, she pushes open the door to flat 23. A breeze flows out, lifting the short hair around her ears. And she knows. She knows Gram's gone. She steps in. Pulls the door shut. It's oddly cold in the room. Her skin prickles. For a moment, she can't look down at the bed pallet. Can't face the reality. At last, she lowers herself beside the pile of quilts and touches her grandmother's cold shoulder.

"Gram, I'm home."

She thought her grandmother would just appear asleep. But the body that lies there is so far from that, that for a full minute, Ruby doesn't breathe. Gram's eyes are closed at least, but they've sunk back in her skull, as if whatever was holding them up has drained away. Her skin has a waxy sheen, the yellow that was already there from her liver disease, now stealing away the flush of pigment that was evidence of her once-beating heart. Ruby draws the old quilt up over the woman's head, but it makes it worse, as if it robs her of identity, turn her into an anonymous corpse.

Beside the AquaClenz is a note from Missus Simpson: *Not good when I left. Hope this goes easy for her and you. Let me know. M. S.* Ruby reads the note several times before the words make sense. The room feels hollow. It's different than being alone, as she often used to be back when her grandmother could still work. Ruby realizes that just knowing someone was coming back, that they weren't gone for long, could fill a space with a different kind of life.

Time passes. She doesn't know how much, but it's long dark when her stupor begins to lift. She expected tears to come, but her eyes are dry. Her mouth chalky. The quiet is like thunder in her head. It's all over. The suffering. The criticism. The teaching. The love.

Another thought comes to her then: she's too late. Not too late to save the old woman, but too late to ask her questions—yet again. Too late for any answers. But somehow, this only makes the chain of the unanswered all the heavier.

"Oh Gram, I'm sorry I wasn't here. I'm sorry I couldn't… I couldn't make it better."

And Ruby Roth, who's been an orphan since she was only a baby, knows she is now truly alone.

The First Offer

The next morning, Ruby moves with a numb kind of efficiency. She walks to the emergency console on the first level, hoping Missus Simpson doesn't see her. Alone. It's alone that she is and alone that she wants to be. She uses the McComb call box, leaves a message with Human Services, and trudges back to her flat. She's sure she sees several neighbors' curtains lift and fall as she nears and passes. Surely word has somehow spread.

Moments later, there's a knock on the door. And despite her earlier sentiment, a feeling of relief loosens her muscles when she opens the door to Harold Sr. Even the usual rush of guilt at the reminder of her dark side isn't enough to stop her from falling against his shoulder. He's only a few years younger than her father would have been. For several years after Harold left the janitorial job at the school, he worked, for a time then, at the same slaughter plant where her grandmother said her father had. It's something Ruby doesn't try to imagine; if her father was like her, the torment of participating in the taking of lives day in and day out must have been a torment.

"Tea?" is all she can think to say when she at last pushes herself away from Harold Sr.'s gentle hug.

"Why sure, sounds good enough." Ruby doesn't follow the man's gaze when he looks over to Gram's pallet, but she feels a grief from him like small needles in her eyes.

Just as they finish cups of dandelion root tea and Ruby starts wondering what to do next, she hears the McComb micromulti pull up to the complex. Something heaves inside her chest, something big and bulging and threatening to burst.

"I got this for you," Harold says, and lets the workers in.

Ruby stays at the table, watching, but not trusting her legs to hold her upright. The team of two, dressed in CC blue, but with dark cuffs and hats of black, works quietly. Efficiently. Their faces and emotions blank. A gurney is rolled in. There's a beep as they use a portable BrandScan to verify Gram's identification. Then they wrap her in a blanket, the same one with the patchwork scraps Ruby always meant to ask about. With practiced moves, they place her grandmother's body in a heavy black bag. A long brass zipper pulls the edges closed.

A sob escapes Ruby. She thinks her chest is going to explode. With all her will, she pulls Gram in, wrapping her arms around her chest in a tight hug. Then, with small nods of sympathy or training, they wheel Gram out.

The flat goes from empty to impossibly hollow.

Gram's pain is over, her pain is over, Ruby repeats to herself. But somehow, it still all seems horribly wrong. How could a long life, a full life—even if lived under the chains of another—it couldn't just end like this, could it?

She almost asks Harold to leave, but he does something that, at first, turns her despair to irritation. He begins to clean. She watches, her arms still crossed, afraid to let go. He bundles the rest of the bedding and, without asking, hauls it away. At first, she wants to scream, *No!* It feels like something precious is slipping away. Surely, she should save the last evidence of her grandmother's end. But her mouth refuses to work, and in the end, she thinks, why? It won't bring her back. It won't give Ruby more time. It won't change anything.

By the time Harold Sr. comes back from the rubbish pit, Ruby has a bucket filled with water and soap powder and is scrubbing the floors. The two of them go on like that for some time. It's only when Harold Sr., just finishing wiping down the cupboards, says, "We ought to get some food in us," that Ruby realizes half the day has passed. Her own stomach suddenly growls. Her belly and chest feel different, as if that swollen bubble inside of her has, perhaps, partly deflated, making just a small space for hunger.

"You wait here," he says. "Missus Simpson dropped a dish of something by earlier. I told her I'd make sure you got it—when you was ready."

Ruby doesn't argue, and when Harold returns moments later, she surprises herself by saying, "Will you stay?" She won't remember what the dish was, or even if it was good, but when she's done, a bit of life seems to pump through her veins. She opens her mouth to thank Harold, but he speaks first.

"I know this ain't the best time, but there's somethin' I been meanin' to run past you." He stares at the newly cleaned floor and shifts in his chair.

Ruby's body constricts. She can't possibly face anything else right now. She stares at the surface of the beautiful table, rubs her hands across the smooth silk of it.

"Your daddy made this. You know that?" At her look of surprise he adds, "Oh, that's not the thing I been wantin' to talk about, but still, it's the truth. Your gram, she told me Nicholas done made this when he first came back from the *other side*. Said she ain't known he got such talent. For my part, I'm still wondering where the wood come from."

She can't sort what Harold is saying. Parts want to mesh with what her gram said just days ago, and she tries to push the pieces into place, but her efforts are leaden with fatigue and sadness.

Harold continues. "But there, look at me puttin' off what I need to say. Now, if you'll indulge me a moment, I gotta get this said."

Then she remembers his worries about HJ and the dreams, her promise to help. "Oh Harold, I haven't had a chance to ask Sister O about HJ and his dreams. Not yet. I'm so sorry."

He holds up a hand. "That ain't it."

"Oh. All right. Sorry. Go on."

A moment, which seems long in the emptiness of the flat smelling of alkaline soap and wet wood, passes. He clears his throat. "I known you for a long time, Ruby Roth. And Little Harold, well, he thinks of you as family, he sure does."

Ruby opens her mouth to agree, to say she feels the same way, but Harold again holds up his hand. The knob of his throat bobs up and down. A tingle of nervous discomfort runs through her. "Harold… I…"

"Let me keep on. You see, I been thinking, given the eviction thing you got and how there's all these new housing rules they be imposin' on us, that there's…" He swallows hard. "… only one thing makes sense. Going forward, I mean."

Then, with words that are rapid and jittery, he says, "If'n you want, it'd make sense if you was to move in with us. It won't be nothing like what people'll think." A blush spreads up his neck. Ruby feels her own color rising. "No sir, we'll keep it just friends, but them McComb folks will draw the conclusion we all want. And Little Harold'll be so happy. It'll be a good thing. I've done thought about it for some time now." He's looking just over her shoulder at the wall, one foot jiggling on the floor.

Of all the things he might have said, Ruby hadn't seen this one coming. She feels both unworthy and beyond grateful. But how to answer? She fumbles for words that won't hurt him. Won't diminish what it took for him to make such a generous offer. "I couldn't impose on you like that, Harold."

He nods, his brow wrinkled in thought. "There's 'nother thing. You see, I been worryin' about what'll happen to my lad if… if somethin' were to, were to happen to me."

"Oh, Harold." Ruby's mind flashes to another micromulti coming from Human Services. Another body wrapped without ceremony in an anonymous black bag. "Are you…?"

Something flashes in his eyes. He drops his gaze. His answer takes too long. "No, it ain't that. I'm doin' just fine, but you know, things… well, things are changing around here. I worry about the lad." His voice is wistful and sad, and whether she takes him at his word or is just too wrung out to question the way he doesn't look at her when he speaks, even she doesn't know. Instead, her mind goes to her own loss of parents. What would have happened to her if Gram hadn't taken her in? Would she have been adopted out like other children? But she can't take advantage of the Harolds, most certainly not without coming clean about her prank so long ago. She just can't. Inside of her the pressure builds.

"I… Harold…" She looks over at the spot where her gram took her last breath.

"I shouldn't've brought it up so soon. I made a mistake. I best be going now. Sorry again about your gram, Ruby. She was, deep down, a good woman." He rises, his posture both stiff and broken. Before Ruby can think of something kind to say, HJ's father is gone.

The Second Offer

Despite wanting to, Ruby can't go after him. It suddenly feels like she can't make a good choice. She let her gram suffer to the end. She's considering helping Colin Tate commit a crime. She's hurt Harold Sr.'s feelings. And Shepherd Downs is… what? Suddenly, she can't stand to be in the flat. She grabs a book she borrowed long ago from the Elohi Outreach and just found while cleaning, walks to the omnibus stop, and waits for the next transport into Denton. Part of her thinks it's a mistake, this seeing Sister O so soon. How will she hold her emotions together in front of the woman? But the peace and calm of the Outreach is the only place she wants to be.

But when she arrives, the scene out front of the building is anything but peaceful. It's another protest. It's either her mood or the fact that this one is different. Her mood vibrates with a rage that rattles through her, threatening the tiny bit of reserve she's trying so hard to maintain.

Her grief swings, replaced by a flood of anger. Why are the ignorant workers protesting the Outreach? Do they not see how the monastics are the only ones here who seem to care about them? How can they believe what Chairman Powell says about their suffering being the fault of the West? She glares at the crowd and shoves her way through, then, at the last minute before she pushes in, she turns. Her eyes scan the motley group. Most people look sickly, wan and in need of something, whether it's better food or medicine. A part of her melts.

"They can help you if you go inside!" she says, her voice cracking.

But her words are lost, swallowed by a different kind of hunger in the agitated mob.

"Don't go in there!" someone shouts.

"They gonna sell you some poison!" another voice yells.

"Traitor. Turncoat. Sellout." The words come like stones.

Go ahead, she thinks, do your best. She pushes through the door. There's a sharp crack. Ruby spins to see a tiny fissure splinter the glass. A small rock tumbles to a stop on the pavement outside the door.

"Inside," says Brother Q, who is quickly at her side, his hand on the small of her back. His touch is warm, a comfort, and suddenly the bubble inside her expands, displacing her anger with pure grief.

Her voice thick, her eyes burning, she says, "Sister O. Can I see her?"

"Of course, friend. Of course."

Ruby nods, keeps her gaze on the floor. She can't bear to have the deep green of Brother Q's eyes boring into her.

In a trance, Ruby walks toward the back room. But a voice stops her. "I'm here, dear one." The Sister, old as she is, is sitting on the floor, her legs nimbly crossed and tucked almost beneath her. Ruby steps close. The brisk scent of lavender tickles her nose. It's a flower, an herb, one she's only seen in pictures, but it has a fragrance she'll forever associate with the monastic.

Sister O is sorting books, spinning the rack before her, and reorganizing the volumes at the bottom. "I'm almost done here. Sister M? Would you put the tea kettle on please?"

"Oh yes! On it," Sister M says from somewhere Ruby cannot see.

Outside, the noise of the crowd dims. Ruby doesn't look back to the glass to see if it's dispersing or she simply can no longer hear it.

"Help me up, will you, dear one?" Sister O extends her ringed hand to Ruby. Ruby takes it, knowing full well that her help isn't strictly needed. Still, doing something, something for someone else, feels like a breath of clean air.

"How about we take that tea in the back room?"

Still mute, Ruby nods. She knows Sister O has figured out what's happened, that her grandmother no longer lives. For that, for not having to tell the tale, Ruby is also grateful.

Minutes later, they're sitting at the small table in the back room. How long has it been since she last visited? Since she was given the dark bottle of pills that sits now, unopened, in flat 23?

"You do not need to speak, dear one, if you do not feel it the proper time. We are here for you, though. Whenever you need us."

They sit in silence and sip a tea Ruby's never tasted before. It's both sweet and bitter, coating her throat and warming her insides. It matches her own feelings, but somehow soothes them too. What was it Sister O told her once about "like healing like"?

In the pleasant quiet, the monastic absentmindedly rubs her middle finger on the curves of the ring she always wears. Once, long ago, Ruby asked about the piece of jewelry.

"Oh my, yes. This, this is a token from my old life, my life before I joined the Elohi Order. It's something most of us do: retain a token of our past. Would you like to try it on, dear child?"

Ruby did. She was so small, her knuckles not the enlarged knobs they were by her twentieth year. The ring spun and hung there, but still she felt a warm glow from the touch of the silver.

She stares at the ring now. The embossed pattern circling the band, the stern-looking bird in stylistic profile adorning the top. There's a chip of pale blue turquoise inlaid over the bird's breast, an empty socket where another must have once defined the bird's eye. It's a thunderbird, Sister O told her. Whether real or legendary, Ruby doesn't know.

"This ring," Sister O says, "reminds me of my past and my future. How one sets me on my way and the other is of my own making."

"How?" Ruby says, knowing already of how the ring speaks to two of Sister O's origin cultures, but not how the ring can say anything about the future, about something so novel as *choice*.

"It is a good question, and most people would not have the deep insight to ask. You, dear one, are exceptional."

Ruby feels a blush heat her cheeks. She almost, almost smiles.

"Our futures, you see," the monastic continues, "hold much that feels beyond our control, but there is always choice. Always. Until the very end."

Ruby gives a little frown. Choice should be something you want. How can it be a choice when the options are loaded with consequences and burdens you don't want?

"When I look at my ring, with its pattern wearing away, one stone already missing, I am reminded that life, the life of anything, has its limits." She studies Ruby for a long moment, then adds, "It will bring scars. It will bring loss. It will bring change. It is up to me how I face it."

Ruby shifts in her seat, trying to scour up some kind of response. Before she can, Sister O speaks again.

"Now, dear one, it is time for you to make a choice." She looks at Ruby with pale blue eyes deep with knowing.

Ruby's stomach flips. The tea churns in her belly. How can the Sister know about Colin Tate? Or is it Harold Sr.'s offer? Both? Her mouth opens, but words stick in her throat. Thankfully, the door creaks open and Brother Q steps into the room.

But there's something in the look he gives Sister O that makes Ruby push to her feet. The room shrinks, the walls closing in. Her breath hitches.

"Dear one," Sister O says, laying a hand on Ruby's arm. "Please, give us a moment. You are safe. Please, sit."

As Brother Q slides a small stool to the table, Ruby lowers back down. She clasps her hands in her lap, unsure why they tremble as if winter has arrived.

A long minute passes.

"Ruby," Sister O says, "as sad as your loss is, it means we may at last tell you the truth. Brother, will you?"

"With pleasure." He turns his emerald eyes to her. "Ruby, we want to take you away from here. We want to take you into the West."

The Dilemma

Ruby stares at the two monastics as if they're speaking another language. They watch her. One pair of pale blue eyes, one pair of startling green. There's no jest in their faces, no twinkle of mirth in their gaze.

"You can't mean that you, you're… um… really… smugglers?" She squints, trying to picture gentle, gray-haired Sister O bundling someone into a disguise or hiding place or transport or something and stealing them away to the West.

"Dear heart," Sister O says, "it's a function, another part of what we do, but a minor one. A risk we take only rarely, and only for a few exceptional people. For you, we would have asked sooner, but your grandmother—it would have been an impossible choice."

"But, it's illegal!" Ruby stares at the supplies for Sister O's illicit medication distribution. "What if you get caught? It's way worse than… this." She waves her hand at the drugs.

"You are not wrong," Brother Q says. "But our purpose here cannot be one dictated by a fear of what has not happened."

"Dear one, we could sit here all day and try to help you sort this, but there is not time." She looks at Brother Q, the crease between her eyes deepening. "There are many changes happening, as you may well have noticed from the growing agitation just here in Denton. The news they allow you to see does not reveal the scope of your country's escalating problems."

"We fear," Brother Q adds, "the Outreaches located in the ASA may soon be closed."

"We may be forced to return to the West."

Ruby stares at Sister O, trying to picture not having the woman to turn to. It doesn't matter that Ruby has no more need for the medication that so helped her grandmother. It comes to her like a sudden gale of wind, knocking the breath from her. Sister O is like family. Who will Ruby lean on if she's gone? Then, something pulls her focus to Brother Q. His eyes are down. The emerald-green shielded by long black lashes. She catches the tiniest feeling of discomfort from him, but then he looks up and it's gone.

"What do you say?" Brother Q says. "Will you let us take you west?"

Ruby thinks of all the times she's talked with the monastics about what it's like in the West, a place where everyone matters, where the land itself, as if it too is a person, has "rights," a place so different, it's as if it's a fairy tale.

Ruby came to the Outreach expecting consolation and comfort. Perhaps even shared tears for the death of her grandmother. Not this. Not a world cracking open at her feet. Not a crevice through which she might fall into a new world.

Ruby swallows, looks up at the monastics. West. Could she really escape all of this and live, actually live, in a world apart? And what if her mother is there, somewhere? Could she find her, maybe, just maybe? Then, as if she's a bird that's flown too high, she plummets back to earth. She falls through the sky of her dreams and lands back at the old motor lodge. The Harolds. Little Harold. She can't leave him like she was left, can she?

"I… I'm sorry. It's just too much right now. I can't think. I can't think." Tears again threaten to fill her eyes

Sister O pats Ruby's hand, the heavy ring clunking on Ruby's knuckles. "Take a few days, dear one. We trust you to speak of this to no one. Not even those closest to you. But know that there is not much time. A window is closing. It may once again reopen, but"—she glances at Brother Q—"this world, your world, we fear, is approaching a change. One that may lead to a better world, but not without great suffering first occurring."

Brother Q slides back his stool and stands. "Think well on it, Ruby Roth. Think well."

The Decision

And she does. So much so that it all but overtakes the void left by her grandmother's absence. Ruby thought being alone would at least afford her a feeling of peace, of not having to keep up her guard under her gram's keen scrutiny. Two days pass in the quiet, purposeless atmosphere of the flat. Below, Ruby hears, more loudly than ever, the voices of the Harolds. She tries to imagine her own words blended with theirs, the family-like sounds drifting up to whomever McComb assigned to flat 23. Then, just when she resolves herself to that being the right choice, her mind flips to the dream of life in the West, to a life without caste, to a life where being different isn't a curse. It's a magnet, this thought, as strong as anything she's ever felt.

There is, though, one easy decision to make: turning down helping Colin Tate with his "petty" crime.

On the fourth day after her grandmother's death, she returns to the hatchery. With no morning obligations, other than readying herself, Ruby arrives on an earlier omnibus. With bold steps that feel as if they are made by some other person, she goes to Colin's office and slides a note under his closed door. As the paper swooshes through, a blade of ice runs down her spine. She almost tries to finger the note back, but it's drifted beyond her reach.

"Mornin', Roth," Officer Downs says when Ruby heads through check-in. His voice holds a faint tremble. There's something in it that makes her stop.

"You got any time, uh, after work?" the Shepherd says.

The question throws Ruby. Shepherds don't ask, they tell. She has no idea how to answer something that feels like a trap.

He clears his throat. A flicker of pity wedges into her reserves, but then her eyes drift to the handle of his zap-crook. It's holstered at his side, but the grip, a dark wood, is glossy and smooth from use.

"Can I go in now?" she says, trying to make her voice neutral.

"Yeah. Sure. Go on in."

She expects him to be waiting for her after her shift. But he's not there, and there's something about that that sends ice through her veins.

Ruby returns to flat 23 distracted, wishing for someone to trust, someone to talk to. When she opens the door, her heart stutters and threatens to stop all together. The flat is empty. Not just of Gram and her spirit, but of the table, Ruby's bed pallet, the old dresser with no knobs, the AquaClenz, everything. Panic runs through her, but then she sees the tag. It's wired to the door handle. The names of people she doesn't know are typed there in capital letters. QUARTERS OF R AND J JOHNSON.

R and J Johnson. RandJayJohnson. Rnjayjohnson. The names become nonsense in her head, rolling and repeating in nauseating waves. How? How did this happen so fast? Ah, of course. The note she left for Colin.

She runs to the landing, looking down in case she walked right past a pile of her belongings. But there's nothing there. What if the corp movers threw everything in the burn pit? She's halfway down the stairs when HJ yells from flat 13.

"Roobs!"

There's a shout from a few doors away: "Shut up, kid, some of us are trying to sleep here."

HJ raises his shoulders and grins as he trots to Ruby.

"Hey buddy." It's an effort to keep the exhaustion and fear from her voice. "You know what they did with all the stuff from my flat?"

"Well, yeah, sure I do. They ain't—sorry, I mean *didn't*—do nothing with it. Come on." He tugs on her hand and Ruby follows, expecting him to lead her to a cluttered, broken pile of her things. Instead, he steps inside the open door of flat 13.

Ruby wrinkles her brow, but then understands. Without her knowing it, without her saying so, a decision has been made.

"We rescued your stuff, Roobs. Me and Missus Simpson, we stopped those corp guys. They were fixin'—fixing—to take it all away! Can you imagine that? But we stopped 'em. Missus Simpson, she was fit to be tied, I tell you."

Ruby's grateful for the boy's chattering. It gives her time. Time to pull herself together. She takes a deep breath and steps into what, evidently, is her new home.

A Different Way

Within days, they fall into a routine that, to Ruby's surprise, offers her some comfort. Harold Sr. divided off a corner of the flat for Ruby's bed pallet, an old blanket hung for privacy—or at least the illusion of such. He works mostly night shifts at one of the McComb Corp grow farms. Each time she's with him, though, she decides it's the moment to tell him about the prank from so long ago. But then something little, such as HJ bounding in or talk turning to putting together a meal or stories from the past, jump in and douse her nerve.

Toward the end of the first week in flat 13, she goes to the Outreach. "I can't leave them, Sister O. I just can't." She listens as Brother Q tries to convince her of the shortsightedness of this choice. He speaks of things such as how soon Little Harold will be sent away, how she must think of her own future, about the new life she'll have far away west.

"I'm sorry, I know you're right. But you're also wrong. I won't be the one to abandon someone counting on me. I won't do it."

Sister O bit her lip, looking at Brother Q with an unspoken question.

"Hmm. Maybe," he says. "Maybe."

"What?" Ruby felt a tiny lift of hope.

"The boy," Sister O says. "What if we could extract him as well?"

"Oh. Oh." Ruby's mind whirls, picturing HJ in the West. No trade school. No life of forced labor doing whatever McComb ordered done. A clear blue sky with nothing but clean air to fill his lungs.

But, but, but… She has to ask. "What about his father? What about Harold Sr.?"

Sister O's blue eyes sparkle with instant tears. She glances at Brother Q, then shakes her head. "Even adding the boy will magnify the risk. No, Ruby. I am truly sorry. However, if things stabilize, then maybe. Perhaps later."

Ruby hears the impossibility in her words. Whether Sister O is saying them to soothe Ruby or herself, she doesn't know. She feels pulled inside out. Everything she wants is here. Nothing she wants is here.

"It's not fair." Ruby hears the whine in her voice. She wants to pull the ungrateful words back, but Sister O gives her hand a squeeze.

"You are absolutely correct, dear one. It is not fair."

Ruby returns to her new life with a sense of impending doom. The monastics are right, but so is she. But there's something else, another shadow that's joined with her since moving to flat 13.

It's only a week later that she notices how thin Harold Sr. has grown.

On his night off, Ruby wakes with a start and hears muffled bursts of coughing. Her first thought is Harold Sr. has picked up a cold, or maybe he has allergies Ruby has never before noticed? The room quiets again. The floorboards above her seem too silent, the new family having not yet moved in, and there isn't even the hint of a ghost haunting the space. She begins to imagine sounds from the old days, when she was still young, Little Harold still a toddler, Gram and Ruby bustling about in the flat above. In some ways, it seems only days ago. In others, another lifetime. She's just dozing off when the concussive sounds of Harold Sr.

coughing again blast her awake. She pushes back against the wall. The room is stuffy with summer heat and humidity, but still better than the second level. When winter arrives, she reminds herself, things will flip-flop and the place to be will be above.

Harold Sr. clears his throat, the effort to still another episode of coughing evident in the sound. Ruby tugs back an edge of the old blanket and narrows her eyes into the dark room. For a moment she sees nothing, then Harold's form comes into focus. He too is sitting, but hunched forward, as if more than a cough is keeping him awake. Then she feels it. Straps seem to tighten around her own chest. Her ribs ache. Something is not right; this is no cold or allergy.

She scoots from her bed, wearing the light set of clothes that has become, for now at least, her habit in such mixed company.

"Harold?" she whispers.

His own hushed voice whispers back, "I'm sorry. I done woke you up. Was trying to not let that happen. The lad here, he still got that child's gift of sleeping through" —he clears his throat and lets a small series of coughs rise— "just about anything."

Ruby stands, trying to sort the best thing to do. He's not well, this much is clear, but a sense of invasiveness flows through her. She's not his wife. She's not even his sister. What kind of role is meant for her? For them?

She turns to something familiar. Moments later, she's lit the kettle and is readying two mugs. Just as she's about to drop slivers of dried dandelion root into each, she stops and instead, selects several chunks of kudzu root for Harold Sr. When she turns, he's sitting at the beautiful table they moved from her flat. He's pulled back the wispy window curtain letting in a swath of light glowing from the bulb outside.

They sip their tea in silence. HJ moans a little, wiggles in his sleep, reaching for his father who isn't there. At last, the boy pulls a pillow to his chest. His breathing returns to smooth, deep rushes of sound that are more comforting than the medicinal tea. Ruby feels her rib cage begin to relax. Harold Sr., too, seems to lift and brighten.

After a deep swallow, he looks up, a pale smile haunting his eyes. "Suppose I oughta tell you somethin'. I been puttin' it off, not wantin' to add more burden, what with…" He looks up to the ceiling. "There's only so much a body and soul can take."

Ruby doesn't say anything, but a fist, one that has nothing to do with the binding, squeezes her heart.

"I thought I'd get better," he says. "Thought it were a passin' thing." There's a long pause. HJ snorts and rolls over, taking the pillow with him. "Well, here's the thing. My super sent me in to see the McComb docs yesterday. They run a few tests. Done give me their opinion." He coughs. A thick, wet sound. "*Opinion*, they call it. Bunch of uppity-muckers. It ain't an opinion, it's a sentence."

Ruby's heart feels squeezed to bursting. "What'd they say, Harold?" But she knows. She knows.

In the unmeasurable beat between seconds, hatred and resentment fill her. This place, their so-called homeland, it's poison. It's killing them all—slowly or too soon. She can almost feel its effects like a sticky film, only it coats her insides, even into her heart and soul.

"Cancer. Not the same as your gram's, but not that different. Kind of a cousin I suppose. I was born and raised across the Bay, you might recollect, in Southern Maryland. My daddy, he worked the Calvert County nuke plant. Still would be workin' there, I suppose, if he hadn't ended it, hadn't seen fit to hang himself."

Ruby can't stop the sharp intake of air. "Oh Harold. I didn't know."

He stares at the table, lifts the mug, but sets it back down with a thud. "I didn't mean to do this to you. That weren't my plan, putting you with the lad and then… ummm… dying on you."

Words fail Ruby. She wants to say it will be all right. But of course, it will be as far from all right as she is from the West. It will never be all right, not for Harold. Not for HJ.

Later, back in her pallet, sleep refuses to come. Her heart aches with what she's learned. Sadness for the boy and even more for his father rush in a whirlwind around her.

Hours later she startles awake. An idea so obvious, so clear she feels knocked on her backside, springs her eyes wide. She needs to talk to Sister O.

Part II
Should Haves

This war did not spring up on our land, this war was brought upon us by the children of the Great Father who came to take our land without a price, and who, in our land, do a great many evil things… This war has come from robbery—from the stealing of our land.

Spotted Tail (1823-1881) Sicangu (Brulé) Lakota

6
Kaileh

Return to Waccamaw

As Ruby wakes to a plan for fleeing west and taking Harold Jr. with her, Kaileh Clearwater Lewis steels herself for the return to the place her brother died. Like the Shelter Rocks enclave, Waccamaw is a border post: a place built and maintained and run in dedication to keeping the Atlantics and their culture from the land. The team boards the train at the Lenape City station in the afternoon. With only a faint whisper, the high-speed Arrow gathers momentum and slips away from the silver, greenery-clad towers of the capital of the Northern Woodlands. Kaileh sits by a window on the right side but misses a final view of the Pontiac Victory Center.

Just as they cross the Ohi-yo, cleaved, at this point, by Headwaters Island, she catches sight of the low knoll where Headwaters Mound rises. Its symmetrical cone is still green despite the summer heat. Someday, she vows, she'll return in early spring when heavy rainfall in the highlands engorges the rivers, turning the waters of the Monongahela or the Allegheny disparate colors: one a chocolate brown, the other a deep moss green. According to the stories, the waters battle like contentious siblings for miles, uniting at last downstream of the island. Her mother Bennu swears such was the river when their family visited the burial earthwork so long ago.

Across from her sit Lena and Bright Hawk, an Osage mixu'ga from the Plains Region. They two have known each other for years, their friendship a reminder to Kaileh of the nation's history, how all the cultures, even those that have historically been enemies such as Lena's and Bright Hawk's, united to keep the invaders from swallowing the West. Bright Hawk joined them at the Lenape Station, having taken an Arrow east from the Plains Region. At the moment, they're deep in an animated discussion having something to do with, of all things, the best wild fermented bread starter. On the seat beside her sits Mateo, equally engaged in the ardent exchange. Kaileh watches the three, fascinated by their ability to speak at once and apparently still be understood. In her family, waiting your turn and not interrupting were rules set in stone. Soon the overlay of voices and passions lulls her back to some other place and time.

"You thinking about Tareq?" Mateo's voice makes her jump.

For a moment, she doesn't answer. Was she thinking of her brother? Does obsessing about Onas Steeprock, Tareq's patrol partner—the man who failed to protect him—count? At last, she shrugs. "He's always on my mind, I suppose."

Mateo rests his hand on hers.

"I know what you're thinking," she says. "And I know it's going to be surreal, being back where he died. I'll be fine, though."

Mateo lifts his caterpillar brows in an "oh really?" look.

"I will." She wants to tell him more. Share her thoughts, the machinations turning wild gears in her mind. Mateo would have solid introspection, valuable input.

When she received news of her brother's death, Mateo quietly stood as she sobbed and pounded her fists on his chest, soaking his shoulder with tears. But then later she told him that upon meeting Steeprock, he'd seemed insincere, as if he were purposefully trying to deceive her, and Mateo brushed it off, saying it likely meant nothing. She convinced herself he was right, a steadfast rock, an anchor to her unmoored emotions.

Now, a year later and knowing so much more, she decides that sometimes an anchor is the thing holding you back.

"Truly," she says, meeting his brown eyes, "I'm going to be fine, it will just take time."

Time. She always thought there'd be more time.

Steeprock's lie had been simple, innocent, really. But inexplicably unnecessary. It was this fact that Kaileh still can't let go of. To her it reeks of innate duplicity, a fatal flaw in Steeprock's character. After all, where there is smoke, there are coals.

She went to see him at the Waccamaw infirmary. He lay there, supine, one eye ringed by a bruise the color of an aubergine, one leg suspended in a shining metal cage with slender pins sprouting like steel saplings from the thick white bandages wrapping his thigh. Sympathy flooded her veins. He'd tried to save her brother, they'd said. She hadn't known yet of the odd discrepancy of where the incident occurred. She hadn't known yet of Steeprock's missing birth records. All she knew at the time was that the pair had been on patrol and only Onas came back.

And one other thing: the administrative aide who gave her the bundle of Tareq's belongings and directed her to the infirmary let something slip, something he'd no doubt assumed Kaileh, being the deceased's sister, must already know.

When she stepped into Steeprock's room she felt pity and a tinge of annoyance that Tareq had not shared the news that he and Onas Steeprock were more than just professional partners. They were more than just lovers. They had sworn their promise to each other, planning their ceremony for the following spring. A ceremony to which she had not been invited, had not even known of. Well, what she felt was more than a tinge of annoyance. It was a rock of sadness and bitterness, dwarfed only by the boulder of Tareq's loss. But in that moment, she believed that burden was hers alone. Something that if her brother had lived, they would have had to work past.

"Hello," she said, "I'm Kaileh."

He shifted in the bed, a flicker of pain flashing in his brown eyes. "Onas. Officer Tareq's partner. But I'm…" He paused to sip water, seeming to need time to compose what he was about to say. He sat the water down with an awkward thump. "I'm," he continued, "sorry for your loss."

There was a coldness to his words that felt directed at her. Did Tareq hate her in the end? Hate her so much that Tareq and Onas both agreed to not tell her about their relationship and the ceremony?

Steeprock spoke again and she waited for the words she needed to hear.

"Tareq was… a good officer. His service will be missed."

That's it? That's all he needed to say?

For a moment, Steeprock's lips parted and she thought he would tell her the truth. What was the point of this lie by omission? Whom did it serve?

Behind where Kaileh stood in the doorway to Steeprock's room, a medic cleared her throat. Kaileh looked back at the woman holding a small cup of medication in her hand, then to Steeprock. "I guess you're busy." She pivoted, then looked back. "Be well."

And that was it. She fumed her way out of the infirmary, past the sprawling winter garden buildings looped in a circle, and to the auto-auto stop. Hoping to never see Onas Steeprock again.

Later, she learned of the tree poachers Tareq and Steeprock had been tracking along mountain ridges north of Waccamaw. How it was just unfortunate timing: Tareq coming upon the armed thieves first, Steeprock somehow far behind. When the team found Steeprock, the femur of his left thigh protruding in a jagged shard, the femoral artery exposed but intact, he'd been dragging himself toward the bloodied spot where her brother had been shot. From the amount of blood, the description of the wounds Onas had seen—one to Tareq's belly, one to the side of his head, releasing twin fountains of scarlet—the enclave's forensics techs concluded the wounds suffered by Officer Tareq Clearwater Lewis were fatal.

But nowhere in the report she was given was it mentioned that Tareq was far from his assigned route. Had it not mattered? Or, was something being hidden? Something Steeprock must certainly know? Was this why he hadn't shared his and Tareq's true relationship? Was it all tangled in with other lies and secrets?

The Arrow slips south into the dark, sliding stealthily along the valleys and foothills of the western side of the Appalachian Mountains. Kaileh dozes, sleeps, Mateo's head resting, at times, on her shoulder. Dreams visit in vivid clarity, then turn to smoke in the ether. She gets up once, around midnight, and walks the length of the train.

As she passes through the lobby car, the train slows minutely. An announcement chimes the arrival of a transfer shuttle. She watches the lights of the shuttle gaining speed, catching the main train, locking on like a lamprey on a shark. The doors of each car open, and for a few minutes, the two are one. New passengers step aboard, a few leave. There's a barely perceptible thud as automated dollies shunt luggage beneath them. Then the doors close and the shuttle disconnects and decelerates. Unseen by the Arrow passengers, it will soon come to a stop, then reverse direction and return to whatever sleepy town in which it began its journey.

Most passengers doze, unaware she's standing over them, studying them, watching them breathe. As she drifts through the train, an otherworldly sense comes over her, and for a long moment, she wonders if perhaps she is truly awake. Maybe she is still dreaming. Or perhaps she has somehow become a ghost. The thought makes her smile, and she walks on.

7

Ruby

Declined and Decline

W hen Ruby was little, she dreamed of the West. Sometimes while awake, sometimes while sleeping, visions of grasslands reaching to the very edge of the earth and capped by a giant dome of pale blue shimmered in her imagination. There were forests too: towering trees grasping toward that blue; cool, shadowy alcoves abundant with ferns; and clear water bubbling from springs. Everywhere there were bison and elk, deer and antelope, bears and wolves. Little creatures as well, butterflies and honeybees, and even slugs and snails.

She wakes certain, the idea bursting to come out. She knows immediately she must take the risk and break her oath to the monastics. She will tell Harold Sr. of their offer, for in the end, he should have the right to decide.

Ruby expects fear, even anger, but when she takes him aside, whispers the golden possibility, his answer is a surprise. There is no hesitation, only a deep sigh. "You go, Ruby. You go and carry my lad with you."

"Harold, are you sure? If it works, and, you know, if it doesn't…" She lets the words linger, sink like a stone in his heart. "You won't ever see him again."

They're standing just outside flat 13 in the early dawn after Harold told her of his illness. It seems too fast for it to come to this, too soon after his announcement of illness. She feels like a scavenger dog, swooping in to take an injured prey before it's breathed its last.

Harold shifts his feet on the grit of the sidewalk running along the length of the old motor lodge. "It's not like I'm gonna have him for long anyway."

That day at the hatchery, she barely notices Downs. She doesn't wonder if Colin is done with her. Even the cold brutality of her work scrapes at only the surface of her emotions.

Her shift done, she goes again to the back room of the Outreach. Sister O and Brother Q sit close, their heads bent so near, strands of hair hanging from each of their russet headwraps' touch, threads of silver twining with walnut brown.

Brother Q says, "We are fighting the clock, Sister."

Ruby chews on the inside of her cheek as the two monastics wrestle with the logistics of getting out not one, but two escaped conscripts.

"Indeed, Brother, indeed. And it is a fight I believe we can win."

The iron in the old monastic's voice straightens Ruby's spine, for even she knows of the growing risk. Just entering the Outreach today meant ducking into the back alley and away from the growing crowd in front of the building. Even as she turned away from the main street, a woman grabbed her elbow. Middle-aged, her skin flecked with pockmarks, Ruby recognized her from the McComb Corp Grocery. Lucy. She was still pretty, but with a brittle look, that made Ruby think she might break if you said the wrong thing. She was wearing a yellow field cap with a serpent logo stitched in black.

"You!" Lucy hissed, but not unkindly. "I know you. Come on now, join us. You're a hard worker ain't ya?" Her breath was hot on Ruby's face. Her pulse jumped; she could feel the woman's feverish passion like a catching sickness. "Don'tcha wanna be able to live better someday? You won't be doing no such thing if this here problem ain't dealt with." Ruby stared at the black emblem of the snake on the woman's cap, the embroidered words *Don't Tread on Me*. For just a moment, Lucy's eyes seemed to narrow into slits that sent ice deep into Ruby's gut.

She'd asked Brother Q about the yellow flag with its black snake when they first started appearing.

"It's a historical emblem, Ruby, created during the colonists' first Revolutionary War with England, not long after my ancestors won the first and second Border Wars in the late 1700s. That's what kept the colonists east of the Proclamation Line. A few years after that, the colonists rebelled against the Crown, desperate to continue their expansion west." There was a pause, then his voice brightened, and his eyes twinkled. "You might be interested to know the original emblem's snake had thirteen rattles, one for each of the colonies. Now, though, there are only twelve."

Ruby glanced again at the woman's cap, then with an abrupt yank, she shook off the woman's grip and ran down the alley to the back door, waiting to knock until her heart stopped drumming in her chest. There'd been something about the woman Lucy's eyes, as if she might herself be turning into a serpent.

Now, sitting across from the two monastics, discussing the plan for HJ and her to leave, knowing the people outside are filled with spite reminds Ruby suddenly of the approach of a hurricane. The air seems charged and oppressive, a warning of what is to come.

"An old acquaintance of mine, a man named Halek," Sister O says, "is due to arrive in Denton in seven days' time. He is an inspector for the International Assembly of Nations. I believe this might be a twofold opportunity." She nods at Ruby, taps her fingertip on the table. "Halek will be inspecting the McComb hatchery and at least one slaughter plant. But then, on the following day, he will visit the Outreach, on personal business." Something in the way the Sister says "personal business" catches Ruby's attention.

Brother Q raises one brow. "Ah. Yes. It will be a perfect distraction. The hatchery staff where you work, Ruby, will be focused on the inspection." He leans back, crosses his hands behind his head. "I should easily be back from… my business in Washington." Ruby almost misses the knowing look he gives Sister O, but she says nothing. The hidden meaning of his words are not meant for her.

The two monastics continue to talk in hushed voices. They speak of protests and documents and withdrawal and boats and ferries and a people called the Brethren. Their voices meld in a gentle hum. There's a suggestion of danger and excitement in their voices and manner. Her skin prickles and her stomach flutters.

"I agree with you, Brother," Sister O says. "When Halek is with us, I believe he will be willing to take the documents that Thomas is compiling in Washington."

"Sister…" Brother Q says, glancing at Ruby.

"I think we are in safe company, Brother, knowing the detail of a name does not put the mission at risk."

"You want me to leave?" Ruby asks, shifting her body to rise. "I don't mind. Really."

"No, dear one. You may stay."

There's a pause, then Sister O resumes the thread. "It is an opportunity we must take as a sign."

Brother Q crosses his arms and leans back. "Agreed."

"That settles it," Sister O says. "Ruby, it may seem soon, but the less time we wait, the less chance of discovery. In a week, you and Harold Jr. will need to be ready to leave with Brother Q. We, all the Elohi monastics, in fact, are expecting to be withdrawn from the States, but not for a few weeks more. I will stay until then, but after that, I will be able join you and your friend just west of the border. There, I will apply to become your sponsor."

Part of Ruby's heart soars. Another plummets. So soon! Though she craves the leaving, the knowledge of its nearness stuns her. Such a short time, and so little left for Harold Sr. to spend with his boy. But she nods. Her voice is thick and she can't hide the shiver of it. "Seven days. We'll be ready."

Before sunrise the next morning, she's about to leave flat 13 and hurry to the omnibus stop when the sound of an engine comes from the road. Ruby's heart sinks when she recognizes it as the blue Reo. Ready to leave, she brushes her lips to HJ's forehead, bows her head to the cord holding her conscript ID, and steps from the door. Heart pounding as if she's just run all the way to the omnibus stop, she stares at Bud Downs's profile in the early dawn. Trying to keep her pace even and worker-like, she walks to his pickup and stands a few feet away. He has the driver's side window down and looks her up and down for a full minute.

"I could order you to get in, but I won't."

Ruby's thoughts race. Why is he here? What is this about? Her skin prickles with goose bumps as if an icy wind has rushed across them: what if he's somehow found out about the plan?

She stays quiet.

"Heard about your flatmate. Real shame, that."

Ruby lifts her chin. "It is. No boy should be without his father."

Oddly, the Shepherd winces. "That ain't always the case. No sir. Not always."

He takes a deep breath. "Ruby Roth, I could force this issue, and I just might. But for now, I'd rather ya choose."

Confusion showers her. What issue? What choice?

"It's a good prospect," he continues, "living as an officer's wife."

Ruby's thoughts grind to a halt. Wife? Oh. Oh no. No. Tiny puzzle pieces click into place. Of all the possible things, he's proposing they be paired.

She feels suddenly dirty and wrong, exposed as if she's forgotten to dress. She orders her voice to work, but her tongue is a brick in her mouth.

He leans across to the passenger seat, and for a moment, she thinks he's going to open the door, order her in. He could demand she comply. Not just with getting in, but with being paired. She has no marriage contract with Harold Sr. She has no one prospecting for her. And certainly no one with Downs's rank. It's then that she wonders if Colin Tate has anything to do with this. It is within his power to order such a thing.

The Shepherd straightens and leans back to the open window. There's a small brown-paper-wrapped parcel in his hand. "This's for ya. Know ya can't use 'em, but I already had 'em." As much to get him to leave as anything, she takes it. He gives a nod and drives off. Her muscles unclench, and she suddenly realizes she's chewed a raw spot into her cheek. The package feels heavy and dangerous in her hands. She runs back to the flat and slides the unwrapped parcel under her pillow. A whiff of tobacco sifts from the wrappings. Then, forcing all thought from her mind, she sprints to the omnibus stop, arriving just in time.

It's somewhere between Denton and the hatchery, as they bump across a bridge over a deep drainage ditch, that it comes to her. She glances down at the silty mud, the brambles almost covering the waterway, and it hits her. She sucks air through her teeth. The woman across from her glances over, but says nothing.

Ruby remembers. She remembers why Bud Downs seems familiar, why he keeps suggesting she should remember him. It happened years ago. An incident, big news back then, but until this moment, a thing forgotten. She was sixteen when it happened. A low free-worker by the name of Arty Downs was found beaten to death in a boggy drainage ditch just outside of town. It was near to where the man lived with his wife and children, or so she recalls now. No one was ever charged, but given the man's low status, it's unlikely the Shepherds tried very hard. Ruby does remember that Gram muttered, when it happened, that the man was an unreliable, disgruntled worker.

But it's what Ruby remembers next that makes her blood run cold. For a while, the main suspect was the man's son, Buddy Downs.

Escalation

At sixteen Ruby's world was in the dawn of adulthood as she faced the end of her only freedoms, the rest of her life to be lived fulfilling the work contract inherited from her father. She didn't know Bud, had only heard of him. The five years' difference was, at that age, as good as a lifetime. But to learn that being from the class above hers did not protect you—or guarantee anyone actually cared when the worst happened—had left its mark.

Something Bud Downs said comes to her as she steps off the omnibus at the hatchery. Tiny hairs on the back of her neck prickle in alarm. She said something about it not being right for HJ to be losing his father. No, that wasn't exactly it. She said it wasn't right for a boy to be without a father. Downs, though, had disagreed.

Who really killed Arty Downs? Though the crime was never solved, Ruby is certain she now knows.

That night at the motor lodge, sometime after Harold Sr. leaves, looking pale and weak, but still required to show up for his shift, HJ and Ruby spring awake to the crash of glass and a shrill scream from one of the other flats.

"Daddy!" HJ calls. "Daddy!"

"It's all right, buddy," Ruby says, rolling from her pallet and scrambling to the boy. "Stay down," she whispers.

Outside, there's a shout. She makes out the words "please" and "no." Without thinking, Ruby rises, moves to the door, but then HJ gives a small whimper. She can't take the risk, not with HJ depending on her. So, instead, she swings closed the inside shutters Harold fashioned for the window. The door, too, has extra precautions originally meant for when he had to leave his son alone. Ruby lowers a thick bar across the center of the door and returns to HJ's side.

A thing she's never felt before crawls across her skin. For despite the squalor of the old motor lodge, she's never before felt this kind of fear, a fear of your own people.

It's spreading then, the violence, she thinks. It's not just the Outreach, not just the shantytown. Suddenly, the monastics' concern, their talk of having to return to the West, takes on new clarity. Even on the radiovision at work, the national news skips a stone across the surface of something big happening: changes that will affect them all.

Only a few days until they leave. Her stomach churns. What if, by then, it's too late?

They wait out the commotion outside, trying to not hear it, but the effort makes it all the louder, all the more terrifying. At last, it fades, becomes the remnant of a bad dream. Unable to sleep, they sit together until morning arrives and Ruby has to leave.

"Bar the door, all right, buddy? Your dad'll be here soon."

HJ nods, but something about his expression rings a klaxon in her head. She studies the boy. "Promise me, Harold Jr. Promise me you'll stay inside until your dad gets home."

He squirms a bit, looking both older and still like a lad just leaving toddlerhood behind. "All right," he says. Ruby can't see his eyes, but she knows he's given them a good roll of annoyance. "I promise."

Arriving at the hatchery, she braces herself for another encounter with Bud Downs. She forces herself to give his words a chance. There'd be some advantages if she were under the protection of a Shepherd. She'd be safe. She'd have more food. She'd even have a house in the Shepherd compound. She tries to think of this as if it's something practical, like counting up your food vouchers. Her skin crawls though, as if she's suddenly a stack of tinned cans of food being contemplated by a hungry worker.

At the BrandScan, it's not Downs who is there, but two new Shepherds. They're young with the bold, ardent look of new recruits. There's something different, though, about their uniforms. It takes a moment to see it. On their lapels are small pins. New and glossy in yellow and black the letters *DTOM* are easy to read. She wonders if these two have been allowed to wear these or if the Shepherd force itself has taken a side.

For the fourth time since waking from the fitful bit of sleep she's gotten, Ruby counts the days and hours until the moment she and HJ are meant to flee. Walls are closing in and Ruby knows that like livestock at a slaughter plant, she's being herded into a trap.

It's on the way home that the thin threads holding their world together unravel.

Just before the shantytown of the adrift, the omnibus lurches to a stop. A man two seats up stands and yells at the driver. "Just go around! Come on!"

In the road ahead, three big lorries are pulled to the side of the road. On the canvas sides of the covered back, the Shepherd logo—zap-crooks crossed over smokestacks, coal, and cotton—boldly announces their ownership. She's seen such lorries only once before, when one of the former self-storage units—barely standing, with piles of rubbish seeming to be the only thing supporting the walls—was forcefully emptied of its residents.

Suddenly, the despair, terror, and anger of those outside the omnibus hit her like a hailstorm. Her body curls in, as if she can make herself a smaller target. Outside, people run and dart, stumbling as Shepherds wielding zap-crooks herd them toward the lorries. Bits of canvas drag from legs. Belongings lie scattered in the road.

The man who stood and yelled throws his hands up and flops back in his seat, muttering something. Throughout the omnibus, people stare, people whisper, people shake their heads. Just in front of her a middle-aged man mutters to his seatmate, "You heard about the compound going up on the far side of town?"

"Yeah," the other man in a stinking, splattered CC-blue boilersuit answers. "Saw rolls and rolls of barbed wire going past the landfill yesterday."

A compound. Barbed wire. Dismay and helplessness fill Ruby's belly like she's eaten something long past its prime. Bile rises in her throat. Then she sees her: the young girl HJ has been so entranced by. She's peeking from the back of the last lorry. It's filled with people sitting on benches running down the sides or standing and squatting on the floor. The girl, wan and thin, sits awkwardly on the lap of a man who must be her father, or at least a relative, given the way his arms encase her protectively, his bearded chin digging into her shoulder. Ruby can almost feel the fatherly embrace, so strong is her connection. Is that what it would feel like, to be protected by a parent? It burns. It squeezes. She both wants to fling it away and for it to never end.

The omnibus driver creeps the vehicle forward. A Shepherd motions impatiently at him. The transport wobbles forward. The man in the front raises his voice. "There, was that so hard? Jesus."

As they creep past, Ruby stares at the young girl. Until this moment, she'd almost forgotten about HJ's preoccupation with the adrift girl. This, and the situation Ruby is now observing, crash together in her mind. HJ's words come back to her. *It's starting, Roobs. You can't stop it.* Still, she has a powerful urge to try to do something, but her movement is bound by both common sense and Harold Jr.'s words.

Where could the Shepherds be taking them? She thinks of all the complaints she's heard from the upper castes and shudders. Could this be the solution they've come to? What will become of them now?

The tent city has been all but flattened. Fires lick the edges of cardboard piles and the remains of structures. Foul, dark smoke snakes into the air.

Ruby stares at the girl, grateful, at least, that HJ isn't here beside her. Then something the girl is holding catches Ruby's eye. It's a stuffed toy clutched close to her thin chest with such fervor and need, it makes her look younger than she is. Something about the toy pulls Ruby's mouth into a scowl. It looks familiar. But probably every child at some point had a toy made of old socks, stuffed with rags and sewn together. Her stomach lurches. HJ wanted to take the girl food and toys. But this toy, this couldn't be HJ's, could it?

But she knows it is.

The boy has somehow done what he wanted to do, despite Ruby's warning. Despite her orders. Suddenly, she needs to be with the boy. To make sure he's all right, and then to give him a stern talking to.

She stands. Pushes past the legs crowding the aisle.

"Hey, whatcha doing?"

"Sit down, girl!"

As Ruby moves forward, the omnibus does too. It's too late. The transport inches past the lorry. She reverses direction, ignores the complaints, and orders and pushes to the back of the omnibus to the rear window. Suddenly the girl looks up and meets Ruby's eyes. There's a hollow sadness to her, but something else too. A spark of defiance. Ruby feels it root into her. Then, she does something before she can think, before she can hear her grandmother's chastisement: Ruby doesn't try to break the bond. With a sudden fierce will, she tries to send something back to this child, this girl on her way to who knows where, or what. The girl's eyes narrow and she gives Ruby a tiny nod as though she's understood. Then, the transport moves on, and the girl is lost. The omnibus passes the lorry.

The tug of their connection almost pulls Ruby from her seat. It tears from her, an almost physical sense of something being dissected away. It burns and chastens her. Gram was right. There's too much pain. Before she can further scold herself, the raven-black shape of a Shepherd emerges from a tin and cardboard shack that is somehow still standing. He drags a woman from the structure, a toddler kicking and screaming in her arms. As they come out of the shack, a little gray dog lunges from the shelter, throws itself at the leg of the Shepherd, and hangs there. The man kicks it off. He draws a gun. There's a muffled crack, and the dog, already cowering away from its earlier bold action, crumples like a rag dropped wet. Ruby's vision goes dark and she falls back into her seat. Not wanting but needing to look, she blinks hard and looks one more time. When she sees who the Shepherd is, it's both shocking and no surprise at all. Of course it's Officer Downs. Of course.

HJ's Dream

The rest of the ride home, Ruby can't stop thinking of the girl, of the tingle of electricity Ruby felt when she purposefully bound to her. It's left a mark, a scar, that makes Ruby shift and twitch. But there's something else, something familiar. She traces it, the line of connection, but finding the source makes her shrink. Those arms, that comfort, that pure love coming from the girl's father, that's what HJ is about to lose. And Ruby will be the one to rip it from him.

With a growing sense of doubt and fear, she rehearses every aspect of her next few days. She must avoid Downs, avoid Colin, continue her work as if nothing has changed, go over the plan with Harold Sr., and above all not let HJ find out. It feels as fragile as an unhatched egg. The pressure closing in might at any moment shatter the shell of it, expose them all. Doom them all.

When she reaches flat 13, a moment passes before she registers the door is open. She freezes at the dark slit. Her hand goes to the small of her back, but of course, she's unarmed. Her hands bundle into fists.

"Ruby!"

She spins around, her hands rising.

"Oh. Harold. You scared me." She almost laughs, but then sees Harold Sr.'s ashen complexion, the creases between his eyes.

"What's happened?"

"Thank god you're home. I've been looking… everywhere… for…" He's gasping and pale. Ruby hurries to his side and loops an arm around his back.

"What is it? What's happened?" she asks as she guides him inside, her stomach twisting in knots. "Where's Little Harold?" But as she says this, she knows. She should have known sooner.

"He, he weren't here when I woke up. Door was unlatched." Harold pauses, breathes deeply for a few moments. Ruby grits her teeth. The young girl. The sock doll. The lorries. The Shepherds. She should have gotten off the omnibus. She should have known HJ would have somehow known. What has he done?

"I didn't see no signs of anyone coming though, so he—" A violent cough seizes him. "Probly jus' out playin'."

"I'm sure you're right. Come on, let's get you to a chair. Some water." She forces her body to move with a calm she does not feel and shuffles him to a seat at the table from flat 23, already cluttered with the remnants of her new life on the lower level: a plate from that morning, a handful of BrandScan printouts from both Harold's work and Ruby's, and HJ's precious drawing pad bought with his own coin earned from the fruits of his mudlarking.

Harold sits and swallows the water she brings him. "Can you use that… that thing of yours to find him?"

For a moment, Ruby doesn't answer. On the small square of the kitchen counter sits a strange cardboard box. From it protrudes several loaves of bread, a box of sugar, a box of flour, and a mesh bag of oranges. Ruby hasn't eaten, or even smelled, citrus in years. She grips the edge of the beautiful table, dizzy suddenly, not from the smell alone, but from knowing who the box must be from. What did he do, part of her mind fixates on, drop this off and then make sure his pistol was loaded and ready to murder a little dog?

The thought spins her around as if she's been struck. Oh god, HJ. No. No. No.

Harold says something again.

"I'm sorry, what was that?" She takes three deep breaths before she looks up. Harold, in his own state of unease, hasn't noticed her distraction.

"Your thing, that gift you got. Can you, uh, use it to find the lad?"

She shakes her head quickly. "I don't know, I don't think so. It doesn't work that way." But she doesn't know how it works, does she? It's a thing she fears, a thing she's worked her whole life to avoid. Her feet jiggle on the floor. She needs to go. She needs to find the boy before it's too late. Before he… The unwanted image of the girl on her father's lap, of a lorry filled with tattered shapes and hopeless souls, won't leave her mind.

"If you'll promise to stay here," she says, "so that if—*when*—Little Harold comes back, he won't go looking for you, then I'll go search for him."

"If you think that's best. Thanks lots, Ruby."

Minutes later, she's out of her boilersuit and garbed in a set of hunting clothes, her favorite pig sticker sheathed at the small of her back. Thinking of HJ's obsession with the adrift girl and the horror that's just happened there, she forces her leaden legs and heavy heart to sprint for what's left of the shantytown.

Reaching it drenched in sweat and out of breath, she's stunned by the eerie quiet of the place. It's like an old graveyard at night, she thinks. The bones of the settlement lie scattered. The stench of burning canvas, plastics, wood, and refuse pools in a thick miasma. At first, there's no sign of anyone remaining, not even curious onlookers. Her heart pounding in her ears, she circles the camp, and there, at the edge near a heap of refuse, she finds HJ. Streaks of tears and dust paint his face. She can feel the agony radiating from him. But he looks unharmed. A huge breath of relief lifts her.

"There you are. You alright?" She forces all rebuke from her words.

"Mmmhum." The boy's voice is rough from crying. He looks up, his eyes puffy and red. Ruby suddenly sees his father in him, the wide-set brown eyes, the strong chin, the tiredness of life. But there's another person there, too. A wave to his hair and the color three shades lighter. Like the mother he never knew. Ruby will never forget that endless night when he was born, that last night his mother was part of his life.

Ruby slides down beside him and puts an arm lightly around his shoulders. "Your dad's worried," she says after several minutes.

"Figured."

"Can you tell me what happened?"

"Mmmhum. Was worried."

"About?"

"'Bout her, about the girl. I tried to tell you. I dreamed the bad men came." There's a tiny bit of accusation in his voice. Ruby recoils slightly, the need to not let the boy down immense.

"You had a dream where the…" She hesitates, not wanting to put words in his mouth. "What bad men came in your dream, buddy?"

His chest heaves. "The crooks. The Shepherd men."

She tries to think of what to say that won't disrespect what the boy's saying, won't dismiss it, or condemn it, the way her gram did of the binding. "That sounds really scary."

"Mmmhum. I had to check, Ruby, I had to. I wanted to help her. I need her to be… I don't know. I just know!"

"You didn't try to do anything, did you?" When did he give the girl the toy? Was he there when the violence happened? Her heart pounds loudly in her ears.

"Oh, Roobs, I wanted to, but… those men… I saw… Why?! Why'd they do that?"

"You were here? When they came?" Her chest tightens. She pictures HJ being shoved into one of the lorries. Pictures never seeing him again.

"Mmmhum. But I stayed back. Stayed hidden. I knew it was hopeless. Hopeless, Ruby." Then he again asks, his voice filled with suppressed rage, "Why? Why'd they do it?"

She sucks in a deep breath. Another. "I don't know, buddy. I don't know why they did it, why any of this is happening. And what you wanted to do, it was good, it was the right thing to feel. But it was also the right thing that you did, not trying to help." She hears the terrible oppositeness of that. The confusing words. Right then, she promises to herself to, over time, help the boy understand how life's a battle, a constant job of sorting good intentions from reality. From consequences.

"Come on." She stands, pulling him up. "Your dad's the one who needs you now." The boy swipes a too-short sleeve across his eyes and takes her hand.

She walks HJ back to the flat and into his father's arms, then stands over the box of groceries, one hand cupped around the knobby flesh of an orange. A powerful urge to know more about her own family floods her. Maybe it springs from seeing the deserted shantytown, a place both frightening and filled with life, with families. Where are those families now? Will they be parted from one another, torn and scattered by no choice of their own? What if her own parents also didn't have an option?

"Can I have one, Roobs?" HJ says from where he's sitting snuggled next to his father on their shared bed pallet. She wonders if they've always slept in the same bed or if it began when they made room for her.

"Why not?" She tosses an orange to him.

"One for Daddy too." He blinks his long-lashed eyes up at his father. "It might make him feel better."

Harold Sr.'s gaze jerks toward her. The question, *Did you tell him I'm sick?* as clear in his eyes as water from an AquaClenz.

She gives a small shake of her head and hands the fruit to Harold Sr. The sharp, sweet scent of the Harolds peeling the rare fruit fills the flat. "Let's keep the peel, all right, you two?" Ruby decides she'll dry it and steep it with the rather foul-tasting herbal concoction she's begun dosing Harold Sr. with.

"Sure thing, Roobs. Maybe it'll smell like this forever!" He's bouncing on his seat.

Forever. Tears burn in Ruby's eyes. As she blinks them away, busying herself by looking at the produce and goods, she sees a slip of paper at the bottom of the crate. Not wanting to, but knowing she must, Ruby unbends the crease and lays the lined paper flat.

Life could be good. I'm a persistent man. BD

Tucked under her bedding is the parcel Downs handed her just a day ago. It's a tin case filled with shiny red-and-white packs of Marlburg smallcigs. The filled tin is worth at least a month of food vouchers, maybe more. But, like some memories, the gifts are too precious to throw away, too costly to open.

She looks over at the two Harolds. The elder is watching his boy relish each segment of the orange with such intensity. He's storing up memories, putting them up like provisions for winter. This she knows. The guilt already riding on her shoulders takes on weight. How can she rob this kind man of his last days or weeks or months of joy? How can she take all that from both of them?

She lifts the note again. *Life could be good.*

Doubt chips away at the guilt. Ruby turns from the Harolds, from the crisp, sweet scent of the orange, creeps behind her curtain, and burrows beneath her blanket. Her eyes close to one simple thought: *Maybe I'm running not toward freedom, but away from responsibility.* But then, moments later, her eyes spring wide. Responsibilities, hers, have always been controlled by others: by the corp, by her gram. But today, she did something different. Today she used the binding to link with HJ's girl, she's sure she did, she's certain something happened. And Gram was right, it did hurt, it did cause pain. But only to her.

Lyng there on her pallet in the stuffy mustiness of flat 13 while listening to the Harolds' breathing, a new thought forms, as weak and tender as a sprouting seed. What if Sister O is right? What if the binding is not a curse, but a gift?

8
Kaileh

The Feather

The morning after boarding the Arrow, Kaileh and the other officers from Shelter Rocks board a small bus in Chota and continue their journey to Waccamaw. The transport traces its way up into the gentle hills separating the Tanasi River Valley from the high mountain valley where the Waccamaw enclave sits. As the elevation climbs, so does her anxiety. Twice she finds herself gnawing on strands of her dark hair. Twice she spits them out, then looks around. Mateo, again beside her, dozes, despite claiming he slept well on the overnight Arrow, a gift for optimizing every opportunity for rest that her brother also had. Bright Hawk and Lena sit two rows back, pointing and looking out the window.

Kaileh follows their gaze. A lump rises to her throat. The road roughly follows the winding Jah'gowa River on its descending path toward the Tanasi. It's fierce in places, riffles and rapids spouting white water, while in other spots placid pools promise fish and cool green depths. Even now, this early in the morning, a group of kayaks and canoes plunge and ride the current. One kayaker, his long, wet hair flying out in a tail, stops her breath. For the briefest moment, it's Tareq. She raises her hand to the glass and indulges in the illusion. It could be true, couldn't it? Where there is no body, no proof, for her there would always be hope. Or rather, she knows deep inside, delusion. She blinks and the man becomes someone who is *not* her brother. But she knows, she knows the way only a sister or maybe a mother could, that her brother did ride this river. Tareq paddled and tipped and bucked, grinning his wide smile with every dip and splash, every close call that much better than the last.

She lets herself wallow in the misery of it, these glimpses of a life she did not share, but by the time they arrive at the enclave, her calm has returned.

"How you holding up, Kai?" Mateo asks, rubbing sleep from his eyes.

"Good. Great," she says, trying to match his smile.

"Hey," Bright Hawk says. "We'll see you at the meeting. Going to find our quarters first."

"See you there," Mateo says. "What about you, Kai? Going to your room or…?" His voice is tight behind the smile not quite reaching his eyes.

"You don't have to worry, all right? I'm completely fine. You go on, I'd like to get to the amphitheater early." He gives her a skeptical look. "Hey, go on." She gives him a gentle shove. "I'll save you a seat, got it?"

"Sure. Sure, Kai. See you there." She feels a twinge of guilt as he leaves, but pivots quickly and heads to the grassy open seating area where in about an hour their orientation will begin.

When she arrives, the morning gratitude service is just ending. Other Warriors move quietly from the space, a variety of expressions on their faces. Most nod a greeting.

The sprawling lawn smells of freshly shorn grass and herbs. Nearby, a flock of sheep graze and baa and bleat, moving in and out of a solar energy forest shading part of the slope. To the west, at her back, the Agiqua River works its way north past the high peak of Mount Attakulla. The highest mountain in the Appalachian chain, it catches the rising sun like a sail. It's all she can do to not stare, to not plunge into thoughts of Tareq dying somewhere up there.

Moments after sitting down, a huge flock of jah'gowa pigeons whirs overhead. Kaileh cranes her neck back and watches the big birds in flight, knowing she's risking the rude ambush of falling excrement. And something does separate from the flock and fall her way, but it's only a small feather. It zigzags down, and to her wonder, settles on her lap. She stares at it for a few minutes. It's short and downy, the soft tip a rusty-rose color as if dusted with blood. A breast feather—a heart feather. A sign, perhaps? Without thinking, she carefully closes her fingers around the tiny quill and tucks it into her own breast pocket.

Voices bring her back to the moment, to the reason she's here. A swarm of trabajadoras lifts from the blades of the solar forest as they orient to the rising sun, their work of cleaning the panels done for that morning. Warrior officers begin filling the space. She sees some she knows from other assignments. Mateo and the Shelter Rocks contingent arrive. Commander Briento steps to the podium at the front. Soon, all but the sheep are quiet, and the orientation begins.

It's mostly what she knows: civil unrest in the Atlantic States, increased illegal crossings of the border, lots of political rhetoric that Kaileh mostly tunes out. But then something xe says catches her ear.

"As I said," xe says, xyr voice rising, "the Atlantic government is using this civil chaos to make sweeping changes, none of which favor the masses. There have been roundups of the un-homed and unemployed, the group they call 'the adrift.' Our intelligence on this is disturbing. We know, without a doubt, that these unfortunates are being packed into internment camps and put to work—on just what, we are not certain. We don't have exact numbers, but the estimates are that hundreds, if not more, have died."

Before she can think, Kaileh's hand shoots up.

"Yes, Officer Kaileh?"

She stands, but xyr remembering her name catches her off guard for a moment. "Um, yes, Commander. I hate to sound callous, but this sounds like none of our business. Don't we still have a hands-off policy? I mean, other than the Outreaches and a few other agreements? This sounds, if you're asking me"—beside her, Mateo coughs—"like the natural result of their 250 years of"—she flutters her hand toward the east where, even from this distance, the dark line of air pollution is visible— "of, well, that."

Mateo tugs at her trouser leg. She slaps his arm away. A few Warriors look at her with raised brows, but others nod.

"You make a fair point, Officer Kaileh. Now, if you'll indulge me, I'll get to the crux of this," Briento says. Feeling both acknowledged and somehow brushed aside, Kaileh sits back down. Xe looks at xyr c-board, then up at the gathering, xyr forehead a washboard of creases.

"One of our covert operators was able to validate an extremely disturbing piece of intel." Xe pauses, seeming to meet each officer's eyes.

"We believe the Atlantic States government is assembling…" Another pause., "… a nascent military."

Mateo draws a sharp breath, and others gasp. Heat rises to Kaileh's face. Her thigh muscles clench and she puts her palms on her legs as if holding herself down. The treaty with the Atlantic States of America has been regularly renewed and enforced since its original signing in 1776. Although the colonists balked at the demand regarding restricted 110armed forces—even testing the limits of it at the dawn of the 1800s with the Second Border War—the stipulation that the ASA not create or maintain an armed force, beyond small domestic police, had been upheld.

Breaking it would be an act of war. Kaileh hears the click in her jaw. A spark flares behind her closed eyes. Could there be a third Border War building on the horizon?

"Here's what we've concluded: the ASA is using the protests as a distraction in order to initially enlarge their Shepherd force. The number of domestic police now exceeds the allowed percentage of the population contained as stipulated in the treaty. And that's just the start of it." Xe looks again at each of them. "The roundups and relocation of their poor may be a part of this. The goal of the ASA may well be, as I can see you've surmised, to form a larger army and break the treaty."

Kaileh stares east. Even the jah'gowa pigeons, whom the colonizers called passenger pigeons, avoid the Atlantic States, no doubt finding few trees for nesting and only the hunter's bullet should they venture near. In the West, the birds are revered as a food source, carefully nurtured to sustain a population worthy of harvest. Kaileh tries to picture her generation facing a repeat of the Great Influx of her parents' time. How the People had to try to assimilate so many with such contrary ways of living, of thinking, of treating the one earth.

Sometime during her reverie, Commander Briento must have finished xyr speech, for the next thing she knows, the crowd is rising.

Kaileh blinks and looks around. The other officers are looking down at their keitais. Typical, Kaileh thinks. Already on their e-utensils rather than contemplating just what this means for their people.

Mateo beside her looks up from his keitai. "Who'd you get?"

She frowns. "What?"

He taps his keitai. "For your partner. Who'd you get?"

"Oh, guess I missed that part."

Mateo gives an exaggerated eye-roll. "Uh-huh. Guess you did. I knew we'd be split up, I got someone named Zeng. Go on, check your file. Let's find out who you'll be training with."

It takes her a moment to find the right section on her keitai. Her fingers fumble with the screen, and for a moment, she feels like a senior Silver whose grandchild has gotten them the gadget. Then, there it is. Her Warrior section has a little raised-hand icon. A new message.

She touches it. It opens. She blinks, looks up. "No. No. No no no no."

"What? What's wrong? Who'd you get?"

She bites her lip, looks at her section again. Then she scans the rapidly emptying space. And there he is. Why did she not think he'd be here? And now, why is she surprised?

He stands down near the front row, his dark head lifted, a single long walnut braid over one shoulder. Onas Steeprock.

Partners

She looks back at her keitai. Stares at Steeprock's name, willing it to disappear. But it remains, solidifies, the letters like hot coals burning her eyes. But then something else pushes forward: the possibility of a war. A major war.

Kaileh grew up in the Pacific Northwest Region, in a small town eponymously named for its river, the Takel, which, like many rivers and geological features of the People, was called what it was: the River. There, so far from the eastern Border Wars that solidified the nation's independence, their history was learned, but was not woven into the cultural fabric with the same vibrancy of those living in the East, along the Proclamation Line. In her part of the Pacific Northwest, it was another fight for which her progenitors were integral in founding the nation. In the late 19th century, hordes of prospectors and merchants and camp-followers and charlatans poured onto the shores seeking gold. Seeking wealth. If the coastal and inland Peoples had not unified, and had the support of their neighbor, Mexico, the West Coast might have been lost.

It was her family's distance from the Proclamation Line that inspired their excursion to the Pontiac Victory Center when she was young. There in Lenape, named—as many border towns were—for Eastern cultures driven from their homelands by the Europeans, her parents strove to make the history of the People come alive. Now, she could be living a new chapter of their nation's long history.

By the time she reaches her quarters during the break between the orientation and midday meal, she's back to fuming. How would things be different if she and her brother hadn't joined the Warriors after university? What if they'd just stayed in their region? Tareq could have become a river guide, for the Takel was one of the most sought whitewater experiences on the continent. He never would have met Steeprock. He never would have been led astray on patrol. What were the pair doing that far off the route? A tiny part of her whispers a terrible thought, one of betrayal to their country, to their sworn oath as Warriors. But no. It's not possible. Tareq would never. It had to be Steeprock doing something nefarious.

But then, she remembers an argument she had with Tareq—one of many. He tried to convince Kaileh that all the Atlantics needed were programs and incentives to "begin a cultural inversion, to break out of the lord-serf dialectic." He always had a way of putting things that made Kaileh roll her eyes, or want to strangle him—or both.

She stops pacing the short length of her quarters and stares into the rising sun, at last fully clear of the haze from the East. "Look where your programs got you, brother," she says to the swath of purple-blue smoke running across the horizon beyond the peaks. Then, before she can stop herself, she's out the door, determined to find Commander Briento.

"Yes?" xe says at Kaileh's knock on the frame of the open door. Xe's staring at the screen of a noto, its ports bristling with dataslips, xyr gray-tipped eyebrows knit together.

Kaileh feels her nerve wavering, but shoves open the door. "I need to talk to you, Commander. If you have a moment." At least, she thinks, no one else is here.

Briento looks up, apparently unfazed. Xe closes the noto's screen and leans back in xyr chair, crossing xyr arms. "By all means, Officer Kaileh. What's on your mind?"

Briento's calm throws her. Kaileh and Tareq's father, Aden, had been that way, able to cool off an argument, or at least Kaileh's temper, with his own expansive equanimity.

"Uh, well…" She resists a sudden urge to gnaw on a strand of her hair. "I'd like to request a change in my assignment."

"That so?" Briento's eyes sparkle.

Is xe amused? Is xe laughing at her? She firms her voice, stands straighter. "Yes. I cannot work with Steeprock. You know… you know, don't you, Commander, what he did?"

Xe lifts an eyebrow. "Steeprock is nothing but exemplary, Officer Kaileh. What happened last year was terrible, and you have my heartfelt condolences, but Steeprock's record is perfect."

"Ha!" She can't stop her laugh. "It's far from perfect, Commander." She chews on the inside of her cheek.

"Go on."

She thinks she catches a bit of interest in xyr otherwise annoyingly calm expression, and before she can stop herself, she tells xyr what she learned from the archivist.

"Ah, I see," Briento says when she finishes. "But a missing birth record has nothing to do with his service record, wouldn't you agree?"

"Uh, yes, but Commander—"

"Officer…" Briento lets the legs of xyr chair drop back to all fours. "Do you trust me?"

She narrows her eyes. "Well, if I'm honest, Commander, not yet."

Xe is quiet for a few seconds, then xyr shoulders begin to shake. Xe's laughing. "Actually, Officer, that's a more honest answer than I've had in some time. Now, let us take this as the first opportunity for me to win that trust. I'm not reassigning you. Understood?" Xe rises.

Something in xyr posture makes Kaileh suck in a breath.

"I… understand." She backs herself to the door. "Uh, thank you, Commander."

As she closes the door her mind twists into a knot, and her feet seem not to know where to go. She should head to midday meal. She should hand in her resignation. She should face Steeprock as her new partner. She should face Steeprock with what she knows. Everything tangles together, wrapping and weaving into a complex knot.

As she walks back to her quarters, advice comes to her from a nearly buried memory. She was eight years old. Her parents had sent her to study with a fiber artist at their culture's preservation farther upriver in the Takel River Valley. There she'd learned to work the downy undercoat brushed from goats, process it clean, then work it into skeins of yarn and thread. Her own work, lumpy and uneven, was a knotted mess her small hands kept jumbling into worse confusion.

"Now, little Kaileh, this is the time for patience and perseverance, not angry hands," the old woman, a masterweaver, said, her eyes stern but with a knowing glitter.

"But Auntie, it's just a stupid wad now. I know, I'll fix it." She lunged her hand at a pair of shears nearby.

"Auk! No, no, no. We don't need to resort to that," the woman said, and took the sharp tools from Kaileh's hand, laying them back aside.

Kaileh puckered her face, picturing the ease of just making a simple snip or two, of freeing the tangle, finding the right ends, and just tying them back together; after all, what were a few more knots in her disaster of a skein? But the auntie showed her instead how to find first one end, then the other. To gently coax apart the knots. Not to insist they reveal their path, but to encourage the coils and confusion to come apart as if of their own will.

Now, as she heads to the dining hall for midday meal, she feels that knot in her mind. But patience? It has yet to come.

She makes it through the rest of the day successfully avoiding Onas Steeprock. And Mateo. Which, she thinks, is probably lucky for them.

By that evening she's exhausted from the effort of evasion. She throws her uniform on the floor, takes a quick shower, and climbs into the unfamiliar bed. Tomorrow, she tells herself, tomorrow. After some time and more effort, she sleeps. But sometime near midnight her keitai buzzes from the small table beside the bed. She jerks awake, stifles a curse, and fishes it into her hand. Her throat tightens when she sees the number. Rosalia, her mother's caregiver.

"Am I waking you?" the healer says when Kaileh answers on the third ring. "I forgot about the time difference, mi amiga."

Kaileh swallows a yawn, brightens her voice. "I'm always ready to answer when I see your number, Rosalia. How is Mother?"

"Mostly as expected, but otherwise fairly good."

"That's a relief." There have been struggles with bedsores, bladder infections, falls, and the like. "Fairly good" in this case is wonderful. Kaileh feels muscles relax that she hadn't realized were contracted.

"It is. I wanted to update you about today, though. I tried to get through earlier. Do not be alarmed. It was just that for an hour or so your mother was lucid."

Kaileh's body slumps. "I wish I had been available." Rosalia did her best to connect Kaileh to her mother during her mother's rare moments of clarity. Each time could be the last. The last moment of clear thinking. The last moment of recognition. It would break Kaileh's heart to miss that. It was hard enough to not simply drop everything and go home. But her mother, a year earlier after Tareq's death and before the disease took her past the point of return, had demanded Kaileh continue her work, saying it would bring her a kind of peace.

"She spoke of you and… your hermano." Rosalia clears her throat. The caregiver is from the canal city Nuevo Tenochtitlán, not far from Mateo's family, a fact that always seems to escape Kaileh's memory until she hears the healer's accent. She likes the woman, and the familiar musicality of her voice, the accent so like Mateo's, is comforting.

"What did she say?"

"She spoke with pride, mi amiga. For both of you."

As she listens, Kaileh toys with the idea of asking Rosalia if she knew about Tareq's planned commitment ceremony, which would mean her mother, too, knew. But would this sound peevish and petty? What if they both knew and hadn't told her? What if Tareq didn't want his sister to know? No, stop this, she tells herself, none of that has any importance now. But she knows that it's another snarled section that's going to tangle her thoughts and trip her forever.

Kaileh sighs and asks, "Do you think it will return? The lucidity?" She went home before with high hopes, doomed for disappointment.

"Ah, there is no way to tell, my friend. But I wanted you to know that for this moment, this gift, it was you and your brother of whom she spoke. She told me a story of the two of you that was quite dear."

Oh no, Kaileh thinks, not now. "Rosalia," Kaileh says, loosening her jaw. Being vulnerable comes as easily as saying she's sorry. "I hate to say this, but my heart is in a tender place right now. And you know me well enough to understand what that means."

"Oh si, si. It means your head, it takes up the slack for your aching corazon, becomes the strong one." Her voice is sweet, amused. Though not family, she speaks as such, and somehow, it doesn't raise Kaileh's ire.

"Si, yes," Kaileh says with a sigh. "But I do want to make a visit. I'm about to receive my travel assignment for the next few months. I told you I'd be leaving the border for inland patrol work. Some of it may be as far west as Takel. And even if not, I'll find a way to make time."

"I am glad to hear it, mi amiga." Kaileh hears the mix of hope and skepticism in Rosalia's voice. Kaileh has promised before.

After the call ends, she wonders if she should have asked Rosalia for advice about working with someone she doesn't trust. But the thought of explaining everything, of trying to catch Rosalia up, was too much. And somehow Kaileh knows the caregiver would have shared sound, logical advice. If Kaileh is being honest with herself, she doesn't really want that. She wants someone to commiserate with her, to take her side. She grips the pillow into a wad and hurls it against the wall. It falls with a soft *flump*. She groans and gets up.

Back in bed, the pillow now over her head, Kaileh muffles a scream into the soft fluff of it. For she knows what she must do—what she will do—even though it's the last thing she wants.

9
Ruby

Five Days

During lunch the next day at the hatchery, David slides close as Ruby sits down with the usual bowl of pinkish-grey stew. "Can you believe the news?" he says. "I mean, it ain't like it's gonna make any difference to us cons, don'tcha know, but still."

Ruby tries to bring her focus to David's words. She woke that morning resolved to purposefully try to bind to someone else. How hard could it be? After it happened with HJ's girl, even without Ruby trying, she thought it would be simple, but it hasn't been. Perhaps it's the years of forcing herself to do the opposite, or maybe the fact that most things and people around her are in a such state of suffering, she'd be a fool to gather them into herself.

Or, she thinks, maybe she's just too tired and distracted—and maybe it's a stupid thing to experiment with only days from when their illegal departure is scheduled.

As David talks, she keeps her eyes on a shredded bit of Cham floating in the thick, muddy liquid. Pushing it around with her spoon, she tries to muster up interest in what her co-worker friend is talking about. After a minute, she sighs and looks up. "What news?"

David scrapes the last bit of stew into his spoon, looks side to side, then at Ruby. His eyes sparkle with gossip. "Colin Tate. Got himself promoted. Yup. Out with the old, in with the new, I say. Least he comes from a bit lower down the food chain. Closer to us and all. You went to school with 'em, right? Used to be friends, right?"

She nods and shrugs and listens as David tells her how Colin's been promoted from assistant to head manager of the hatchery. Stella Fletcher, his now former boss, one of the few women in McComb management, has been accused of doctoring accounting records, skimming money from the corp's golden pot.

"He did it. Somehow, he did it," Ruby mutters.

"Wha's that? Yeah, suppose he did. Yup," David says, scraping his teeth across the spoon as he takes in his last bite. Ruby wraps her arms around herself, hiding a tremor.

"Turns out"—David continues— "the corp uppity-mucks got no qualms 'bout turning her out and putting a man in her stead. Didn't even wait for some kind of hearing or such."

Colin. He must have found someone else to help him. He must have accomplished his petty crime and now she knows what his intent was. At least Stella Fletcher's departure is no loss. Under her oversight, the required output of the workers was increased. Instead of productivity bonuses, inefficiency penalties were instituted. Not that Tate could possibly be that much better.

A feeling of blandness comes over Ruby, like they're all just bits of Cham being pushed around by a giant spoon. Then she reminds herself: only five more days. That's all. Then she'll get herself and HJ away from this place.

Earlier that morning, she watched for Downs at the BrandScan, but he was oddly absent. Instead, there were three new Shepherds on duty. When she leaves after her shift, the sight of the three shiny new officers snaps her from her fugue. It's rare to get a new Shepherd, much less three at one time. And there's something even more disturbing: each has a gun holster hanging from their belt. Black like the uniform, with a sinister matte-black pistol grip nosing out as if wanting to be stroked.

As she nears them, her feet stumble to an abrupt stop. The worker just behind her mutters a curse. Ruby forces her legs on, but she feels them, these new officers. She's not trying to bind, but there's an energy, like the humming power lines running past Denton on their way to bigger towns; the officers vibrate, electrified by the need for something to go wrong, for a reason to handle the pistols at their sides.

"Keep moving, con!" one of them barks.

Ruby steps forward. Then, at the edge of her vision, just as she takes her BrandScan printout, she sees Downs. He leans against the wall where he first offered her a pull on his smallcig. Ruby doesn't meet his eye, pretends to not notice. But his presence is strong. She can almost hear his words from the note: *I'm a persistent man.*

Ice runs through her veins. *Focus*, she thinks. *Keep your mind on one thing.* Five days. She must avoid him for only five more days.

It's when she gets off the omnibus in Denton to head to the Outreach that she hears another voice. She has her head down, determined to keep it there and remain focused on work, on normal, everyday work.

"You've been a busy girl," Colin Tate says, stepping from the door of the McComb Corp grocery as she passes. His face is smug. For a moment she wonders if he's looking for congratulations on his promotion—or maybe a new kind of respect, like maybe she'll give him a bow or something. It almost makes her laugh. But she holds it in. Nothing would be stupider right now than getting into trouble. *Go on like normal*, Brother Q said. *Don't change anything.*

It takes her a moment to compose her face, her response.

"Mr. Tate," is all she can muster. Perhaps she's not done such a good job concealing her dislike, for Tate's assurance slips from his face.

"What can I do for you?" she adds, trying her best to sound like the obedient conscript he expects. She even summons a tight-lipped smile.

He stares at her, eyes shifting back and forth. "Do for *me?*" He smirks. "It's about what I can do for you. What, in fact, I've already done."

A chill tightens her pores. Despite the manic look on his face, or maybe because of it, Ruby knows this is not leading to something that will make her feel any better.

"Oh," Tate says, "I see you don't know yet, do you? Well then, let me be the first," he says, the sneer lifting both sides of his mouth, "seeing as how we go back so far and all, to offer my congratulations,"

Congratulations? Confusion swirls in her like a dust devil in the hot summer air.

"Ah, you didn't hear? Well, that's a shame. Sure enough, I signed the acquisition form just yesterday. It's sitting on my new desk in my new office right now, as it happens."

Acquisition? No no no. He's sold her contract to some other corp. When? When will she leave? And where? Is there time? Her lips move, but she can't speak her questions.

"So, please," Colin finishes, "you all let me know when the happy date is set, alrighty? I'll make sure you and Officer Downs get a day or two off for the…" He chuckles. "… honeymoon."

It hits her like she's been slammed into a wall.

He hasn't sold her contract to another corp. He's approved Downs's request to take a wife. To take her.

"You can't do that," she says, her mouth as dry as sandpaper.

"Aw, see, that's where you're wrong, Roth. Sure, most cons find their own mates by now, but seeing as how you're still *available*, it just makes sense."

"No, no that's just… that's just not… You can't."

He shrugs. "I offered you another way, now didn't I? But take heart, Roth. You'll be marrying up a class. That's a good thing. Life could be good for you."

Goose bumps prickle her arms. Downs's words repeat in her ears.
I'm a persistent man.
Life could be good.

Acquisition Form M-100

People pass by, some unseeing, others scowling, and one or two casting long looks of pity her way like Ruby's some starving stray dog too weak to beg or bite. At last, pain in her palms causes her to rouse. She looks at her hands. Dark red crescents dimple her skin. Her pulse thuds in her ears. The fury and frustration welling inside her have nowhere to go. What would she do if HJ weren't counting on her, if others wouldn't suffer for her actions? She can see herself chasing Tate down, sinking her fingernails into his slender neck, feeling his pampered flesh tear like it's made of paper. But their plan counts on her acting normal. No, not normal, but obedient, compliant, passive. Part of her wonders if she even knows how to stand up for herself—to anything other than a stray dog or a group of girls on the street. And she didn't really even stand up then, did she? No, she had help.

A sense of inadequacy settles on her shoulders. If she makes it to the West, will she be worthy? Will all the danger and trouble others are taking have been worth it? But then she stops. Gone, if it ever even existed, is the luxury of thinking only of herself. This is not just about her, it's about HJ too.

Maybe she's a fool to reject Downs? Maybe it would be better to do the sensible thing. Ruby gathers in the ragged bits of her worries and heads down the alley for the back door of the Outreach. Just growing nearer to it pivots her mood, as if proximity to the monastics is like stepping into a sunny day with blue skies above.

She taps on the door twice. It opens with a snap, but only a sliver. Sister M looks out, her headscarf tipped to one side, her face scrunched with worry.

"Oh, Ruby, it's you! Come in. Come in." Sister M pulls her through. The monastic's hand quakes. Concern pushes Ruby's angst to one side. Something has happened to her friends.

Inside, Sister O is bent over Brother Q at the small table where she usually prepares medicines. He looks up. His own headwrap is off, a bloodied cloth held to his right temple. For the first time she sees his hair in full: short and dark with gentle waves. Sister O says, "Keep still now, Brother." Despite his dazed look, he gives Ruby a smile.

"What happened? Is he, are you, all right?"

Sister M wrings her hands. "It's just terrible! Those, those horrible people." She sounds as if she's holding back both tears and what she'd really like to call them.

"Sister M," Sister O says with firm kindness, "will you take Ruby to the front?"

"I'm all right, Sister," Ruby says, forcing her breathing to a less panicky state. It's apparent that Brother Q, though bruised and bloodied, is truly fine. In fact, other than Sister O, he seems to be the calmest person in the room.

Sister O looks at Ruby, her eyes narrowed. "You then, Sister M. Would you kindly keep an eye on the front door? Don't stand too close, dear. Just let me know if anyone shows up with another brick, or the like, in their hand."

Brother Q chuckles. Sister O straightens and shakes her head. "Truly, Brother, it is nothing to laugh at."

He shakes his head, winces. "I was just thinking that perhaps what you've said in the past is true, that my head is indeed harder than a brick."

Sister O laughs quietly as she puts drops of a healing oil she's told Ruby is made from a tree in Australia on the small gash and wraps it with clean gauze, the crisp, medicinal scent filling the room. As she treats Brother Q, she tells Ruby that earlier, in front of the Outreach, Brother Q interceded when a pair of off-duty Shepherds began harassing some of the poor lined up to receive care. "Why one of the men just happened to have a brick in his hand," she says, "the gods only know."

The gods. Several months ago, when her grandmother first took to bed, Ruby asked Sister O, "What religion are you? I mean the Elohi monastics." Ruby almost never thinks about a god, other than to acknowledge the many old, sparsely attended churches in Denton. After all, the motto of the Atlantic States, said first by Chairman Calvin Coolidge in the 1920s, is *Every Factory is a Temple, Every Worker a Supplicant.*

Sister O smiled kindly and shook her head. "Our order is not one of worship, not directly. The Elohi are dedicated to service, as you already know." They were standing at the book rack in the Outreach where Ruby was attempting to choose between the biography of the world-famous Osage ballerina, Elizabeth Ki-He-Kah-Stah-Tsa, and the latest in an adventure series by Olympia Nage about two Western sisters who travel the world solving mysteries.

Sister O tapped the adventure book titled *Into the Night* and said, "Did you know that Olympia is my twin sister?"

Ruby's mouth must have dropped open, for Sister O laughed. "Yes, yes, I have a family other than my monastic siblings. My name in that life was Odyssia. My mother, whose parents fled Greece during the British invasion of the 1920s, was determined her daughters bear names from the land and mythology of her parents." She took the book from Ruby's hand. "It is a joke of the gods, and within my blood family, that I was named for the legendary traveler, King Odysseus, while it is my sister, Olympia, who passionately explores the world."

She told of her Greek mother's love of the Pacific Northwest, where she and her sister were raised, and of the culture of her adopted country. How the ring she passed on to her daughter honored her mother's ancestors with its circlet of a Greek meander overlayed by the thunderbird. "When we Elohi give up our other world and aspirations, most take with us a single tangible token. A reminder.

"But, dear one, I've *meandered* off the path of your question of religion," she said, giving a soft laugh. "Those in the Elohi Order dedicate their lives to serving others. Some are healers, others scientists, but all are committed to… hmmm… there is no perfect translation, but basically to *easing or preventing suffering.* This means treating suffering when it is manifest—present—but also, working to ensure its prevention through education and opportunities."

Ruby puzzled over this for a few moments. "You mean like the books here that show us better ways of doing things?"

Sister O nodded. "But ultimately, we want to change the hunger of the species from one of greed to gratitude, for it is seeking and desire that are truly the rootstock of all suffering."

Ruby liked the idea of a world where God or gods or any deity couldn't be blamed, or credited, for the good, the bad, and the rest. But mostly, it was the ring, the symbols of Sister O's heritage so proudly worn, that sparkled in Ruby's imagination. She wondered what it would feel like to know *who* you came from. To have a legacy worthy of pride.

What kind of legacy will I leave, she thinks now, *if I stay here, marry Downs, try to help raise HJ? A dismal one, at best. But if we flee, and are caught, then, well, that's no legacy at all, is it?*

Finished dressing the wound, Sister O sends Brother Q upstairs to the living quarters. He gives Ruby a wink but doesn't argue.

"Ruby, we are going to have to be extremely careful. Your leave date is almost here, but the risk has increased more quickly than we had hoped. If there were a way to expedite your departure, trust that we would."

Ruby opens her mouth to share her doubts, to bounce the ideas and concerns and confusion off Sister O. But before she can speak, Sister O says, "We have one more duty here, besides your extraction. You may have parsed this out from overhearing earlier conversations: there is critical information we must get to the West."

There's a bang out front, then another and another. Ruby and Sister O jump. It comes again. Not a gun, but something hitting at the front of the building.

Sister M throws open the door. "Sister O, dear me, Sister O, they're back. They're throwing things. Oh my. Oh dear."

"Out the back with you, dear heart." The look the monastic gives Ruby stops all protest. She leaves, still not remembering why she originally went to the Outreach. Sister O's words take shape in her mind. Critical information. That must get to the West. Is she to take it? Or is her trip part of that bigger plan? It consoles her, this thought that there's something else at play, something more important, she's sure, than one person's legacy.

10
Kaileh

A Second Feather

The next morning Kaileh wakes groggy, her head filled with rocks of fatigue. After hanging up with Rosalia, all she could think about was her mother, and although she tossed and dreamed the rest of the night, she's still managed to oversleep. There's barely time to make it to the first session, much less have morning meal. She jumps from bed, reaches for her unpacked bag, and realizes with a groan she forgot to pack a second uniform top. Nor, of course, has there been time to do any laundry. She scrounges through the mess of yesterday's clothes on the floor and lifts the rumpled shirt. It smells far from fresh, but she pulls it on, smooths the wrinkles as best she can, and hurries to the morning assembly. As she squeezes in next to Lena, her stomach gives a vengeful growl. Lena looks at Kaileh with a "well that's what you get" grin.

As the class begins with the prayer of gratitude, Mateo, several spots to the side, leans forward and mouths, *Good morning*, but she barely notices. She blinks, her mind refusing to fully enter the moment. Something about the brisk morning air, the sudden shiver that runs through her, triggers a replay of one of last night's dreams.

She is five, Tareq seven. The family stands along the rocky bank of the Takel River at Ti'lomikh Falls for the annual salmon ceremony. It's early summer, the sun just rising, but everything is in ice, the falls a frozen cascade. Tsinuk salmon hang suspended above the rocky leaps, their silver, rose-tinted bodies glistening. Frozen drops of water are caught mid-drip. Everyone is frozen but Kaileh. Even the Silver seated in the story chair, her net extended and filled with icicles, is a statue. But then something moves: a mature, sinuous Tsinuk undulates up from the frozen water. Ice splinters shatter from its body and fall like a rain of crystal. The fish flies with ease, soaring through the air toward her. As it passes over, it grows, seems to fill the sky. A scale falls from the fish's belly and drifts down, impossibly slow. She holds out her hands, notices how tiny they are. She catches the scale, and it begins to melt, only it doesn't turn to liquid. It becomes a snow-white feather.

If she were back at Shelter Rocks, she'd be able to talk to her spirit healer, Nibaa, about it. Nibaa, of the Wendat culture, has a special interest in the belief of dreams as hidden wishes of the soul. Kaileh is rather enjoying trying to imagine what Nibaa would make of a flying, molting fish when she catches sight of Onas Steeprock sitting several rows toward the front. But today, he looks different. She tips her head and realizes the way she thinks of him has changed. The shimmer of a mirage has lifted. He's just a man. A man concealing something. It might be hidden from her at this very moment, but it doesn't have to stay that way. It's as simple as finding the other end of the yarn, patiently working the knot of lies and truths all tangled together. She's certain that somewhere at the center of the knot is an answer.

"I'll find the truth, Steeprock. Just wait," she mumbles.

"What's that?" Lena says.

"Uh, sorry, nothing." Kaileh gives her a grin.

Then, before she has a chance to reorient herself, the assembly is rising, dispersing. Kaileh looks around for contextual clues, hoping to bring herself into the hoop, Mateo is beside her. "Well, that was short and to the point," he says. "Glad we have a break to process this. I mean, we all expected this, but I'm not going to lie, it makes me uncomfortable."

Kaileh grimaces at her—once again—loss of focus. Before she can grit her teeth and ask Mateo what she missed this time, he gives her a nod and walks toward his new partner. Kaileh studies the pair, feeling a twinge of jealousy when they greet each other like timeworn friends.

Someone touches her shoulder. She turns, expecting it to be Lena, who was just at her side. "What?" But it's not Lena. It's Steeprock.

She looks again toward Mateo. He's walking out with his new partner. That's when she notices everyone is pairing up. This is it then. No more denial. Partners have been assigned, and she, somehow, has been stuck with Onas Steeprock. A sudden thought pushes aggressive words from her mouth. "Was it you that made this happen? Did you request we become partners?"

"Well—"

"Because I'm not him. I'm not my brother."

"I didn't think you were."

"Well then?"

"Well what? I'm not sure…"

"I… I…" Kaileh hates how she's sputtering and spins away. "I'll catch up with you later." She makes it three steps when something pricks the skin above her right breast. It's itchy and uncomfortable and demanding immediate remediation. Annoyed, she stops. Her hand lifts to her pocket, and she feels the sharp point of something dig in further.

"Gods of rot." She opens the flap and slips her hand inside expecting to find a twig or stick or hairpin. But her fingertips brush the soft end of the feather she put there yesterday and forgot. Her fingers close on the tender softness. It feels bigger than she remembered. When she gently works it out and holds it before her, it isn't a feather. It is two. One is the dove-gray-and-rose plumage she remembers. The other is snow white. They shiver in her palm; a tremor runs through her and into the earth. She drops onto the grassy bench and stares at the tokens cupped in her hand.

Onas lowers himself slowly to the grass a few feet away. "Jah'gowa feathers."

"No," she says, shaking her head. "Well, one is."

"The other, too. But from a white, leucistic bird."

She scowls at him. "How do you know?"

He meets her stare. She feels repulsed by the tear poised at the corner of his eye. A frustrated growl builds inside her. "Go ahead. Say what you want."

"Your brother. That's what he, we, were protecting. The day… it happened."

There's a long silence. Part of her wants to accuse him right then and there of… of… of what? Of leading her brother a kilometer off their assigned route? It most likely means nothing, their straying off course. All she really has is her intuition that there is more to the story than she's been told. That somehow the gap in Steeprock's own record is related. Still, she wants to act, to accuse, to find a granite reason to dislike Steeprock. Her mother, not unlike the old auntie masterweaver, would tell her it is patience that reveals the truth, then dive into an anecdote of her archeological work. And then, even as Kaileh's contrary nature labors for reasons why that's a bad idea, she knows it's not. Working with Steeprock, watching him, even listening to his stories, might uncover the truth. Her hand lifts a hunk of hair to her mouth, but then she throws it back down. Onas says no more, and even though Kaileh feels as if she's the fish being taunted with a lure, she has to bite.

"Tell me more."

They walk down the slope to the Agiqua where they sit on a bench. She at one end, he at the other.

"We were watching the tree," Onas begins, "a mature mountain maple, for weeks. The jah'gowa pair had a nest there."

In all the American cultures a nesting tree—of any bird species—is revered, respected, and not to be touched. And for the Woodland people in particular, the jah'gowa is a gift to be managed and honored. A nesting pair is as safe as a bison calf in a circle of adults.

"We were fascinated by the white one." He gives a soft laugh. "Tareq, he was obsessed, really. The female, we thought, was the leucistic one, but of course, they share nesting and parenting duties, so it was hard to tell. But it was cause for much conversation with us…" He pauses, looks into the distance.

"The sound of the chainsaw, the smell of petrol fumes that morning, caused us to, in retrospect, act rashly." The image forms from his words: the poachers wanting the maple for profit, the sound of their tools of slaughter shrieking in the forest, the utter disregard for the lives of the tree and birds.

"Tareq got there first. He was fast."

"That I know." She remembers the footraces of their youth, how she always thought one day she'd beat him. They were the same height, but her legs were longer, her stride light and lengthy. Still, no matter how she tried, Tareq always made it to the finish a hair ahead of her.

"As you know"—Onas shifts his injured leg—"I was too late." He swallows twice. "Do you want me to go on?"

Kaileh considers. She stares at the two feathers. How did the white one get into her pocket? It's impossible, isn't it? Of course, she remembers the dream, but that was the most impossible of the impossible—the stuff of fireside stories, one she could hear Tareq, had he lived, repeating at every family gathering. Another thought comes: did Steeprock somehow get into her room, planting the feather? It was as unlikely, but at the same time more plausible than a dream manifesting. The feathers are striking, lying beside each other. Such symmetry, such difference. She shakes her head. "Only this. Did the tree survive?"

He pauses for a moment. "Yes. Yes, I believe so. I have not yet returned."

She rises, turns her back to him. "All right. All right." Then, carefully cupping her hand over the pair of feathers, she walks away.

The Other Partner

Later that day the officers gather for another group assembly. They spent most of the day in classes on Kaileh's least favorite thing: politics. She did her best to soak in the information, even though she cared little and wanted desperately to argue the pertinence of such study. They were border patrol officers, after all. Wasn't this new job simply an escalation of that role? As the day went on, though, once again a gnawing sense of having missed something critical ate at her.

Now, as they gather again at the amphitheater, the sun nearing the western foothills cupping the high valley, she catches bits of gossip drifting from the other officers.

"I can't believe we'll have to work with *them*."

"For my life, I cannot understand how this idea is going to turn out well."

"The whole thing makes me ill."

At last, Kaileh nudges Mateo's shoulder. He turns from where he and his new partner Shoushan Zeng, from far across the Pacific in their ally nation of Zhongguo—a culture even older than Mateo's Mexica heritage—sit on the grass in front of her. "What's up?" Mateo asks, breaking off from some story he was probably boring Shoushan with.

"What's all the talk?" Kaileh whispers.

Mateo rolls his eyes, but she sees their warm glimmer as he revels in, once again, being the one to keep her informed. "It's just speculation, but I think we're about to find out. If it's true, it's going to be a real bone in the fish."

"Do you—" she starts, but Mateo has turned his attention to the front where the commander has taken the podium.

"If everyone will settle, we can begin." Briento, she thinks, looks tired, deflated. The observation does nothing to settle Kaileh's growing anxiety. She'd thought her bad news was over. What is it going to be this time?

"We begin this assembly as we did this morning, with thanks to the prophets Neolin and Tenskwatawa, with thanks to the vision of the woodland peoples, with thanks to the sacrifice of the early Warriors."

The assembly rises as one, faces the east, and in a singular voice says, "With thanks."

"And now," xe says, "I am thanking each of you for the sacrifices you are willing to make for the People, for the continent, for the cultures." It's a familiar line, but something about the way the commander says it sends a chill up Kaileh's spine.

Briento scans the crowd. To Kaileh, it looks as though xe doesn't want to speak aloud something xe must.

Mateo looks back at her, his brows knit, a question mark on his face. This time it's Kaileh who shrugs.

"So," Briento says, "we've come to the hard part. You may have wondered why so much time was spent today studying the internal affairs of our neighbors to the east." Xe says the word "neighbors" with a touch of cynicism and a very good impression of an Atlantic accent. It puts a smirk on Kaileh's lips. The word "neighbor" in many languages of the People means much more than "one living beside or next to you." The irony of its use now is not lost on the seasoned group of Warriors.

"I've told you the basics of our mission, that, for the first time, we will extend our search beyond the border itself. This may sound futile, a waste of time, a waste of resources, but as you may have gathered from your classes today, political machinations often work in seemingly contrary ways."

Kaileh knows of this from her mother's work as a Silver for their people. Her reports of necessary maneuvering and compromise and posturing always left a bad taste in Kaileh's mouth.

"So now we get to the crux of this gathering. This news, in all truthfulness, I've been reticent to share. But I, as you, must bow to the wisdom of our Silvers and fulfill our honor through our service." The assembly is utterly still in the long pause that follows. A long shadow drops over the crowd as the sun dips into a cloudbank to the west. Another day, another sunset on a secure border. What now would they have to do to keep it so?

Briento clears xyr throat. "I suppose delay will not excuse me. I ask that you hold your comments and reactions for later. Perhaps even in private would be for the best."

Lena, sitting next to Kaileh, leans over and whispers, "Gods, this sounds bad." Just down from them sits Onas Steeprock. He's close, but has left a respectful distance, as if she's a shy fawn and he's trying to gain her trust.

"A major reason for our creation of this new task force is to create a buffer of time in which to retrieve all of our people from the East. Correct?" Most nod, and some verbalize an affirmation. Everyone has heard of the Outreach monastics and inspectors and other Western citizens needing time to make it safely west.

"Before I tell you the next part, I want you all to keep this truth in mind. Yes?" Xe waits a moment. "Is that a yes?"

"Yes, Commander!" Kaileh adds her voice, but something crawls along her skin.

"As part of this effort, we've made a deal, you might call it, with the ASA." Xe sighs. "In brief, each team here will be accompanied by a representative from the Atlantic States as part of our, *eehum*, diplomatic maneuvering."

Lena beside her says, "What does xe mean by 'representative'? I don't like the sound of this…"

"Trust me," Commander Briento says, "when I say this is a strategy perhaps only the eagle sees. And with that, I think it is time to stop circling the prey." Xe grew taller. "The representatives you will be tasked with working side by side with are members of the ASA domestic police force."

Everyone is silent for only a heartbeat.

"Shepherds?"

"No!"

"For truth? Shepherds?"

Kaileh's mind whirls. How can this be what their leaders have decided? It's ridiculous. It's preposterous. It's untenable. She feels like a knife is being held at her back. She stands without realizing it. Her eyes somehow find Onas Steeprock. The fact that he's looking back at her pushes the blade deeper.

Without thinking, she whirls, pushing her way past the legs of others.

Commander Briento stands patiently, giving the assembly time. Kaileh drops her head as she plows past others. She's at the edge of the crowd, just breaking free into the open, when she stops. Inside she roars. What is she doing? She can't keep running from everything, either in her head or with her feet. With an exasperated groan, she lowers herself at the edge of the crowd, pins her stare at a point just past the commander's head, rubs her aching jaw, and listens.

11
Ruby

The Happy Day

Never before has time moved so slowly for Ruby. She feels chained to a cart, her load growing heavier with each step. She watches for Downs at every turn, expects another yellow notice to be tacked to the door of flat 13 announcing her relocation to wherever it is the Shepherd lives. One day passes. Then the next. Then, on the third day, before escape is at hand, and just as she starts to relax the tiniest bit, he intercepts her after work.

He stands against the wall in the place she's come to think of as *his*. A brown envelope is clutched in one hand.

Suddenly, Ruby smells the stench of poultry clinging to her, despite having showered, despite having changed, despite having worn gloves for her entire shift. It's repellent, a reminder of her status even more than the CC blue of her clean boilersuit. As she covers the few yards between the BrandScan exit and Downs, she lets her mind picture, just for a moment, life without the clinging musk of feathers and yolk, life without CC blue.

"Ruby," Downs says. She looks down quickly, feeling as if she's forgotten an essential piece of clothing; he's called her by her first name alone.

"Officer Downs," is all she can muster.

He grunts. "Guess for right now, that'll have to do." He looks at his feet, stubs one toe of his black boot into the dusty earth. It's such a contradiction—what's the word Sister O uses? A paradox. A Shepherd officer that only days ago dragged a poor woman from her shelter and put a bullet in a tiny dog like he was squishing a mosquito, standing before her now, apparently as shy as a little boy. It does nothing to erase her memory of the other Bud Downs.

"You'll come around," he says. "You'll see. I can wait. Here." He lifts a hand to the pocket beneath his Shepherd ID and slips a note from it. "This here's the date it'll be on the books. But I'm gonna give you some time. Get your affairs in order, and such." He lifts his eyes. There's something behind the hazel gold of them. Not gold, she decides. False gold. Fools gold. She's relieved that at least with Downs, there's not even a whisper of the binding. The man is a blank.

He leaves her then. The note quivers in Ruby's hand. She gasps in air and realizes she stopped breathing at some point. The date. She knows, of course, it's the date his marriage acquisition is to take effect. She looks at the folded paper. It's shaking now as if a storm is blowing in. She's been acquired. Like a piece of property. But of course, that's what she's been her whole life. Property. Generational property. Inherited or passed on or traded or sold. With no way out but one.

A new thought comes. Children. Will there be children? Her stomach heaves and she runs around the corner and vomits. A thin stream of seaweed-green bile, along with bits of Cham, still disturbingly undigested, trickles from her mouth onto the dry dust. Then she laughs. Her children, should there be any, would be born into the free-worker class. That's something, isn't it? She laughs again, a note of mania in the sound. Children. Something she was determined to never have. To never bring innocent life into this horror of a world.

When later she pushes into flat 13 and HJ runs into her arms, Ruby has no memory of getting home.

"What's that, Roobs?" HJ says.

"Huh?" She follows his gaze to the note, now a sweaty wad clutched in her hand.

"Oh. That's nothing. Just my… my BrandScan printout. You know those." She shoves it into her pocket.

HJ tips his head, suspicion clear in his face. But he doesn't challenge her. "If you say so, Roobs. But hey, you heard anything about them?"

Ruby blinks, trying to steer her mind back on track. "Them, buddy?"

"Yeah! The folks from the shantytown. The girl and her daddy, you know?"

"Oh." She thinks about the rumors at work. It wasn't just Colin's promotion that was buzzing around the lunchroom, but tales of more roundups, of beatings, of a nearby camp where they were taking the adrift. Will telling the boy this reassure him, or make it worse?

"No," she says at last. "Sorry, buddy. No news."

"All right," HJ says, his voice accepting but sad. "If you say so." He squirms a toe into the scuffed floorboards. "But I had another one of those dreams though, and I think she's close. I think it's going to be all right. I'm pretty sure, anyway."

"That's good, buddy. That's real good." Ruby gives him a pat. Her hand feels heavy. "I gotta rest now, all right?"

"You should. You look tired, sure enough. Real tired."

Ruby climbs behind her curtain, not bothering to remove her clean boilersuit and hang if for the next day, and, despite the heat, pulls the quilt to her chin.

Only two full days until they leave. It's soon, so soon. *I can do this*, she tells herself. *We can do this.* She and Harold Sr. have everything planned to the minute. How they'll rise at 3 AM, tell HJ of the surprise adventure Brother Q has planned for them, then hike to town, reaching it, hopefully, by 3:45. Even with Harold's lagging energy, they should make it by 4 AM with time to spare. Brother Q is to meet them in the back of the Outreach promptly at 4.

She can sense the bulk of the note in her pocket. She hasn't read the details of it. Downs said he'd give her time. But what does that mean? Can she just ignore it? Pretend she doesn't know? But of course, that won't matter. McComb knows. Colin knows. Bud Downs knows. Fact is, it's about as official as a thing can get.

Anger simmers inside her. She wads the quilt in her hands, twists it, and tries to tear it apart. She stays quiet, a scream deafening in her head, echoing into her heart. The unfairness of her life feels magnified by the nearness of escape.

Sometime later, she hears Harold Sr. come in from the maintenance chores he does for a few other residents. Ruby tried to talk him out of keeping up the extra labor. "Your health," she said. But he shook his head, told her things needed to keep on as normal as possible for not only the lad, but for him too. Outside her curtain, he whispers to his son, thinking, she guesses, they don't want to wake her. Soon, he says his farewells and heads to his shift.

As he leaves, a wake of exhaustion trails out behind him. She can feel it tugging at her. Only when it's gone does she realize how his health has plummeted. How, she wonders, is he carrying on like everything is fine? It's a thing she'd like to be: strong as a parent.

Ruby falls asleep at last, the note with the "happy date" shoved under her mattress and unread.

The Sock-Monkey Doll

On the morning before Ruby and HJ are to meet Brother Q for their escape, Harold Sr. and Ruby go over the plan. They're to take nothing but the clothes they're wearing and whatever they might pack for an innocent outing. Knowing she's leaving everything behind, even trinkets and everyday objects she's never before valued, it becomes surprisingly difficult to say farewell.

"I want to send the boy with somethin' to remember me by. That make any kind of sense to you?" Harold says. They've sent HJ outside to play, even though it's barely dawn. The past few nights and days at the old motor lodge have been peaceful. Even the tension in town is less. But it's the kind of lull Ruby is certain is bad. Like the center of a storm, there's something about the very air pressure that's filled with foreboding.

Ruby nods at Harold's sentiment. "I'll tell him about you every day, Harold. I promise." She finds it hard to speak without a tremor in her voice. She knows now is the last time, the very last opportunity, for her to confess what she once did to the man. Ruby opens her mouth, but her gums are suddenly dry. It feels greedy almost, as if the confession would be truly for herself alone.

"I been looking for one thing, though. Somethin' that rightfully belongs with the lad. But I ain't been able to find it." He glances at the door. They both tip their heads on tense necks, then relax when they hear the sounds of HJ quietly playing outside.

"I'm sorry," Ruby says. "Is it anything I know of?"

Harold stares at her for a moment, chewing the inside of one cheek. "Well, maybe you done recall that old monkey doll his momma made?"

Ruby nods again, then it dawns on her that she knows what happened to the worn toy. The young girl has it, or at least had it when she was taken away. "Oh, Harold, I'm sorry, I thought you knew. HJ, he gave it to the… to a young friend who… who was moving away."

For a moment, Harold looks like the earth has been pulled from beneath his feet. Then, with a weak laugh, he shrugs. "Ah, you mean that youngun from the shantytown he was always talkin' about, don't ya? I was worried that was what done happened. Well, I suppose that there's done and done then." He gives her a strange look, like he too has a secret to confess, but after a moment, says nothing more about the lost toy.

Ruby wonders then about his woman who left, about HJ's absent mother. Are there stories she should have learned about her, things Ruby can tell HJ when he's older? Before she can ask, the McComb shift clock now on the wall of flat 13 clangs. It's time for her to leave.

One more shift. One more day.

If all goes well.

And it seems to. There are even fewer chicks she must cull during her shift, no equipment breaks, no workers are penalized, and at lunch, in addition to stew and stale bread, each worker is given a tiny bowl of canned plums. David elbows her. "You'd think it was Christmas, all this bounty they're serving up. Guess that Tate is making good on a touch of his promise."

Ruby doesn't answer. The plums, no matter what their source or reason, are sweet magic in her mouth. Even the Cham stew she swallows with a kind of determined nostalgia, chanting silently: this is the last time. The last. The last. The last.

But at the end of her shift, Downs is there. Not at his spot. Instead, he sits in his dark blue Reo. She almost doesn't notice him until the hair on the back of her neck begins to prickle. She looks over, tries to make herself smile. But he doesn't respond with anything but his continued stare.

She boards the omnibus. Her pulse rises into her ears when she sees him pull out and follow the transport. Her mind spins. It could be innocent. He could just be… be… be what? Making sure she gets home safely? No. Something is going on. For no apparent reason, as the transport enters Denton, Ruby's ears pop.

She steps to the platform to await the omnibus to the motor lodge, trying to not look back at Downs's pickup. But she still sees it. There in the periphery of her vision it lurks.

An omnibus is reloaded with another shift of workers for one of the other McComb plants outside of Denton. As it pulls away, Downs drives past. He drives slowly, passing just feet from where Ruby stands. She knows it would be smart to look up. To smile. To do something that doesn't raise his ire or suspicion. But wouldn't doing those things seem suspect? What is normal, or at least what would Downs think is normal for Ruby? By the time she decides it's better to meet his eye, he's gone.

One more day, she tells herself. *Less than one, really. By this time tomorrow, I—we—will be far from here. Then I'll never have to see Bud Downs again.*

The Road to Denton

"Oh boy," HJ says, rubbing sleep from his eyes. "Is it time?" Despite their determination to not let on to the boy about the early-morning outing, there was no way to hide their final packing, no way to conceal their own agitation, so they told him their lie just before bed.

"Yeah, buddy. Time for our adventure with Brother Q."

It's dark outside. The clock on the wall says 2:43 AM. Ruby has been awake most of the night, her skin itching, her mind unable to calm.

"Daddy, why can't you come too?"

Harold Sr. swallows. His Adam's apple bobs madly. "Got stuff needs doing here, lad. Like I told you. But I'll be walkin' you and Ruby to town, sure enough, that I will. Ain't nothin' gonna stop me from that."

A fist grabs at Ruby's heart. It squeezes like it's trying to stop the beating. "Come on, buddy," she says, her voice cracking, "grab your satchelpack. We'll eat a pemmican bar on the way."

She hoists her own pack up. A clink comes from inside. Ruby feels a twinge of guilt. She's packed one, not two, things that aren't necessary.

Ruby stands, studies HJ holding his daddy's hand. There's still time to change their minds. She hasn't told Harold Sr. about Downs, but she suspects he's heard. Could she get Downs to let her take HJ in with them… after…? Doubt again washes over her. But then the image of the little dog trying to defend its mistress flashes in her mind. And Downs's father, killed, maybe by his own son. *No*, she tells herself. *Besides, Brother Q needs us for some part of what they're doing. He, they, the monastics, need me.*

The International Assembly of Nations inspector from the West, Halek, Sister O's friend, arrives sometime today. It's a thing tied to the timing of Ruby's escape as well as a link in the tangled chain of events she doesn't fully grasp.

Ruby uses the night bucket in another curtained corner, rinses her hands in a bowl of water in the kitchenette, tops off her AquaClenz, and looks at the stock of herbal remedies she's mixed up for Harold. Each task, each motion seems slower, every step of it fixing in her mind like a photograph.

"You remember to keep taking the concoctions I made, right, Harold?" she asks. HJ wrinkles his brow at her. "When I'm at work, I mean."

"I know, I know, Ruby. I'll eat as much fresh chickweed as I can stomach, and kudzu greens next spring, and…" Harold trails off, his eyes pinned on his son as if they've never before caught sight of anything else quite so precious. Which, of course, is the truth.

They close the door to flat 13. The air outside is still, quiet, only a few insects grating and chirping and clicking in the night. They walk a brisk pace, the road to Denton peaceful at this hour. At first, Ruby keeps glancing behind them. Certain she'll see or hear the dark blue pickup. Certain Downs will be watching her, expecting something, and ready to stop it. But no one follows. No one passes. A few stray dogs bark. About halfway there, a mangy pair burst from a hedge of briers, cross the road, then plunge snarling into the scrub on the other side. Ruby puts a hand to her chest, her heart thumping like a hammer.

The three walk abreast, a trio of shapes in the dark. HJ ambles along between them, one hand holding his father's, the other Ruby's. The boy's hands feel big to Ruby, and she thinks of all the growing up he has yet to do. How will this sudden loss of his father, of learning they left him behind to die, how will that change who he becomes?

On schedule, they reach the far edge of the remains of the shantytown. Even in the dark, Ruby can make out the graveyard of broken shelters and bones of pipes and metal not yet scavenged for salvage. Here and there come sounds, and a light glimmers in one far corner. The camp is already home to a scattering of new people. Bumps lift on her arms; maybe they're ghosts.

About a quarter mile from the center of town, Ruby hears something. "Hold up." They stop. For a moment, only their heavy breathing fills the air. Then, it comes again.

"What's that? What's that sound?" Harold Sr. says.

"Come on, Daddy, we don't want to be late."

"Shush, lad."

It comes again. A muffled crack. A blur of yells. Then a single sharp pop. The two adults share a look.

Ruby tries to fill her expression with what she hopes looks like competence. "Come on," Ruby says. "This way's better. It'll be fun."

She leads them toward Franklin Street, a detour around the center of town. They turn west and pass an old tobacco warehouse, boarded and chained, a few abandoned businesses also secured, and come out one block below the Outreach. The noise has grown, but they're still well clear of it. A glow like a too-early sunrise lights the sky, rising, it seems, from the Outreach itself. But maybe that's just her imagination. She does her best to quench the increasingly loud beat of her heart and focuses on the sweaty grip of her palm around HJ's hand.

"You both stay here," Harold blurts. "Lemme go and get a look." Before Ruby can argue, Harold Sr. trots off. She feels the effort it takes for him to maintain a normal gait, how the increased pace makes his lungs burn. Ruby has a sudden image of the worst, of Harold Sr. pushing too hard, of passing out or even worse, right in front of his boy. What if this is what does it? What if, in essence, *she* kills Harold?

As they wait, the glow from Market Street takes on a bluish hue. Not a fire then. Ruby feels a small bit of gratitude. Harold is back quickly. His face, even in the dim light, has lost color. "It's them protesters. They're out front of the Outreach. Got some big ol' searchlights and a lorry. It don't look good."

"That's all right," Ruby says, "we should go around the back way anyway. That's where we're meeting Brother Q." She struggles to keep her voice light.

"Daddy?" HJ says, doubt spilling from his words. He leans close to his father.

Ruby squeezes HJ's hand and forces her smile big. "See buddy, didn't we promise you an adventure? For this part, you'll pass the test if you just do as your daddy and I say, got it?"

They head back the way they came for several blocks, then turn and walk casually across the main thoroughfare, Market Street. Ruby stares down the long throat of it toward the Outreach, keeping her body firmly beside HJ, blocking his view. People fill the street. Some have placards, others wave the yellow snake flags of the DTOM movement.

Just as the three are about to pass behind the dark building at the corner, the Outreach door swings open and several figures step out. Even from this distance, Ruby knows the silhouette of one of them. Bud Downs. He's with two other men. She's not sure, but it seems as if none are in uniform, though they carry zap-crooks and something she's sure are guns. Another sharp *pop pop* confirms her guess. Now, two of the men wave these weapons, barrels pointed to the inky sky like they're aiming for God.

More figures stumble out. Men with zap-crooks prod the figures forward. Ruby stifles a gasp. Two of the shapes have sacks over their heads, their hands tied behind their backs. A sob heaves from her chest. She clamps her hand over her mouth. The figures, one tiny with a slight stoop, the other straight and regal and holding her heavy chest with pride. Even with the hoods, even with the poor visibility, she'd know the shapes of Sisters M and O anywhere.

Beside her, both Harolds stiffen. There's no ruse left. This is not a game, not an adventure. Frozen, they watch as the hooded shapes of the monastics are shoved into the back of the lorry.

Ruby's feet move a step toward the scene. Harold grabs her arm. "No, Ruby, you can't. There ain't nothing we can do."

"Do you think…?" She leaves the question unasked. Only two shapes. Two matronly shapes. Maybe Brother Q escaped? Surely he would try to save the Sisters, right? Shouldn't they do that too?

She moves again toward the scene. They're closing the doors on the back of the lorry.

Then, a single figure slowly turns toward Ruby and the Harolds. He stands in the glare of the searchlights, no way to see up the street, or so Ruby tells herself. The shape solidifies and her heart stops. She grabs HJ's hand and pulls him into the side street, Harold Sr. right beside them.

"It's the bad guys," HJ says. "The bad men." His hand trembles in Ruby's. What has she gotten them into? What has she done? Uncertainty drowns her. Its waters fill her lungs and she can't breathe.

"Ruby," Harold Sr. says, but his voice comes muffled.

Then another voice works its way down through the heavy water. *This is bigger than just us.* Sister O. What would she tell Ruby to do right now?

She sucks in a deep breath. "Come on." Hating herself, she leads the way a short distance farther north to the opening of a narrow lane. They turn and follow its parallel path back toward the Outreach. The sounds of the raid grow nearer. They reach the corner across from which the Outreach sits. The lane continues on the other side, the back entrance to the building visible in the dark. But it doesn't matter, for Brother Q and the waiting car are not there. For a moment, they say nothing.

"Maybe we oughta go back home? No one would be the wiser…" Harold Sr. whispers.

Somehow, Sister O still buoys Ruby from the flood of doubt. She shakes her head. "Brother Q might have gotten away. Hold on a minute." She dashes across the road intent only on the goal, failing to look first toward Market Street, toward the danger. As her feet fly, Ruby realizes her mistake, but it's too late. She reaches the door, pounds her fist on the steel slab with one hand, shakes the handle with the other. Her heart thuds in her throat. Her hands tremble. She tries again. No one answers.

Then something catches her eye. A slip of paper sticking from the threshold. Ruby crouches down, grabs it, and unfolds the torn piece of paper. It's a note, written in haste, barely legible.

old can car BQ

She can't process anything but the fact that it has to be from Brother Q. She clenches it in her fist and runs to the edge of the building. Across, hidden in the lane, the Harolds wait. This time, before she crosses, she looks toward Market Street.

Two figures stand staring down the side street toward her. They're silhouetted by the bright light, dark shapes with no features visible. But she knows. She knows. She *knows*. They begin to move toward her.

Ruby doesn't think. She sprints across the street. "Run!" she screams to the Harolds, and points north toward the river and the old cannery, the *old can*.

"Stop! I see you, Ruby Roth. Stop, now!" Bud Downs shouts, his voice punching through the noise from the street and the pounding in her ears.

But she's across now, closing the gap between the Harolds and herself.

"Don't make me shoot!" Downs's voice is close, but muffled by the building between them.

Harold Sr. shifts his feet, not yet in motion. Ruby reaches them, resists shoving the man into flight. "We've got to run, come on," she hisses.

He takes a few steps, then stops. "Don't think I can make it, Ruby. Don't think I can. You go, take my lad."

"No, we can make it." She shoves them forward, then jigs to the side into the thick gnarls of a smelly boxwood hedge gone feral.

"Take HJ to the river, to the old cannery," she pants to Harold Sr. "I'm faster. I'll loop out and lead 'em away, then find you. I can do it. Go!" HJ is oddly quiet. It both encourages Ruby and scares her.

"Ruby, you know I can't make it." Harold Sr. shakes his head. "But this here, this here's somethin' I can do." His words are breathless, husky.

"Daddy?" HJ's voice is small in the dark.

"S'alright son. You do as Ruby says. You gonna be fine. It's all gonna be fine."

"Come on out," Bud calls. "You can't hide from the Shepherds. I can make this go away for you, Roth. You know I can." The singsong words seem to come first from the left, then the right. It comes to her that he's turning as he calls. He doesn't know where they are.

Her heart screams for her to argue with Harold, to give him these last few moments with his boy. But her brain stomps on her emotions;

she knows he's right. With an effort beyond anything she's ever felt before, she nods, then draws his tall thin body close.

"Ruby. Come on out now," Downs says, closer now. "Stan, you go around the other side. They're here somewhere. I know it."

Stan. Ruby knows that name. Bud's younger brother.

Harold kneels awkwardly, the leaves and branches of the hedge scraping at his clothes. He pulls HJ into a fierce, almost violent embrace. A sob wells in Ruby's throat. Then, without another word, Harold turns and pushes through the underbrush, moving away from them. HJ gives a small whimper. Ruby prepares to hold him back, but the boy doesn't resist.

The sounds of Harold crashing through the brush puts weights on her feet. She knows she needs to go, to run, to get away, but she can't move. A second passes, then HJ does something odd. He takes her hand and whispers, "Come on, Roobs, we gotta go."

From just feet away, Downs curses. "Goddamnit, they're movin' that way. Come on, Stan, let's bring 'em in." Footsteps stomp past, fading at last as the two men run after Harold.

She gives in to HJ's tug and somehow finds the will to move as quietly and quickly as possible toward the river.

Race to the Bay

They sprint through alleys and across empty lots occupied by only the charred remains of structures. They circle around mounds of rotting salvage, rusting appliances, soggy low spots reeking of decay, and always the grasping branches of brambles and vines. Holding HJ's hand in a fierce grip, Ruby pushes them to the limit. HJ, an air of somber acceptance surrounding him, doesn't complain, and soon they're not far from the old cannery. *Old can*. Is that what the note really meant? She wonders if they should stop, try to find better light, and read the message again. But she keeps on. Her chest burns, the air both too cold and a fire in her lungs. She breathes deeply, not only from the need for more oxygen, but in the hopes of catching the telltale smell of the Outreach sedan, for it runs not on petrol, like other cars. Instead, the old diesel sedan is powered by buckets of spent frying oil the monastics salvage from one of the McComb processing plants, puffing out the scent of something like batter-fried chicken in its wake.

HJ's hand twitches. He hiccups and sniffles as he pumps his legs beside her. Behind them somewhere is Harold Sr. It's both a whip and a tether, knowing the man will be caught.

She can't let his sacrifice be in vain.

The growing light makes Ruby guess it's near five o'clock; they're at least a half hour behind their goal. From Denton they're to travel to the Bay where a small watercraft waits at the Kent Narrows dock. It's all Ruby can do to not picture those watermen growing impatient and motoring away without them.

"I need… to walk…" HJ stumbles, pulling them to a halt, clutching his side. In the sudden quiet, the fading night is filled with sound. The howl of a dog, a loud engine, then two pops of what Ruby hopes is a car backfiring. The noise makes her cringe. HJ gives a single sob. Would the Shepherds really shoot Harold Sr.? She thinks, she hopes, not. Certainly McComb Corp wouldn't be happy to lose property.

After a few more gulps of air, Ruby lifts HJ's hand. "Come on. We can do this, buddy." They set out, walking now, with long, tired strides on wobbly legs.

After only a few more steps she smells it: the sweet, gamey odor of combusting fry oil. Ruby squints into the pale morning. There, up ahead, the skeleton of the old cannery rises from a tangled pull of briers and vines. They reach the stretch before the road turns east, and there stands Brother Q by the tan diesel sedan, pacing and scanning back and forth. Energy returns to her legs, her lungs, her heart. She and HJ break into an awkward lope and cover the last yards to the car.

As they near him, Brother Q flings open one of the back doors. "Quickly now. In and on the floor."

She helps HJ, tosses in her satchelpack, and throws herself in. They do their best to hunker low just in front of the back seat. Brother Q pulls a blanket over HJ and Ruby and climbs into the front. "Were you followed?"

"I don't know," Ruby pants, still trying to catch her breath. "Maybe. Harold, he led two Shepherds—I knew 'em, and they know me too—

away from us." She coughs, her throat tight. "I don't think they know which way we went."

"Unfortunate. But I understand."

The car begins to move, and with it, the throbbing in Ruby's ears slows. It's all she can do to not crumple into tears. They're pulling away from Harold Sr. Leaving behind a beloved friend in need.

HJ squeezes her hand. She squeezes back so hard the boy flinches.

"Even if you were not followed," Brother Q says, "the Shepherds will certainly alert the force, or, at least, attempt pursuit on their own. If Harold is caught…" He doesn't have to finish. HJ's father knows only the direction they're headed: west. But there's only one car route from Denton west to the Bay. Ruby tries not to think of the consequences if Harold tells the Shepherds—or, perhaps even worse, if he refuses.

"I am heading toward the old bridge. It will add time, but perhaps it will be unexpected." North of Denton, where the newer McComb processing plants are, Shore Highway has been modernized: a new bridge, suitable for heavy lorries, spans the Choptank. The old bridge in town is used mostly by local drivers and foot traffic. The sedan's diesel clacks along about as stealthy as the clattering wagon of a peddler. The cab is lit by only a dull charcoal light, but outside, the day is brightening more rapidly than seems possible.

The hum of the tires changes. Ruby guesses they've mounted the old bridge. She hears a thump, and they're across. The clack rushes into a purr as Brother Q accelerates. He lets out a small exhale of relief. As the sedan bumps and jostles, Ruby fights the nausea of not being able to look out. But it's more than that. It's the chant in her head of Bud Downs's words: *I'm a persistent man.* What will that mean for Harold Sr.? What will that mean for them?

Kent Narrows, where the boatmen wait, has two ports. The one on the north side handles ferry traffic and boats from the big towns of Annapolis and Baltimore. The smaller, southern dock serves local boat taxis and watermen. Sister O told her that the watermen helping today are part of a secret group who aid the monastics when they can.

Ruby suddenly realizes again she's been thinking only of her situation. But there are others, not just herself and the Harolds, who are in danger today. "I'm sorry, Brother Q. I… I saw the protesters take the

Sisters. Do you know if they…" Ruby holds back the words, as if not saying them aloud will keep the worst from being true.

He clears his throat. When he speaks, he sounds as if a belt is clipped tight around his neck. "It is not your fault, Ruby. We should have been more prepared. I did not… None of us thought the violence and danger would escalate this rapidly. We thought we had more time."

For some minutes, no one says anything. The sedan slows, and a line of bright streetlights fill the cab with their brilliance.

"We are passing the Refudyne sorting station at Queen Anne. The shift change is happening." A minute later, they pick up speed. Ruby risks pulling back the blanket and sees Brother Q glancing repeatedly in the rearview mirror. He must sense her, for he says, "We are still alone."

After a mile more, he speaks. "There is much I wish I could tell you, Ruby. But for your own safety, it is best you know as little as possible. I can tell you there are operatives in place to deal with a situation such as the Sisters' capture. I have confidence those good women will be safe. Your country—your old country, let us hope—cannot afford to raise the stakes too high. At least not yet. If these protesters are, whether they know it or not, puppets of the government, then Sister O and Sister M should remain unharmed." The unsaid possibilities shout to be considered.

Soon they slow again. "Passing through Wye Mills. Not far now." He takes a deep breath. HJ sighs from under the blanket.

"Ruby and Harold Jr.," Brother Q says, his voice now even and strong. "I need you to listen closely to what I am going to say. Your safety—and mine—depends on doing exactly as I tell you. When we arrive at the dock, our friends should be waiting. But we must assume the Shepherds are not far behind. When I tell you, I need you both to leave the car and run to the boat. It will have its engines on and two men on board. It is likely the only craft preparing to leave, but if you are uncertain, both men are bearded and will likely be wearing brimmed hats. The boat has a wide red stripe running around the hull. Do you understand?"

"Yes Brother Q," they repeat from under the blanket.

"I wish there was time to say farewells. But as soon as possible, I must leave you and attempt to intercept Halek."

For a moment, the name means nothing to her, the tension in her body and mind not allowing thoughts beyond the moment. Then its syllables take on a shape and meaning: Sister O's friend, the one they were to give the documents to. But Sister O is gone. The Outreach, for all purposes, is no longer. Brother Q must have these important papers. He must be hoping to catch the inspector at some other point. As if hearing her thoughts, Brother Q says, "I will attempt to intercept our friend from the IAN arriving soon at the north port. Now, tell me again, do you both understand?"

"Yes," Ruby says.

"Me too." HJ's brown waves lift from beneath the blanket. "Brother Q, you'll take care of my daddy, won't you?" The lump already lodged in Ruby's throat expands, threatens to choke her. Brother Q extends an arm into the rear compartment and lays his hand on HJ's head. "Yes. You have my word. I'll do my best, Harold Jr." Ruby's heart lurches. It's a promise as big as the sky and one she has no idea how he'll reach.

He pauses, then says, "Two minutes and we'll be there. Get ready."

Then, just seconds later, Ruby hears another engine. Her whole body tingles. Her bowels churn. Brother Q stares into the rearview mirror.

"The Shepherds."

The Edge of the Continent

"Brace yourselves!" Brother Q calls as he hits the brakes. Everything spins. Ruby's caught in a whirlpool. Her brain tips. Her stomach flips. Gravel sprays and clatters as he brings the car about. There's a sudden silence, then the rear passenger door flies open. Brother Q is already outside. "Stay low, but go! Go!"

Ruby tries to get her bearings. Nausea and something else paralyze her. Once again, HJ takes the reins. He prods her. "Roobs, it's time to go."

"Right, buddy." She sucks in a breath and begins to crawl backward out of the car. The sound of another vehicle sliding to a stop fills the saline-tinged air. Her knees hit sharp rocks, but she's numb to it. With one hand, she yanks her satchelpack from the back floor. With the other, she guides HJ out and onto the ground. Her calves and thighs quiver from the earlier exertion. Then, for a surreal moment, her vision fixes on the details of the gravel as if it's a thing of wonder. There's a scattering of smallcig butts, a wad of pink chewing gum, torn shreds of canvas.

"Come on out!" Downs calls. "We gotcha now! You too, holy man!"

"Ruby." Brother Q is crouching by the front fender. He looks back at her, biting his lip, studying her for something. She blinks, knows she's supposed to act. The scent of brackish water fills the air, blows away the diesel's familiar fumes. There's the purr of an engine from the docks.

She scrabbles her legs under her, begins to rise.

"Wait." Brother Q crawls back. HJ is kneeling, quiet, and eerily calm beside Ruby. Before she realizes what he's doing, Brother Q is shoving an oilskin-wrapped packet into her satchelpack. He puts a hand under her chin, lifting it to meet his disconcertingly green eyes. She wonders if this is the last time she'll ever look into them.

"I am sorry to add this to your burden, Ruby. This was not the plan." He gestures his head toward the unseen Shepherds. "Sister O will not be able to meet with her IAN friend. I was hoping to intercept him. But now—well, I see no other way. I need you, *we* need you, to get this across the Bay and on to the West. We cannot risk the Shepherds finding these on me. It would be the end of all we have worked for." His gaze darts left and right, watching both ends of the car.

For the first time ever, Ruby feels a fragile binding to the monastic. She follows it, unable to resist the chance, her last, she's sure, to feel close, to feel connected, to this intriguing, kind man. It's a wire, the connection, tight and strong, pulling her toward him. She senses his resolve; he isn't afraid for himself, just of failing, of not accomplishing what he's supposed to do: for Ruby, for the mission.

Downs calls out, his high voice an intrusion, poisoning the connection.

"Come on out! It's too late, Roobee." He drags the syllables out. The sound sends a long shiver through her.

"Ruby?" HJ says. "I need to tell you something." But Ruby's stare stays fixed on Brother Q, on what she's steeling herself to do.

"I'll take it, Brother. I'll do it."

She thinks then that he'll send them on down the gangplank, but instead, he reaches to his throat and tugs at something. When his closed palm comes away, two slender black cords dangle from either side. He again pushes his fist into her satchelpack. "Keep this. Do you understand? I… I… There's so much I wish I could explain. I am not even certain why, but I think this token might help you. I don't—" The sharp *pop* of a shot cuts his words short. Ruby's ears ring.

"Go! Go now."

Then, before she can respond, Brother Q is moving round the front of the sedan, crouching low. "Let them be, Officers! I can explain!"

More yelling now, but from the water. "Run to us!" Ruby glances down the gangplank, seeing the men on a red-rimmed boat, just as Brother Q described. One holds a long thick rope running to a cleat on the dock, then back to the boat. His body leans backward, battling to keep the craft from moving away.

Ruby lifts from her crouch. She readies to run, but something holds her back. She can almost see it, the wire binding her to Brother Q. She doesn't want to let it go. She doesn't know if she can.

HJ tugs at her. "You gotta hurry, Roobs, you're almost out of time."

Something about HJ's words sounds wrong. She shrugs off the sense of needing to suss it out, slings her satchelpack, heavier with the documents and token, over her shoulder, and forces her cramping calf muscles into action. They prick and zap, asleep from staying too still for too long after the frantic run to the old cannery.

Another sharp crack of a shot rings in her ears, and suddenly, there's a new agony. Fire, shooting through her shoulder, but not *her* shoulder. She knows what's happened. She looks back through the car's windows. Bud Downs stands fifty feet away, his gun aimed low, pointing to the ground beside the car, to where she knows a newly injured Brother Q lies.

Downs's brother Stan is beside him, his zap-crook like an extension of his arm, pointing while he grins at the same spot. "Good shot, brother!"

Downs ignores him. "Just stay down. Don't make this any harder, holy man."

The pain in Ruby's shoulder is a red-hot poker. Fear floods her veins. She knows they need to flee, but she can't break her connection to Brother Q.

"Roobs, come on."

She doesn't answer HJ, but drops back down, presses her cheek to the gravel. On the other side of the sedan Brother Q lies on the ground. His eyes find her, his mouth moving, telling her wordlessly to run. His right hand is just over his collarbone, dark blood oozing onto his burgundy monastic shirt. Dark. Not bright red. Not arterial. Not fatal then, at least she hopes. She can just make out the words he's mouthing: *Go, I'm all right. Go!*

And she tries, but the wire of connection is strong. It pulls her toward him. Then she hears Gram scolding her for her weakness, warning her of the dangers of the binding. *It be the thing what got your daddy killed. Don't you ever forget that, gal.* And Ruby knows, she knows she's doing that now, bringing risk to everyone. Causing pain. Causing harm.

She strains and rises, feeling the connection ripping something apart inside her. She and HJ turn again toward the dock, toward the frantically gesturing watermen, toward the waiting boat that will take them away from here.

Then, another engine roars over the small rise of the land bridge between the north and south ports. A sleek black car roars into the car park and brakes parallel to Bud. At first, she's certain it's more Shepherds. Reinforcements. The men on the boat call. HJ pulls on her arm. Downs orders her to stop. Brother Q bleeds, willing, she knows, them to run.

With a huge effort, she takes several steps backward toward the dock. Two men leap from the black car. One holds a badge of some kind before him. He's tall, older, with silver streaks at his temples. Not a Shepherd, but moving with obvious authority. It's enough to draw and hold Downs's attention. Ruby continues to back toward the boat. Downs yells something at the man with the badge and points to where Brother Q lies, then to HJ and Ruby. The second man from the car wears a McComb chauffeur's cap, bright red hair sticking out from beneath. He strides toward Stan Downs with a lilting gait. Stan shakes his head at whatever the redheaded man is saying. He pivots and begins to march toward the sedan. Toward Ruby and HJ.

Suddenly, strength fills Ruby's legs. She feels the wire unravelling, releasing her. HJ heaves on her hand, pulling her toward the boat. "Ruby, you gotta go, gotta go, gotta go!"

In her head, Ruby only vaguely hears the "you." She doesn't wonder why the boy isn't saying "we," not right at that moment.

"Yes!" one of the watermen calls. "Yes! Keep coming!" The boat's bow lifts, its hull moving side to side, impatient, needing to break free.

They're halfway down the gangplank, then three-quarters. They're going to make it. Suddenly, her arm is yanked backward. She turns, thinking HJ's tripped, and the boy *is* on the ground, but with Stan Downs on top of him. She still has HJ's hand, smooth and soft, but it's slipping from her grasp.

Just feet away, one of the watermen yells, "For the love of god, you must come to us. Now!"

Ruby's frozen. She can't leave. She has to free HJ from Stan. She's promised he'll have a new life in the West. She's promised to watch over him. To be there for the boy. She grabs his wrist with her free hand, strengthens her grasp on his palm, and pulls with all her might and more. Even dislocating his shoulder would be all right, a fair price paid to free the boy. HJ kicks and knees Stan. Ruby pulls HJ a few inches free. Stan grunts and scrambles. Ruby braces her feet and pulls harder. HJ slides a few inches more.

Then Bud's voice comes. Too close. Too confident. "Stay right there, Roth. It's over." He's on this side of the sedan. His gun is lowered. But he has a pair of handcuffs clutched in one hand. The tall older man is several paces behind. He looks defeated, sad, angry, frustrated. Without trying, Ruby senses the man's deep desire to help, but something holds him back. Ruby strains, leaning back, bracing her feet. HJ's almost free. Downs takes long steps down the gangplank, rapidly closing the distance. He reaches out. The handcuffs jangle.

Then, without a word, HJ opens his hand. For Ruby, it happens in slow motion, one finger at a time, until her palm is empty. He looks up at her with his wide brown eyes. "You need to go. It's all right, Roobs. I'll be all right."

"No," she says, but backs away, the nearing form of Bud Downs repellent.

"You jus' stay right there, Ruby Roth. Don't you move. Don't you make me…" He doesn't finish, but shoots his eyes to the gun in his hand.

Ruby's ears fill with blood. She can't hear anything, but she can feel HJ willing her on. She can feel Brother Q, still alive, being tended by someone. He wants her to go, to run, to take the packet to safety.

Bud is almost an arm's reach away. His expression brims with vile confidence. White spit clumps at one corner of his mouth.

"Go, Roobs. Trust me," HJ says, his sweet voice penetrating the muffled roar in her ears.

"I'm so sorry. I'm so sorry. I love you, HJ," she calls, her voice more tears than words as she runs the last few yards.

The waterman holding the line releases the boat from its tether. It starts pulling away, moving parallel to the dock. Her legs fly. She tries to stop thinking. Stop feeling. There's a sharp crack just as something flies past her leg. It leaves a graze of heat on the side of her thigh. Then she's even with the craft.

"Throw your pack!"

She does.

"Jump! I will catch you!"

Ruby looks back one more time, then, despite the stone in her heart, makes the leap.

Part III
Exodus

This we know, the earth does not belong to man;
man belongs to earth. This we know.
All things are connected like the blood which unites one family.

Chief Seattle (Si'ahl), 1786-1866)),
Suquamish and Duwamish leader

12
Kaileh

Tracking

"T he Reo automobile is a thing of beauty," Shepherd John McConnell says in the drawling voice that, after a long month working together, still makes her grit her teeth. The Shepherd sits across from Kaileh and Onas Steeprock on the Sunrise Express, still extolling the magnificence of the automobiles of the East.

How many kilometers has it been, Kaileh wonders, since his diatribe began? She puffs a sigh onto the window of the Arrow, continuing her scrutiny of the passing landscape with her own intensity. It's a habit now, this staring at everything but the ASA officer McConnell.

Her body senses a subtle change as the train mounts the long expanse of a wildlife overpass, seeming to levitate over the prairie below. She scans the horizon, hoping to see a herd of bison flowing toward the underpass. It was a magical part of crossing the Plains Region; she'd experienced it once before, passing at almost six hundred kilometers per hour over a brown-and-black river of animals thundering beneath. At this moment, though, the tallgrass prairie is a tranquil sea of greens and golds shimmering in the midday sun. It seems vacant of life, a thing the early colonial invaders chose to set deep plows to, but it's anything but. The long grasses, easily reaching over her head, hide a bounty of life. The thought of what is out there, unseen, watching her as she searches for it, sends little sparks of electricity all the way to her toes.

"I grant you," Steeprock says to the Shepherd, "there are stylish lines on many of the models, but how can you see it as beauty when there is such an economic cost? Not to mention the detriment to the environment."

Kaileh glances at the Shepherd without moving her head. He nods as if Steeprock's words are a revelation. His slate blue eyes seem to sparkle with what she's certain is espionage. But, when she's honest with herself, she's found little of substance to dislike about the Atlantic officer—other than his bright blond hair and exceedingly pink complexion.

"I suppose you've got a point there, Steeprock. I must admit, I'm fascinated by the nifty tek you all have got here. Still can't quite wrap my mind around that, what'd you call it, nanopore tek?"

Kaileh blinks. Maybe that glint in his robin's-egg eyes truly is a glimpse of nefarious purpose. Although, she reasons, if the Shepherd is here in the United West for something such as burgling secrets from its citizens, he's certainly going about it in a blatant, blundering manner.

Onas prattles on in response, as he has for the month since they were introduced to the ASA officer. In another truth kept to herself, Kaileh grudgingly admires his approach. He's somehow found a way to sound as if he's sharing nuances and secrets, but it's all data available through the World Science and Teknology Bank. The tiniest part of her whispers disappointment at Steeprock's skill; she's waiting, she's been waiting, for him to slip, although she's uncertain just what she thinks she'll learn. But every time she listens to the quiet words of reason speaking in her mother's voice, something else—another, equally quiet voice—tells her to not give up, to not let her guard down. Onas Steeprock, this voice insists, is not what he seems.

The trio is traveling east to the Northern Woodlands Region, their destination the Sacred Site Park in Chalagawtha, home to the greatest concentration of ancient geometric earthworks on the planet, known to the People as the Great Gathering. Even before the formation of the United West, Chalagawtha was the spiritual heart of the nation. Ironically, or so it still seems to Kaileh, it was also the first Sacred Site Park to open a few years earlier to foreign tourists. Since then, as she'd suspected would happen, petty theft, almost unknown in the citizenry, had seen a drastic increase, with pilfering of keitais, bangles, and wallets now a real problem. Just why Briento thinks her team will find anything there, she isn't sure. And no one seems to be inclined to listen to her opinions on the matter.

"But your cars are all designed and built by the government!" McConnell is saying. "I mean, there's just no style—no offense—to them. At Reo, we have a heritage to live up to. And the horsepower, my god, let me get you into a well-tuned V-8 and you'll be singing a different tune." McConnell's enthusiasm makes Kaileh's stomach hurt like someone punched her in the gut a day ago. But Onas laughs as though he can picture the veracity of what the Shepherd is saying.

One thing she does appreciate is McConnell's choice to not wear the draconian black-and-red uniform of the Shepherds. Rather, he accepted the offer made to all the visiting officers of donning a version of the United West Warrior garb, dark putty in color, but without any official Warrior insignia. Kaileh's sure it was done to avoid attention from the citizens. As far as she knows, though, McConnell is the only one. Does that mean he's not the same as the others? More likely, she thinks, he's just better at duplicity. She stares now at his chest where his ASA Shepherds' badge is pinned. It, at least, is honest in its blatant industrial domination: crossed Shepherd crooks, a trio of industrial smokestacks, a sheath of tobacco, and several lumps of coal.

Kaileh focuses on the thread of Onas's and McConnell's words. Amazingly, annoyingly, they're still talking about autos. Innocuous and innocent. Too innocent, she thinks. It's then that she realizes she should be paying more attention to McConnell's words. To Steeprock's too, for does not the finest subterfuge happen right under people's noses?

When she was at Shelter Rocks, her tracking was a journey serenaded by the creaking leather of her saddle and her mule's unshod footfalls soft on the leafy trail heading up Nemesis Peak. She'd watch his jackrabbit ears pivoting to and fro, scooping up sounds as she scanned the earth for a clod of freshly turned humus and the vegetation for the broken tip of a sapling. Little things easily missed by the untrained and unfocused eye and ear.

Onas laughs, dragging her back from the pure, clearly defined work of the border.

"Well," he says, "of course, that's why ours run better, run cleaner, run longer. We don't let style overrule function."

Perhaps the entire exchange is truly innocent. Perhaps Steeprock thinks he can change the man's nature the way Tareq believed the entire culture of the East could be manipulated. Maybe he hopes to send McConnell home inspired to make the ASA's petroleum-burning behemoths a thing of the past. And wouldn't those reasons, simple, naïve, and hopeful, be far less big-fish than some clandestine exchange of... of what? Onas is no upper-level Warrior officer or administrative aide with access to secret documents. She gazes out the window, soaks in the blur of beige and green and brown, and wrinkles her brow.

"You all right?" Onas asks, making her jump.

"Fine."

The men stare at her. "Just eager to get to work," she says. "Trying to keep my mind on the job ahead."

And she is. For perhaps at Chalagawtha, a discovery awaits.

Two days later, Kaileh still has seen no hint of Steeprock being anything other than a dedicated Warrior. She tells herself she should feel relief. Her brother's death was a simple, horrible tragedy. And Steeprock's missing birth records? Maybe they too can be easily explained.

Besides, there has been a small victory. After only forty-eight hours of investigation, they arrested three people connected to the crimes of petty theft, and two were undocumented Atlantics. The third, though, was one of their own citizenry, confirming another thing she suspected would happen: the viral infection of European greed and want.

"You people have a precedent for dealing with this sort of thing?" McConnell asks after the three detainees are put in temporary holding cells in the back of one of the park's admin buildings.

Kaileh tries to keep a sneer from her voice. "You are correct in that, unlike the East, this is indeed rare. But our forces have planned for every scenario." Although this might not be precisely true, it's close. Standing between the two, Steeprock's face looks forced into an irritating mask of neutrality. *What?* she thinks. *I'm not saying anything that isn't true.* Still, part of her wants to erase the roughly spoken words, or at least polish the sharp edges. How her mother, or anyone, ever functioned as a Silver is beyond her.

"We will, of course," Onas says, "work closely with the ASA regarding your two Atlantic citizens, but as the crime was committed here, I'm sure you understand why we will be holding them until it's resolved."

McConnell pulls his lips in, his head nodding. "That'll work fine by me. I'll be reaching out to my superiors, find out if the pair has any outstanding records or debts back in the States." When the couple were arrested, the first thing McConnell did was roll up their sleeves and check their forearms for embedded corporate identification chips. There was triumph in the way he pushed up the sleeves of the couple. She grinned to herself when the pair's arms were free of brands or chips or removal scars.

Kaileh ends the day with a mixed sense of validation. Part of her longs to let her private mission recede, to simply do the job she's been assigned, and maybe even enjoy the wonders of the earthworks. But a tiny worm still eats at her, gnawing away at her equanimity, insisting that were she to drop her guard, that's when it would happen: that's when she'd miss her chance. Still, maybe she can do both.

Serpent Mound

Early the next morning, trying to latch on to the previous evening's resolve to appreciate the wonder of the earthworks, Kaileh strolls to the mound closest to her quarters. Since leaving Shelter Rocks, she's tried, and mostly failed, to continue her walking meditations. But now, as she reaches the Octagon and mounts the flat top of the huge earthwork enclosing over twenty hectares, she realizes how much she's missed it. The sun is just nudging away the gloom and washing the sky in light. The singular peace of night fades as the world begins to gain color.

The great earthworks of Chalagawtha rise from the Appalachian Plateau, resting on a wide sweep of natural earth carved by a surrendering glacier some 12,000 years earlier. The Octagon, a berm of perfect geometric symmetry, was erected at least 2,000 years earlier by the ancient ones. There's an energy here that holds her. She almost doesn't want to breathe. It's as her mother, a world-renowned archeologist specializing in earthen monuments, has always said—or used to say, Kaileh reminds herself: "earthworks absorb and emit. They hold the memories of the People and honor their wisdom in a way that embellished structures never can. They are us, we are of the earth, and to the earth we will return."

It's this nostalgia that cloaks her when later that morning Onas leans close. "I'm borrowing an auto this afternoon and heading down to the Great Serpent Mound for moonrise service." It's another place she's never been, a mound even older than the geometric earthworks. As Bennu, her mother, often reminded her, Serpent Mound reigns as the world's largest surviving effigy mound. In some ways, it is the opposite of the ruler-straight geometric earthworks.

She nods. "That sounds nice."

"You want to come?"

Then, before she can think, she hears herself say, "Sure."

Unlike the earthworks in Chalagawtha, Serpent Mound isn't open to foreign visitors—unless accompanied by one of the People. The rest of the day she frets over the possibility that Onas will invite McConnell. On the one hand, it would be another opportunity to scrutinize the two. But riding together… in an auto? If she hears another word about regenerative braking versus the thrill of eight cylinders gulping petroleum, she'll throw herself out the door.

That evening, with the night once again settling gently over the Allegany escarpment, Kaileh grits her teeth and studies the back of Onas's head as he steers the borrowed auto over the rolling hills and south to Serpent Mound. As she feared, McConnell joined them and rides in the front. At least he's quiet, scanning the dark hills as if, she thinks, he's imagining locations for an auto factory or some other big industrial mess of a complex.

After several kilometers of quiet, she surprises herself by saying into the quiet space, "Do you believe what the two Atlantic prisoners are claiming? That they're puppets?" For the two swore they'd been brought here to work, trading their smuggling into the West for an enforced stint of theft. It irritated her, this suggestion that it was the citizen of the West who'd orchestrated it all.

"They seem sincere," Onas says. "Desperate enough." He glances at the Shepherd. His voice holds a tone of sympathy that brings her molars together with a snap.

"How do you mean?" Kaileh says. "Desperate how?"

McConnell's back stiffens.

Onas glances at the Shepherd, who seems to be purposefully avoiding engaging.

What I wouldn't do, she thinks, *to know what this man is really thinking.* This is the closest they've come to discussing the dismal conditions in the East—and the Shepherd force's role in it.

Onas looks back to the road. "The situation they tried to escape, being unhomed and starving, had to have made them vulnerable to such a scheme."

"They're not the victims." She pulls her hair from its confines at the nape of her neck, catches up a single stray strand that was tickling her face, and cinches it back with a yank.

"Not the only victims, of course. But think about what they were facing back there. They lose their jobs as workers and then face the horrors of the street." He looks again at the man riding across from him. McConnell seems to have shrunk into the seat. "You have no idea how bad it is for them," Steeprock finishes.

She loosens her jaw, searches for a remembered wisdom from her spirit healer Nibaa. The first thing that comes to her she almost says aloud: *You can't sow rotten seeds and grow flowers.*

Onas says, "I am interested, of course, I am, in seeking out the real culprits, the ones convincing these people it's more worth being smuggled west than working off the debt over time. Sounds like they are just a new kind of enslaved worker."

"I don't disagree with that." She hates the tightness in her voice, like a reed flute being squeezed shut. "But everyone's responsible for their own actions. These two are criminals. If we start feeling sorry for them, before you know it, the Atlantics will be…" She clamps her jaw shut with an uncomfortable clack. Why does McConnell have to be included in this? And why is he so blasted quiet? Maybe he and Onas are waiting for a chance to be alone? But then why invite her?

A bead of sweat trickles into her eye. She blinks it away and leans back against the seat, studies the backs of the two men's heads. They have to be hiding something, don't they? Or will all her vigilance and suspicion be for naught? Is she just a hungry mosquito on a bison in its full winter coat?

The last few kilometers are traveled in thick silence. Kaileh sighs when they at last pull into the parking lot for Serpent Mound. Several other autos pull in just behind them, and many are already there. A trail of people, small handtorches lit, thread up the slope toward the top of the hill where the serpent coils along the peak.

Then, as they move to join the procession, she has an idea. One last test, then she'll give up the hunt, let it go, move on. Patting her trouser pocket where her keitai hides, she looks up with a shrug. "Apologies, I'm expecting a call. Or a script. From my mother. I need to take this." She slides the e-utensil out, looks at the blank screen as if it's lit with important information, and feels like a child trying to trick their mother into looking away while they steal a treat. "You two go on ahead. I'll catch up." She keeps her gaze lowered, waving them away with her other hand.

"You certain?" Onas says.

She ignores him, turns, and cups her hand to the keitai as if needing privacy. From the other side of the auto, with her body turned sideways, she watches the pair from one eye as they recede in the darkness. And of course, nothing happens. She trails behind them, staring at their silhouettes, backlit by the trail of lights. For several meters, the two men walk with the ease of the innocent.

She's being a fool, stalking along like she's some sort of criminal investigator.

Just as she's about to close the gap it happens. She almost misses it, so subtle is Onas's movement and McConnell's response. The two men's hands lift with one motion, threading near one another like lovers absentmindedly reaching for each other. Although she cannot clearly see what is passed along, there's the faint glint of what looks like a small metal case as it bridges the gap between their hands. A dataslip, maybe? And then it's gone. Both fists close. Both hands return to the men's sides as if nothing has occurred, an innocent brush of fists, spontaneous or accidental. Were it not for her looking at just that moment, she never would have seen it. But just what has she seen?

She lengthens her steps, growing closer, unsure if she will confront them or feign naivete. Which would be of more value? Three steps before she reaches them, her keitai vibrates. Kaileh yanks it from her pocket, glaring at the screen, bright in the dark night. The hard lines of her face melt. All thoughts of challenging Steeprock evaporate. Has her own deception manifested this? For there on the screen is a script from her mother's caregiver Rosalia, the message: *Call me as soon as possible.*

As her shaking fingers rise to dial the number, the keitai vibrates again. Her heart leaps, and strength drains from her knees.

But it isn't home. Instead, Commander Briento's name glows from the e-utensil. She answers the call.

"Hello." She tries to smooth the anxiety from her voice.

"Officer Kaileh. Is Onas with you? I know it's late."

"Uh, yes." At her voice, Onas stops. He and McConnell pivot toward her. In the dim light, she thinks she catches a hint of surprise on both men's faces at her nearness.

"Good," Briento says. "There's been a development."

A few moments later, she hangs up. Onas starts to say something, but Kaileh holds a finger up, shakes her head, turns, and calls Rosalia. She paces slowly back down the hill as she listens to the familiar voice of her mother's caregiver. Her shoulders wilt with each step. At last, she pivots and trudges back to the men, feeling as if a decade of time has passed.

"What has happened?" Onas says.

"There is news. Some changes." She forces her mind to skim the surface, to not dive below the facts floating there. "I have to go home. My mother has taken a turn." She clears the emotion from her throat, swallows hard. "Also, the commander called. As soon as possible, Briento wants the two of us, just the two of us"—she keeps her stare on Onas only—"back to Waccamaw. There's been…" She repeats Briento's cryptic words. "… a development."

13
Ruby

Crossing the Bay

The boat moves beneath her curled body lying on the deck. She pulls herself tight, wanting, no, *deserving*, to disappear, to die, to shrivel up and be made dust. It seems impossible, but somehow her ears continue to hear, her body to feel, her heart to beat. Sounds pummel her from the receding land: yelling, the sharp crack of gunfire, but they're almost inaudible over the drumming in her chest. The bow of the craft lifts and falls, slapping the still water of Prospect Bay. A gentle breeze lifts the short fringe of hair around the nape of her bent neck. Sweat crisps into a salty crust on her skin.

What has she done what has she done what has she done? She rocks and moans and questions her every act up until this moment.

The sounds from the dock gradually fade. They're away. They've made it. Only *they* haven't. If she had the strength, she'd roll over and tumble over the side. Swim back—or drown. Either would be acceptable. Only the important documents anchor her to the deck.

You can leave them. Leave them for the watermen. You can go back to HJ, to Brother Q.

Yes. Yes!

She shifts to her knees, crawls a few feet. She's almost at the low cable running a ring around the deck when a sudden surge of water, the ripple from a faraway ship or barge or ferry, slaps the side of the boat, tipping her back to where she lay. Even this, even something so simple as dropping over the side, she can't do properly.

One of the watermen comes over. She sees his feet from her slitted eyes. "I need to go back. Let me off," her voice croaks. But it's either lost on the breeze or the man ignores her. She feels a blanket settle over her. And there, at last, in the semidark, she lets herself weep.

The sun is well up, as happens quickly on the flat plain of the peninsula. Despite trying not to, she becomes aware of the widening of the Bay. She's never seen the Chesapeake proper, just inlets, and only one time, long ago, when practically the whole town had marched to the wide mouth of the Choptank to see a dead whale.

At last, she hoists her head like a blade of grass bent from a storm. With a deep breath, she turns and looks back. The south dock at Kent Narrows is out of sight. Even if she wanted to swim back, could she? And does she even know how to swim?

Images of what might have happened after she came aboard the boat torture her. Is Brother Q in the Shepherds' custody? What will they do with HJ? Guilt, as thick as tar, coats her thoughts. If she'd not lingered, if she'd not let the binding hold her in place, at least HJ would be with her now. How did this happen? After all the preparation, after all the fear and worry over what the Shepherds would do, in the end it had been her. It slaps her with the force of a physical blow: Gram was right.

Ruby pushes all the way up onto her backside, hugs her arms around her knees. Then, despite the warm sun and the blanket wrapped around her, her entire body begins a deep, teeth-rattling shake. She tries to make it stop, but she might as well have just been pulled from a deep snowbank.

One of the boatmen, taller than the other, glances from the wheel, then back to the open water. The other man goes to a trap door, hunkers over it, and fiddles with something. From the growing roar, Ruby guesses he's done something to the boat's diesel engine. He gives a thumbs-up to the other man, whose eyes reveal a smile behind the tangle of grizzled muddy-brown beard.

Perhaps it's the smile, the two of them working quietly together, for Ruby's shivering gradually fades to an intermittent shudder.

The water feels deeper now, like she can sense the bottom receding away. Bits of debris float past. A froth of soapy foam clings to the odd knots of junk. The shorter man, his own beard still solid brown, but just as wind-tossed, moves to the bow and scans the surface. Using a long pole with a hook at the end, he dips it into the water and pushes larger pieces of flotsam and jetsam out of the way. Once or twice, he signals the other man to steer to one side or another.

A wave of desperation hits her. This is it. These are her last moments to face what she's leaving behind. She scoots frantically around, turning her body toward the vanishing wake of the boat. Something catches her eye, a small shape, brown, moving fast. Is it another boat? She leans closer, certain she'll make out the determined shape of Bud Downs in pursuit. Salty air pulls through her clenched teeth. She glances at the two men in their wide-brimmed hats. They must not see it. She opens her mouth to call out just as the shape lifts from the horizon and flies into the air. Birds. Just a small, clustered flock of waterbirds.

The boat continues on. Ruby's shaking lessens. But despite the buoyancy of the boat, her body grows heavier. The men still don't meet her eye, nor do they make any attempt at speech. She's delayed them. She's put them at risk. Thankfully, she feels nothing from them, a thick fog with only vague shapes that look something to her like resentment, like how Gram would seem when Ruby didn't do as expected.

A wedge of land, which has been flanking their path and must be the southern end of Kent Island, grows closer. She realizes the boat is heading toward it. Soon, the clattering throb of the big diesel becomes a low boom and the boat slows. The older man lifts longviewers and scans the water back the way they came. He nods at the other man and noses the boat toward a narrow channel. He's seen something, she's certain. They've decided it's too much of a risk. *She's* too much of a risk.

The older man at the wheel cuts the throttle even more. The younger one is again at the bow, prodding floating trash and branches out of the way.

They should put her off the boat. It would be for the best. They could flee to safety; she could return and face the consequences. And the packet. She can leave it with them. Her mission, at least the part that matters beyond herself, will have been completed, at least in part.

The channel narrows. The younger man uses the long pole to lift vines and thick drapes of brambles. The sides of the boat screech as the craft chugs further inland. She keeps her eyes on the land, looking for a safe place for her to go ashore. Ruby takes slow, steady breaths. A calm comes over her. This is right. This is the fair thing.

At last, they stop under an arched bower of yellow-green. The engine coughs to a stop, the silence overwhelming. A small spit of dry, solid-looking land is just visible between the vigorous growth. A trail. It's a trail back.

The older man is beside her. "We stop here." He extends his hand. "Come. Up you go now."

"I'm sorry I delayed you. I'm sorry about the terrible risk. And Brother Q." She says it in a way of facts, without pleading, without negotiation. She moves to the low cable, wondering how to clamber over and reach the dry land.

The younger man says, "Brother, she…"

"What?" The older man's eyes, brown ovals set deep above sunburned cheeks pitted with small scars, widen. "Ah, no," he says to Ruby, putting a wide hand on her shoulder. "This," he waves his hand in a circle, "is where we wait. If there is pursuit, then we'll be safe here. I am Noah, by the by, and this is my brother Levi. Fear not. You are with the Brethren now."

The Bay

The brothers tell her even if they wanted to put her off, this part of the Eastern Shore would swallow her up. They tell her that the other members of the Path, the loose web of people helping folks such as herself, know the risks of what they do. They tell her in words both blunt and gentle that she must not give up.

"Come," Noah says. "There is peace in labor."

Levi hands his brother a can and two brushes. He takes a similar small container, its edges crusted with dried globs of pale blue paint. The color, so close to CC blue, sticks Ruby's hands to her side when Noah holds it out to her.

"You want me to…?"

"Do as I do," he says when she at last takes the can. *It's just paint. It's the color of the sky in the West. Of Sister O's eyes.* The thought makes her own eyes burn. She keeps them lowered to the can of paint. Noah pops off the lid. Fumes trickle up, burn her nose, at least giving an excuse for the tears still threatening there. They kneel at the edge of the craft. Ruby feels the side lower closer to the water and stills a small gasp. Noah, undisturbed, angles his arm under the cable, looking over the top as he begins to repaint the dark red stripe.

With a sigh, Ruby pushes back her sleeves and mimics his position, his movements. Her first dip of blue splatters onto the deck. She yanks her hand back. "Oh! I'm sorry." The water already in her eyes brims, and she feels like a clumsy child.

"It is no matter," he says again. He dangles a towel over the side, lifts it dripping to the deck, and swabs off the mess. "We shall keep this at the ready. What say you to that?"

They work their way around the deck, meeting at the point where Levi, counterbalancing them on the other side, began. The boat no longer has a red stripe. It is only when leaning close that Ruby sees the myriad layers of colors. This, then, is nothing new to the watermen. She is one of many. It calms her, this knowing she is not that special. Not really. But guilt still fills her gut like a tumor. She's grateful for the ungainly mass of it. It's something she deserves. Something she needs.

The painting done and drying, the brothers finish the transformation by changing the set of numbers on the boat's side and erecting a canopy over the aft part of the boat. Wooden baskets and boxlike cages come up from another trapdoor. These, she'll soon learn, are crab pots.

As Ruby pulls the sleeves of her shirt back down, she sees the scar on her forearm and gives a yelp.

"What is it? Have you been bitten?" Levi asks.

"My micro-ID. Can they, can they track me? What if we are stopped?" Before they can answer, she has her short pig sticker out and is aiming the sharp tip at the edge of the scar.

"Stop!" Noah says. "Calm yourself."

"But the micro-ID. What if it gives us away?" She imagines more guilt, the mass in her belly taking on weight with every thought.

"Again, I say calm yourself." He is at her side now, a wide, calloused hand on her arm.

Levi comes to them. "You have no need to fear at this moment. It can only be scanned from a very short distance. But you are right in that it needs to be removed, but I ask you, what would be more conspicuous than a newly made wound in your arm?" He gives his brother a look. Ruby shrinks.

"There now, be still," Noah says. "Let us get underway."

"It will be done later," Levi says in a reassuring, patient voice. "Here," he says as Noah starts the engine, "put these on." She takes a plaid vest and a wide-brimmed hat from the man. At first, she feels silly, but the hat's canopy not only shields the glare from her eyes, it somehow makes her feel almost invisible.

As they work their way from the inlet, Ruby settles again on the deck and slithers her hand into her satchelpack. There, her fingers find the corded piece Brother Q tore from his neck. She doesn't pull it into the light, but caresses it. She's seen him wearing it, a glimpse of black, a flash of silver. Now, her fingers slip around the flat disc, exploring it. Imperfections come alive despite the thick pads of calluses on her fingertips. The piece feels hammered by hand. In the center, held in place by a ridge of silver, is a smooth stone. What is she meant to do with this token? Why did Brother Q have the impulse to give it to her? Perhaps at this moment, he's regretting the choice.

They emerge from the tip of Kent Island and, seeing no signs of any other craft, enter the Chesapeake proper. Ruby gasps. North to south, it's like a sea. Far to the west, a long line of grays, purples, and greens runs in a streak across the horizon. The Western Shore. The edge of the continent proper.

They reach the other side several hours later and motor slowly south along the Western Shore. They stop here and there at bobbing markers and reel in dripping wet crab pots. Some are empty; others hold a few crabs of pale blue-gray with almost iridescent blue arms. The color reminds Ruby of the turquoise in Sister O's ring. What, she wonders again and again, has happened to the Sisters?

Levi sees her staring at the crabs. "These with the blue, they are Jimmies. The males. We only take these and only if they are mature. This here," he plucks one from the basket with red-tipped claws, "is a grown female. Some call her a sook. These we return." He drops the crab, the sook, over the side. There's a small splash that almost makes Ruby smile. The sook, for now at least, is free.

The Western Shore

Late afternoon the next day, the boat chugs into the wide inlet of what Levi says is Mobjack Bay. "We are in Virginia now," he adds. Far on the north side, three tall smokestacks erupt from a massive building. They look threatening, a trio of bullies lurking tall over Ruby's shoulder. Smoke billows in ominous black clouds.

Levi says, "That is the Tri-State Energy Corp's coal plant. One of them." The look he gives it is as dark as the noxious smoke. Ruby can't stop staring at the looming giants. They feel like gatekeepers, watching for someone such as her who has strayed from her bounds, and then she realizes why: they're almost the same as the stacks on the Shepherd insignia.

The sun is low in the trees, the north and south arms of the inlet growing closer, when Noah turns the boat into a nearly invisible inlet on the south side. Its banks are thick with brush and wear a lacy collar of multicolored litter. None in pieces large enough for salvage, as the watermen did crossing the bay, with most too small to retrieve with the net. The waterline surges up as the boat passes, making the trash bob and dance. Levi glances at her. "That there we leave as a kind of camouflage. To keep this route from appearing special."

At last, the boat throttles down and coasts with a dull thud into a heavy trio of pilings lashed together. Levi throws a rope around one and cinches the boat close, leaving a little slack, which Ruby supposes is for the breathing of the tide.

"Come," Noah says, and helps her step to the piling. He takes a long stride to the soggy shore, then pulls and lifts her arm as she jumps.

She follows the watermen up a winding, silty path carved through dense undergrowth. Her legs feel jellylike on the unmoving earth. Soon they reach a clearing in the scrub, a small home and a few little buildings crouching in the middle. Warm light glows from the windows, and crickets chirrup. The flash of lightning bugs catches Ruby's eye. She stops and stares, her eyes darting with the insects' magical dance.

She jumps at a sudden clang and a loud cry from an outbuilding. Levi gives a soft laugh. "That is Noah's girl, Betsey, finishing the milking."

"A girl?" Ruby says. "It sounded more like, well, I don't know."

He looks at her with a puzzled expression that quickly turns to a smile. "Ahh, yes, the cry. That there is one of the milch goats. Betsey, she is tending them."

Goats! Ruby's never seen a goat and feels her legs tug in that direction. But she stops, a wave of guilt dousing the wonder. She was not meant to be seeing new things without HJ at her side.

She follows the brothers a few steps farther to the clapboard house. Even before the door is fully open, impossibly wonderful smells wrap around Ruby and pull her forward. She smells unfamiliar spices, yeasty fresh bread, and a meat that's not chicken. Despite the weight in her belly, her stomach gives a loud rumble and suddenly she is ravenous.

A slender but strong-looking woman with light brown hair tucked under a white headscarf steps from the stove. She wipes her hands on her smudged apron and holds her palms out to Ruby, who takes them, thinking of all the layers of paint, thinking of all the meals this woman has likely fed to others in a similar plight.

"I'm Rebekah, the wife of Levi. That there is my sister-in-law, Noah's wife, Ida Marie." The other woman looks up from the table she is setting and flashes a wide, easy grin. She's dressed like Rebekah but in a fuller, more ample cut of clothing.

"You look like real sisters," Ruby says without thinking.

"That is the truth of it!" Ida Marie calls out. Her voice is more powerful than Rebekah's and hints of a ready laugh lying in wait.

Rebekah shakes her head, but she's smiling. "Yes, yes, we are that, too. It is never quite clear which fact should come first." She shrugs her shoulders and squeezes Ruby's hands, still in her firm grip. "Come in. Be at peace here." Before Ruby realizes what's happening, she almost binds to Rebekah, so strong is the feeling of warmth and love that radiates from her. But she twists her mind to her failure, to the tonic of guilt, and shuts down the connection. No more, she thinks. No more.

They send her to a small washroom off the kitchen. There, she finds soap, blessedly hot water, and a change of clothes. Someone either knew her size or guessed well.

By the time she comes out, she finds the long plank table almost filled with people. Levi and Noah sit at each end. Along the benches is an array of children. There's one slip of a spot left. Ruby slides into it.

After a prayer, Ruby guesses, but does not understand the odd words and language used, she's introduced to Noah and Ida Marie's fourteen-year-old son, Rafe, and ten-year-old daughter, Betsey, the goatherd.

The lump in Ruby's stomach expands. Ten years old. Almost the same as HJ.

She can't dwell long though, for next she meets Rebekah and Levi's little girl, who, before they finish introducing her, sticks her hand in the air. She first holds up five fingers, then works to get just one to pop up on her other hand. Six digits at last extended, she looks up at Ruby with a glow on her face. Ida Marie, setting a pot on the table, gives a low chuckle.

Rebekah says, "Not for a month yet, Booboo." She flutters her fingers in some kind of pattern as she speaks.

Despite Ruby's fatigue, her hunger, and the burden in her belly, Ruby says, "Booboo?"

Everyone laughs. Ruby's cheeks burn.

Rebekah says, "Booboo, show Ruby your elbows." Her hands again do a series of fancy moves. The child, with wiry red hair unlike anyone else in the family, proudly lifts her two arms and displays a collection of scrapes, both old and new.

"The Lord saw fit to give our child a special gift and a special challenge," Levi says. "She cannot hear. But this has not stopped her from the adventuring. It is a challenge for her mother and I." Levi says the words with warm affection. Rebekah rolls her eyes, but Ruby feels the joy the little girl brings; she's like a burning coal that won't go out. Ruby looks down to hide the hot burn in her eyes.

When she looks up, Booboo is pointing to what looks like slices of Cham on a platter near Ruby's place at the big table. The little girl waves stubby fingers toward it. For the first time, Ruby hears Booboo speak.

The words, round and spoken as if she has a stone in her mouth, sound like "an-hoss."

Ida Marie says, "She asks for the pannhaas. Hmm, you would call it scrapple? No?"

Ruby swallows. Happily, she passes it to Rebekah who is closer to the little girl. The stuff looks too much like fried Cham for Ruby to want to try any.

"What do you say?" Rebekah says, holding the platter up but not putting it down beside Booboo.

The little girl makes a circling motion, her gray eyes sparkling with pride.

"Good girl." Her mother sets it down. Booboo takes a piece with one hand, then touches her chin with the other. It's easy for Ruby to understand she's thanking them.

Ruby goes to bed that evening with her guilt intact and her determination to never let her weakness hurt others pounding in her head like a klaxon. Tucked into a small room, part closet, part pantry, Ruby settles onto a thick mat of bedding. The golden scent of straw puffs up around her. Soon, fatigue blurs the earlier part of the day, the choices she's made, and she sleeps, blissfully unaware of what is to come.

14
Kaileh

Partings

Kaileh tucked her knowledge of the exchange of what she's sure was a dataslip, loaded with who knows what kind of national secrets, between Onas Steeprock and the ASA Shepherd aside—for the time being. Her mother needed her. Rosalia needed her. Even Commander Briento said, "Go, be with your mother. We'll catch you up when you return." So she found herself once again on the Arrow, this time streaking west, praying she'd make it before it was too late.

Now, thousands of kilometers from where she left Steeprock and McConnell, Kaileh Clearwater Lewis is home. She steps from the Arrow transfer shuttle into the warm, arid blanket of late summer at the southern edge of the Pacific Northwest. The air is thick with the sweet tang of hot pine needles, and another sense, beyond that of the eyes, ears, and nose, ambushes her: that deep, almost drowning feeling of being home. It is an almost tangible thing, and her brain and heart wrestle with competing desires to succumb or flee.

An abundance of acorns, small and reclusive, clings to twigs of the white oak, almost invisible among the dark green of the leaves. A mast year, she thinks, a time when the species comes together in unspoken agreement and reproduces en masse—not unlike, she thinks in a rare literary moment, the coming together of the many cultures of the People at the end of the 18th century.

Near her family's community, white and black oak grow in abundance. In a good year, the sound of nuts falling on the rooftops is like fireworks. Along with all the children of their community near where

Apserkahar Creek flows into the Takel, she and Tareq gathered the yaná crop, bringing the bounty to the community preservation kitchen or taking sacks home for their own families to process.

A sudden memory of a family outing, another one of their parents' efforts at occupying their two offspring with productive, educational activities, hits her as she hoists her backpack. They took horses and rode all day, following Apserkahar Creek to near its birthplace. There, they pitched a night camp beside a memorial to the historic battle of the late 1800s when Takel chief Apserkahar led local forces, along with Klikitat Warriors from the north, to victory in the Gold Wars, driving the last of the prospectors and their mercenary troops from the region.

There, while roasting acorn flatbread and a freshly caught brook trout over the campfire, Tareq had announced he would join this tradition. He would enter the Warriors after his formal education was complete.

Now, as she waits for an auto-auto to take her to their community, Kaileh decides while home she'll try her hand at making a batch of the soured acorn flatbread that was her father's specialty. Her mouth waters, remembering the early mornings after Tareq left home, rising to the tangy scent of smeared smoked tallow on the flat hot cakes, maybe a drizzle of honey, of her father telling Kaileh to tear the disc into two, and then he would always choose the smaller of the two. Where was her mother during these mornings? The fact that Kaileh doesn't know suddenly bothers her. It's a minute thing grown suddenly important. A thing she'll now never know the answer to.

Inside the small self-driven vehicle for the twenty-minute trip home, she keeps her face pressed to the glass, watching for glimpses of the Takel through the thick trunks of trees and leaf-heavy branches where it winds in a meandering, generally northern direction. When she was little, Tareq told her that deep in the river lived a giant gray-green water snake, its tail the beginning, its mouth at the sea. It's the kind of memory that still brings her a shiver of pleasurable terror. When she swam in the river, even as an adult who should know better, her body always felt puckered and repulsed as if certain the slither of wet scales was about to slide against her skin.

The auto-auto stops halfway to her village at a rocky point, not far downriver from Ti'lomikh Falls. The door opens for a waiting passenger. A teenage girl squeezes into the seat beside Kaileh, holding a basket of strawberries in one hand and a mesh bag of leafy greens in the other while smelling of sun and sweat and youth.

"Pée túu auntie!" the young woman says,

"Pée túu," Kaileh answers, her native tongue rusty in her mouth.

The girl chats companionably, switching with fluidity between Takelma and English. Kaileh feels a pinch of envy. The girl stops, at last taking a breath, only when they arrive at the Apserkahar community.

The girl's easy laugh comes when Kaileh, too, steps out. "Guess we're neighbors! Maybe I'll see you around!"

Kaileh stands for a few moments and takes in the familiar community, seeing it differently with each visit home, each year of age that passes since she left. It sits on two flat plains cleaved by Apserkahar Creek just before it flows into the Takel. Mountains flank the area and funnel upstream toward the site of the battle and the expansive hunting, camping, and foraging grounds of the People, of her people. On the mile walk to her family's cabin, she passes the large community garden, lush with mid-summer abundance: corn well beyond knee-high; sunroot in full bloom; squash leaves sprawling languorously and promisingly; and borders heaped with mounds of woody herbs, their scent released with every brush of a gardener's legs. One or two people at work raise a hand or call out, "Pée túu!" as she strolls past. Kaileh answers, her responses growing more confident with each greeting.

The smells of the garden fill her with nostalgia. How she misses the touch of rich earth under her nails, the faint yellow tinge left by the tomato leaf, breaking off a nub of purslane and nibbling on its lemony tang in the hot sun. The umbilical tug of home is powerful, and for a moment, she wants to forget Steeprock and McConnell, forget the dataslip, forget that no molecule of her brother has been returned to the land, to them.

"Hola, mi amiga," Rosalia says as she opens the door of the Clearwater-Lewis family's log cabin, sitting in a small grouping of several others. Rosalia's voice is warm and welcoming, but Kaileh feels suddenly out of place. She isn't sure what she expected, maybe the scent of baking or a hearty stew, but instead, the alien scents of cleanser, soap, and a faint, maybe even imagined, burn of ammonia hits her.

"Rosalia. It's so good to see you." She lets the woman, about twenty years her senior, tall and willowy like Kaileh, pull her into an embrace.

"I'm the one who's glad. You arrived just in time," Rosalia says as she releases her hold. Kaileh's heart flies to her throat; a little choking sound catches there.

"Oh, no, no. Your mother is still on this side. But in two days, the aunts, uncles, and cousins arrive to celebrate your mother's life. And… to say farewell. For you to be here for that, that is the perfect timing."

Kaileh exhales and imagines the small cabin packed with milling bodies. It is, of course, the way of her people and what her mother would want, but Kaileh dreads it. The heavy cheer of those with less bitterness toward death than she isn't going to be easy to endure.

As she passes through the rooms of their cabin, heading toward her mother's room, she feels a gloom trailing her like the tail of a comet. She's the last of their first family. Is there a word, she wonders, for someone who is beyond a simple orphan? There should be a term for someone forced by tragedy into being an only child.

Inside the room that used to be her parents', Bennu Lewis lies on the peeled pole log bed that came with the house. Kaileh stands in the doorway, her palm slicking the doorknob with sweat.

"She sleeps mostly," Rosalia says beside her.

"Is there… Is she… hurting much?"

Rosalia hesitates. "There is pain. I will not lie. We treat it, of course, but still, there is pain."

Kaileh bites her lip. "I suppose it's to be expected."

"Yes, yes, that is true, but truth can still be hard to accept, can it not?"

Kaileh feels the burden of her truths heavy on her shoulders. "Yes. Yes."

"Come, my friend, let us get you settled. Morning is the time she's most alert." Her eyes drop to the inert form of Bennu Clearwater Lewis. "Perhaps in the morning."

Kaileh wakes just before dawn the next day to an aching jaw. She expected to dream of Tareq or her parents, but instead, she dreamed of Steeprock. Dreams of duplicity and pigeons, of dataslips and feathers, dreams that in the light of morning won't hold still long enough for scrutiny. She walks softly to her mother's open door. Bennu looks the same, like she might at any moment swing her legs over the side, rise, stretch, and embrace her daughter. But she remains unmoving, lying on one side, pillows propping her in place. For a few moments, Kaileh watches her mother's narrow chest rise and fall. There are pauses. Long pauses that make Kaileh's own breath stop. But each time, each time, her mother's rib cage lifts again. Shaking herself, Kaileh pulls the door partly shut and walks to the kitchen.

"Morning, Rosalia." She wonders if the caregiver has risen early or been up most of the night. She frowns. She should have offered to take a shift.

"Coffee's ready. You help yourself. Made it the way you like, I do believe."

The scent is robust and filled with life. It's stronger, somehow, here at home than anyplace else she can remember. "Any changes in Mother?" she asks after her second soothing sip.

"It is subtle, but there. I turn her less…" Rosalia lets the obvious remain unspoken: what worry are bedsores or pneumonia at this point? "At least that way," the caregiver adds, "there is less pain."

"That makes sense. Thank you. If it's all right, I'd like to walk to the creek, while mother is still sleeping?"

"You go, amiga, you go." Rosalia tips her head to her keitai on the counter, her eyes saying she'll call if anything changes.

Coffee cup refilled, Kaileh opens the door to the steep slant of the morning sun and winds her way through the community of tiny cabins and the larger community of pavilions and buildings. Some windows are dark, but most glow with light. Still she feels invisible, like an outsider, an intruder, even.

An outsider looking in. Suddenly, when the mystery of Onas Steeprock is the last thing on her mind, an idea forms. She pulls out her keitai and rings Mateo.

"Morning… Yes, the trip was good. Good enough." A longer pause. "Thanks, yes, the visitations start soon…I know… I will… Hey, Mateo, I have something I want you to do for me. You know that relative you have at the Southern Archives? Well, I need a favor. It's about Onas Steeprock."

A few minutes later, she taps off.

She's near the steep edge of the creek's bank. Steps lead to the gravel bar below, and just as she considers going down, a whir of wings rushes overhead. Instinctively, she ducks. In the growing light, she watches the silver-and-white plumage of a large osprey as it dives toward the water. A pool shimmers just beyond the base of the steps; a shallow overflow glistening where it escapes over a shiny swath of stones slick with summer algae. The pool, she knows, is both a refuge and a trap. She waits. The bird rises, and for a moment, Kaileh thinks it's caught a fish. But it's just the silvery glint of water falling from its empty talons.

Sweet Sorrow

For the next few days, Kaileh fills the long hours as best she can. Rosalia has her help cook for the celebration, or, more likely, pretends Kaileh's unskilled chopping and measuring is of assistance. Following through with her promise, Kaileh ferments a few scoops of yaná meal overnight, then makes a batch of xník flatbread. To her surprise, it's almost as good as her father's. Mostly, she sits with her mother, soaking in as much of the woman's last hours as possible. Bennu Lewis is only seventy-three and has, until the end, aged with beauty. Even now, supine beneath a soft, downy blanket smelling of sweat and the end of life, there's something regal about her. She's too young for this, everyone says, but Bennu, before her memory began to depart, said everyone has a date, a time when they are to leave; hers just arrived a bit earlier than some.

Late the third morning, Rosalia steps into Bennu's small room where Kaileh's spent the morning waiting. Waiting and hoping her mother will wake one more time.

"You want me to give you a break?" Rosalia doesn't say what she's probably thinking: *You should freshen up.* In an hour, the guests will start to arrive: the friends and family, who Rosalia says will ensure Bennu never dies the third death, never fading from the memory of the living.

"No. I think I'd like to stay." *There's still a chance* hangs silent in the atmosphere.

Rosalia nods. "You let me know if you need anything, all right?" She sets a strong hand on Kaileh's shoulder, squeezes once, and steps out.

The room is quiet, the sounds from the kitchen a comforting clatter. The window is open, and bursts of hot air bellow into the room, their momentum purely from convection, for outside, the shiny green leaves of a large madrone tree are still. For a while, Kaileh stares at the green berries on the big tree, remembers herself and Tareq racing to gather the bright red pearls of fruit in the fall, before the seasonal flocks of *T. migratorius*, their red breasts only a shade lighter than the berries they favored, swooped in to devour them all. Her mother would sit them down, needles and thread ready, and have Kaileh and her brother string handfuls of the berries into beaded pendants while she washed and spread the rest out to dry.

Kaileh is in this reminiscent state when she hears a sound. A whisper. She blinks back into the moment to meet her mother's open eyes. Kaileh's heart quickens. But Rosalia said to not expect clarity.

"I'm here, Mother. I'm here, Níxa." Kaileh leans in, pushes a strand of her mother's lank hair aside. Much of the natural kohl black remains, but it's blended with silver so as to look steel gray. Kaileh's breath catches as Bennu lifts a hand. Her skin is still remarkably smooth. A few age spots nestle in valleys between ropey tendons and veins. Kaileh remains like a deer with a fox sniffing nearby. The hand flutters like a broken-winged bird, but at last grasps a strand of Kaileh's hair. It's the reason Kaileh hasn't cut it, her long hair the thing that once made them so alike, the thing her mother might still remember.

Bennu's lips part. They quiver silently for a full minute.

"Do you want some water?" Bennu blinks, and there's the slightest dip of her chin. Kaileh uses a tiny dipper to transfer a bit of cold water to her mother's mouth. For a moment, she fears she's made a mistake, that her mother will choke, that she'll have made her mother suffer more. But then Bennu swallows.

A moment later, her mother's rusty voice speaks. "So altúu… so beautiful." Kaileh struggles to make out the syllables and hopes she's understood.

"It's like yours, Mother." Tareq took more after their father's side, even bearing hints of the Irish origin of their paternal grandmother, Maggie, adopted from an Irish orphanage when just an infant, but raised in the nearby Modoc culture.

"We are… too… alike." Her mother speaks as though through a mask of cotton, but a smile strains across her lips. It's something her mother's said before. Something Kaileh always balked at, but now, suddenly, she wants it to be true.

"You should rest, Mother, save your strength." She feels her keitai buzz in her pocket but ignores it.

Bennu's head moves, a small side-to-side. "Soon. Forever rest… is soon."

Kaileh's eyes burn hot, and her vision blurs. She traces a finger along the plump channels of blood still pumping through her mother's diminished body. Kaileh feels the sudden urge to scream at the disease, to call it out for the rot of a coward it is, taking her mother from her long before it took her life.

There were still *things* that could be done for her mother—or at least that could have been even a few weeks back. Medications. Treatments. Special care. But Bennu long ago made her wishes clear. "I want to leave this plane with the gods' first invitation." She said this at a family meeting some three years earlier, when the diagnosis was made and the disease was a nascent thing. It seemed a future far away, then. Not only that, but it was a future Kaileh thought she'd be sharing with Tareq. She had this vague, hopeful thought back then that it would bring them closer.

"I love you, Mother." Kaileh stares again at her mother's arm. Tries to not imagine seeing her veins deflate, feeling her warmth recede, watching her muscles clench in rigor.

There is to be a ceremony at Lake Giiwas. What Rosalia calls the second death. A pyre at one of the Sacred Site Park's many funeral alcoves along the rim of the ancient collapsed volcano. Her mother's ashes will drift and settle somewhere near those of her father, Aden, along the steep banks of the caldera. Some might even float like tiny feathers down to the water, coming to rest on the pure blue below, clouding, for just a moment, the crystalline clarity of the water. A brief blink swallowed by geological time.

Bennu's voice catches. "Tell him… I miss him."

Kaileh frowns. "Who, Moth—Níxa?"

"He… needs you… Don't forget." Her eyes flutter low, like a dying moth leaving the flame, and she is still.

"Momma?" Kaileh strokes Bennu's cheek. Her mother's pulse beats a faint throb in her neck. Sleep, then. Only sleep.

Bennu never wakes fully again, and for three long sunrises and one sunset, the people come and go: colleagues, friends, and family from nearby and afar. It is a blur of stories, laughter, tears, and farewells. On the night of Kaileh's fifth day home, her mother dies the first death.

On the Arrow east, a few days after the body that was Bennu Lewis is returned to the elements, her energy set free, Kaileh feels as adrift as her mother's ashes.

People warned her, "Knowing the thing is coming is never enough," and, "It's going to be difficult," and, "Don't expect too much from yourself." She'd shrugged the statements off. What did it matter if they were right? But now, she sits on the high-speed train, barely aware of the gentle hum of its movement, the blur of the passing land, feeling like a hole has been carved in her middle. No, not carved; it is as if something rooted there has been ripped out by its deep, sustaining roots.

Not long after boarding, she at last looks at her messages. Most are simple scripts from friends and family, the kind of thing she's dreaded and expected and appreciates all at the same time. She brushes her finger along the screen, finally finds the one from days ago. The one she's purposefully ignored.

Mateo: *Hope you are doing well enough. Call me or script when you have time. I have some information, for what it's worth. No rush.*

Kaileh lets out a long sigh, thinks of her mother's lungs deflating that one last time. How innocent their breaths seem, how mundane, how routine… until they cease. She's heard people are born with a countable number of heartbeats and breaths. From the time they take their first, they are running down the clock. A fact. Facts. But until now, they were cold truths, easily ignored.

Losing her mother is one thing. Tareq another. Something gritty pulses through her veins, scouring her, reminding her of her duty, her promises. She taps *reply* on the keitai's screen.

"It's me," she says when Mateo answers. "Thanks. Yes… yes. Very peaceful… I know. Thanks." A long pause. "I'm ready. Go ahead."

When she disconnects, she's learned nothing new. As she requested, Mateo connected with the person he knew working in the Archives. She thought maybe, just maybe, the archivist at Lenape City had missed something—or kept something back regarding Steeprock's past. But like the Northern Woodlands contact, Mateo's found only the innocent-seeming birth-record discrepancy. Otherwise, the Warrior's record is as bland as the Atlantic's white bread, a past free from both demerits and commendations. She thanked her friend for trying, then touched disconnect before he could probe her intent.

She chews on her lip, waves away the attendant asking if she'd like a hot washcloth. Something about what, or how, Mateo shared doesn't sit right, like a bite of food that tastes fine but is tainted. Finally, she picks up the object on the empty seat beside her. It's a hand-carved box about the size of two large books. Its aesthetic is beyond rustic, more akin to crude. It was made by Tareq for their mother when he was a young boy, spending summers at their culture's preservation. Kaileh was too young to now remember when he brought it home. It was just always an object that was there on their parents' dresser.

"Tu madre wanted you to have this," Rosalia said as Kaileh repacked her bags before leaving.

"Hmm?"

"Bennu told me your brother made it for her many years ago. Inside, I do not know what it contains. But they are things important to Bennu, and even more so, muy importante to pass on to you."

"I'll miss you, Rosalia. Truly. Even just seeing your scripts has become part of my life, a part muy importante," she said with a thin smile.

"Oh, you'll be hearing from me, mi amiga. I have grown fond of this family. You are a part of me now. Your mother is a part of me, too. It is how we live on." She lifted her arms but didn't put them around Kaileh.

Instead, she waited for Kaileh to step into the offered embrace. It didn't take long.

Now, the Arrow streaks through the short-grass prairie. They are somewhere near the midpoint of the trip east. It is time. Kaileh opens the box.

Sometime later, she lets the lid on the box drop, presses down on it, trying to trap the words inside. But it's too late. Tareq's letter, his words, repeat and echo and etch onto her brain.

Thank you, Mother, for understanding why I need to do this. I know if Father were still alive, he'd want me to help the refugees too.

15
Ruby

Discovered

A hand clamps over Ruby's mouth. She panics awake, arms flailing, her mind at a loss as to where, and even when, she is.

"Shhh," a soft voice whispers. "It's Rebekah."

Rebekah. Rebekah. It takes Ruby's brain long seconds to come awake. She nods her understanding. The hand lifts and her memory returns. She's in the small pantry of the Brethren family. She's on the other side of the Chesapeake. She's here without Harold Jr. The weight of the dawning knowledge almost makes her sink into the floorboards upon which she lies. But Rebekah's firm hand lifts her.

The room is dark. Outside the doorway, there are muffled voices, a flickering lamp seeping its light beneath the door and the narrow slit left open.

"Is it morning?"

"It is just past one o'clock. You must rise with haste. We have received a warning from other Brethren in our community. The Shepherds are moving down the coast, raiding our homes. We believe they are searching for you. Come."

Ruby's body and mind shed their protests, responding to the tightness in Rebekah's voice, the vibration of fear in her body. Ruby grabs her satchelpack, not thinking of the documents, not considering that perhaps she should leave them with the brothers. She feels instead for the reassuring bulge of her sheathed blade. A small sigh escapes her when she feels it still strapped to her waist. She pushes herself to her feet—glad she slept in her clothes—and follows Rebekah to the kitchen. A lantern, half-shuttered, glows on the table. Levi and Noah busy about, seemingly looking for signs that they've had a guest. Rafe and Betsey sit on one bench, Booboo between them, her red head nestled in Betsey's shoulder. She looks up at Ruby with a big yawn. Their faces seem calm, tense, but not overflowing with fear.

Rebekah answers Ruby's unasked question. "We have planned for this, practiced with the children." Her voice is steady, but Ruby feels the motherly fear so strongly, it makes her stomach ache. She never should have come here, never should have endangered more children.

Noah is at her elbow. "You and the children will leave. We have an escape route. Rafe and Betsey know the way. You would be wise to listen to them. To do as they say."

Ruby swallows the dry lump in her throat. A glass of water on the counter sends her hand reaching before she can think. She downs the cool, clean liquid in three swallows. "I will," she says. "What about all of you?"

"We must stay. Our absence would confirm their suspicions. I fear the Shepherds at Kent Narrows observed us better than we prayed. But perhaps not. These raids happen, for no reason, so it seems. Still, it is safer to remove the children."

"Brother?" Levi says, holding the outside door open. "Shall we finish our preparations outside?" Noah gives Ida Marie a light kiss and follows Levi out.

"But, what…" Ruby wants to ask where they're headed, try to pin her place on a map of the Western Shore. She knows she's left Maryland and is now in the state of Virginia, still near the wide bay of the Chesapeake, but where will they go now? But Rafe's at her side, the hooded lantern in his hand. He wears a satchelpack much like Ruby's, as does Betsey. Booboo is dressed the same as the others: long sleeves, long trousers, a dark cap pulled low.

"What say we head out?" Rafe says, sounding so much like his father it makes Ruby's heart swell. His smile is warm, and his eyes, almost the same gray as his sister's and cousin's, brim with a confidence that puts his age to no meaning. Is this what happens, she wonders, when a child has a set of parents, or even a single, loving parent, to do more than simply bring you into the world?

There's a tap on her arm. Booboo is grinning up, a dark gap, like a missing fence picket, midway on her widely spaced bottom teeth. She signs something Ruby doesn't understand. She continues to looks up, a question in the sparkle of her eyes.

Betsey says, "She wants you to carry her. But you don't have to. She is strong."

Ruby hoists the little girl's boxy body to her hip. Chubby arms wrap around her. Although the little girl's scent is different, she feels so like HJ just a few years ago, Ruby's eyes burn. She briefly snuggles her head into the soft, red waves and hides a sob there. Sweetly, Booboo gives her a squeeze.

"Thank you, thank you," Ruby whispers to Rebekah and Ida Marie as she follows Rafe out. At the door, her feet stop. She feels held back, like there's a rope connecting her to the room or to someone.

"Come," Rafe hisses. From a distant place, dogs bark. The night is dark, not even the moon looking down on their flight. Ruby follows Rafe, with Betsey in the rear, along a short path to the small barn. There's the vague tang of crushed leaves and coal smoke in the air.

Inside the rustic building, one of the goats jumps when the door swings open. The space smells of dried grasses, earthy manure, and something else: a pungent, fermented smell. Inside one of the pens, over which a hand-lettered plank reads N*anny & Ninny*, Rafe fiddles with a hay-stuffed feeder. It clicks and swings aside. Below is a wide flat piece of wood. He slides it away, revealing a dark maw, the top rung of a ladder barely visible. Without a word, Rafe hands Betsey the lantern, and she slips down the hole. Booboo squirms off Ruby's hip, leaving her feeling too light, like she might float away. The little girl throws Ruby a toothy grin, then follows her sister into the dark hole. Rafe nods at Ruby. She takes a deep breath, finds the first rail with her foot, then squeezes through the opening.

Ruby's maybe ten rungs down, submerged in the cool, inky black, when she hears the scrabbling sound of Rafe following. Her foot finds the bottom. It's soft mud. The sound of dripping comes from all around. She tries to stand erect, but her head brushes the roof. A bit of cobweb brushes her face, making her gasp. Then, Betsey turns on the lantern. They're in a small space from which a horizontal tube opens into more darkness. The tube looks to be made from a ridged culvert, shiny and wet. In the wet season, she thinks, this must flood with water.

Without warning, a tight band locks around her rib cage. Her throat strangles. A cold sweat breaks across her forehead and chest.

"I… I…" Ruby tries.

"Oh no," Betsey says. "Rafe, we gotta get her out."

Rafe spins Ruby toward him. "Look at my face, not up, not down, not around. Look at my face. Now."

Sweat stings Ruby's eyes, and she sucks in a tiny sip of too-wet air. She does as she's told.

"Now, you must breathe with me. No, with me." His voice is stern, so much older than his smooth skin, his uncreased eyes, the little details of youth Ruby forces herself to focus on.

Slowly, so slowly, the band loosens just a bit. Her vision clears, and she can again breathe.

"No, keep looking at me," Rafe orders when she flicks her eyes to the side. "This is what happens next, all right, Ruby?"

"Yes," Ruby answers.

"You will close your eyes and keep a hand on Betsey's shoulder. I will follow. I will keep a hand on you too. You must, you *must,* think only of our touch. Nothing else. Can you do that?"

She nods.

"Close your eyes."

She does as he says. Rafe's hand pushes her head down. For a moment, Ruby's mind fixates on what this means: the ceiling closing in on them—even more. Her free hand brushes the side of the passageway, the cold, ribbed metal of a too-small space. A shudder runs through her. It's all she can do to not reach out with her other hand and confirm presence of the tight, narrow tube.

She keeps her feet in motion. Forces herself to think of nothing but the feel of Betsey, the touch of Rafe.

"We're almost there. Keep breathing," Rafe says. Her hand on Betsey begins to shake and the band around her chest tightens.

"I see the opening!" Betsey says. Booboo makes a cooing sound. There's a tune to it, and Ruby thinks the little girl is humming a song, maybe a real one, maybe made up. Its discordant notes fill her mind and she takes a breath. The band loosens.

A few steps later Betsey says, "We're here."

"Ruby," Rafe says, "I'm letting go of you now, but you should be all right. You can open your eyes if you want."

She feels his body move past her. But her eyes are stuck shut. There's a click, a latch opening. Ruby waits. A moment later, Betsey tugs her forward. A rush of cool night air floods across her, filling her lungs with coal-smoked air that smells like heaven. Ruby opens her eyes at last.

They're outside the mouth of the culvert. A drape of vines and roots covers most of the opening. Betsey, standing to one side, drops the camouflage back over the hidden door, then turns off the lantern.

"Wait here," Rafe says, and shimmies up the bank.

Minutes pass. Sweat dries cold on her skin and shirt. She tries not to think of the narrow space and how it closed in on her. It's a terror all the more traumatizing for its unexpectedness, the shock of learning a weakness of which you never before knew.

Never again, she hopes. Never again.

Bits of dirt clatter down the bank, Rafe sliding after them. He lands on his feet and shakes his head at Betsey.

"No," her voice squeaks.

"We won't know until later," Rafe says. "They may all be fine."

"What is it? What'd you see?" Ruby says.

"Our farm. There are lights. Too many lights. The Shepherds are there."

Booboo

Betsey buries her face in her hands. Booboo leans against her cousin's leg, a thumb plugged into her mouth. Rafe's face, eerily lit by the hooded lantern in his sister's hands, is dark, creases of worry between his eyes.

Ruby's stomach churns. The children's emotions hit her like fist-sized hailstones. She crosses her arms, bites the inside of her cheek until she tastes blood, then says the only thing she can think of. "We should go back. We should do something."

"No." His voice is certain. "That would be the wrong thing. The Shepherds, it is their way to teach a lesson, one our family is meant to share amongst our people. But I don't believe they will harm them. Martyrs are something the Shepherds do not want."

She pictures all the other horrors the Shepherds could bring to these gentle people. Because of her. "But I could…" Ruby begins, meaning to say she could turn herself in. But then she realizes that would only confirm the officers' suspicions. She would likely incite more punishment of the Brethren family.

"Come, we must continue. The underground route is meant only to delay the hounds, should they use them. We must move on." He puts an arm around his sister, gives her a squeeze, ruffles his cousin's head, then leads the way forward. Something holds Ruby back, a tug of connection, a long, slender chain leading back, back across the Bay. She knows the heaviest link is Harold Jr. Where is the boy now? What about Harold Sr.? And now the endangerment of the Brethren's farm. She should have just stayed in Denton. Accepted her fate. Tried to make a better life for HJ there.

But it's too late now. Too late to undo anything.

She grits her teeth and vows to not let anything happen to these young people. Then, lifting her heart and feet, she follows them into the darkness.

They trek through fallow fields, across sluggish drainage ditches, and circle around a poultry grow farm owned, Rafe says, not by McComb, but another big corp named Blosser Birds. It shifts something in Ruby, having been raised in a world where everything, everything, was related to McComb. The stink oozing from the Blosser farm is a familiar ammonia-laden stench. The same stink, Ruby thinks, just with a different name.

For stretches, Ruby carries Booboo, or her cousins` do, but mostly the little girl chugs along on her own stubby legs. The child's resolve pulls Ruby forward.

The sky is still a black swath when they reach a large drainage ditch where Rafe comes to a stop.

"This is Aberdeen Creek," Rafe says. "We follow this to the York River."

Several moments later, the group rounds a bend, and Ruby catches the sweet, rancid odor of rotting flesh. Booboo gives a strangled cry just as they round another bend. They freeze.

Just feet away, partway down the silty bank, a small pack of wild dogs snarls and snaps. The slit of light from the lantern makes the eyes of two who turn their way glow into red orbs.

Another set of bright ember eyes lifts. There's a growl. The slash of sharp teeth. Another dog, its muzzle buried in the rib cage of something small, suddenly flashes up and bites one of its packmates. The injured dog shrieks and takes a step back, raises its whimpering muzzle, and stares at the children. Ruby can almost feel it sizing them up, its desperate need to conquer something weaker than itself. For a brief moment, she thinks of the pack of girls on the Denton street; this primal need is not limited to wild animals.

Rafe takes a step backward, one arm held behind him. "Don't turn your backs, but look down," he says in a low voice. Booboo, now in Betsey's arms, gives another whimper, her stout little arm pointing at the gruesome feast.

Ruby holds her breath, her pulse loud in her ears, as they continue to slowly back around the corner. The dogs snarl and rip and snap, apparently thankfully uninterested in something fresh to hunt. Ruby's pulse slows. It's then that she realizes she's withdrawn her knife. She stares at it, turning it back and forth. It feels heavier than usual, its glint showing its sharp two-sided edges in the growing light. Ruby slides it back into her sheath and stares at the glowing band in the eastern sky.

How is it that only a day has passed, only one day, since she and the Harolds set out?

The little group has traveled several yards farther back when Booboo, still in her cousin's arms, makes her dove sound and signs something.

Rafe says, "She doesn't fear them, those dogs, though it would serve her well to do so."

Ruby frowns. Rafe answers the unspoken question. "Boo senses the animals themselves. These, she says, make her sad. 'They so hungry, scared,' is what she said." He turns them into the brush, following a wide arc around the spot where noise of the wild dogs still comes.

The skin on Ruby's arms tingles, not just from the carnivorous sounds, but from what Rafe said. Does he mean Booboo can do something like binding with the dogs? Could that happen? Her job on the hatchery line, a task of selective, coldhearted murder, what would it be like to have the little girl's curse and work there?

The light continues to grow. The sound of the dogs fades. The group's footfalls are heavy with fatigue, growing noisier. Around her, the scenery takes shape. It looks much like the Eastern Shore: flat, overrun with scrub and vine, many places to hide—or for something, or someone, to be lurking. A watery vegetable scent grows stronger with every step.

"We're here," Rafe says a few moments later. "The York is only a few yards farther, but the daylight will not be our friend." Rafe steps toward a heap of vines, mostly kudzu, and parts the long drape of it. "After you," he says with a grin.

They squeeze through, dropping to their knees under the low roof. Beneath the vines is a small open space supported by rotting beams of what must have been a low-roofed shed. For the briefest moment, the band of panic threatens to cinch tight. But then Ruby focuses on the light filtering through the many openings in the covering, and her breath comes again.

The ground beneath their hands and knees is surprisingly free of debris. Ruby feels certain it's a space that's been kept ready for just this moment. She takes a long drink from her AquaClenz, refilled by one of the Brethren just before they left. Rafe hands out strips of dark, spicy dried goat meat. The flavor is robust and rich, seeming to expand in Ruby's empty belly.

"We'll sleep through the day, if possible," Rafe says. "Come nightfall, we'll put in and paddle upriver. There, Lord willing, we'll rendezvous with friends at Werowocomoco."

Werowocomoco. Ruby rolls the strange name around in her mouth. Somehow, the exotic syllables make her flight more real.

Sometime later, Ruby wakes and stretches. The light through the canopy speckles green brightness across the earthen floor. A pebble, feeling as big as a boulder, presses into Ruby's hip. She rolls over with a low groan and sees Rafe sitting up, his head bowed. Betsey and Booboo are curled together in a sweet, sisterly ball. Rafe's head lifts at her sound, his lips moving in silent words.

"Sorry," she whispers.

"I am finished." He seems to study her. She's certain there can't be more than ten years separating them, but the impression of Rafe being older than he is, is strong.

"We have been blessed thus far to have not been pursued," Rafe says. "Our family has prepared for this, but still, it is an oddity to be living it."

As the other two sleep, Rafe tells her more of the collective of Brethren families still following the old ways. But some, such as theirs, take great risks to help others. "My father and uncle believe a new day is coming and that the Brethren will once again flourish."

There's something in his voice that makes Ruby pause. "You don't believe it too?"

"No, I do, but I see a great tribulation coming first." He lifts his gaze and looks at his sister and cousin, then drops his head again.

Ruby lies back down, certain no sleep will come.

It's just growing dark when her eyes snap open. At first, she's surprised to have truly slept the entire long summer day. But then the hair on her neck bristles. Something's not right. Ruby pushes up on one elbow. Betsey is still asleep, on her stomach now. But Rafe and Booboo are gone. As she tries to sort this fact, Betsey stirs, and Rafe slips through the canopy.

"Booboo, have you seen her?" He looks side to side, panic twisting his expression, vibrating from his body.

Betsey sits up, rubs her eyes, and looks around. "Booboo! Where is she?"

The small space is a cavern without the little girl's presence.

Booboo is gone.

The Hounds

Ruby leaps to her feet and moves to the opening with only one thought: *not again*. She'll find the little girl before it's too late.

"Wait," Rafe says. "We need to think. We need to do this right. Let's search in circles around the shelter." His hands twist together. His voice is urgent, but thoughtful. "Ruby, go that way. Betsey, stay with me." He points Ruby to the left. She nods, happy to follow his orders, for surely he must know this area, and his cousin, well. Her mind is a storm of images: the little girl running, pushing through tangles of vine, being scratched and torn by brambles and bitten by angry black flies. Fear fills them all, she can feel it as strong as the carrion rot of the night before. She walks her circle, staring at the ground, the shrubs, the leaf litter.

In the fallow fields and scrub around Denton, Ruby learned a different kind of seeing. Where some might see a long, leafy stretch of soil, she learned to catch the almost invisible pattern left by the passage of beast and human. It serves her well now; on her second loop, she finds Booboo's path leading away from the makeshift camp.

The girl's trail leads away from the river, away from their route of escape, and heads back the way they came.

"Might she have tried to go home?" Ruby says as they stand over the signs.

Betsey remains quiet. Sleep has mussed her light brown hair into a wad of tangles, and her gray eyes are wide, gleaming in the fading light.

Rafe says, "No. At least, I don't think she would." But Ruby hears the doubt in his voice, the growing terror.

They resume their search, following the nearly invisible trail of one so small. The light fades, and soon the tiny bits of turned earth and broken twigs are swallowed by the night. Even with the lantern, they fail to find her tracks. They stand still, hearing nothing but the rising sounds of night, the buzz of insects, the howl of a distant dog, the hoarse croak of a bullfrog, and Betsey crying quiet tears.

Ruby's earlier sense of contribution is long gone. None of this would have happened were it not for her.

"Rafe, what should we do?" Betsey says, wiping her nose on her sleeve. To Ruby's surprise, the girl slips her hand into Ruby's. She feels suddenly frustrated and angry, but with no one thing to focus on, it buzzes around in her head like a nest of angry hornets.

Rafe opens his mouth, but no words come. Ruby can't see for sure, but she thinks he too is crying. He turns his head back toward the York. Back toward his duty. He takes a step in that direction.

"No," Ruby says. "We can't give up." The thought of leaving behind another innocent child is unacceptable. She feels the weight of the documents in her satchelpack, but suddenly doesn't care about national secrets and politics.

"I won't leave her," Ruby says. Betsey squeezes her hand.

Then they hear it, the hungry barking and baying of dogs threading through the night. It comes from the same direction as their flight, the same direction in which the little girl went. For a moment, Ruby wonders if it's the rangy pack they encountered earlier. But then the long *boowhoowhoo* of a tracking hound sings out.

"Shepherds," Rafe says.

Ice runs down her spine. She slips her knife from its sheath.

The baying is still distant, but its progress toward them is obvious.

"I… I… We must take to the water." Rafe turns and heads toward the York.

Quietly sobbing, Betsey slides her hand from Ruby's. It becomes HJ's. She feels the boy's fingers slipping away, the look on his face, the stone it put in her heart.

"No!"

Rafe turns, opens his mouth, closes it, opens it again. "My father and my uncle, their orders… their orders were clear." His voice wavers, uncertain, a young man trying to do the right thing.

"Just give me a few more minutes." Not waiting for an answer, Ruby crouches low to the ground. She hears Harold Sr. asking if she can do "that thing." Should she try now to connect to the little girl? But what if Booboo is hurt and the feelings overwhelm Ruby? She remembers the terrible lock Brother Q's pain had on her. How it paralyzed her, kept her from doing what was needed to keep HJ safe. If she tries it now, will she again be immobilized? Will she endanger them all?

"Give me your lantern," she says to Rafe. She unhoods it close to the ground, casting an angle of light across the cryptic scattering of leaves. At first she sees nothing. She crawls forward, not caring about the sticks and mud and rocks biting into her knees, checking every inch before them.

Something makes her stop. She tips her head, changes the angle of the lantern, and there it is, the faint pressing left by a small foot on the moist earth.

"Come on." She's up now, moving, not waiting for the siblings to follow her.

The baying grows closer. The dogs can be no more than a quarter mile away.

"We must go to the water. We must," Rafe says in a hoarse whisper.

Ruby ignores him, runs with the lantern low to the earth, ignoring the scrape and slap of branches on her arms and bent head. Quiet scuffles and panting come from Rafe and Betsey not far behind.

The sound of the dogs grows steadily closer. She's running toward danger. She's taking Rafe and Betsey toward terrible peril. What if she's wrong and they're all caught? Her feet fumble in doubt. She almost shields the lantern and comes to a stop. But then, as they round a corner not far from where they encountered the wild dogs the night before, a sliver of moon lifts above the horizon. Moments later, Ruby sees Booboo. She's backed against a pile of deadfall at least three times her height and wedged between the gnarled roots of a long-ago tree.

At first, Ruby only has eyes for the beautiful sight of the girl. Then she realizes what stands between them. It's not the pack of feral dogs, but something almost worse. A huge wild sow faces the little girl, pawing its cloven hooves, ready to charge.

The Sow

The massive old hog's sagging teats swing as she grunts and sways her craggy head from side to side. Her tusks gnash as she smacks her long black snout. Streams of saliva glisten and drip.

"Get Betsey back," Ruby hisses, swishing her arm behind her.

She takes long breaths, trying to calm herself, trying to think. She's faced wild boar before, but never an enraged, full-grown sow.

"Hey! Pig!" But it's as if Ruby isn't even there. The sow keeps her small eyes locked onto the little redheaded girl before her. The hog's muscled haunches tense. Ruby stomps on the ground, hears Rafe behind her yelling at the pig. The distance to Booboo is too far for Ruby to cover in time. Almost without thought, she raises her arm, her brain calculating the trajectory toward the most tender spot on the huge beast. With her small knife, even a perfect hit won't kill it, but she can surely get its attention. There's a reason this kind of knife is called a pig sticker.

She throws.

As the knife leaves her hand, it seems to slow. The silver blade arcs slightly up, righting itself on the downward leg, the tip of the blade dipping toward… toward… That's when she sees it's going to miss. It will sail just past the point she targeted, just behind the sow's ear. Ruby will be left unarmed, with only her body to throw at the beast.

But then a miracle happens. The sow swings her big feral head toward Ruby, as if sensing the predator suddenly behind her. And just as she does, the knife sinks deep in her eye socket. An earsplitting squeal of fury and pain echoes into the night. The sow spins around to face this new enemy. Booboo, too, screams. Ruby hears sounds of scrambling behind her. Facing Ruby, the sow charges, but robbed of binocular vision, the animal's aim is off. Ruby dashes into the pig's blind zone. She tears away for the deadfall, grips her hands to Booboo's chest, and with all her strength, tosses the little girl up into the pile of dead wood. She hears snorting and a flurry of debris as the sow pivots, then the pummel of hooves coming for her. Ruby has one foot on the root ball at her feet, and another hand on the slender log above, when the sow hits the pile of wood with the force of a small car.

But she's missed Ruby's dangling leg. A moment later, Ruby is higher, pulling the little girl into her arms. Booboo squeezes her. Low-pitched sounds grumble and tumble from Booboo's mouth.

Below them, still so close, but just out of reach, the old sow gives it one more try. The crash shakes the pile, and a few branches and thin trunks snap and crack, but Ruby and the little girl keep their seats. There's a moment of pure quiet, then with a grunt, the sow ambles away.

In the quiet, the sound of the tracking dogs comes again. Close. Too close.

Ruby scrambles from the pile, finds her knife in the churned earth. Rafe lifts the little girl and squeezes her so hard she starts to squirm. Betsey's hand covers her mouth, but even in the dark, Ruby sees the joy sparkling in her eyes. Booboo's face is covered with scratches, and dirt clings to her clothes, but otherwise, she's unhurt. She pats Rafe on the head, scrambles down, and climbs back into Ruby's arms. Touched in a way she didn't expect, Ruby lets herself cry, burying her head in the girl's small shoulder for just a moment. If there was time, if their lives were not in danger, Ruby would dive into this moment, pretend, for just a second, the small body is that of HJ, and tell him again how sorry she is.

When she looks up, Booboo is saying something with her hands.

"She says the sow was sad. Bad dogs kill her babies," Betsey interprets, but there's something in her voice, a tone like a question, or doubt.

It's then, as if someone temporarily deafened them, that they again hear the dogs. The bays and barks and low growls are impossibly close, as if they're about to spring from the underbrush.

The reunited children run, tearing through the entanglement of vines, ignoring the clutch of branches reaching for them. Ruby's hand, pushing away a branch, finds the green oval leaves of a pawpaw. She strips off a handful and thrusts them in her pocket. Their feet suck and slog through the thick, sandy banks of the slough as they near their destination. The sounds of men urging the beasts on is a zap-crook crackling at Ruby's back. And then they're there. At the edge of the inlet where a canoe has been hidden by Noah and Levi. The flat black shimmer of the York River is a beautiful glossy expanse beckoning them outward.

Without hesitation, Rafe splashes into the water, throwing back branches and vines, revealing the canoe.

"Let me take her," Betsey says, holding her arms out to Ruby. "We have done this together before." She hoists her little cousin up and wades after her brother. Ruby follows, glad she's not tasked with holding the little girl as her feet skid and slip, almost landing her in the water. She partly climbs, partly falls aboard. Rafe strains his feet into the deep silty muck and pushes the canoe out. The craft tips and lists as he too scrambles in, the girls crawling forward to keep the narrow boat upright. Paddles in hand, Betsey and Rafe begin to propel them away from land.

The gap slowly widens. So slowly. They're only thirty feet from the shore when lights flicker through the scrub. There's a flurry of mad barking as the dogs burst through. Then one, no, two of them, send up triumphant howls that send ice through Ruby's veins.

A man calls out, not yet seeing the canoe now almost fifty feet away, "Here! They was just here!"

Another voice yells, "Loose the dogs!" There's baying, snarling, a yelp as the animals crash down into the reeds and muck and water.

They're sixty feet out, then at least seventy. And suddenly, the canoe slips from the inlet and into the river proper. Its width, nearly invisible in the night, is a vast, comforting presence. Rafe, in the bow, and Betsey, in the stern, work the paddles, their heads bent, their efforts on moving as one. But Ruby sees the younger girl lagging. The canoe's nose wobbles to one side with each strong pull by her brother.

"Here," Ruby says, and takes Betsey's paddle. The girl doesn't protest, but shifts quickly into the middle of the canoe and nestles low with Booboo. In the short lag, Ruby glances back to the shore. Lanterns and handtorches fan out where they pushed off. The yellow beams sweep greedy arcs across the water and toward them. Rafe and Ruby lean into every stroke. Then a light finds them, skipping across the water, then reversing, pinpointing the boat.

"There!" a husky voice yells.

Another light hovers close, then pounces on the canoe.

Ruby and Rafe paddle with all their strength, not worrying about splashes and sounds as the wide wooden blades hit the water.

There's a staticky crackle from the shore as a loud-hailer is switched on. When a voice pours through it, Ruby's blood turns to ice. It's the too-high pitch, the singsong cadence, of Officer Bud Downs.

"You ain't gonna make it, Roth. Turn around now, and I'll make sure things go easier for you!" A pause, then, "And whoever's helping you. They the ones gonna pay the price if you don't do what I say!"

She doesn't answer. The sound of the paddles is almost drowned out by the dog's frustrated yelps. One or two splash into the water. Downs's words and their meaning bloat in Ruby's mind. A sudden vision of Little Harold mudlarking along the Choptank flashes, his hands sieving the dirty sand for a trinket of value.

Downs calls again. "Oh, and in case you were wondering, we've got your little friend!"

Ruby's arms stop working. The paddle trails uselessly on the water. The canoe noses to the side, exposing more of the craft to the lights.

Rafe looks over his shoulder. "He's lying. Keep paddling. Please, Ruby."

But she can't move. From her head to her belly, a razor edge seems to slice her, opening up all the hurt she's been packing there. She opens her mouth to call to the shore, unsure of what to say, but needing to speak. Only a small croak comes out.

"Betsey," Rafe says, now alternating his paddle on either side of the canoe, "take her place."

"You best be makin' a good choice now, Roth! You don't wanna make others pay for your mistakes, for your crime." Betsey tries to take the paddle, but Ruby's fingers refuse to release their hold.

"That's it, Roth, Ruby. Come on back now. I'll make it all better."

Rafe hisses, "Ruby. He's lying." Then, when Ruby remains paralyzed, he adds, "Who do you trust more?" From the middle of the boat, she hears Betsey whispering something.

Who does she trust more? She looks at the young man in the bow of the canoe. Of course. Of course. There's no contest. She dips her paddle into the water, hesitates, then digs into the thick black of it, propelling them away from the lies.

Swearing comes from the shore. Then, a tiny splash *ploops* near the back of the canoe, the crack of a rifle following right behind it. There's another shot, closer now, plinking into the water only inches from Ruby's paddle.

Suddenly, seemingly from nowhere, a finger of gray mist reaches out for the canoe, wraps them into its shelter, and tugs them into a deep bank of fog.

Betsey whispers, "Thank you. Thank you."

Downs continues to yell, but his voice fades, muffled by the water droplets filling the air. Two more wild shots ring out, but land somewhere unseen, far from the canoe. The mist dampens Ruby's face with brackish dew, hiding her tears. HJ. *Does Downs really have him locked up somewhere? How much of what he said is a lie?* The thought won't leave her mind, the image of the boy in some dark, lonely cell.

They hear one last *boowhoowhoo* from a hound before the fog snuffs the sounds completely.

They paddle in strange, solitary silence for many minutes. Ruby's shoulders ache, her biceps burn, but it's a sweet distraction from the wound in her heart, broken open anew by Downs's words.

At last, Rafe turns, his voice a hoarse whisper. "We cannot risk following the eastern bank north, as we had planned. Instead, we shall cross the York. It is some distance." He turns his attention back to the nose of the canoe, back to putting space between them and the Shepherds. Ruby wonders, will Downs alert another contingent of officers on the other side? Will they paddle straight into the waiting shackles of more Shepherds?

As they progress across the wide body of water, an odd sensation begins to creep over Ruby. It's not like her earlier claustrophobia, but something different. An awareness of the deep water below. Its dark, cold depths grows. If they capsize, what down below might be waiting? The canoe suddenly feels ready to unbalance; an unsafe, thinly hulled vessel. Her pulse rises, her breaths shorten. With a huge effort, she does what Rafe commanded earlier: she stares at only the back of his head, just visible in the dense fog.

Moments later, there's the feathery whisper of tall grasses brushing the canoe. Ruby reaches out and strokes the slender stalks, tugs on the firm rootedness of the sharp fronds. The shore must be close. And then, as if by magic, the fog retreats. Before them lies the dimly lit bank of the western side. They guide the canoe into a small inlet, marsh grasses stretching to either side, and come to the crumbled remains of a one-lane bridge. Rafe steers the canoe under one of the sections drooping into the water. Beneath it is a sort of cavern, a wedge of dark shadows that swallows them as he guides the canoe in.

In the shelter of the bridge, Rafe snugs the boat to a post of rusted iron. On shaky legs, they step out to a narrow shelf of pebbled earth. A black shape slithers from a corner. Before Ruby can process what it is, she lets out a little cry, the sound amplified in the small, stony space.

"Only a rat snake," Rafe says.

She nods, feeling foolish.

"We are at Carter Creek. We'll be safe for the day. Tonight, we'll paddle north to find our friends and hopefully news of our parents. Lord willing," Rafe says.

"Lord willing," Betsey echoes, her hands signing Rafe's words to Booboo.

Booboo lifts her fists and speaks as her small hands work circles into her eyes. This time, even Ruby understands her words. "Ord ehlling," the little girl says, and tips her heart-shaped face to Ruby with a tired, honeyed smile.

16
Kaileh

The Precipice

On the Arrow whisking east, away from her homeland, empty, now, of family, Kaileh sits stunned. The box Rosalia handed her is still on her lap. One of Tareq's letters flutters in Kaileh's shaking hand. Kilometers blur past before she at last lays the letter down, closes the box's lid, and tries to fold her mind around what she has learned. Her brother was a traitor. There is no other word for it. He was helping illegals cross the Proclamation Line, helping the very people that were to blame for their father's death, their mother's grief, and, in the end, himself passing too early.

And their mother had known; not just known, but kept it secret.

A sudden thought makes Kaileh's stomach swirl, and nausea spasms her throat. What if her mother even endorsed his subterfuge, his betrayal of vows to the nation? Kaileh's not ready for the death of her brother's honorable memory, much less her mother's.

For the first time in many weeks, Kaileh thinks of the jah'gowa feathers from earlier that spring. She still has them, tucked in an envelope and buried somewhere inside her luggage. For a brief time, she convinced herself they were signs from the gods, a symbolic reminder that despite her and Tareq's differences, they were from the same family. They had the same ideals, goals, and sense of honor. It was stupid, she realizes now, a pathetic desire made manifest by her own childish longing. When she gets back to Waccamaw, she'll find the envelope. She'll burn the evidence of his betrayal.

Then she frowns, thinking of the other item in the box. Nestled at the bottom lies an unsullied gesture from Tareq. A token made with his own hands. Meant for her alone. And it has nothing to do with his traitorous politics.

"No," she says aloud, making the passenger beside her, a young man with his nose in a book, jump. *No*, she thinks, *I'll never wear it.*

By the time she arrives at Waccamaw the following morning, she's exhausted but determined. She knows what she must do, even though it will rip her heart from her chest. She messaged Commander Briento from the train, requesting a meeting with xem as soon as possible. But first, she needs sleep. She falls onto her bed, her mind caught in dizzying loops. It spins with what she'll tell the commander of her brother's betrayal, and not just that, but of her suspicions about Onas Steeprock, suspicions made all the more plausible given his partnership and romance with Tareq. She'll wash all the guilty knowledge from her with one painful confession.

She tosses and turns. She punches her pillow, beating a deep valley into the middle, settles in, then puts another pillow partway over her head and begins counting backward from a thousand. Somewhere around four hundred, her brain wades into a dream.

She's far from here, in a place it takes the still-aware part of her a moment to recognize: the ruins of Dán Aonghasa. She's at Inishmore on the Aran Islands of County Galway, Ireland, surrounded by her family—a place she's never actually been, a place her mother once made her and Tareq promise to one day visit. There they are, all still alive: Tareq, Bennu, and their father, Aden. The rolling green hills spin about them. One hundred meters below, the North Atlantic crashes and foams. They're at the homeland of her father's mother—adopted during the great European famine of 1955. Kaileh, weightless, drifts near her mother, who's saying something to Tareq. Something from her archeological knowledge. "These ruins are two millennia old, yet even then, they are young compared to some of the earthworks in our country. Never forget that, my son. Never forget. Never forget." Her voice lifts and drifts on the salt-tinged Atlantic breeze.

Above, atop the wall, Kaileh's father hovers. She turns from her mother and brother and floats toward him, calling out. He turns but doesn't seem to see her. She feels herself shrinking, down, down until she lies as a baby in a crib. She's not herself, but her grandmother, squalling in the filthy orphanage crib during the horrific famine. Her legs kick weakly, the weight of a sodden diaper pinning her in place. Hunger. A hollow belly. All she wants is to be lifted from this place, to be held, to be fed.

Then Kaileh's herself again, back on the high bluff where the ancient walled fort sits. Her mother is drifting up to her father. Bennu waves, but not to the invisible Kaileh, to a little boy at the edge of the precipice. No! Kaileh thinks. Get back! You're too close! She tries to run, but her legs are thick and heavy, each step a massive effort. Somehow, she reaches the child. It turns and becomes Tareq grown.

"I'm sorry!" she screams, unheard, into the wind.

Birds, so many birds, swoop toward them, and feathers drift down, covering her brother. "Look," Tareq says, "I have wings." And he does, but they're the stuff of Icarus. Doomed. He steps nearer the edge. She tries to pull him back. *No, no, no*, she pleads in her mind, *don't go. Don't leave me.*

Suddenly, he turns. Seems to see her at last. His arms wrap around her. They're real wings now, full, pinioned wings that encase her, their tips crossing again around her brother.

Tareq whispers in her ear, "Do you trust me?" And he pulls her over the edge.

The Inspector

Kaileh rips awake as she slams onto the floor of her quarters. Her bedding ripples down after her, covering her head. She lies there for a few seconds, almost wanting to laugh. Falling out of bed? She can't remember even doing that as a child. She stays on the soft rug and lets the dream sift back to her. It's mostly there. The blanket of feathers surrounding her, their firm encasement, feels almost real, even now. *Do you trust me?*

At last, she rises, picks up the knot of bedding, then empties her bag onto the messy bed. The envelope with the feathers isn't there. Did her own desire to destroy it manifest? Suddenly, she wants it back more than almost anything. She plunges her hand into every pocket and on the second round, finds it, extracts the delicate feathers, and tries to remember Tareq's wings in the dream, the kind of feathers sprouting there.

An alarm on her keitai sounds. It's almost time to meet with Briento. Will she still take Tareq's letters to xem? Is she truly ready to confront Onas Steeprock right there in front of their commanding officer and force him to explain his murky past and the dataslip he gave to the Shepherd McConnell? There's one thing she's sure of: it has to be Steeprock who led her brother into the broken vows the letters tell of.

She caresses the two feathers, one rose gray, the other snow white. So different. So identical. Color, after all, is just a trick of the light. Some might even say color doesn't really exist, or that more colors exist than we can see. She tucks the tokens carefully into the envelope and lays it inside the box with her brother's damning letters.

Five minutes later, she's out the door, but she pauses, her hand clinging to the knob. With a deep sigh, she goes back into her room. Moments later, Kaileh is again in the hall. She buttons the top closure on her shirt and pats her neck, feeling Tareq's gift hiding there.

When she lays her hand on the door to Commander Briento's office, her conviction has mellowed. She will still objectively report what she's learned. After all, Tareq is dead, safe from consequences—save the loss of his honor. And her mother and father are gone too. She is the last of their family. She will bear witness to her brother's crime. She will accept the dishonor.

But, she'll wait until after the meeting, no matter what her own agenda is. Suddenly, it's more important to be brought back into the hoop than expose her family.

So, when she steps through, she is completely unprepared for seeing not just Onas and Briento but two others, both strangers to her. Their expressions are grim. Even the air in the room feels charged with electricity.

Briento rises. "Ah, Officer Kaileh, welcome back. You know Onas, of course, but not our guests. Here we have my old friend Halek Tuskenugee of Seminola. Halek is an inspector for the International Assembly of Nations, his wife Sarin a Silver for their people. And here we also have Sadie, a member of the Junaluska Black Brethren, not far north of here." Briento rubs xyr hands together and points to an empty chair.

Kaileh's mind, still on her own dilemma, spins with all the names.

"First, you have my deepest regards concerning your loss. I trust," xe says, and locks xyr wideset eyes on her, "you will fill me in at another time."

Kaileh drags her gaze away. The intensity in Briento's expression threatens to crack her open. She knows at some point she will have to let her grief bloom, but this is not the place or time.

"There have been a few developments since the event that precipitated your and Onas's recall to Waccamaw. I apologize for leaving you out of the hoop, but let us rectify that now."

Kaileh darts a look at her supposed partner and marvels at how he looks so innocent.

Briento turns to the older man with two silver streaks winging back from his temples. "Following the intelligence that precipitated your recall to the enclave, Halek shared news of a more personal, yet equally compelling-to-our-cause nature. He has come directly to us following a brief but traumatic ordeal in the Atlantic States. Now, he is before us ready to share his story, augmented in part, thanks to the confessions" — xe blows air out through pursed lips—"of Onas and Sadie."

Kaileh feels tripped. As if she's suddenly looking at the sky instead of the finish line. Briento's words make no sense. Confessions? What does xe mean? Her mind races. Questions pile up in her mouth. It's all she can do to hold her tongue.

Briento turns to Onas, who drops his gaze for a moment, then with a deep breath, straightens his shoulders. "Some of the things you are about to learn may be hard for you to hear, Kaileh," Onas says with apparent effort.

Oh gods, she thinks. They know. Steeprock has already told the commander about her brother.

"I wish we had time," Briento continues, "to preface it more gently. But time is of the essence. To sum it up, Onas, it would seem, has been participating in an illegal program, helping bring select Atlantics, travelers, he says they're called, across the border."

Kaileh feels robbed of breath and more, as if something she hoarded has been stolen. Or someone she was about to punch hit themselves in the face first. She turns her gaze to Steeprock. He is a traitor. Well, at least she was right about that. Then her breath catches. Suddenly, she doesn't want Tareq exposed. Not yet. Not now. And, at the minimum, she doesn't want Onas, of all people, to be the one to reveal it. Briento speaks first. "Onas has told me this of his own volition, a thing that will not be forgotten." It's then that Kaileh realizes the commander has been referring to Steeprock as simply Onas. Not Officer Onas, but plain civilian Onas.

"In conjunction with what Halek told me earlier," Briento continues, "and what we have since learned, Steeprock's illicit activities may prove beneficial." Xe clears xyr throat. "Now, if Halek, Onas, and Sadie will kindly summarize what we've learned, together we can come up with a plan."

She opens her mouth to speak, whether to tell what she knows of her brother or something else, she's not sure. But the time feels wrong, so instead, she does something equally difficult: she listens.

And two hours later, the poles of her world have reversed. Kaileh Clearwater-Lewis finds herself agreeing to be part of a plan to help one specific illegal migrant somehow carrying a packet of vital information cross the border.

17
Ruby

Goat Cheese

As Ruby and the Brethren children doze in fits and starts on the hard ground beneath an old bridge on a forgotten stream in Virginia, Ruby dreams of HJ. In some, he's in chains in a cell, his little boy arms weighed down by iron links. In others, Harold Sr. is well and healthy, happy Ruby left his son behind. When she wakes, usually only for a few moments, she feels hollowed out, a fish gutted but somehow still breathing. Sometime after midday, she pushes up to sit on the narrow bit of land, rubbing grit from her eyes. Is this to be her life now? Tortured by all she's caused? Sister O once lent her a book of Greek myths. The story she remembers now is of a god doomed to roll a boulder up the same hill over and over for eternity.

Betsey sleeps in a curl around her redheaded cousin. Booboo's scratches have dried, and Ruby knows bruising will follow today. She'll make a salve of the pawpaw leaves to drive away black flies. Even bitten and bruised, these children look impossibly beautiful to her. Ruby stares at Betsey's light brown hair, so like Ida Marie's, while her nose matches the chiseled shape of her father's. Ruby's hands lift to her own face and hair. Parts of her she knows must come from her father, for her grandmother always told her so, but what of the rest of her? Is it wrong, selfish and premature, to dream of a mother that lives? That maybe looks a little bit like her?

An hour or so later, Ruby is still awake. At last, her legs aching from the hard ground, she stands and braves ducking behind a chunk of concrete to relieve herself.

Soon the others are squirming into consciousness. But there's leisure in their movements; it's still too bright out to consider leaving.

Rafe scratches at an angry welt on his neck. It's then that Ruby remembers the pawpaw leaves in her pocket. "Rub these on your exposed skin," she says, realizing as she pulls the leaves from her pocket that there's no point, no time, and no supplies to make a salve. The leaves, though, will still useful on their own.

"What are they?" Betsey says.

A puff of pride buoys her, fills a bit of the empty space; somehow, she's found a way to contribute. "Pawpaw leaves. My gram taught me to use them. They'll help keep the biters away."

She passes a leaf to each member of their group, wishing she'd grabbed more.

"Here. My turn," Rafe says, and hands Ruby a sliver of something hard and white.

She lifts it to her face to sniff it, ready to take a bite.

Betsey and Booboo giggle.

Rafe gives a small laugh. "It is soap," he says, and points to the water.

"Oh." She scoots gratefully to the sharp lip of their hideaway. Soon, her hands and face, at least, are scrubbed clean.

Rafe passes around chunks of fried pannhaas. It still looks far too much like Cham, but suddenly, even boiled Cham doesn't sound that bad. Ruby nibbles a corner of the piece Rafe handed her. Her tongue waters at the sweet meat of hog, lots of savory herbs, and something else she can't identify. Betsey hands a small oiled drawstring bag to Ruby. "It is dried goat cheese." She adds, with a shy smile, "I make it."

Ruby tips up the bag and plops several dried cubes in her mouth without hesitation. A flavor she's never before tasted, sweet and tangy, salty and buttery, bursts in her mouth.

Betsey watches keenly. "Good? I do most of the milking. Ma says the goats, Nanny and Ninny, are practically mine." She darts a look at Rafe. "At least their care is mine."

Ruby wants to smile, but something makes her look at Booboo, who's been watching them talk, reading what she can from their lips. The little girl's eyes are pooled with tears. Ruby can't tear her gaze from the girl. Something deeply sad shines from her. Ruby stops chewing, sets her jaw to resist binding.

Rafe follows Ruby's stare. "What is it, Boo?"

Booboo shakes her head, pulls her lips tight.

Betsey tips her head to the little girl, lifts her chin to meet her gray eyes, the twins of Betsey's own. "Booboo, what's wrong?"

Booboo's lower lip quivers as her chubby hands slowly flutter the story into the world. Without need for interpretation, Ruby guesses the meaning of one sign, as Booboo's index fingers tip up from her head like horns. *Goat.* Then a waving motion from the ground into the air that Ruby can't make out. But the horrible meaning is clear, for Betsey bursts into tears. Death, or leaving the earth, or heaven, perhaps.

"Why!? Why… would… they… kill… them?" Betsey's words are thick, shattered by the hitches in her breath.

Rafe's eyes meet Ruby's. She soaks in his helplessness, a powerful desire to be older, stronger, a protector. His arms wrap around his sister. "They are unholy men, *veesht* men, this you well know."

While he's patting her heaving back but saying no more, Booboo crawls into Ruby's lap and brings her thumb to her mouth. Ruby thinks of the sow. Was it only yesterday the little girl was close to being killed? She'd left the shelter, following the pull of something. Maybe it wasn't the deaths of sad dogs or the even sadder mother sow, but the deaths of Betsey's Nanny and Ninny.

Ruby squeezes Booboo tight, closes her eyes, and pretends—just for one glorious moment—she's holding Little Harold. She hears his words again, his utter calm when he said, "I'll be all right." Then she feels something that must be her imagination. It's HJ's hand, small and firm on her back, like a pat or a push. She squeezes the little girl one more time with such force Booboo squirms.

In silence, they wait for the sun to douse itself into the west. When all is in shadow, they haul themselves once again into the canoe. Ruby's body is all cricks and boards, *like a shack groaning 'neath the kudzu*, as her gram used to say. For a moment, Ruby can almost hear the woman as if she were just behind Ruby's shoulder.

The children, despite their obvious fatigue, do not complain. Ruby, too, holds her tongue. Without words, they paddle from beneath the ribbed underbelly of the fallen bridge, through the marsh grasses, faintly green in the last light of the day, and back into the York. There, they nose the canoe north and paddle on.

Werowocomoco

The canoe glides steadily north and west. They stay a hundred feet or so from shore. Progress feels slow, the shoreline a repetitive scene of scrub, brush, a few pilings leaning in the mouths of inlets, snaggy and menacing like the tusks of the old sow. Before long, even those details are swallowed by the night.

"I'm surprised there aren't more boats about," Ruby says, trying to tear her mind from other thoughts.

Rafe's quiet for a moment, as if considering how to answer. "The York was settled early by the colonists. They called it then the Charles River, or so it is told. Near here is Yorktown and Williamsburg; what remains of them. The York watershed long ago fell to industry, then that too moved away. Now, not many people are here, but nor are there fish or shellfish, at least healthy specimens."

The rhythm of his paddle slows. "Across the river and a throw north is, or was, Werowocomoco. That's where we're headed. It's a special place, sacred to some. There once sat an ancient village of the first people. It was also a meeting place of the Powhatan Confederacy. It is there we hope to find our friends."

"Are we… also moving west?" Ruby asks, feeling muddled by the dark and the crisscrossing of the waterway.

"Indeed, yes."

They paddle on, switching arms and changing the pace here and there. They stay to the side of the somewhat faster current toward the center. Rafe tells Ruby there's little elevation change along this stretch of the York, making it more bay than river.

The hours pass. The night sky above them reveals only occasional glimpses of faraway stars. She feels both concealed and exposed, as if the past and the future are looking down at her, judging, perhaps, her small life. At some point, Betsey wakes, taking Ruby's place for a while. Ruby tries to doze, but gives up after only a few fitful minutes.

"Can I ask you something?" Ruby says to the girl.

"Sure." In the bow of the long, narrow craft, Rafe continues to paddle, automatically matching his sister's strokes.

"Your people, the Brethren… I'm not sure what I want to ask, it's just, well, I've never met anybody like you all."

Betsey's quick flash of white teeth makes Ruby relax. The girl sits with her back straight as she paddles and speaks. "The Brethren, we are not many now, but are what is left of the people of the Old Order. Anabaptists, they were called, when they fled Europe, and persecution, two centuries ago." Her words come easily, but bear the pace and tenor of a school lesson well learned. "The Brethren," Betsey adds, "are mostly *bouwers*."

"Bowers?"

"That is our word for farmers," Betsey explains. "But now…" She shakes her head, and her words seem to wilt. "Now, there is hardly land for us."

"Why?" Ruby asks, thinking of all the brushy scrub through which they passed, land that could be cleared and sown for crops or livestock.

"The corps," Rafe says from the front of the canoe, "they took most of it. A thing they call eminent domain. But they don't use it either. Mostly, it just sits. Fallow and taunting our people. Some of us, we would break these laws, but mostly our people are pacifists. Some though, the younger ones, wonder if it is time to… reassess."

"Why don't you flee? I mean, why don't your people leave?" Ruby asks, feeling like she must have missed something important. "Couldn't you go west and be safer?"

For a time, no one answers. Then Rafe's voice sags. "Yes. But do you see the pattern, the problem? Our forebears, they left the old country. And some of our people *have* left the East. In the United West there are those calling themselves Lappites, and there are the Black Brethren of Junaluska. But they all came from here, from the Old Order. Some of us go back and forth across the border, helping those such as you." He keeps his voice low, the open water ready to magnify and carry their voices to unseen ears on the shore.

Ruby shifts, the canoe's seat suddenly uncomfortable.

"Many of us have decided to remain," he continues. "To hope to one day make things better, to stay for those who cannot leave, and to serve whatever role the Lord sees fit."

They progress slowly up the York. By the time the moon rises, they've crossed to the eastern side. The night is thick with smells and sounds. Ruby listens for hounds, for any sound hinting of the presence of Shepherds somewhere on the shore. Where is Bud Downs at this very moment?

The paddles dip, the buzz of insects floats from the shore, the hoot and call of a hunting night bird echoes across the water. Ruby picks up a salty iron smell at odds with the organic nature of the rest. Moments later, the canoe drifts past the towering hulk of a long-derelict petrol tanker. It lists on its side, like a dead whale of their own manufacture. Though likely long empty, Ruby is sure she sniffs the scent of fuel oil.

Rafe whispers, "It is from the time before. In the 1900s England still sent crude petrol from the North Atlantic. There was a refinery farther up." He gestures north.

They're near the shore now, still paddling north. No signs or sounds of friend or foe come to them. They cross a small, open body of water, Purtan Bay, Betsey tells Ruby, then enter a channel into the marshes. It snakes and winds, as if determined to lose whoever traipses in. Ruby stares at the confident pulls Rafe sends through his paddle. Despite his age, it's easy to picture the boy as a man. She wonders if that's what surviving in the Atlantics does to some: grows them up fast, maybe too soon.

At last, they thread into an even narrower channel, and the canoe nudges ground. "This is called Purtan Island," Rafe says. He glances at the lighter gray in the eastern sky as they step ashore on tired, wobbly legs. Betsey and Booboo squat without self-consciousness on the spongy ground, relieving themselves.

"I've got to…" Ruby points to a clump of brush. There's a brief rush of blood to Rafe's face as he nods.

When Ruby returns, the canoe is gone. Rafe and Betsey, settling their satchelpacks on their backs, seem unconcerned. Still, it unnerves Ruby; what if the dogs burst from the grasses or a shot finds them? Won't they need the canoe quickly? Her pulse ticks up. She touches the pig sticker and readies her mind for vigilance.

Still, somehow, the man is upon them before she notices. His deep voice says, "I've found you."

Zill

Betsey shrieks as Ruby spins toward the voice behind her. The young girl runs past in a blur of dark colors and leaps into the outstretched arms of a tall man. "Uncle Zill!"

He sweeps her up into a wide hug, then swings her around to ride on his back. He turns a wide smile to Rafe, Booboo, and Ruby. "Glad you all decided to show up."

"We had some… trouble," Rafe says.

"Heard. Come now, got a meal going for you all just in case you made it this morning." He leads them from the soft, swampy earth and onto proper land. Zill looks to be about Harold Sr.'s age, but with dark blond hair held back at the nape of his neck, and a field cap of dark green pulled low, but not hiding the streaks of gray near his temple. A dark copper earring dangles from one earlobe.

"Given what I heard happened," he says, "you done good, Rafe. You got the traveler here all safe and sound." The tall man gives Ruby an appraising look. She feels studied, like a specimen, an oddity like the dead sei whale she saw rotting on the bank where the Choptank met the Chesapeake so long ago.

Partway up the slope, Rafe hoists Booboo on his hip. With Betsey still bouncing along happily on Zill's back they continue up a narrow trail that climbs a low bluff. Ruby's legs ache, the muscles shortened by sitting for so long. But it feels good to be on land, to have places to run, to hide. She stares at Zill, Betsey bouncing with his every stride. Harold Sr. used to hoist his lad, as he always called the boy, up the same way. Where is HJ's father now? Will she ever learn what happened to him?

Her mind hitches; maybe it's better not to know.

The trail crests on a flat plateau only a hundred feet or so across. Before them lies a lush vegetable garden, gray-green in the growing dawn.

To one side sits a small shelter, more lean-to than hut. Before it, a campfire gives off a faint wisp of blue smoke. It smells clean, not of the acrid chemical stench of the campfires of the shantytown or the foul, eternal smoldering of the Eastern Shore landfills. A blackened steel pot hangs from a tripod over the coals. Ruby's heart surges at the same time her stomach growls.

They settle on old stumps and watch Zill ladle thick porridge from the pot into a single metal bowl cupped in an old cloth. He pushes a wooden spoon in and hands the bowl to Rafe sitting next to him.

"Ruby, you go first," Rafe says. She hesitates, but then, smelling the starchy porridge, takes the bowl. Heat fills her hands, soaking easily through the rag. The spoon sits in thick golden cornmeal mush specked with dark, nutty seeds.

She must look at them oddly, for Zill says, "Those little bits are wild amaranth."

Ruby tries it, wants more, but passes the bowl to Betsey. Soon, the bowl empties, is refilled, and passed again.

"Heard after you fled, your people got visited by the crooks?" Zill says after the bowl has made two orbits. The derogatory term, so often used in the quiet of conscripts' homes, tugs at Ruby, making her feel both far away from and closer to her own people.

Rafe grimaces, then, in a voice that sounds as if he's aged many decades, says, "Have you heard any news of our parents? Were they… harmed?"

Zill runs a hand over his stubbled chin. Pulls his cap off and resettles it. "Talked to Zara yesterday. We anchored together up Morris Bay— heard rumors of a late run of croaker. Caught one, but didn't look fit to eat. Zara, as usual, caught aplenty." He takes a bite of the porridge, passes it to Betsey. "Zara, she heard the crooks let 'em be." He breaks off, glancing at Betsey, seeming to hold back something. "Well, they were trying to get information. They left, but came back with dogs. They, uh, did some other damage, but then the crooks' hounds picked up what no doubt was you all's scent."

Betsey must catch Zill's hesitation, for she says, "I know what happened, Uncle Zill." She stares into the bowl, stirring the porridge in slow circles. The turmoil in the girl radiates out to Ruby. She's trying so hard to be mature it hurts.

Zill shakes his head, wrinkling his nose as if he's smelled something foul. "Least your parents are unharmed. Once we reach Zara, we'll send a messenger with news of you. Knowing your folks though, they're already heading to the next point." Ambiguity and worry fill Ruby, but she stays quiet, her acceptance the only support she can properly give.

After breakfast Zill and Rafe cover the fire with half an old steel barrel, snuffing the flame without making smoke or steam. With the sun bright, they follow Zill down the other side of the plateau. There, in an inlet only slightly larger than the one where they left the canoe, bobs a small shantyboat. Weathered boards overlap the outer walls. They're hung with traps, nets, and drying plants, and decorated with symbols painted on or burned into the wood. A line of letters across the bow makes Ruby squint, but they're either just marks or in a language she's never seen.

Aboard the boat, Zill shows them into a tiny living space. It's cozy and warm and calm. Inside, for the first time in days, Ruby feels safe. And there's something about the idea that the small house can just float away at the whim or need of the inhabitant that makes her heart happy.

"You all should stay in here as much as possible, or at least only come out one at a time—case the crooks got any of those air surveillers we've been hearing about. Help yourself to whatever you need in here. There's even a, ehhem, night bucket, should the need arise." His face flushes a color not unlike his copper earring. "Got any questions?"

"Uh, it's nothing important," Ruby says, "but what does it say on the boat, those big letters?"

"Ah, Rafe here knows. It's written in a language almost lost now. Even my people only know a handful of words and phrases—though I hear tell in the West you can get books written completely in Cherokee."

Ruby swallows, aware, maybe for the first time, of her ancestors' role in this loss.

"The saying on the boat is in Cherokee, but it is a phrase from the Mattaponi, from my people. Impossible to translate to English and not lose some of the gist. But maybe something like this: 'we belong to the land. The land does not belong to us.'"

Zara

The Brethren children and Ruby succumb to the rhythm and lull of the shantyboat as it chugs slowly upriver. Booboo and Betsey make no attempt to remain awake, but snuggle together on the small bed at one end of the cabin. For some time, Ruby can't tear herself from gazing out of a small porthole on one side. She feels something like a responsibility to take it all in. Will she ever be able to share the trip with Sister O or Brother Q? The thought of HJ missing all this, in addition to the horror of a life he's now doomed to, keeps the crack in her heart wedged open wide. It might never close, she realizes. A new thought comes to her: is this what life was like for her gram? How many more losses did she have besides her husband and her son?

Ruby's legs at last begin to shake and she slides down to the floor. Rafe, who did the same minutes before, says, "We shall soon pass the remains of Port Richmond. Before that, long ago, it was a village of the Mattaponi called Cinquotek. It... Well, now there is no one."

"Why?" Ruby asks, trying to picture a big port town being abandoned. He tells her of the loss of crude oil coming from England, of the failed nuclear plant that followed and sealed the city's fate.

As her eyes grow heavy, Rafe says, "We shall soon meet Zill's sister, Zara. It is only fair to warn you... she is... well, different."

Ruby waits. The boat rocks gently. An occasional whiff of diesel tingles her nose.

"Zara has a gift, stronger than what Booboo has with the animals. But there's something else. She is not like most. You may, at first feel... hmm... as if she does not like you, I suppose." Rafe continues to speak, each word duller in her fading mind. And soon, though she's sure she's still listening, she's asleep.

Her head jerks awake. Her neck pops and her head throbs. There's a bumping sound that vibrates through the boat. Beside her, Rafe mumbles and rubs his eyes.

"We must be here."

Betsey shrugs out of the nest of blankets she and Booboo have burrowed into. "Are we at Zara's?"

"Believe so."

"Booboo," Betsey says, "we're at Auntie Zara's." Her voice is soft, but excited. Even the hand signs she gives her cousin seem different. But after Rafe's warning, Ruby's not sure what to expect. Nervous sweat dampens her underarms and palms.

"You all can come on out now," Zill calls with a knock on the door.

The light through the porthole is still bright, but without the harshness of midday. Time has blurred for Ruby though, and she wonders how it could be the same day they boarded the shantyboat. Rafe opens the door, and more light pours in. Ruby takes a deep breath, bracing herself for she's not sure what, and steps into the low rays of the sun. The boat is snugged near another, looking so close as to be its twin. Booboo scoots around Ruby's legs, almost unsettling her.

"Boo!" Rafe says, unheard by his little cousin.

"It's all right." Ruby takes her hand from the doorframe. Booboo scuttles across the deck, her scratched-up arms chugging the short distance. She leaps at the legs of a woman standing beside Zill. Zara's hair is dark where Zill's is light, but otherwise, they are so obviously siblings, Ruby wonders if they might be twins. The woman is tall, powerfully built, a few years younger than her brother, but leaning hard on two canes. Though she doesn't show it, Ruby knows immediately Zara's in pain.

"My girl," Zara says, squatting down to embrace Booboo. Zill reaches for his sister's elbow, but she swats him away. He pulls off his cap and resettles it with a grin that says he's unsurprised by his sister's reaction.

"You, my little one," Zara says to the little girl, "you've been the source of worry for some."

Booboo, staring up with an open mouth, watching Zara's lips, shrugs and nods.

Zara lifts her gaze as she stands, bracing one hand on the side of the boat and the other on a can. Her eyes are a green so like Brother Q's, it slices into Ruby's heart. She braces herself, expecting critical scrutiny, to feel dismissed as Rafe warned. Zara's eyes do not meet hers but instead brush across Ruby, coming to rest on her shoulder.

"Ah," the tall woman says, "the traveler." Ruby feels pinned in place. The woman's emerald eyes bore into Ruby's shoulder as if her heart is displayed there for all to judge.

The curved handles of Zara's canes are glossy from wear. She arches side to side as she moves across the deck toward Ruby. But she covers the distance with practiced surety. This is not a new injury. The agony binding Ruby despite her best efforts to repel it is old, one Zara's accepted, learned to master, but… not quite. It worsens, even as she nears Ruby.

"Ah," Zara says, standing close now, "it is as I expected. You are one who feels."

Ruby's mouth pops open. "I… I…"

"My pain, you are reading it," Zara says. For a moment, the woman's disconcerting eyes flick up to Ruby's. Her knees weaken, but she holds herself to her full stature, petite beside this bent yet towering woman. It feels like a test, this scrutiny, and for some reason, Ruby feels desperate to pass it.

"The dear Sister told us you were special, did she not, brother?" Zill nods.

Ruby's breath hitches. "You know Sister O?"

Zill chuckles.

"Of course we do, we of the Path work as one."

Travelers. The Path. The Brethren. It's like she's seeing puzzle pieces joining to form a picture where she'd thought only randomness existed.

She sucks in a breath and blurts, "Do you know if Sister O and the others are all right?"

Before Zara answers, Zill says, "How about we all get settled first? There'll be time to catch up, some anyway, before the others get here."

"Who's coming?" Rafe asks.

"You'll be happy to know it's your father and your uncle," Zara answers. "They radioed a few hours back."

"Pappy!? Pappy's coming!" Betsey spins in a circle, then dances with Booboo, swinging the little girl back and forth. Booboo coos and rumbles a secret song. With a pang Ruby wonders what HJ would make of the little girl. She can almost see the two—despite the gap in their ages—as fast friends, developing a secret language and sharing adventures.

Soon they're all settled on boxes or sitting on the deck. Ruby breathes deeply of the watery scented air. It's different here, cleaner somehow, greener even. The rushes whisper around the boat. Overhead, a bird, a hawk or other winged hunter, calls a long, hungry screech.

Zara settles onto the only chair, her canes clutched between the knees of her trouser-clad legs. She sits just apart from the others, and for a moment, Ruby fears it's something to do with her, but then remembers what Rafe said. She notices, too, that Zara meets no one's eyes, except, so it seems, Booboo's.

"You asked of Sister O," Zara says, passing a small sack containing bits of something that reminds Ruby of the pemmican bars Sister O used to send her home with. "Sadly, we do not know much. She, along with Sister M, were taken captive, but I believe you already know this."

Ruby nods, remembering the proud profile of Sister O, the stumbling steps of Sister M as they were loaded like livestock into the waiting lorry. It can't be the last time she'll ever see the monastics, can it?

"Of Brother Q we know nothing," Zara adds.

Before Ruby can hold it in, a sob bursts from the hollowness inside her.

"Perhaps," Zill says, "Levi and Noah will have heard more. Certainly, they will have been in touch with others of the Path."

"Yes, yes," Zara says, "let us hope that is true." She shifts in the chair. Ruby feels the moan the woman holds back.

Suddenly, Zara looks directly into Ruby's eyes. The deep green pulls her in, locks her like steel to a magnet. They stay that way for what feels like hours. A sense of being seen more deeply than she's ever been seen strips Ruby bare. She squirms but forces herself to not look away.

Zara tips her head at last, and her gaze drops. "You don't believe in your power yet. You should. You must. It will be your savior. Or your undoing."

Ruby lets a smile lift the corners of her mouth. She doesn't want to correct the woman, doesn't want to tell Zara just what happens when she lets her so-called power rule. It's a path to failure, a different kind of undoing.

At dusk, the Brethren brothers Levi and Noah arrive. The *putt-putt-putt* of their small motorboat clips through the growing dark, sending jiggles of excitement through all the children, even Rafe. Ruby feels his need to pass on his heavy load. She'll be relieved for him, she realizes. In her satchelpack, the packet of documents is her own burden. She asked

Zill about them earlier. "Hold on to those. They are not meant for me," was all he said.

Ruby stands back as Noah and Levi step aboard, their children a swarm about them.

Betsey hangs onto Noah the longest, her head buried in his chest, sobs shaking her shoulders. Booboo, for her part, clings to her cousin, sharing the grief of losing the goats. "They were good friends and good providers," Noah says. "We won't forget them." His understanding and compassion, for both the animals and his daughter, shakes Ruby. He didn't say what she expected, something like, "We'll get new goats," or, "They were just animals." It leaves her feeling sad, but it's a sweet sadness, a feeling of both her own lack of nurturing parents and her joy that they do, for some, exist.

"We must go," Noah says after only minutes.

"No, Pappy, not yet!" Betsey says.

Booboo wraps her arms around Levi's legs as though she's trying to anchor him to the boat.

Rafe squats down and pries her off. "Come on now. How about we'll stay and help Zara fry up those croakers she caught?" He looks at Ruby over the clinging shoulder of his cousin.

Something passes between them.

He's almost ten years her junior, but in so many ways she knows this boy to be more of a man than some she's met. It's not a physical attraction she feels, something she's sure she'll recognize if it ever happens, but a deeper connection. Her eyes fill with tears, not just for losing this, but for all they've done for her.

"Come," Noah says, the waterman captain once again. "We must waste no time." So much goes unsaid, both in their farewells and in his portentous words.

Minutes later, they're in the little boat, putt-putting away. Ruby glances back, not trying to hide her tears. She catches Zara's eyes one last time, and she can't be sure, for the night is now earnestly upon them, but she thinks the woman mouths something. *Believe.*

That's when a new thought comes to Ruby. Maybe Zara meant a different kind of power, like what Betsey believed in when she seemed to have summoned a sheltering fog, or what the children believed in that did indeed come true when their families remained safe.

Believe.

No matter its meaning, its power and use are as distant to Ruby as Harold Jr.

Crossing Carolina

It's only when the small motor boat nudges onto land that Ruby remembers what else she holds in her satchelpack, besides the documents and Brother Q's token. There's the dark amber bottle of pills. They are for pain, so strong that if too many are taken, death can result. But in small doses? They're a powerful relief.

"Noah?" she says as they follow a narrow path into the brush.

"We're almost to our pickup," he says.

"No, I mean, that's good, but I have something that—"

"Hush now, wait until we're well away."

A dog barks, sounding too close. Its excited noise turns to frightened yips. There's a human yell, another yip. A home or farm must be close.

Yards later, they emerge onto a small dirt road. An old pickup, its back shrouded by a hand-built cover, is nosed into the thick shrubs alongside it.

She walks without hesitation to the side door, but Levi motions her away. "I wish that could be where our travelers ride, but the hours on the road are long, the risk too high."

"Of course. I'm sorry." Her cheeks flush, unseen by the men in the dark.

"No need to apologize, no need at all. We have prepared the back for you."

Ruby swallows, not liking the boxed-in look of the covering over the pickup's bed. She's seen sweat boxes behind the Shepherd headquarters in Denton. She knows how they work. And now, after the tunnel the night they fled the farm… it's as if she's already entered one of those boxes, a horrible tool of the Shepherds. Cold perspiration beads on her forehead, runs down her chest. But she forces her breathing normal as Levi opens the back hatch.

From a fog, she hears the driver's side door open. The pickup shifts, squats a tiny bit, and the door closes. Ruby looks inside the back. Relief fills her. It's small, but looks comfortable, with high, narrow slits for fresh air cut into the sides. A thick rug covers the floor. On one side sit tubs of carpentry tools, lengths of wood, an assortment of bottles and buckets, some filled with bits of hardware. On the other side, a gray blanket is draped across a piece of furniture. From what Ruby sees, it looks like a chest of drawers, finely made, crafted with the kind of skill employed in making the beautiful table she left behind in Denton. She thinks of the small chunk of wood in her satchelpack, the memento she slipped from the table's only flaw.

Levi, seeing her stare, says, "That is our handiwork. And our livelihood. It is also our cover. We hold a permit to transport such things, and our customers, mostly those who quietly support the Path and its mission, live in many places ready to accept a delivery if one needs to be made."

"But," she says, "what if you're stopped?" The sweat has dried now, but threatens to bloom anew.

"There," he says, and points to what Ruby assumed was another tool chest tucked against the cab. It's a long box, spanning the width of the cab, and suddenly, it no longer seems an innocent vessel for tools. It looks like a coffin.

Breathe, she tells herself, *just breathe. You're not inside. Not yet.* What was it Gram used to say when Ruby was little and fretting about something? "Don't cross the worry bridge twice."

Levi has crawled into the covered back. "If we are stopped, I will alert you. Then, here, you must push here." His calloused fingers slip along an edge, lifting a piece of hardware Ruby doesn't recognize. There's a click, then the lower portion of the box drops open, revealing an impossibly small space. The thought of shimmying in is unbearable. She blows air out through her mouth, as Levi, not noticing, shows her how to close the hidden door once she's inside. A tiny part of her brain takes it in, more terrified, perhaps, of not being able to escape the contraption.

After Levi backs out and stands waiting for Ruby to take her place, she finds her feet are glued to the ground.

"What is it?" There's concern in his voice, but it's salted with impatience and urgency.

Somehow, despite the fact that she's been on the run for days, has crossed the Chesapeake, has torn through the night, made it through a dark tunnel and the panic that gripped her, fought a wild sow, escaped tracking dogs and, for now at least, Bud Downs, then paddled up the York River to meet two remarkable survivors, this moment, standing here at the brothers' pickup has a finality to it that the crab boat and the canoe and the shantyboat did not. The brothers told her they would drive through the night and the next day, reaching the borderlands by nightfall. In a mere twenty-four hours she would be at the Proclamation Line; a line of no return.

The driver's door opens. The pickup creaks. "We must leave," Noah says as he steps around the back.

"Ruby?" Levi asks.

She tries to not think of everyone she's brought harm to: the murdered milch goats, punishment for Harold Jr., risk for everyone. All to help her. The documents she carries, of course, hold a value that she cannot define. But there's something else: she again feels the small hand of HJ on her back, the whisper of his breath hot in her ear. "You need to go, Roobs."

Air fills her lungs. She does need to go. She needs to complete what others have worked so hard for. There's a life for her to the west. There's blue sky to the west. There's hope in the west.

Exhaling, she climbs in.

The brothers drive through the night. Ruby sleeps. She wakes. She lets tears and sobs free of her body in the solitude of the covered pickup bed. The tools clank. The chest of drawers creaks. The engine rumbles. Whiffs of petrol and metal and sweat and dust fill the dark.

Once, only hours from dawn, they stop, each of them making short trips into the brush to relieve themselves. Without words, they hand Ruby strips of goat jerky and an apple, withered and leathery from storage. Without words, she takes them and returns to her hideaway.

Several times, vehicles overtake them and pass. Each time, Ruby's heart wants to burst, and she doesn't breathe until there's no sign of a roadblock ahead, no sign they'll be stopped.

All the time, the coffin-like box sits and waits.

As the morning comes, Ruby climbs to the tall, narrow slits and looks out. Levi said they would be passing along the back roads of North Carolina. The land rolls, the flatness of the Eastern Shore stark by comparison. They pass factories, more poultry farms, a few smoldering landfills, signs for big mining operations pointing up into the hills. Once they pass a series of fancy houses, each huge and grand, even over the span of long, rolling lawns, green moats keeping regular folk at a distance.

The day passes, and although there's no sign of them being followed, no sign anyone is waiting for them, Ruby feels something. A presence. As if she's being observed from above like a tiny ant certain of its journey while a foot hovers above ready to stomp. She tells herself it's just her imagination, that she's crossing the worry bridge before she needs to. But the unsettling sense refuses to leave.

And then she hears another car gaining on them, the engine roaring as it passes. As it pulls in front of them, she peers through the front window, past the brothers, and falls back, her heart thudding like a hammer on tin. It's a dark blue pickup, impossible to make out its brand, not from where she sits. She holds her breath, certain the pickup will slow, that the brothers will give her the signal that will doom her to the horrible confines of the hiding space. But nothing happens. As her heart beats slow, she laughs at her silliness, for surely there must be hundreds, even more, of the same vehicles. She's not just in the backwaters of the Eastern Shore anymore, but crossing the more peopled state of North Carolina.

They continue on. Through the front window she sees the distant gray-blue mountains growing closer. She knows their presence means the border is not far away: the Proclamation Line, as it's officially named, although she's never thought to ask why. Close. She's getting close. A tiny whisper of hope dances in her mind. She might make it. Alone, and leaving so many behind.

Then, just as the afternoon parts ways and evening sets in, she sees *him*. Or thinks she does. They're stopped in a small town, waiting for a shift of workers to cross the road. A man steps from a corp grocery, two filled bags in his arms. He doesn't wear a Shepherds' uniform, but dungarees, a plaid shirt, a bloodred field cap. The burlap sacks brimming with supplies block most of his face. But there's something… something about the posture, the way his head tips forward, that reminds her of Bud Downs.

As the brother's pickup continues past the store, Ruby ducks down. Does she feel the man staring? Does she give off some kind of signal that shouts, "I'm here!"? Seconds pass. As with before, nothing happens. At last, she looks out, but the town, the store, and the man are long gone.

The Proclamation

Shortly after leaving the town, the brothers turn onto a narrow dirt road. Ruby bounces in the back, her stomach threatening nausea as the wheels hit and jolt along the rutted track. She knows the brothers won't be taking her across the border, but someone from the other side, working for the Path, will meet them and guide her across the Proclamation Line.

Only days ago, during her lunch break at the hatchery, she heard Chairman Powell on the radiovision broadcast. He called the border the "discrimination" line, saying Atlantic citizens, hardworking citizens, were being kept from success by not being allowed access to the unlimited resources of the borderlands. Even Ruby knew he really meant the corps were being kept from more wealth at the cost of the land and the real workers.

The sun is swallowed by the mountains into which they now ascend. Outside the enclosed back, Ruby senses the stillness, smells the powdery dust, and wonders who waits for her. Who will take her the last few miles to freedom?

As if in response, the micro-ID on her arm, the pink knot of scar tissue, begins to itch, as if the nearness of freedom is causing a kind of allergic reaction. Soon, she thinks, soon it will be removed.

Just when Ruby wonders if the road will ever end, the engine dies and they roll to a stop. Have they broken down? Or is someone out there, making them stop? She massages the tiny scar and takes slow breaths, trying not to cough in the cloud of dust roiling over them. The headlights flash on and off, on and off, three times. Minutes pass. Then a tiny light blinks back at them. It bobs closer. One of the brothers turns on the headlamps and brings life to the silhouette of a man only feet away.

Levi knocks on the window. Not once, but three times: one slow, two fast. The signal. Not to hide, but to emerge.

Ruby opens the back and climbs out, pulling her battered satchelpack and its precious documents with her. For a moment, her legs seem locked in place, just as when she first climbed in. But it's close now, the end. For better or worse, her flight will soon be over.

She walks to the front of the pickup. The stranger, tall and broad-shouldered, steps forward, a slight limp making his gait bob. He raises a hand. "Welcome, traveler. I will be your guide for this last portion of your long journey." His voice is tired, his words measured and sounding almost forced.

Ruby feels suddenly itchy. Something about the man's demeanor seems off.

First Noah, then Levi, embrace the man like an old friend. Levi leans away and says, "Is everything all right? Is something...?"

Ruby stiffens. It's not just her then.

The stranger hesitates, but then says, "Fatigue, my old friend, nothing more. It is good to see you both. I wish we had time for a proper reunion."

His exhaustion is evident and true, but Ruby's sure it hides something else.

Noah says, "We too wish for this. We are glad our message got to you in time. Our Brethren from Junaluska, well, we count on them at times such as this. If you see Sadie, please give her our regards."

"I will. I most certainly will." He looks back at Ruby, then farther over her shoulder and into the night. "Were you followed at all?"

"There was much trouble initially. Shepherds. But we believe we lost their trail far to the east."

A knot tangles at the back of Ruby's throat. Should she tell them what she thinks she saw? But how could it have been Bud Downs? If he was still leading the chase, certainly he'd be not only in uniform, but with other officers. Jumpy, she decides: she's just nervous. It's not the time to trust her own interpretations.

"That is good," the guide says, then to Ruby, "Traveler, let us get you… across the border to safety."

This is it then. The last distance to the Proclamation Line, to the border, to freedom. Her heart pounds with the realization. She turns to the brothers, words and messages and gratitude so crowding her mouth, none can get out.

"Go on, get now." Levi plants a wide hand on her shoulder and squeezes. Noah smiles and nods.

She wants to tell them thank you, to send final goodbyes to the children, to Zill and Zara, to Rebekah and Ida Marie. But her voice only croaks a small, "Goodbye."

"Come." The guide motions for her to follow. Something makes her stop. Not the same tug from behind, from what she's leaving, but something from this man. Part of him doesn't want her to follow him. She can feel it. It's not menacing, but sad. Maybe, she tells herself, he's worried. Fearful of the risk. Or is it something else? Something that, though it should be impossible, feels like a trap.

"What is it?" he asks.

Ruby clears her throat, swallowing the tightness. "May I ask your name?" It's not what she really wants to say, but it seems suddenly important.

"Yes," he says. "My name is Onas. Onas Steeprock."

"I'm Ruby," she says.

"Yes. I know."

The Ambush

Ruby follows Onas into the night. Her chest tightens again as she hears the pickup turn around and drive off. Its engine fades into the chirrup of crickets and buzz of insects. In the distance she hears another engine, far away, on some other dirt road perhaps. She thinks of all the people who must live out in the wilds—others on the fringe, perhaps, like the Brethren. A new thought comes to her. In the last few days, she's met more new people than ever in her life, and all of a sort drawing her to them. Is this how it will be once she's really free?

But what of the man before her now with his contrary sense of reluctance?

They've gone only a few hundred yards, still following the pockmarked dirt road, when a shape emerges from the darker shadows.

Ruby jerks to the side, her hand flying to the blade still strapped to her back. She was right, it is a trap.

But Onas stands without alarm. He lifts his handtorch and slides it across the figure. It's a woman. As tall as Onas, but vibrating with energy and unconcealed emotions Ruby cannot fully block or decipher, so rapidly do they shift between anger, repulsion, elation.

Onas turns to Ruby and suddenly she knows the source of his own conflicting emotions. It's this woman. "Try not to be frightened. Everything will be all right. In the end." A pause. "You have my word."

The woman says, "Ruby Roth, citizen of the Atlantic States, you are now in the custody of the United West. Extend your hands." A pair of restraints, flat-black and evil-looking, jingle in her hand.

Confusion floods Ruby. Onas seems unsurprised, as if he expected this. Maybe this is how the Path works. She'll be taken into custody and… and… and what? Her thighs twitch. Her calves burn to run. But where? Where would she go? Back into the hands of Shepherds, back to work for the corps, or worse? Surely she's better off a prisoner of the West than of the Atlantic States of America.

Onas says, "Those are not necessary."

The woman ignores him, moves closer to Ruby. "Don't move."

"It will be all right," Onas repeats. Ruby hears a clattering sound and realizes it's her teeth clacking together.

"You have something that belongs with us," the woman says.

"Can we do that later?" Onas says. "Look at her, she has been through enough. I mean it."

"We have to make sure it's really her. It's what she has, if she even really has it, that we want."

Ruby stays still. She feels at once invisible and beneath a magnifier.

"We agreed that bringing her across is part of the deal. Everyone," he says, "agreed."

"Let's at least make sure she has what we've all risked our careers to get. Can we at least do that?"

Onas sighs. "All right. Ruby, did a man, back when you first fled, give you a packet of documents?"

Ruby blinks. Then it's as if clouds part and she can at last see a pure blue sky. "Are you who they're meant for?"

The woman's demeanor relaxes a notch, but her dark eyes keep their keen focus. She reminds Ruby of a hungry raven waiting for the right moment to dive. "We'll take them, but you are still in our custody until this gets sorted."

"They're in my satchelpack." Ruby lifts it from her back, its weight suddenly lighter. The woman rips it from Ruby's hands.

As Ruby opens her mouth to explain about her personal items inside the worn pack—the gift from Brother Q, the small bit of the table her father made—something makes her turn. An icy blade runs up her spine. There's the crack of a branch. Then, before any of them can react, they hear the shot.

A thunk splits the bark of a dead tree just feet away. Another plinks into the dirt just ahead of them. Onas pulls Ruby to the ground, extinguishing the handtorch as they fall. They hear Kaileh scrambling into the brush on the other side.

For a moment, the night is quiet. Even the insects are hushed by the intrusion. Then the blast of a loud-hailer slams into the pause. "This is an officer of the Atlantic States of America. You are trespassing on Atlantic States soil." The voice. *His* voice. If Ruby wasn't already on the ground, she would have crumpled.

"Release your captive ASA citizen, and get on back where you belong. I'll give you one minute to clear out before me and my officers get serious."

Onas hisses to the woman, "I will cover you. Get the documents across the border. I will bring Ruby."

"Thirty seconds!" Downs singsongs.

"Go!" Onas calls to the woman. Rustling sounds come, then light footsteps and she and Ruby's satchelpack are gone. Relief and loss hit Ruby at once. The documents will be safe, but her few things: the tiny piece of wood from the table, Brother Q's pendant, and the pack itself seem suddenly like treasures lost.

"I got eyes on you, Warrior. You best follow that woman now and get on. Leave the girl. She's not your property."

"She is no one's property," Onas yells. The conviction in his voice, the sudden rigidness of his body, surprises Ruby.

"Oh yeah? That what ya think, Warrior man?" Then, without warning, a bullet hisses overhead.

"No no no," Ruby whispers.

"Next one's for ya if ya still feel the same. Don't forget, I'm well within my rights to take ya down."

"Come." Onas tugs Ruby's arm. "You heard the way the woman went? Follow her, but give me ten seconds to lead the Shepherds aside. I'll loop back for you."

"No," Ruby says again.

Another bullet kisses the air. Closer now. A tiny red light dances past them. Downs has a laser scope. As if to prove her right, the dot of bloodred pins on Onas. Ruby's breath stops. Downs will do it. She knows he will. If nothing more than to punish Ruby. The beginning of her punishment.

"No," she says a third time, her voice stronger now. No one else will suffer. "Bud!" she yells. "Don't shoot. I'm coming out." Before Onas can stop her, Ruby stands. The red dot spasms across her chest, then to her still-prone guide.

He scrambles to his knees, grabbing Ruby's arm. "You must not go back." There's pain in his voice, a hollowness that Ruby knows comes from something deeper: from another, greater loss. This, her loss, he will get over.

"I'm coming, Bud. I'm coming." But then Onas has her, his arms around her waist, pulling her toward the West.

The next bullet whistles past Ruby's ear. "Uhh," Onas jerks backward, his arms slipping from her. Another shot burns past her arm, leaving a fiery path in its wake, a bright white in her head. She spins to see the guide clutching his upper arm. The smell of copper and iron are strong in her nostrils.

The loud-hailer screeches, "That was a mistake. Might wanna think about what ya gonna do next, Warrior man."

Onas's arm oozes dark, sticky blood. It slows and he begins to rise. It's then that she understands he won't stop. He will die trying to save her. He will die because of her. She pivots toward the source of the loud-hailer, and before Onas can recover enough to stop her, she marches away from the West, away from freedom.

"No, Ruby," Onas pleads. She keeps marching.

"There ya go," Downs calls. "That there's the right choice."

Then, as she closes the distance, "Told ya I was a persistent man, now didn't I?"

Part IV
Belief

*We cannot save ourselves from corruption
by doing only little, easy things!*
Tenskwataw, the Prophet (1775-1836)

18
Kaileh

The Documents

Kaileh, crouched low and moving fast, hears the shot. Her stride falters, then resumes. She's pulled on her nightseers hanging from a strap around her neck. The landscape passes in ghostly grays and diluted shadow. From one arm, the pack swings. The weight of the documents within gratifyingly heavy. Kaileh's done it. They've done it. The information Halek obtained during his captivity in the States was correct: the illegal, Ruby, had indeed been transporting missives meant for the West. Kaileh hadn't quite believed it. Part of her wants to open the packet and take a quick look, just to be sure.

Another shot sears the night. She hesitates, but then marches on; if Steeprock puts aiding the Atlantic woman over his own safety and gets himself arrested, well, that's not Kaileh's fault. She can't control his sympathies for the Atlantics and how it misguides his heart. From the direction she came, she hears an amplified voice, the words garbled but almost taunting. Then, another shot. Doubt trips her steps. Suddenly Tareq is there beside her, a ghostly memory settling a heavy hand on her shoulder, bringing her to a stop, begging her to consider his former partner and her own conscience.

"Rot it all," she says, and, gritting her teeth, turns back.

She arrives back where she left Steeprock just in time to see the retreating form of Ruby Roth, hands held high, walking toward the Shepherds. Kaileh still has her nightseers on. The eerie shape of a solitary man is clear in her sights. He holds a loud-hailer in one hand, a long-barreled rifle resting over one shoulder. The fugitive is almost to him now. Kaileh looks to either side, waiting for other Shepherds to step forward. But nothing happens. There's no movement, no rustle of branches or flash of steel. It's then that she notices something even more odd. The man holding the rifle and now placing restraints on Roth's wrists is dressed in plainclothes. He wears no uniform, no insignia of any kind that she can see. Didn't she just spend weeks with Shepherd McConnell, who, even though willing to wear his temporary Warrior garb, still proudly pinned his chest with the Shepherd badge?

The man with Roth is now shoving her toward a vehicle, barely visible until its cab opens and the light, magnified by her goggles, burns bright. The auto, too, is one of civilian use, not a Shepherd cruiser. Is Steeprock seeing this, she wonders? She turns her head and sees Onas, on the ground, leaning against a rotting stump. For a second, just one brief blink, her heart stops. Has she let a fellow officer be killed? Is she now the one to have abandoned her duty? Who will hate her as she hates Steeprock for losing Tareq?

Then he groans and rises to his feet, one hand clutching his left arm where a dark stain blossoms. She walks quickly to him, looking to the side at the sound of an auto roaring to life, then pulling away. Roth is gone. But it's no matter, Kaileh reassures herself: they have what they came for.

"I tried to stop her," Onas says as Kaileh bends down to inspect the wound. Nightseers off, she holds her handtorch to his dark shirt and the spot where blood is already starting to dry on the night-camouflaged shirt.

"Let's take a look at this." Kaileh nudges his hand off of the spot where he was hit.

"They got her, didn't they? The Shepherds?" he says as she inspects the wound. It seems to have passed through his biceps completely, leaving two seeping wounds, but apparently having missed bone and major blood vessels. He flinches as she moves his lower arm to verify the integrity of it.

"You'll live," she says.

"Thanks for the good news."

"Let's get going. You will be fine to walk, too."

"Did you see them? The Shepherds? They didn't harm her, did they?"

Kaileh gnaws on what she saw. It won't help Steeprock to know he just lost his prize to one man. A Shepherd maybe, most likely given his weapons, but just one, and whether his capture was official or not, she had no idea.

"Yes. She seemed fine." She bites her lip, then adds, "You did all you could."

"Rot it, rot it all to the underworld. I let her down. I let the Path down."

Kaileh scowls, unseen in the dark. "You need to just give up now. It's over. You did your best. We have what we came for."

He gives her a look then that unsettles Kaileh to the core. She feels like Tareq is suddenly there. There with his damned rhetoric and logic and well-thought-out arguments.

She puts a hand out and more gently says, "We cannot do more now. Let's get these"—she pats the satchelpack—"home."

19
Ruby

Buddy Downs

When Ruby sees it's only Bud Downs who has come for her, she's not surprised. It feels like destiny. As though since that spring morning when his pickup first appeared, she was set on a path toward this moment. Yet this moment is not the end. No. It's a beginning. A horrible, unwanted beginning.

Her body feels rag-like as she lifts her hand to the bindings he holds before her. They reach his pickup. He helps her in the passenger side, his hands hot and grimy and making her flinch away.

"Quite the little chase ya led me on. Thought I'd done lost ya, but those ignorant farmers thought we'd left 'em alone after putting the torch to their barn."

As numb as Ruby feels, the knowledge of how Betsey's goats were killed makes her want to shrink into a tiny ball and disappear. She aches for the girl, how such a horrible thing, how seeing the charred remains of the barn and perhaps even of her beloved animals, will rob her of the kind of innocence that can never be regained.

"Yup," he continues. "Like following a baby with a broken leg."

The image makes her flinch; there's such violence in it, such hate.

"Did you… did you…" she can't say it aloud. Levi and Noah, their own pickup heading back down the trail. Did they encounter the Shepherd? Did Downs do something beyond harming animals?

She stops her questioning. She doesn't want to know. She can't know.

But Downs answers. "Ah, ain't you the softy? Naw, those two hicks that carted you out this far kind of done me a favor. So I done them one and didn't kill their trespassing carcasses." Then Downs adds something that makes her knees give way. "Besides, I ain't really got no need to punish them. The end is coming for their kind. It's just a matter of time now."

He catches her elbow as she crumples and with a gentleness that makes her nauseous helps her into the cab of his pickup. Within minutes after pulling away, feeling as if there's nothing left to care for or worry about, Ruby falls into a restless sleep.

It's almost dawn when the pickup comes to a stop. The sudden lack of movement startles her awake. She opens her eyes expecting to see that they've arrived at a Shepherd station, not in Denton of course, but where else would they be headed?

Bud opens the door. He straightens her shirt, removes the wrist restraints. "We're here. Get out."

Ruby rubs her hands over the ache and scans the view.

"Here" is not a station, but an old farmhouse sitting between a treeless slope, a gnarled old orchard, and a well-worn dirt road. Even in the gray light, the hill behind the house reveals wrinkles of erosion, scrub brush sprouting in between. To all sides, there are only scarred hills, a couple of broke-down vine-covered pieces of farm equipment, and a shed or two. From one, an engine rumbles. Ruby catches a whiff of coal smoke and guesses it to be from a working power generator.

She feels neither relief nor despair at being somewhere other than a Shepherd station. Her acceptance feels like she's been drugged, and she doesn't even care if it never wears off. It makes her think of the amber bottle of pills. She meant to give them to the brothers for Zara, or for whoever. And now, if she had them herself… for which purpose would she use them? An escape for herself? Or revenge?

Inside, the house is tidy: a table, two chairs, a couch, a bed, a single bare bulb illuminating the space. Two windows pierce the front, but the back wall's blank except for two doors. Both closed. Ruby stares at the bright bulb glowing in the small kitchen.

"My daddy had a generator put in for his folks," Bud says. Her head takes a moment to process this. *His daddy.* The man who died. The man Bud likely killed.

"He done cared more for his own ma and pa than us, his own children. Didn't deserve us. Still, when he died"—the word is low and layered with something—"he done left me this place way out in the backcountry of… Well, it don't matter, but fancy that, will you? Often, I thought about coming back here after I finished my first assignment, that was up in Baltimore working at Marlburg." He scans the room, his eyes finding and holding Ruby. "But something drew me back to Denton."

Claustrophobia bands around her chest, threatens to steal her breath.

"Still, I kept the old homestead." He looks again at the room. "Figured it'd come in handy one day." A smile, too wide. She catches the wet brown of tobacco bits stuck to his teeth. "Sit down," he says, pushing her to a chair.

There's an old icebox humming in the small kitchen. Downs pulls a bowl out and sets it on the table. Something congealed and brown jiggles when he thunks it down. Next come two bowls, two spoons, a glass, and a filled AquaClenz pitcher.

"Eat."

Ruby looks at the bowl. Her stomach feels bloated, although it's been since dinner with the Brethren that she ate a proper meal.

Downs narrows his eyes. "Eat. I said to eat."

Her hands still cuffed together, she dishes a spoonful of the stuff into her bowl.

"It don't look like much, but it's, what do they call it? *Nutrient dense.*"

Ruby watches her hand grip the spoon, dip into the thick, cold mess, then lift it to her mouth as if someone else is guiding her. She wills her mouth open. The spoon slips between her lips. She tries to not breathe, tries to not focus on the jellied texture.

Bud digs into a bowlful. Did he abandon the Shepherd force at the York River? Has he chased her on his own since? As she tries to make sense of what has happened, she forces down a few more bites, then drinks gratefully of the water.

When he's cleared the table, he lays a document down, pushes it over to her, pivoting it with the tip of one nail-bitten finger. "Accordin' to this, ya belong to me now, or as good as. As you already knew, we're man and wife." He chuckles out a sound somewhere between a snort and a laugh.

Ruby sees the heading: *Aquisition Form M-100*. Colin Tate had not lied then, when he said he'd signed it. He'd bartered her away for something, maybe just spite. "Tate," she says before she can stop herself.

"Ha! Yeah, that Tate's a rabid weasel," Bud says. "I'd just as soon crush his head 'neath my boot as anything, but he's paying for his past in a different way."

She's too wrung dry to parse out what he means. Although she's not sure that knowing would make any difference.

"So, look around, Ruby Downs." Bud tips his chair back, balancing it on two legs, his arms crossed behind his neck. "You'll come to realize this here's a mighty big step up for a con such as yourself. And don't you worry, I'm getting myself transferred out this way. Yup. It's gonna work out fine."

Ruby tries to sort this, tries to find some logic in it. Does Downs really believe they'll somehow become a happy little family? Or has he gone mad? Or maybe it's the same thing.

She gulps more of the water. Downs's glass remains empty and she wonders if he's waiting for her to fill it for him, testing out whether or not she needs some training as a wife.

Bud clears his throat. "Less ya give me trouble, that is." His eyes narrow again.

Her mouth opens. She could ask him about HJ and Harold Sr. and Brother Q, couldn't she? Or is it too soon? Would he just use her desire to know against her—or, even worse, punish her with a brutal truth?

Then, before any words come to her mouth, she sees two of him. She blinks, but everything is doubled. Then the room begins to swirl. It tips to one side, then the other. "Whaa…?" she mumbles.

And Downs laughs. It's almost a giggle, like he's a little boy who's pranked his mother. He nods at the water and gives a shrug.

For the first time since she started marching toward Downs, leaving her dreams and hopes behind, a spark glimmers inside of her. She forces her eyes to lock on the side groove of Downs's neck, the pulse of life there. She reaches for her knife, or tries to. Her hand slips, lifts again, finds nothing at her waist but her own skin.

Downs's head elongates to one side, his mouth a wide black hole. "Lookin' for that ol' pig sticker?" Another laugh.

As her eyes close to the spinning room, she hears:

"I…

"ain't…

"no…

"rookie."

Tethered

It's almost dark when Ruby wakes. Whether it's the same day or many later, she cannot tell. Her head pounds and her mouth is a dry cave lined with sandpaper. She's on the bed, her legs straight, her head on a pillow, a blanket pulled to her chin. Though covered and still clothed, a terrible vulnerability floods her. She knows he's touched her, lifted her to this place, even undressed her, for she now wears an old calico dress that comes to her knees. Although there's no evidence he's done anything worse, her skin creeps and she wants to wither into herself, the things he could have done somehow all the more terrifying for her not having been aware.

There's a click. The door. Downs steps inside, a cloth sack in his arms.

"Oh good, ya're awake." His voice is light, happy, like Ruby just took an innocent nap. Before Ruby can stop herself, she feels her legs cross and her hands grip the blanket to her chin.

He stares at her, makes a tsking sound. "Ya can cut that out. I'm not like that. I may be many things, accused murderer"—he laughs a hard bark—"or even a real one, but I ain't no rapist, no mo-lest-er. I ain't my daddy." He spits a wad of greasy brown chew into an empty can sitting on the window ledge. "May he rest in hell."

And Downs is true to his word. Days pass. Ruby loses track of how many. Sometimes he forces her to drink whatever sedative it is he's using, other times he stakes her ankle to a line tethered to a ring in the floor, saying he knows she needs time to accept her new situation. Ruby feels like a pet dog being trained to a new home.

Through one of the two doors in the back wall is a true luxury: a functioning water closet, with a toilet that flushes and a small sink. The chain on her foot extends just to the inside, but prevents the door from closing. Downs tells her, "There ain't no need for privacy amongst married folk."

The other door is locked. Ruby never sees Downs open it—or where he keeps a key. She doesn't fight the tether, at least when he's there. The first time she's alone, and not in a state of stupefaction, she goes to the bolt anchor in the floor and turns and pulls and twists, trying to unthread it from the floorboards. But it's either too stuck or has a nut on the underside holding it fast. Another time, she wets her foot in the sink, soaps it up, and tries to slip off the ring around her ankle. The result is an angry bruise on her anklebone that later that day, when he returns, Downs sees as he runs his eyes down her bare legs to her ankle. His eyes darken, his face contorts, and he scrubs his hand over his mouth.

"Now why'd you go and do that? I thought we were gettin' somewhere." The next day, when he leaves her alone, he stirs in a broken capsule of powder into a glass of water and forces her to drink it.

So, she stops trying. Stops caring. She thinks she might really be broken. Worn to submission like an abused dog. Is that what most training is, she wonders? Just wearing something or someone else down until they give in?

"Time you start doing your part," he says one morning as he readies himself to leave for whatever it is he does now. "I'm gonna add a bit of length to this here chain. I'll be expecting a clean kitchen, floors too, by the time I get back. That works out, I'll set you up for some cooking."

Ruby says nothing.

Downs sucks air in through his teeth. "A *thank you* too much to ask for?"

Ruby looks up. She avoids meeting his gaze as much as she can. It's just easier that way. And now, she wishes she hadn't looked. His face is red. A flash of something just past impatience in his eyes. For the first time in days, Ruby feels afraid.

"Thank you." She does her best to keep her voice from cynicism. Her neutral, mechanical response makes him blow out the held breath and shake his head. When he leaves, the small farmhouse rattles with the slam.

So, she cleans. She cooks. She scrubs. And she watches out the front windows. For what, she's not sure. The landscape surrenders no clues of where they are, no hints of hope for rescue. She hears no other people or the distant sounds of cars, lorries, or trains. In the long hours of solitude and boredom she imagines things both wonderful and not. The documents are in the West, helping in ways she'll never know. Her guide, the man, Onas Steeprock, is healing fine. HJ, being a child, has been forgiven and returned to his father's care. Or maybe, Missus Simpson stepped up, took the boy in if Harold Sr.… could not. And then she thinks of all those things, only with the worst possible outcomes having happened.

For a few days, Ruby's domestic skills seem to placate Bud Downs. Over meals he begins asking her questions about her life. Casual things, the way one might do if they were actually courting a prospective mate.

One evening, on what Ruby guesses to be her second week of captivity, he says, "Ya ever think about having kids?" He's chewing on a battered and fried turkey tail. His fingers slip it around inside of his mouth, his tongue working off the bits of fat and meat. She tries not to watch.

He brought the paper-wrapped pack of fresh tails home the evening before. At first, Ruby wanted to laugh. The tails were both an indulgence and an insult. A statement of their poverty. One step up from Cham or Cherky.

"Well, what about it? I know ya was abandoned by your parents, and me, well, that's another story. But ain't it those that learned from the worst that be the best equipped to do something better?"

Ruby can't stop herself. Her laugh comes from nowhere and everywhere. It's both nothing and everything. She laughs hard, not caring that bits of batter and grease slip from her mouth. Downs's face reddens. The veins on his forehead thicken into ropes. And she can almost hear his teeth grind together.

"With you?" she says, knowing it's a mistake. She's poking the coiled snake, taunting the terrified dog. And she doesn't care.

"You think you'd make a good father? You think I would want to bring a child into *this*? Into this life? With you?"

For a moment, she thinks he's too stunned to do anything other than sit there. And she should stop. She knows she should. But she can't. She just cannot.

She laughs until his hand stops her. The blow is hard and fast, coming almost before she realizes it. It spins her around and off the chair. Copper fills her mouth. She spits blood and a single ivory-colored tooth onto the freshly scrubbed floorboards.

But still she laughs.

20
Kaileh

Debate

Two weeks have passed since Kaileh limped Onas back across the border. After finding him wounded, she'd alerted the commander. Medics met them at the boundary and took the wounded Steeprock into their care and off her hands. Now, still stuck at the Waccamaw enclave, she's bored. She's called and scripted Mateo several times, hoping he's at last heard from his archivist relative, but he's only replied: *still working on it*. Even Commander Briento has been distant, busy, dealing, she's certain, with the documents and the fallout of their mission, for now, she realizes, there was no way to hide the existence of the Path—and their own people's involvement—from the United West government.

She expected Steeprock, at least, to be put on suspension, herself to be debriefed. But there's been only the commander's repeated, "I'll let you know. For now, relax, enjoy the area."

And she's attempting a version of that now.

"I'm saying, again, it doesn't matter," Kaileh says as she steps over a dead log as she and Onas, his arm still in a sling to hold the mending wound still, trace their way along the ridge of the mountain range north of Waccamaw. They're on their way to the location where her brother was slain.

"And again," Onas says, his voice pitching a tight note higher, "I'm saying it does. The woman Ruby Roth, she matters. We were, we are, wrong to abandon her." They've argued about it several times—not the fact that they had to leave her behind that night, but of not trying to help her now. Kaileh watches Onas's back. His braid sways, always a bit more to the right, opposite his shortened stride.

Kaileh blows out an exasperated puff, but doesn't, once again, repeat the facts. The documents they risked their lives to get are in the hands of those who can use them. That was the purpose of the mission. And it has been accomplished—whether or not their content was of value is almost beside the point. They did the job they were assigned. She tells herself, even if Steeprock won't listen, that she should feel relief, a sense of pride even. But instead, there's a hollowness in the days following their return. Part of her wonders if it's not having anyone to talk to. They've been ordered to not share news of the event with anyone. And even if she could, other than Mateo, who is left?

As she follows Steeprock toward the site where he says he and Tareq had been defending a jah'gowa nesting tree, she thinks of the crudely carved box back in her room. Nesting inside, on top of Tareq's letters, are the two jah'gowa feathers. She knows it will take a long time to forgive her brother. But love is something entirely different. Like the two feathers, set apart yet the same, defying the rules.

As they trek the ridge and dimples of the mountains, the glory of autumn is not lost on her. The oaks and maples are following the buckeye and locusts and transforming their verdant greens into those of the heavens: fiery sun golds, sunset crimsons, glowing sunrise tangerines. From the ridge where she stands, it looks as if one can take flight: leap into the air and skim across the sea of color. It has been some time since she's dreamed, by night or day, of flying.

The trek would be therapeutic if only Onas would drop the topic of the young woman, Ruby. They still don't know who she really was, much less who the operative was that had entrusted the documents to the fugitive's hand.

"I can't let this go," he says. "That woman sacrificed herself for those papers. For us, for our cause, really."

She sighs. "Will you just drop it? For the last time, that's not the way I see it." She comes to a halt, breathing deeply the brisk air, the alluring scent of crisping leaves and a forest readying for winter's sleep.

"There," Onas says, pointing down the slope to a towering mountain maple. A somewhat less imposing tree than some other *Acer* species, this one, at about ten meters, is probably at the peak of its height. The gash made by the poacher's chain saw is still visible, the wound stopped by a clot of the tree's own blood, a gnarl of amber pitch now encrusted with bits of debris collected over the year.

Somewhere, there in the leaf litter, her brother too had bled. But unlike the tree, he succumbed. It hits her in a way news of his death did not. This, this is where it happened. This is where the earth sponged the last beats of Tareq's living heart. Around them now stand the witnesses, silent, unmoving, uncaring, perhaps, about the fragility of the two-leggeds. For the forest, for the earth, time was something entirely different. Her chest hurts, feels expanded with something primal and urgent, something desperate that needs to be released. A scream, she realizes. If she were alone, she would scream until there was nothing left inside of her.

Then she spots the nest. Vacant now, a half-meter-wide conglomeration of sticks, twigs, moss, and a few downy feathers all wedged between a fork in the branches. Kaileh squints at it in wonder. She realizes she'd wondered if Onas lied about the nest, for this region is not the jah'gowa's normal nesting area, which is far to the north. She chews on her lower lip, trying to find meaning in the oddity.

As if he read her mind, he says, "I know. It shouldn't be there." He lowers himself to the ground, awkwardly dropping the last few centimeters. She hesitates but finally folds herself down beside him.

"That was part of why Tareq was so enamored of the pair. We weren't sure if one had perhaps been injured, and they remained, grew fond of the place." His voice is distant, his gaze even more so. "They are gone now. I don't know if they ever came back. I could not bring myself to check—until now."

"Loyal to the end," Kaileh says. "The birds, I mean. Mating for life as they do."

"Indeed." A light breeze stirs the rust-brown and gold leaves of the trees around them, seeding a shower of foliage. It drifts like a colorful snow to the forest floor. Part of her expects a feather to float down, some sort of stick-to-the-head sign she is supposed to interpret. But, like the osprey back home, swooping up from Apserkahar Creek, no feather falls. She takes a deep breath. Even this close to the border, with its intrusion of air pollution, the crisp scent of summer radiates from the soil, the decaying leaves: death bringing new life.

She almost asks him then. Her lips part. Words hover in the back of her throat. *Where were you really born? Why are your records hidden?* She has the sense that he would tell her the truth. But something stops her. She's not ready, just not ready to hear words. A story instead, maybe, that will foster forgiveness, maybe even bring them closer. There's a comfort in the distance; the barrier shields her, and for this, for now, she is glad.

Revelation

The next morning Commander Briento sends Kaileh a script: *If you'd like an update, come to my office after first meal.*

Onas, sitting across from her as they both finish eating, looks up from his keitai at the same time as her. "This should be interesting,"

"So," Commander Briento says after both she and Onas are seated. Xe seems to have aged years since this all began. It shifts something inside of her. The magnitude of what is happening seemed lost for the last two weeks, diluted, maybe by the waiting, the visit to the place her brother breathed his last.

Briento steeples xyr fingers and studies the two officers. For a moment, she thinks they're in more trouble. "Suffice it to say, the documents retrieved from the ASA are proving to be of utmost value. I cannot go into details, as I'm sure you both appreciate." Xe reaches down beside xyr chair and lifts the would-be refugee's satchelpack. "We have more information about the young woman." Xe glances at xyr timepiece. "I'm waiting for Halek to arrive. He's just returned from a visit home. A well-earned rest."

As Kaileh soaks in the fortifying news that the documents held information of value, there's a knock at the door, and Halek steps in.

"Ah. Welcome back. You know officer Kaileh and Onas, of course. And although Onas will be leaving us, due to his confessed role in aiding immigrants and this Path operation, our little conclave has some loose ends to knit together."

Leaving us. It's official then. He's not just suspended, he's to leave the service. It's all she can do to not look over at him, but it's the microscopic twinge of discomfort that surprises her. She cares. Not much. But some. With intent, she shifts her focus to the inspector. Halek is a tall man, sturdily built with the bearing of a diplomat. He looks tired but has lost some of the fragility that surrounded him at their first meeting.

"Halek told you," the commander says, "of his captivity in the ASA and how it brought him together with the Elohi monastic, Sister O. That it was her concern over the documents and Halek's realization that they were likely given to the young woman by a man she called Brother Q during the incident at Kent Narrows. Well, it turns out there's more to the story. It's information that may guide us in another direction. Halek's agreed to reveal all of that now." Briento gives xyr old friend a look Kaileh can only interpret as exasperation. She narrows her eyes. Glances at Onas, who looks at her and shrugs.

Halek steeples his fingers, and for a moment, the gesture is so like Briento's it's easy to imagine them as longtime friends. "I'm ready," Halek says.

He turns to Kaileh and Onas. "You already know I work for the IAN as a human rights inspector. Before I fill in some of the, um, things I omitted, I want to clarify that I'm in no way a part of the movement of undocumented migrants, this thing they're calling the Path. I was indeed unaware of the organized nature of how… this young woman—or, from what I'm learning, many others—came to us." He clears his throat and shifts in the chair. "I say this not with any concern for my own reputation, you understand…" He shakes his head. "Or, maybe there is a molecule of that. But let me get back to how I came to be involved.

"I left out much, partly because I thought you would succeed in bringing her, the woman Ruby Roth, back with you, and partly because things were… well, still muddled in my mind."

Kaileh can feel something, some momentous piece of truth, hovering just at the edge of the story. Without realizing it, she scoots forward in her chair.

Halek takes a deep breath. "I arrived on the Eastern Shore, early the morning I was scheduled in Denton to perform inspections on several of the massive poultry facilities." He looks at Briento. "But you all already know this. Forgive me, Toma."

"It is no trouble, my friend. Please continue." Kaileh hears Briento's tone. Whatever Halek is working up to, the commander already knows.

Halek nods, rubs his forehead. The silver at his temples has spread, turning his dark hair a brittle iron gray. "When the ferry docked, my driver drove us off the boat. But then, as we proceeded on, something happening at the south port caught his eye. He brought the auto to a halt and said, 'Sir, are you of liberal mind?' There was great anxiety and hope in his voice. I answered, 'I do believe you might call it that. Why?' He didn't answer but turned and accelerated into the smaller harbor's parking area. Quickly, it became apparent there was some sort of altercation occurring. Two men, Shepherds it turned out, one armed, were intent on a tan auto. Then, I saw a man lying on the ground near it, apparently shot. The sight was disturbing, but still, I had no real right to intercede. My driver, though, he was greatly agitated. And then, for reasons I thank the gods for, I decided to trust this man, who had won me over in ways we don't need to go into. All he said when he braked us to a stop was, 'Sir, it's time to put that IAN badge of yours to a purpose for good.' I must admit, it was the best part of my time there." Halek rubs his hands together, his eyes glittering. "I sprang from the auto like a young man, brandishing my badge. The taller man holding the gun told me they were on official Shepherd business and to get back in the auto. But I felt eager to interfere with these domestic enforcement specialists." He scoffs.

Kaileh thinks of the single Shepherd, or man pretending to be one, at the border. How she'd have loved to interfere. Not necessarily to rescue the Atlantic woman, but to take him down a few rungs.

"I was only able to do so much, though. As I dealt with the older Shepherd, his partner turned on two others, the woman Ruby and a young boy who were attempting to flee to a waiting boat. My powers were limited though, and only the woman escaped to the waiting boat." His eyes gaze into the distance. Kaileh feels a tiny surge of joy at the fugitive Ruby's escape. She tells herself it's only because of the documents.

"As the boat pulled away," Halek continues, "I pulled the smaller Shepherd from the boy, who seemed remarkably calm and unharmed. That Shepherd, well, he attempted to punch me, but," he chuckles, "my days of wrestling, long ago, to be sure, came into use."

Briento laughs. "Halek and I have known each other since university, where we both were on the wrestling team." Kaileh remembers when she thought Briento had likely once played lacrosse. "I also," xe adds, "stood in witness at Halek and Sarin's binding ceremony."

"That was a good day. A day when all was filled with hope." Halek's voice has a melodic tone. It's sweetly familiar: the same way her own father used to speak about Bennu, her mother. Words and affection that used to make her squirm, now a time that she'd do just about anything to bring back.

"With the boy under my watch," Halek continues, "both Shepherds ran down the dock, I presume to attempt to stop the fleeing boat. By then, I felt fully invested in the young woman's escape, and the boy seemed fine, so I proceeded down the gangplank to attempt delaying them further. The Shepherds cursed my arrival, likely as I kept placing myself between them and the fleeing watercraft."

A "Ha!" comes from Kaileh's mouth before she can stop it.

Halek gives her an appreciative smile. "The older Shepherd screamed even more curses when he turned back to the parking area and saw the tan auto fleeing, no sign of the young boy or the injured man. They too escaped his governance.

"From there, my driver, Percy, quite grateful for what I'd done, took me on to Denton. Sadly, tragically, there we found a mob, most wearing the colors of the so-called DTOM movement. They were looting stores, shouting at onlookers, and, worst of all, burning the Outreach."

He digs the heels of his palms into his forehead again.

"Would you like a break?" Briento asks. Kaileh, for the first time, considers what the older man has been through. Like Briento's lifemate, he was held captive by the enemy. A twinge of guilt twists her stomach.

"No. This feels good. Feels right. I will continue. Percy, who I suspect is a part of this underground—the Path—tried to get me from the scene. And he would have succeeded had I not been so determined to see to the monastic's safety. As we now know, Sister O had meant to ask me to get these documents out. But it was I who initially arranged the meeting. It was… for a very personal purpose." The way he says "personal" makes Kaileh straighten. She knows they've at last come to the meat of the nut. "I will try to be succinct. As you've likely noticed, being short-winded is not a problem from which I suffer." Even Kaileh laughs at this, feeling an intense liking for this man.

"You see, I've been—I mean we, Sarin and our daughter Hahsi—have been on a search for many years. A search that led me at last to Denton." He glances at each of them and rubs his hands together again as if chilled. "It's a long story and one that deserves a separate telling, perhaps." He takes a long, slow breath. Kaileh's so close to the edge of her seat now, she worries she might slide off.

"In Denton, I hoped to at last have our search bear fruit. I'm still not sure, but what I learned during my captivity with Sister O indicates that the young woman, Ruby Roth, may be… my… may be our granddaughter."

21
Ruby

Prayers

The day after Downs struck Ruby, he bursts through the door, returning from whatever it is he does. He catches Ruby sitting on the bed with her eyes closed and her lips moving around the clotted gap in her mouth so recently vacated by Downs's hand.

"What the bloody hell ya doing?" The door bangs shut behind him, but not before a breath of the outdoors enters, bringing the earthy smell of falling leaves, lichens, cooling soil. It gives Ruby a sudden powerful desire to find a patch of earth, burrow down into those fallen leaves, and sprout into something else.

She doesn't know how to answer his question, for she's not even sure herself. Some, she supposes, would call what he caught her doing praying.

He whips his head to the kitchen, where she's supposed to have been scrubbing pots and kneading bread. "Why ain't your chores done?"

Despite her weakening muscles, the ache in her jaw and neck, she jumps up. The long chain on her leg clatters and clanks. She knows the disaster of the previous evening should have inspired more vigilance, more effort to placate this man, her captor, but somehow, it's done the opposite.

"Well? Whatcha got to say for yourself?"

She doesn't answer. Doesn't even know what to say, as if his blow has struck all speech from her. That's how she thinks of it now. She'll not speak again. It's the only power left to her, or so it feels. So she stands there, mute and unmoving.

He sets a parcel down on the table with a thunk and walks to the kitchen, fuming and muttering. He comes back and sits at the table. She holds her breath. Expecting everything and nothing, but what he says is far from anything she could have anticipated.

"This ain't working out." He rubs his forehead like he has a headache. For the first time, Ruby dares to hope.

She breaks her vow. "You can let me go. I won't tell anyone." Her voice squeaks of rust and fear.

He rubs his forehead again, swinging his head side to side. He takes a deep breath and looks up. "I done give ya enough time to make the right choice. To"—he motions around—"appreciate what's being offered to ya. To see that we're meant to be together, you and me."

Ruby looks into his eyes. The gold flecks in the green-brown of them seem to have spread.

She stares at the package. Ice drips cold rivulets down her spine. Whatever is in there, it's not bolt cutters to set her free.

Then, from nowhere she hears a voice. *You must believe.*

Ruby almost looks around the farmhouse, so clear are the words. But, of course, the source is not there. Zara of the Mattaponi is far from her. How did she sound right there, just behind Ruby's shoulder? *That's it,* she thinks without surprise, *I am going mad.*

"Get in there," Downs says. "Evidently, playing nice ain't gonna cut it. If this is what it takes… so be it." He stands, goes to the door that, until this moment, she has not seen him open. A key slips from his pocket and into the lock. The door creaks open. Ruby's pulse beats erratically in her ears. He reaches inside, and though she cannot see what's in the space, the object he pulls out is immediately identifiable: a zap-crook.

Immediately, her body vibrates as if already shocked. She tries to move toward the kitchen. Maybe it's not too late.

The first zap is like lightning striking. Her entire body goes rigid. Urine leaks from her, and her eyes pour unbidden tears.

"I don't wanna do this. Ya know that, right?" Ruby can't answer, can't look at him, but even through her pain, she hears a tremor in his voice.

Then, before she can respond to his order—with defiance or acquiescence, she doesn't know—he presses the crook to her once more. "No. Please," she manages through rattling teeth.

"If ya'd just do as you've been asked, we'd been right fine. But if convincing is what it takes, maybe my daddy… he was partly right." He moves his arm toward her for a third shock, but Ruby stumbles just beyond reach.

You must believe, Zara's voice says once more.

In what though? Ruby tried to be like Rafe and Betsey, praying to a god that, if real, has been as absent in her life as her own parents. And it didn't work anyway.

With her last bit of will and her fingers quivering, Ruby begins to scrub the dirty pot soaking in the sink. That was her sin, leaving it to sit, hoping time and water would ease her labor.

"There ya go now, that's the right choice." They're the same words he called at the border.

She thinks of Onas Steeprock and the Warriors of the West. Do they believe in a god? In gods?

Elbows bent, Ruby scours the old stained pot as if years of burned meals cling to the bottom. She tries not to make a show of it. Tries to walk the narrow tether keeping her from being hurt.

Believe.

What can she believe in?

The pot cleaner than it's probably been in years, Ruby balances it on the full drainboard. The plates beneath it shift and clink, protesting under the weight.

"All right then," Downs says. "That weren't so bad, eh? Come on over here, I got something for you." He points to the table, the packet still sitting there.

Ruby's body trembles. Then she hears a sound. At first, she thinks it's her own teeth clattering. But then, there's a clank, and another, and another, from behind her. And before she can spin and reach out, the stack of dishes supporting the heavy pot gives way, and the entire construction crashes to the floor. Dishware explodes across the space. The pot hits with a brittle bang. When it ends, she looks up. Downs's face is rigid, the only thing moving the throbbing veins on his temples.

After a few ponderous seconds he speaks, his words slow as a fire just taking light. "Goddamnit, Ruby." The fire catches. His fists rise. "Ya stacked 'em like that on purpose, didn't ya?" As his voice rises, so does her fear. She backs to the limit of the chain at her ankle. Downs bends over and picks up a piece of broken dishware.

"These were my nanna's. Passed down to me. Now just look at what ya done to 'em."

Ruby knows she cannot escape, yet pulls against the band around her leg with more force than ever before. The steel bites deep, but she hardly feels it. She leans away, the far counter against her back. He bends down again and reaches for another broken shard. It's then that Ruby realizes what she needs to do. She squats down, as if trying to help clean up the mess, and reaches for a knife-shaped piece of ceramic.

Then, just before she can stand, just before she can use it as a weapon, his booted foot kicks her hand, sending the shard spinning. "Ah, now that'd be a mistake." His voice has changed. It's deep, measured, as though he's not even the same person. And then, even though she's certain of what's about to happen, knows she'd be better off curling into a ball amidst the jagged bits, she stands her ground and stares as he pulls back his bunched fist.

The first blow sinks into her eye socket. His knuckle bones meet her cheekbone, her eyebrow, the side of her nose. Her body is thrust backward, though there's no place to go. The shackle yanks her foot from beneath her and she falls. There's a brief thought, a belief, of sorts, that she's about to be murdered. Then the back of her head hits the counter and she remembers no more.

More Prayers

She wakes on the bed, still wearing the same belted housedress and ratty sweater Downs put her in when she arrived. She keeps her eyes closed at first, partly because they seem to be glued shut and partly because she's afraid of what she'll see. So, she listens. And after a time, she's certain she's alone. Her eyes peel open with effort, and Ruby rubs the congealed goop from her lashes, flinching as her fingers touch her swollen, aching left eye.

The farmhouse is in darkness, the two windows gray squares. It's not cold, but Ruby's body shivers as if she's stepped into a Maryland blizzard. She tries to move. At first, she's sure she's been bound in place, so stiff are her limbs, but then the chain clanks against the steel bedframe. Her ankle is still restrained.

She tries to rise to her elbows and falls back with a gasp. The back of her head feels like a melon that's been dropped on tarmac. Fumes rise with her movement, drenching her in a stench of urine and old sweat.

How long? How long has she been like this? Did Bud just cart her to the bed and drop her there? Has he abandoned her? What if he went back to Denton, his little experiment in domestic bliss gone amuck? How much food did he leave?

Get up, she yells inside her head. *You need to get up. You need to do something.* But the dark and pain and despondency are heavy weights keeping her in place.

The next time she comes to, it's daylight. She's still alone. Every part of her body still aches, but her head feels mildly less swollen in the light of day. The sandpaper of her mouth frightens her almost more than anything else. The more she tries to make it go away, the worse it gets. A kind of claustrophobia closes in. Memories of the tunnel, but now with her mouth filling with powdery dry earth, almost transport her back to that overwhelming panic. Then she sees one of his portable AquaClenz bottles. It's close. Just beside the bed. Bud must have put it there. Even in his fury, he did that. In a way, it turns her stomach, the kindness more disturbing than the abuse.

And she's fairly certain it means he will return.

She drinks, she sleeps, she even crawls to the water closet and performs a feeble and mostly futile ablution that leaves her breathless. She's hungry, hungry in that odd way you can't feel anymore. She forces her feet into the kitchen. He's cleaned up the evidence of her failure, of his rage. Inside the icebox, she finds no food. Nothing on the shelves. Nothing. Just the water.

You must believe.

Go away, she thinks to the voice of Zara of the Mattaponi. *I'm going to die. I believe in nothing. Nothing. Nothing.*

You must believe.

She sighs, her breath heavy with a chemical smell she knows to be a sign of her body beginning to eat itself. *Please*, she thinks, *save me or leave me alone.*

Believe. Fine, she thinks, and climbs back into the filth of the bed, clamps her arms around her hollow belly, and tries again to pray.

Universe. World. Nature. God. Gods. If you are listening, if you care, I'm here. I want to care. I still care.

She dozes again.

Sometime near the end of the day, something rouses her. Bud. She's sure he's returned. Her mind scrambles for a response, a plan, a point of going on with this charade. Would playing along be something she could do? Her brain says yes, what do you have to lose? But her soul recoils. She'd rather die.

The sounds come again. Voices. Two. Outside. Voices, neither of which are of Bud Downs.

Ruby tries to call out. A squawk comes from her lips.

One of the voices, male, says, "Hello? Anyone home?"

Then, a second voice. A young girl. "Pops, boost me up. Lemme peek inside."

A girl. A young girl. Ruby reaches for the water. Her head hammers. She drinks and croaks out a hello. Its faintness is drowned out by the sounds of the unseen man and girl talking.

"Nah, we ain't gonna stoop to snoopin'. We shouldn't anyways. What if someone sees us?"

"Aw, Pops, there ain't no one around but us."

"You do as I say now, all right?"

"If you say so. But knock again. Knock real hard this time."

He does and calls out, "We ain't lookin' for no handouts, just wanna camp nearby for the night."

"I'm hee-er… helllp… muh." Oh please, oh please, gods, if you're there… Ruby thinks.

"Come on, gal, ain't nobody there. We gotta move on."

Footsteps recede, dragging the tiny morsel of hope with them.

Ruby lets herself cry. But no tears come. Just dry, croaking sobs into her pillow.

Prayers. Belief. What is the point?

22
Kaileh

Answers

*G*randdaughter? Kaileh's brain stumbles over what Halek has just revealed. There's a *what* and a *how* perched at the tip of her tongue, but like Onas and Briento, she stays quiet, processing the plausibility, the possibility.

Outside the window of Commander Briento's office comes the discordant honking of a flock of sasa geese. It nears, then fades, a noisy signal of the coming winter. Kaileh's eyes burn with sudden tears as she wonders if the large birds have arrived yet in Takel. Her mother adored autumn: the whip snap of frost in the air, the way the animals adapted and the scenery altered. Is this how every season will be now, Bennu's daughter wonders? Tracking the things her mother is missing. That Tareq is missing. That her father is missing.

But she's not the only one in the room folding loss into their soul.

Making her voice as gentle as possible, she asks, "Granddaughter? How?"

The man rubs his palms together. His knuckles are slightly enlarged, the hands of a man who's done more than sign papers and inspect working conditions. He sighs. "It is a long story, as I've said—and you can probably guess how much I relish the telling of such." Briento gives a small, understanding laugh. "But," Halek continues, "I shall do my best to be brief.

"When our daughter, Hahsi, she's thirty-six now, was a teenager, our community in Seminola participated in a program aimed at making small, generational changes to the culture of the ASA. You remember, Toma?

That lofty hope that by showing a few a better way to live we could influence the whole?" Halek shakes his head in a sad wave. "Anyhow, the program brought a handful of candidates from the States into the United West on work/education passports. Was not that the program, Toma?"

"Yes," xe says. "It was meant to imbue a seed of cultural change in the youth of the ASA. The ASA government agreed, perhaps hoping to use it for their own purposes, nefarious or simply to try to stem the flow of immigration that happened during the Great Influx, but our councils believed it was worth the risk."

Onas clears his throat. "Sorry to interrupt, but why haven't we heard of this? Wouldn't we have learned it during training or history or something?"

Briento shrugs. "It's not a guarded secret, but it lasted less than a year. I suppose it's only a footnote for most of us."

"The young man," Halek say, "named Nicholas Washington, was assigned to our community to learn woodworking skills." Halek went on, describing Nicholas as a gifted and emotionally sensitive young man who won their community's heart and, unknown to them at the time, the Tuskenugees' daughter's affection.

Halek pauses, looking at each of them, his eyes seeming to see some other place, some other time. "When the program abruptly ended, Nicholas returned to the Atlantic States, leaving behind a pregnant young woman. Hahsi wasn't aware of her condition until sometime after his departure. Nicholas, back in the ASA, would have been ignorant he was to be a father. And that's the way it should have stayed. That is, until—well, I'll get to that in a minute. As the pregnancy advanced, we learned our daughter was carrying twins."

Kaileh chews on her lip. He's implying this Ruby Roth was born in the West. Not just that, but that she has, or had, a sibling. Kaileh finds herself wanting to hurry Halek along. If this were a book, she'd skip to the end.

"When her time drew close, Hahsi experienced some complications. She was nursed at one of the Elohi natal centers. That is where we met Sister O, who was a maternity healer there. All went well, and we returned home with two beautiful, healthy grandchildren. A boy and a girl. A few weeks later, we held the naming ceremony. The girl became Araminta, the boy Frederick. We chose the names in honor of two of our cultural ancestors who were heroes in their own right: brave people who escaped that part of the Atlantic States long ago." He sighs. "There I go…"

"It is fine, Halek, take all the time you need," Briento says again. Kaileh studies the commander. How much of this did xe already know?

"Not long after the babies were born, my daughter took a dangerously impulsive step, something we perhaps should have anticipated, being aware of her spontaneous nature as we certainly were." He takes a deep breath. "Without consulting us, Hahsi sent not just a letter to Nicholas via McComb Corporation headquarters, but a photograph of herself with the babies." He clucks his tongue. Kaileh pictures the foolhardiness of such a thing, then feels like she's aged suddenly into a stodgy Silver berating the ways of the young.

"We shall never know if McComb passed the letter to Nicholas or if he found out some other way. And fortunately, McComb Poultry Corp had no rights to the children. That was until…" He pulls a kerchief from his pocket, blots his forehead. His larynx bobs up and down. He tells them that months later, Nicholas made his way to the border near Port Tomochichi where he tried to cross into Seminola. Fortunately for him, it was the Warriors that took him into custody, and not the Shepherds on his trail. To these officers, Washington told his story and requested asylum. Halek and Sarin were notified and traveled immediately to the asylum center. "Hahsi, despite our requests, followed us there—with the babies.

"I still shake my head, considering how different things might have gone. If Hahsi had just been patient and let the border officers and amnesty office do their work, well…" He looks around, lets his gaze linger on Kaileh and Onas. "If you ever have children, you will understand the surety of the young person is quite a force to be reckoned with."

Kaileh holds back a laugh; she lost count of the times her mother had said much the same to her.

"During one of the visitations at the holding center between Hahsi, the babies, and Nicholas, the young couple decided to stroll the trails of the wildlife refuge that abuts the grounds. Nicholas was only lightly guarded, being no threat and having already made a good case for asylum.

The center is quite near the Tomochichi River, with all of its wandering forks and tributaries, and Hahsi still swears they did not intend to go near the patrolled area of the border."

Briento clears xyr throat. "Ah, I always wondered why that area is now off-limits for civilians."

Halek nodded. "You can thank us for that. Well, as you have probably guessed, the young family was apprehended by Shepherds; likely they had tracked Nicholas to the border. Hahsi, attempting to use what tools she could, produced her papers and claimed Nicholas to be her legal mate, the children their own. That straying over the border had been an accident. But to no avail, for Nicholas still wore the barbaric brand applied in the days before the… the equally barbaric micro-ID."

Kaileh wants to ask if perhaps the couple hadn't strayed. What if the Shepherds were the ones to penetrate the boundary, and they later lied about where he'd been arrested? But she keeps the thought to herself; it won't make any difference now.

Halek blows air through his lips. "They took Nicholas. They took the babies. They took our future, truth may it be." Halek's voice grows thick. He pauses for a moment, appears caught in reverie.

"At least they let Hahsi go. Our border patrol found her near hysteria, brought her back to us. What became of Nicholas and our dear little Araminta and Frederick was unknown for many years."

"Even with all of your connections?" Onas asks.

Halek nods. "It was like they no longer existed. But we knew that the young man's corporate link was McComb. Their operation extends into two—no three, of the neighboring states. Of course, there was the risk his contract, and the children's legacy contract—yes, that's what they call it— would be sold to another corporation, but for years, I focused my attention on monitoring any McComb documents or communiqués we received, watching for the last name Washington, for I expected the children's names to have been changed to match his. We never considered they'd been orphaned or their names changed—at least not until very recently."

Kaileh can't help herself, patience never was her granite. "Do you know what happened to the father? To Nicholas? And if this Ruby is the girl, Araminta, what happened to Frederick?"

"We aren't sure about either," Halek answers. "But as there's no evidence of Nicholas ever having existed—that we can find—we came to suspect he was 'dealt with' officially or perhaps fought his capture and was killed. We know he never returned to Denton. And little Frederick, well, let me get to that." He massages his forehead with his fingertips and takes another shaky breath.

"We immediately filed paperwork to retrieve our little ones. I wasn't as integrated with the upper machinations of our leadership or the IAN at that time, so nothing moved quickly. What I've just told you took years to piece together." He shakes his head. "As far as we can determine, there has never been a case such as this. Therefore, there was no precedent to guide the process. Toma, I am correct in this, am I not?"

"Indeed," xe says, then adds, "Halek and I have known each other since university, as I told you. We formed a close bond. Over the years, I've kept up on the matter, and although unable to do anything substantial, I kept an ear to the earth. But the last thing I expected was to find a possible match for Araminta knocking at our door."

Halek says, "Your support, my friend, helped my family maintain a bit of hope." He glances at his timepiece. "And I want to apologize for not having initially told you of my ulterior motives for visiting Denton…"

Ah, Kaileh, thinks, so the commander did not know that part of the story, which explains the earlier hint of xyr exasperation.

"Our search stagnated. Then, I became a full inspector and was able to put my feet on the ground in the ASA. Earlier this year, I was assigned to the Delmarva Peninsula, an area comprising parts of three states and almost totally owned by a single of their giant corporations, McComb. It was then the stars began to form a guiding constellation."

"Excuse me," Kaileh says. "I'm sorry to interrupt again, but where was your daughter during all this?" Onas glances at her, and Briento raises one eyebrow. "I don't mean to imply she wasn't contributing. I'm just curious."

"I understand. I understand. Truth may it be, Hahsi did not handle the loss of her children, nor her role in it, well. Most certainly, there is no surprise in that. But it did more than depress her, it…" He rubs his hands together, and a few knuckles pop and snap. "It derailed her life. She turned to… she turned to abusing hallucinogens and alcohol. There would be times, months, even one time over a year, when she seemed recovered. Moving forward with her life. But then, something would trigger a relapse.

"We haven't told her about this possible match with the woman Ruby Roth. And of course, it will be bittersweet if we are only partly successful—if we find only one of the children. Either way, Hahsi has just completed the Peacemaker Recovery Program in the Black Hills. No, if this turns out to be yet another phantom match, I won't put her through it. Not again. Her mother and I will bear it. Privately."

Kaileh has never wanted children, and if she did, she'd adopt, keeping up a family tradition of sorts. But a loss such as the man described, and at such a young age, is easy to fold her mind around as life-altering.

"So, other than matching in age and being associated with the same corporation," Onas says, "how does this woman fit the description?"

"I mentioned the connection to Sister O, how we knew her from when the babies were born. When I was assigned the inspections in Denton, I found out Sister O was stationed there, at the Denton Elohi Outreach. We hadn't kept in contact, but it seemed a serendipitous opportunity. If anyone has their pulse on the inner workings of a community, it's the Elohi monastics. So, I arranged a visit.

"You all know this next part, of my arrival, the scene at the dock, the chaos in Denton, and my own captivity by the extremists. It was during that short time, in a locked cell with the monastics, that Sister O told me of the documents obtained by this Brother Q. She said she didn't know what had happened to him, that, on her insistence, he'd taken the documents and fled the Outreach when the mob arrived early that morning. She told me then too of the planned extraction, that very day, of two Atlantics. This is how I learned of the monastics' role in this Path movement. Of course, once she told me this, it was simple to put it together with what I had seen at Kent Narrows. When I described the scene, she suggested that Brother Q, believing the Shepherds were about to arrest him, would have given the documents to Ruby in hopes she would make it to the border.

"After Sister O's frank display of trust, I shared my own ulterior motive for the appointment I'd made with her. I queried her about young men and women in Denton with the last name of Washington. She knew of none. But then I told her more of the story, how the children and father were taken at the border, the father possibly dead, and how old the children would now be. It was then the pieces began to fit together. I could see it in her expression—and I must tell you my heart skipped a beat or two in anticipation of news at last. She told me, 'I do not want to raise your hopes, and perhaps this is too much of a coincidence, but Ruby Roth, the young woman at the docks, lost her father along the border. She has just turned twenty-three, the age your granddaughter would be. I don't know her father's last name, but I know it was different from hers—her grandmother adopted her and gave the child her own last name. But I'm sorry to say, she has no siblings.' So, you see," Halek continues, "if her father was Nicholas Washington, and the baby was renamed Ruby Roth…"

"And you heard no word about a young man bearing the same description?" Toma asks.

Halek shakes his head. "I've tried to not be discouraged by this. I know there are several possibilities: Frederick was killed along with his father, Frederick was given to another family, or this isn't even the right match. But it's too close to ignore. Too close."

Kaileh says, "You're still not one-hundred-percent certain."

"No. And believe me, Officer, I've been disappointed before. I am completely prepared to be chasing the wild turkey once again. But never, never, has anything come this close. She's the exact age, phenotype, location, and backstory—discounting the twin brother." Briento's head bobs in enthusiastic response.

Onas says, a suppressed smile in his voice, "Commander, are you, perhaps, considering an attempt to retrieve Ruby?" Kaileh expects him to glance triumphantly her way, but he doesn't. Her ready expression of dismissal fades.

Briento scans the three people sitting before xem. Xe says, "I think we have no other choice. Besides that, it's the right thing to do. Let's meet back here first thing in the morning. I need to get some particulars aligned before we proceed." Xe stands, and Kaileh sees a flush in xyr cheeks just before she steps to the door.

"Hold up, Officers. I almost forgot to ask you about this."

She turns around and watches Briento plunge xyr hand into Roth's satchelpack.

"This," xe says, "was at the bottom, under some of the woman's clothing." In xyr hand is a black cord from which dangles a silver disk, the center a bezel-set translucent brown stone.

Kaileh's hand flies to her neck and closes on the pendant still suspended there, twin to the one Briento now holds. Onas steps toward Briento and sucks air through his teeth.

At the same moment, they say, "That is Tareq's."

23

Ruby

Answers

"Wake up."

Again, through a dark mist, a voice says, "Ruby, wake up."

Harold Sr., a part of her subconscious declares the voice to belong to. *He's here. He found me. We'll all be together again.*

"Wake up goddamnit." Water pours over her face. She sputters awake.

"Jesus Christ," Bud says. "You shouldn't scare me like that."

The room comes to life. Her reality comes to life. She's still here, still in Bud's family's farmhouse.

Still his captive.

"Get up and clean yourself. Clean this place." He tosses a small paper bag at her. The greasy brown wrapping is warm in her hands. The smell of the fried meat within, the touch of the oily paper, almost makes her swoon from hunger.

A memory comes to her then of a dog she once saw back in Denton. She was walking from the McComb Corp grocery to the Outreach by way of the back alley when she came upon a small crowd gathered in a tight circle. They cheered and booed and cried out as if their lives were at stake. Inside the ring two dogs snarled and ripped and tore at each other. One of the men had a whip. Ruby guessed him to be the owner of one of the dogs, a squarely built piebald, for the man used the lash when the animal attempted to flee the circle. The thin tip bit into the poor creature's hide, turning it to face its four-legged opponent. She'd fled then. Ran from the obvious pain of the animals as much as the brutal emotions from the onlookers. Later that same day, she saw the piebald dog, the apparent loser of not just the match, but his owner's loyalty. The dog cowered, his mostly white coat splotched with mud and dried blood. He stood, back arched, along a fence as three teen boys, free-worker class, their lime-green ID's dangling, poked a stick at him. The animal didn't snarl, didn't run, didn't respond with anything more than a lifted brown eye when Ruby, too frightened herself to intervene, passed.

"I've thought about it," Bud says now as he watches Ruby finish the meat, trying to pace herself, and begins to pull the soiled bedding from the mattress. "I shouldn't a hit ya. I never meant for it to come to that, but ya know ya done pushed me too far. If this gonna work, you're gonna have to do better." He taps out one of his smallcigs and lights it, sits at the table. She sees the brown parcel from before is still there. Still unopened. Still, she supposes, for her.

Ruby saw that piebald dog one more time, several days later, even thinner, even sadder. It stood in the road as the omnibus came into the station. It seemed transfixed by something on the tarmac at its feet, unaware of the danger of its position. The transport's klaxon rang. The dog's ears perked the tiniest bit. Its lowered brown head swiveled toward the heavy vehicle bearing down on it. But it didn't move. It didn't even yelp when the omnibus thumped into it.

Is this her now? Is she just waiting for the end? Has she become that beaten cur?

She yanks at the bottom sheet, the bedding catching on the metal springs.

"Don't ya tear that!"

Ruby crouches down on shaky knees. Her hands trembling, she works the tangled fabric free. And then she sees it. Just beneath the bed where the edge of the quilt hung lies a long, sharp slip of pottery from the dishes. It's been there the whole time. An answer to her prayers.

Ruby tugs the freed sheet toward her, not even noticing the stench of it, and scoops the knife-shaped shard into the bundle. She hobbles to the kitchen, drops the bedding into the big sink, and begins to pump water. Her back to Downs, she wraps the end of the shard with a washcloth and tucks it beneath the sweater and into the cinched belt. Her heart pounds. Her knees shake, and she's uncertain how much of that is simple weakness from lack of food and inactivity and how much is fear. She's that piebald dog about to make a different choice, about to turn on its master.

Ruby pumps the handle, fills the sink, pours in a handful of soap flakes. Then, without a word, she turns and walks to face Downs. This is it. She will leave. One way or the other.

"Whaddya think you're doing?"

"I need the key." She looks down at her chained foot. "I'm leaving," she says, her voice rusty and rough. Her right hand rests under the sweater, her palm around the grip of her makeshift weapon.

He scoffs. "Yeah, don't think so." He sets the smallcig in an ashtray on the table and in a movement so quick she has no time to resist, pulls Ruby onto his lap.

Her blood suddenly pumps so slowly she wonders if she'll freeze up, like the piebald dog. Her hand holding the makeshift pig sticker trembles. But she's close to the soft flesh of his belly. So close.

"My daddy, he used to hit our momma. Did it when she tried to stop him from hitting us kids, or worse." Bud's breath is hot in her ear. It smells of onions and beer and tobacco and old meat. "I swore I wasn't gonna be like him." He raises a hand. Ruby flinches. "Tsk, tsk," he says, and strokes her filthy, matted hair.

"I'm not like him. No sir. Just look around. We never had things this good back there in Denton. You're special, Ruby Roth. I've known that for some time." His hand is in her short choppy hair. Where his fingertips meet her scalp, the skin burns. It's all she can do to not pull away. But something tells her to remain still. To wait for just the right moment. From the corner of her eye, she sees the paper parcel still on the table. An edge has come undone, a swath of lacey white fabric just visible.

"My daddy, he done stuff to us. Mostly to my sister, though. Momma couldn't stop him. Stan couldn't stop him. But I sure enough did. 'Course, it was too late by then. Liza, she was already gone. Already succumbed and took her own life."

That name. That name. Ruby knows it. Her brain flops like a beached fish trying to find water. She needs to know this.

"That's why I had to kill him. Weren't really killing, more like putting down a rabid dog." His voice is distant, husky. But then it perks up. "You ever see one of those? Sad thing, that.

"I never forgot what ya tried to do, though. Liza, she told me how you helped her. Had my eye on ya ever since, Ruby Roth. Knew we'd be a good match. And that weasel Colin Tate, he actually tried to making up for his past a bit by taking my side in the matter of us getting together. Still don't forgive him, 'course. Would kill him too if I could get away with it. It was easy with Daddy."

Liza Downs. It comes to her then. Liza. The last time she saw her was after Ruby hit her tormentor with a rock. To know, even now, years later, why the girl had become the boys' target, how she'd been long before beaten down—and by her own father—breaks what's left of Ruby's heart.

Downs still holds her on his lap, but with his arm just starting to give a little.

"Liza, she was special," Downs says. "She and me, we was true friends. I ain't never forgiven myself for not stepping in sooner." He's looking into the distance. "Liza, she had something special." He runs his hand from Ruby's head to her throat and traces a line down to her collarbone. "Just like you."

Zara's words fill her mind. *You don't believe in your power yet. You should. You must. It will be your savior. Or your undoing.*

You must believe. Its meaning unfolds like a printed cloth at last revealing its pattern. Believe. Not in something or someone else. Not in a god. *Believe in your power,* that's what Zara said. *Your power.*

It will be your savior.

Bud's fingers toy with Ruby's collarbone, light as a songbird's feet, but heavy as bricks. Her breath catches.

Believe.

"That's right. Ya know fate's done brought us together. I think it's time we stop puttin' off the inevitable."

In your power.

His hand slips lower. Ruby flinches away, pivots her makeshift knife.

"Goddamnit, Ruby, I've had enough of ya tempting and yanking it back." His hands grip her face and force it around. Her arms are suddenly free.

Believe.

She stares into his gold-flecked eyes and wonders how they will change when the jagged piece slices into his skin, through the fascia, and into his bowels. There will be fear, pain, the sudden realization that death, slow or fast, is upon him.

Your power. Ruby freezes. Her power. Zara did not mean Ruby's physical strength or skill with a blade. No, of course not. The binding. But Bud, she cannot read him, not just because she fears it, but because he's always been a blank wall. Always.

Still, she tries. One last time. For whether Downs deserves this death or not, she knows she does not deserve to be the one to inflict it.

She closes her eyes. Thinks not of what Bud Downs is intent upon doing to her, but instead of his poor sister. And the little boy Bud was, little Buddy Downs, who couldn't protect his sister Liza.

And suddenly, like she's become jelly, she slips through a crack and into the Shepherd's feelings. For a moment, just a fraction of a second, she teeters on the edge of an abyss. Back is safety. Over the edge is truth. Then, with her own will, she falls. Down, down, down into the writhing hurt that is Bud Downs. There she sees it. She sees his pain; she sees what she needs to do.

When she speaks, her voice is somehow strong and clear. "This here, what you're fixing to do, it's what those boys did to Liza." She holds her makeshift blade poised, still an innocent, unbloodied shard.

Her eyes still closed, she feels his chest hitch, but he keeps working his fingers down her top. "This is what your daddy did to Liza."

He stops fully now. His hand trembling on her chest. Ruby is hit by a flood of emotions, as if a dam inside Downs has broken. Betrayal, failure, hate, love, fear, revenge, regret.

Regret.

Regret.

For a moment, Ruby thinks he'll continue, that she'll have to take his life, or try to.

There's an infinite moment during which Ruby's entire existence, one that ends now and one that goes on, slicks out before her.

But then Bud Downs shifts. She opens her eyes. For one flicker of a moment, he meets her look.

She says, "Your daddy shouldn't have done it." His face contorts like someone's pulling a string from inside, trying to turn him inside out. His eyes widen, the gold now almost all she can see.

He pushes her from his lap, but keeps one hand on her arm with such a fierce grip she fears her bones will crumble. There's a long pause. Should she say more? Should she remain still? She dares a quick look at his face. His eyes seem to have lost the gold flecks, as if something inside of him has burned out.

Then, with one trembling hand, he pulls a key from his pocket, drops it on the table. There's another long minute. Her hopes rise and fall in rapid succession. Her palm feels the bite of her makeshift blade.

At last, he releases her arm, lifts both his hands, and buries his face in his palms.

Through them he says, "Go. Go now."

24
Kaileh

The Pendant

K aileh tugs at the cord, suddenly thick and heavy around her neck. She pulls the pendant she found in her mother's box over her head and lays it beside the one Commander Briento drew from the pack. They are twins. Flat silver discs, bezel-set golden brown stones, a tiny pattern embedded in the icy silver.

Briento's eyes shift between Kaileh and Onas leaning over the desk. "One of you want to go first?"

"Kaileh?" Onas says.

She realizes she is holding her breath, her hand pressing her lips. Slowly, she releases the captive air. "I didn't know about either one until a few days ago. My mother… she had this one. It was in a box of keepsakes. A note with it said that Tareq had made a pair, one for me, one for himself. He, um, he sent the one for me to our mother. The two of us were, well, not exactly communicating at the time." She touches her index fingers to both pendants, one still warm from her skin, the other icy cold.

"Tareq found the stones," Onas says. "We were exploring the islands of the Salish Sea. Kayaking, camping. It's where he proposed…"

She can picture her brother planning a rugged, romantic holiday, walking the pebbled beaches, poking into the sand with a stick. He'd always had his head down—or aimed at the stars—looking for evidence of other worlds, those unseen by most.

"Tareq picked the agates up the same day. A few weeks later, he had polished them into this shape, pounded out the silver, and formed the pendants. From the beginning, he intended one for you, Kaileh." Onas flips both over, exposing the flat disc of the backside. "If you look closely, you'll see, other than the subtle variations of the stones, how they differ."

Kaileh and Briento lean forward, almost bumping heads. A wisp of her hair loosens, falls forward. With a frown, she tucks it behind her ear. On the back of each pendant are the faint lines of an etched image. A snake, she thinks. But then she looks closer. They are indeed serpents. They loop back on themselves, fanged jaws open, biting their own tails.

"The Ouroboros," Briento says.

Kaileh shrugs, then squints again at the pair. "I don't see any difference."

"They face opposite ways. Tareq told me," Onas says, hesitating, "that is how the two of you were. Always busy, always chasing what lay just in front of you. So that you could not see each other."

She considers her earlier thoughts, of her brother's interior conversation with the stars, the stones. She never thought of the two of them as similar. It peels a layer from her, this learning that Tareq thought they had something so essential and intimate in common.

Halek steps between her and Onas and gazes down. "Of course, it's also the symbol, in many cultures, of rebirth and renewal."

Rebirth. Renewal.

Then it hits her. "This." She nudges the pendant Briento pulled from the sack. "This could mean Tareq is alive, could it not? But how did Ruby Roth get it?" She can feel Onas stiffen at her side. She sends him a glance and realizes he is waiting to be accused of abandoning Tareq: alive Tareq, not just his corporeal self. She won't deny the strong pull of that old condemnation still exists, but now a new reality threads around her, and pulls her toward it: Tareq might be alive. She might have another chance. *They* might have another chance.

She pivots toward Halek. "What did the man who was shot at the docks look like?" She knows the man who was injured and gave Ruby the documents was healthy enough to flee the scene with the young boy. He was alive, at least when Halek last saw him.

Halek tells them, describing her brother so precisely she wants to scream, to run back the clock and somehow be there with Halek at the dock, to help Tareq, to have saved him from whatever he has somehow been caught up in.

Halek puts a hand on her arm, and says, "If only I could have found out more from Sister O before the IAN peacekeepers raid freed me. If only she'd not been moved just hours before their arrival. And now…" He swallows hard. "When we spoke, the Sister and I, I never felt she believed Brother Q was anyone other than who he said he was: a monastic sibling of the Elohi Order. But I could be wrong. She was…" He clears his throat. "She is… a woman committed to her beliefs and causes."

Tears burn in Kaileh's eyes. She clamps her molars shut until an electric shock shoots through her mandible. What could it mean? Why has Tareq let them believe he was dead? Why has he let her suffer? Is he playing some cruel game? She narrows her gaze on Briento, then Onas. Maybe Tareq is embedded purposefully, taking his belief in the cause of this Path to the extreme. Her mother's last words come to her, almost forgotten until now: "He needs you; don't forget that." She shakes her head. None of that matters now. What matters is trying to find him. And to do that…

"We need to find Ruby Roth," she says. "She's the link."

"Agreed." Onas's voice is husky. Kaileh avoids meeting the "haven't I been saying that" look she knows must be in his eyes.

"If you're willing, Commander," Onas says, "I'd like to bring one more person into this. Someone who I think can help. Another member of the Path."

Betrayal

Over the long hours waiting for the arrival of yet another citizen of the West who'd seen fit to illegally help Atlantics cross the border, Kaileh gnashes her teeth over who it could be. Her thoughts keep returning to the Lappite Jakob from Shelter Rocks. A man she always suspected was up to something nefarious. It makes sense: Sadie from the Black Brethren in Junaluska is a sympathizer, and the men who escorted Ruby Roth to the border are too. Why not one more?

So, when she, Onas, Halek, and Briento gather in xyr office, and the knock comes, the last person she expects walks through the door. Mateo. Her Mateo.

Many things rush through her mind: he's here by coincidence, or maybe to at last give news of what he's learned from his archivist relative about Onas Steeprock. But Mateo and Onas, who Kaileh believed didn't know each other before they met at Waccamaw, embrace like brothers, she feels the floor give way. If she wasn't already been sitting, she might have crumpled to the ground. But quickly, her pulse leaps, her face flushes, and anger pumps through her veins.

Not him too. Not her friend.

After Onas releases Mateo, Mateo turns to her, a big, sappy, embarrassed grin on his face like he's some kind of puppy who's just wet the floor. It crumples when he sees her own look of granite.

"Oh, Kai, you can punch me, kick me, scream, whatever you want—and I deserve it—but if Tareq's alive…" His words fade, seem to retreat, choked perhaps by Kaileh's flat affect, her rigid body. Her gaze falls to the floor, her eyes burn with the fire of betrayal, and she can barely tolerate being inside her own body, much less looking at this person she thought she knew, this person with whom she's shared so many secrets and to whom she's almost given her heart.

Mateo tries again, his voice smaller now. "I can't tell you how sorry I am, Kai, to not have been able to tell you the truth, really, but right now, I'm incredibly happy to know Tareq is alive. I mean, probably alive. No, he is. I know it."

She tries to speak, but her jaw is locked, her teeth grinding in slow circles. Finally, she looks up. "Not sure why I should believe you—or even trust you in the slightest at this point. I honestly can't even start into that. And well…" She spins one hand in a circle, ignoring the varied expressions on the other's faces. "It's rather not about me right now. So, just go ahead with whatever you all are going to do anyway." Mateo blinks as if struck, his brown eyes too bright. She lifts her chin and turns away.

"Commander Briento," he says, his voice tight, "I know you'll need my resignation after this. Onas let me know that coming in would have long-lasting repercussions, and I'm truly dismayed to have let you down. I hope that if we get Officer Tareq out, or at least learn he's alive, and if these documents he obtained are as useful as they sound, it will have all been worth it."

"Noted," Briento, who's been standing with xyr arms folded, a solemn knit to xyr brows, says. "All right people, there's a lot to be done before we can hope to accomplish this without starting another Border War. I'll get our reconnaissance units on this. It will take some time to learn what we need to before crossing into the ASA. And you all…" xe looks pointedly at each of them. "You all go work out whatever you need to. By the time we are ready to go, I want you all acting as a team. Got it? Good. Now go."

Another Truth

Kaileh makes it to the door first, but then, in the hallway, she realizes she doesn't want to be alone—and not simply because of Briento's orders. Onas and Mateo follow her, shifting around her as if she's a coiled snake rattling its tail. Halek's tall form disappears around the hallway corner. Kaileh, with nothing else to do, decides to follow him. But then, not even knowing she's going to do it, she spins around and faces the two men: one her former friend and bedmate, the other a man she'd just began to consider trusting. Words gum in her mouth, her throat too dry to spew out the proper vocabulary to adequately express the betrayal she's feeling.

The two men stand, their patience a pebble in her shoe.

What other things have they kept from her? And something else: what confidences she's entrusted to them, Mateo in particular, have been betrayed—for this thing, the Path? The Path. Tareq. Her chest deflates. If she could just get him back, she knows she'd forgive him in a heartbeat. For everything. Why then can't she let Mateo and Onas's betrayal go?

She wants to talk about her brother. About the possibility he lives. Of course, this Ruby Roth could have just found the pendant, or been given it by one of the poachers that stole Tareq's body. If he was still alive when they dragged him back across the border, what does it say about Onas? Does it help excuse him? Or further implicate him in losing her brother?

But when she at last opens her mouth something else comes out. "So, Onas, is this Path thing why your birth documents are missing?" She glares at him, his brown eyes, his long braid of walnut brown, but hopes Mateo hears her unheard jab at him: *You knew. You knew.*

Steeprock blinks. "What?"

Mateo's eyes dash between the two. He's standing the same distance from Onas and Kaileh, like they're some kind of tripod. She wonders how long he's straddled this fence, kept a foot planted in two camps.

"My birth documents?" Onas's voice makes it sound as if he's been asked something absurd, something ridiculous.

"Kai found out about your missing birth records." She glares at him, at last understanding why he put off helping her.

Onas, though, looks blank, his expression annoyingly innocent.

Mateo says, "Oh. I didn't know. I mean, I didn't know *you* didn't know."

Kaileh fights an urge to laugh. She can't laugh. She won't. She's still mad at Mateo. Beyond mad.

Onas says, "I know I was adopted, but there should be records. It's not something I ever questioned. I… I… are you sure? I know they had to be reviewed for Warrior Academy… didn't they?" Onas shifts his weight back and forth. "Are you sure?"

The thrill of her accusation slips away. That too, so it seems, has been stolen. Then, it dawns on her. Mateo knows something neither she nor Onas does. She meets his eyes. She opens her mouth.

But Mateo looks side to side and says, "Not here. Let's go."

He leads them to the vacant amphitheater. Kaileh can sense Onas's confusion. This should be interesting, she thinks.

They sit at the center of the grassy expanse, buffeted by ambient sounds from the enclave, the river, the sky, the forest. It all sounds the same, as if nothing has changed. How, she wonders, can the world just go on without a pause?

"You knew," she says to Mateo. "You already knew—you *know*—and you pretended you didn't. Do you even have a relative in the Archives? And when I asked for your help, how could you lie so easily?" She sounds, even to herself, petulant, like a child whining about fairness.

"Oh, Kai. I'm sorry. It wasn't my story to tell, and I honestly believed he knew." He turns to face Onas. "Friend, you were adopted, but—I can't believe your parents never told you."

"Told me what? I know about my birth parents; they died when I was two."

"No, my friend. Well, your adoptive parents might have believed that—and it might even be true. But there's more to it. To put it bluntly, you're not from *here*."

Kaileh rolls her eyes. "What does that mean? Would you just say it?"

"Hold on, Kai, this isn't just about you." It stings, this rebuke, but she holds her tongue.

"Your parents," Mateo says to Onas, "the people who raised you, what did they do as professions?"

"My first mother was, still is, a teacher, and my second was a Warrior. She served along the… Proclamation Line…"

Mateo lets this sit. A wind blows up from the river, sending a chill through Kaileh's light clothes. "You think he's from… from there?"

Still, Mateo waits.

Onas stares back and forth, then his eyes widen. "Oh. Oh. You… are you saying I was…"

"Yes. I believe so. One of your mothers was a border officer during the Great Influx, correct? There's no way to know without asking your mother, but everything I could find, with the help of my uncle in the Archive Department"—he gives Kaileh a look—"points to you having been one of those children sent across the border by relatives or friends or someone. I think your Warrior mother scooped you out of the system. I'm not sure why she, or they, didn't make it official, and maybe they did, and the records were misplaced."

Onas's expression is impossible for Kaileh to read. Does he feel his own kind of betrayal? Or does he feel even more connected to the people he's been trying to help?

"You honestly did not know?" she asks, not even sure why it matters. Is she looking for a way to forgive him or another reason to condemn him? Then she remembers the dataslip he passed to the Shepherd McConnell. That had to mean something. Maybe that's what she should be asking now. As she opens her mouth to fling this new accusation, Steeprock rises.

"No," he says. "No, I did not." And before Kaileh can say a thing, Onas rises and walks down toward the river.

25
Ruby

The Girl

Ruby stumbles down the steps of the farmhouse, not noticing as the pottery shard clatters onto the bare wooden stoop. Her bare feet find the earth at the bottom of the steps. It's cool and dusty and leads her away. She wants to cry but seems to have forgotten how. At her back, she can feel Bud's presence. It looms, it pulses, and she knows at any moment he'll burst through the door and haul her back in.

Move. Move. She must keep moving.

Her feet lift and fall, her soles somewhat toughened from her time on the boards of the farmhouse floor. But even with that, tiny pebbles and bits of twigs bite and snap, and soon, her feet moan in pain.

She listens and listens for the sound of pursuit, every rustle or pop making her spin to face from where she came. At the end of the lane to the farmhouse, Ruby turns left, toward her best guess of what must be the route into town—for it's the route Bud takes when he leaves. But isn't this a mistake, her muddled mind asks? When Bud at last realizes what he's done, surely he will follow. He'll start up his pickup and be on her in moments. She does her best to run, but it only lasts a few paces.

It's late afternoon. There's a chill in the air that punctures her sweater and thin house dress. Sweat plasters it to her body, turning icy despite her labored pace. Her chest heaves with effort. She stumbles every few steps. But soon, the farmhouse is out of sight; the sound of the generator fades into the quiet. Only a few insects rattle in the brush. She smells neither woodsmoke nor any other scents of habitation. She is alone.

Minutes pass. Maybe an hour. Dusk arrives. A few bats sweep from some hiding place, happily diving and darting in the dark, finding prey, finding food, finding their way without effort. It feels like a taunt to Ruby, a reminder of her trespass into a place where she has no right. At intervals, she scans the roadside for late-fall berries, even a tuber or root she might scrape from the soil with her chipped nails. But there is nothing.

She hears something in the distance. An engine, or a motor, she's sure. Her pulse already pounding in her ears, Ruby stops, tries to calm her breath and heart enough to parse out the mechanical sound. But when at last everything quiets, the engine noise is gone. Maybe, she thinks, it was never there.

Then she hears something else. Something more terrifying. It's close. Footsteps. He's simply followed her on foot. It was that easy. Ruby doesn't bother looking for a place to hide. It's pointless.

As she waits in the gray light for him to round the corner, the footsteps suddenly sound wrong. There are too many. One too many, she realizes just as two figures emerge from the growing dark.

As they close on her, one calls out and says something that makes no sense. It comes again, words called from the mouth of a young girl. Ruby knows she's just imagining it.

She laughs, a cackling sound that reminds her of a madwoman she once saw outside the Outreach.

"Ruby? Ruby Roth?" It comes again. This time from the taller figure. A man.

She says nothing. She's gone mad. No point in denying it. No point in running. So she waits. Her body swaying like she's hundreds of miles to the east, back on the boat crossing the Chesapeake Bay.

"It's her, Pops, it's her!"

From the back of Ruby's mind comes a memory of that voice. She's heard it before.

"Looks thatta way, gal, looks thatta way."

They are beside her now, arms slipping under her quaking elbows. Ruby feels struck dumb. Everything's mixed up in her mind. She's heard these voices. She's seen these people somewhere else. But how? It makes no sense… but… but…

"Do I know you?" she finally manages.

"Well now," the man says, "we ain't been officially introduced."

"But we do know you!" the girl, maybe thirteen or fourteen, chirps.

"Been looking for you for some time, Ruby Roth," the man says. "Come now, people are waitin'."

The Cabin

Ruby realizes she doesn't care that her brain refuses to put the pieces together. She senses nothing from the pair. Their words sound warm and genuine and suddenly she's just so relieved to not be alone.

"Come on now," the man says, "let's get you someplace safer."

"Pops, Pops! She *was* there, in that farmhouse. Told you! You shoulda let me peek in the window like I wanted."

"Well now, that might be, but we can't buy nothin' with shoulduvdones, now can we, so let's get goin'."

The pair keep talking, but Ruby's mind seems to want to shut down. Her body, though, like some kind of automated thing, keeps going. They walk three astride, the man with his arm gently around Ruby's waist. At first, she recoils from the touch, but when she stumbles and almost goes down, she accepts the support. When the girl, too, puts her skinny arm around Ruby. It feels both frail as a dry reed and as comforting as a warm blanket.

They limp her a little farther down the road before turning off it. Ruby's certain at least one time she hears an engine from behind them, but soon they're traipsing up a leaf-covered slope, their footfalls crunching loudly. Ruby can no longer feel the bottoms of her feet, and even though part of her knows she'll later pay, for now, she's grateful.

There's little talk, but partway up the hill, the man says, "This way ain't the easiest, but it's the safest."

Ruby nods, an invisible gesture in the dark. The man has a small handtorch, but mostly, he leaves it off. They stop here and there to listen. At one pause, she hears it, the mechanical sound of a car engine or some kind of motor. The man and girl grow rigid.

"Hunker down."

Ruby whispers, "Is it him? Is he coming?"

"Hush now," the man hisses back. They listen. Ruby's body aches. Some of the numbness threatens to leave her feet. The motor sound comes near, but soon fades. "That was one of them overhead surveillers."

Most of what he's saying is lost on Ruby, but she knows Bud is not yet right behind them. It eases some of her cramping muscles and tired heart. Still, the *not yet* echoes in Ruby's brain. *Not yet. Not yet. A persistent man.* She shudders. Something, maybe just her own terror telling her lies, promises her she will see him again.

They continue. Time blurs. Maybe she even sleeps as they guide her along. The landscape undulates, up and down, down and up. Over small hills and through dry gulches. The brush scrapes at them, the path narrow, more of an animal trail than one made for humans.

"We're almost there," the girl whispers. "You doing great, Ruby."

Ruby smiles in an unseen response.

They're tracing a zigzagging route down a hill when Ruby sees the flicker of warm yellow light through the branches. Her feet scrape to a halt.

"It's all right, that's where we're headin'. Come on now. Folks won't believe we found you."

"Hello inside!" the man calls out as they near a small structure squatting low to the ground. The door opens. A tall figure steps out. A smaller shape darts past him and into the dark. Toward them. Coming fast. Ruby flinches.

"Roobs!"

Time stops. She must have died, she thinks. This is impossible. Not here. Not in the borderlands.

But then the boy is upon her. His arms fling around her. His body plows into her and, were it not for the man, and even the slender grip of his daughter, Ruby would have fallen.

It's his scent that makes her believe. She lowers her head to his hair and breathes in the precious smell she thought she'd never again encounter. HJ. Little Harold.

After a minute, he begins to squirm. "Roobs," his muffled voice comes. "I can't breathe!"

"How?" she says. "How?" If she had the strength she'd shake him until the answer fell into her ears.

"Let's get you inside," says the tall figure in the doorway. "There's a lot to explain, but first things first. Water and rest, I believe, are in order." His arm is in a sling from Bud Downs's bullet piercing his upper chest, but Brother Q stands there, alive, well, and here. In a trance, she follows him into the golden light of the cabin.

Reunion

Ruby wakes in a nest of blankets. They're not clean, not exactly, but they smell nothing of the farmhouse. She buries her nose in them and pulls in a deep breath. It's the scent that makes her believe: she's free, of Downs at least. Someone wiggles beside her. She turns over, holding in a gasp at the pain in her head, the aching of her entire body, and the fire burning on the soles of her feet. Something soft has been wrapped around them and she catches the familiar smell of Sister O's tea tree oil.

"You're awake!" HJ says, elbowing up from where he was curled on top of the blankets at her side. Without moving his head from near her, he yells, "She's awake! Ruby's awake!"

"I am now, buddy, that's for sure." She grins, feeling the corners of her mouth crack a little.

Daylight streams through a single window, filling the small room with enough light to take in the details. Bedding lies in piles and corners, making Ruby wonder... "Your dad?"

HJ's face crumples. It's an answer.

A voice says, "How do you feel?"

She pushes up and rubs her eyes. It really is Brother Q. As impossible as it all seemed. It really is true.

"Be... better." Her voice is rough and dry. A portable AquaClenz is suddenly in her hands.

"Roobs, you need to drink more." She lifts the bottle and pulls a long swallow. It's cold and tastes faintly of algae. As HJ takes it from her, empty now, she links her hand in his and meets his brown eyes. She tries to see the answer to the question she most wants to ask: what happened to Harold Sr.?

HJ blinks. His eyes brim sudden and fierce. Ruby squeezes his hand. He gives her a nod that's packed with wisdom and a maturity he shouldn't have to bear. She won't ask more now. There's no need.

"Speaking of water, my young friend," Brother Q says, his voice husky, "would you assist the others in the morning forage? Take the other water bottles to the spring; remember the most important thing?"

"'To never run low on water.' I'm on it, Brother Q," HJ says as he whisks up two other bottles sitting nearby and gallops out the door.

"Chew on this," Brother Q says, and hands her a strip of jerky. The sight of it almost makes her weep, thinking of Betsey and the Brethren and of all those who have helped her along the way. She focusses on the rich flavor of the meat and tries to not think about Harold Sr.—or any of the others she's left behind.

After a few bites, she says, "I'm so confused. How did you find me? How did you get here? It's just so, so…"

Brother Q laughs. "You are not wrong, my friend. It's Harold Jr. that you have, for the most part, to thank. It is a long story, and one I am happy to tell, but we must prepare to move. Our time is running out."

Ruby stares at Brother Q, soaking in the impossibility of it all. His head is bald, or nearly so. Shaved, Ruby sees from a little red nick on one side. He doesn't wear a headscarf, nor does he bear any other signs of being a monastic. A knobby, pale scar sits just above his right temple. It's old and well healed, but it still makes Ruby flinch. She wonders, had she not heard his voice, would she have recognized him?

"Ruby, I would rather not query you now, before you have had a time to rest, but the packet I gave you, is it still in your possession?" His voice is strained and it seems as though he's rehearsed the question, rehearsed his reaction to bad news.

"No, Brother." She sees his slow exhale and realizes he misunderstands. "No, Brother, it's—" she begins, but then the door opens and the young girl and her father step in. After sleep and some food, Ruby's mind is just beginning to sort the jumble of her memories. As the morning light hits the man and girl, it comes to Ruby how she knows them. She last saw them in the back of a lorry being hauled away from the destroyed shantytown at Denton. The impossibility of all of this, of all of them being here together, so far from Denton, takes her breath away.

"Mornin'," the man says. "Heard our newest member was awake." He and the girl grin with nearly identical smiles. Ruby returns them, but holds her lips closed, aware, suddenly of her missing tooth.

"Indeed," Brother Q answers. "Any signs of surveillers or trackers, Tyrell?" Brother Q asks.

"None. All's peaceful."

Mary gives him a funny look. "But Pops…"

He scrubs a hand through his daughter's greasy light brown hair. "Mary here thought she heard commotion down on Blue Gulch Road, but I didn't hear a thing."

"But—"

"Now Mary, let's let Miss Ruby get her strength back. Border's not far away." His daughter nods, runs to one of the bed pallets, and grabs something. At first Ruby thinks it's a small blanket or a wrap, but it's a thing she'd almost forgotten: the sock-monkey doll, looking about as loved and worn out as anything. It makes her think again of Harold Sr., how he put so much value on the raggedy old thing. Still, she's happy it's here. Happy, in a way, it's back with HJ too.

Mary. Mary and Tyrell. Ruby practices the names in her head. She realizes she never wondered what HJ's girl's, as Ruby's always thought of her, real name was.

Mary pivots and walks out, her father behind her. How, Ruby wonders? How did they all come together?

Brother Q says, "Let us hope that Tyrell's hearing is truly the more accurate. Ruby, apologies again, but the documents?"

She exhales, relieved to be able to explain even in the presence of others. "They are across the border already. I… Well… it's a long story, but a Warrior took them from me. There were two of them, a man and a woman. One was shot. By Bud, by Downs. But I know, I think, anyway, they made it back across. With the documents." It feels like a long speech. Her voice rusty and her mind even more so.

Then something dawns on her. "Oh, Brother Q, I lost your pendant! I mean, I didn't lose lose it, it was in my bag. They took it… I'm so sorry."

Brother Q's expression shifts back and forth between relief and something else, like a question he cannot think of is balancing on the tip of his mind. "That is wonderful news. About the documents. And the pendant, it is, it was, only an impulse to give it to you. But—"

There's a pause. Brother Q's face shifts through several expressions, settling on something that, to Ruby, looks like confusion. "Ruby, can you describe the Warrior officers that met you and took the documents?" There's something in his voice that catches Ruby's deeper attention, like he's searching for a clue to a mystery as yet undefined.

A sudden sound outside sends Ruby startling back onto her bedding. No door. There's no back door. There's no way to escape. These things her brain tells her in a flash, though she knows here she is safe.

HJ steps into the cabin, Tyrell and Mary at his heels, erasing their conversation as if it never began.

The Trek

A short time later, Ruby stands with Brother Q in the small clearing before the cabin. To one side, a dry creek carves through the landscape. Just up the gully, a verdant green pocket hints at a spring, the source of their water, she's sure.

"What is this place, Brother Q?" she asks as he guides her to a low bench along the front of the building to sit. She leans her back against the cabin wall and sighs, trying not to think of the long hike ahead of them. "Here"—he sweeps his arm in an arc—"is where I became Q. It saved me once before, or the women who brought me here did."

Something in the way he says "became Q" makes Ruby want to ask more, but she holds her tongue. It feels like the kind of thing that he'll tell her when, and if, he's ready.

Inside, HJ helps Tyrell and Mary pack. The two young people chatter in rapid succession, like they're longtime friends. "Come on, Mary, hurry it up," and, "You just mind your own business little boy," and, "I can't believe we found her," and, "Actually, it was me an' Pops what found her," and, "Yeah, but I'm the one told everyone she was nearby."

Brother Q follows Ruby's sideways gaze. "They have been like that since we all set out together. That's another story. But to your question about this place…" He touches the scar on his forehead. "This happened to me over a year ago. I still don't remember how. Even my real name is something that hesitates just at the edge of my mind's vision. But here is where I awoke. I was tended to by two women. It was they who found me and brought me here. Eventually, when I was stronger, it was they who introduced me to the Path. I had a hope they would still be here… but they are gone."

Into the silence of the hollow where the cabin sits comes a sound that doesn't fit. A whirring of mechanical parts. A motor. She's sure.

"Brother Q?"

"I hear it too. A surveiller. Come on."

Inside the cabin doorway, Brother Q stands beside Ruby. Behind them, HJ, Tyrell, and Mary stop moving.

The whirring sound fills the sky. Ruby's breath stops. They wait. She's heard of the tiny craft used by the Shepherds to hunt for escapees. But she's never seen one. It's then that she realizes two things. Here, near the border, there will be more vigilance. Every step closer to freedom means a step closer to danger. But another thing bothers her even more. Bud Downs. How long will his regret over taking her captive overrule his regret for letting her go? She's sure it can't last long. If nothing else, certainly he'll start to worry someone else will capture her. Another Shepherd. A fellow officer to whom she might tell the story. No, he'll want to get her first.

The sound of whirling blades fades. They wait, like rabbits fearing a prowling fox. At last, Brother Q steps out of the cabin. "All clear."

They spend the rest of the day organizing for what Brother Q says will be a hard march to reach the border. He prepares them for the possibility of surveillers they cannot avoid. "But, know there is a chance some of these could be from the West. There, the teknology is even more advanced than what the ASA is able to acquire. It is possible this will be to our benefit. It is our goal to be captured, so to speak, by Warriors."

"But what about people from the Path?" Ruby says. "I thought it would be those that meet us."

Brother Q nods. "Ideally, it would have. But our little expedition is not scheduled. There will be no one from the Path to meet us." The cabin, even smaller with all members of the group present, is quiet. "But, fear not. I will be able to explain. Ruby, if the documents indeed reached the right hands, it should not be too long before our case is justified. And either way, we are better off captured by the West than risking arrest here."

Better. Better. Ruby remembers thinking the same thing. Was it only weeks ago, or days? She suddenly realizes she doesn't know what day it is. And at this moment it seems pointless to ask.

Sometime after the sun begins its arc toward the west, Ruby feels as ready as she can be. Tyrell has given her a pair of his own shoes. Normally they would be too large, but with the bandages rewrapped and doused with drops of tea tree oil from Brother Q's supplies, they fit well enough. She touches the makeshift sheath clipped to her hip. A knife, not as good as her old one, lent by Brother Q, rides there. Just the weight of it makes her relax a notch.

"In an hour's time, we will begin our push," Brother Q says. "Now, let us all eat well—and pray it's our last meal ever this side of the border."

Pray. Someday, Ruby thinks, I want to know what that really means.

They pass supplies back and forth and chew and swallow and do it all again. There's a businesslike sound to their meal. The empty space where Harold Sr. should be occupies much of the small room. She both doesn't want to think about it and feels bad when she doesn't. Still, she has to know. "Is there time now to tell me how it is we are all here like this?" she asks between mouthfuls.

"I believe so," Brother Q answers.

"It was Brother Q," HJ says around a wad of dried bread and apple in his mouth. "He got me away from the docks while that darned Bud and his brother were shooting at you, Roobs. I didn't want to leave, but he told me we had to go find..." His voice catches. He sits straighter and opens his mouth to try again. Ruby's heart aches for the boy. He cuffs tears from his eyes, his open lips wordless.

Brother Q says, "Shall I continue the story?" HJ nods and stares at the dried apple slice, bitten halfway through, as if he doesn't know what to make of it.

So, Brother Q tells of his and HJ's escape from the dock, thanks to the distraction of the man in the black car, then their return to Denton, of finding the town in chaos. There were riots, fires, and no sign of the Sisters or Harold Sr.

"And the IAN inspector who helped us at the docks was nowhere to be found. I don't know how he chose, or even knew, to help us when he did. Before, I had hoped that after I delivered you and HJ to the Brethren, that I could intercept him at the north docks. It was a risk, yes, but with the Sisters taken and the Outreach in danger, it was the only thing I could attempt. And then, after being wounded, I was certain the Shepherds would capture me with the documents. That is why I gave them to you."

Clouds part in Ruby's mind, revealing her role in a grave error. The man in the black car. It was the same man, the one the monastics had planned to meet with the next day. Halek. Sister O's old friend.

"I shouldn't have taken the packet!" Ruby says, picturing herself on the boat speeding away and the inspector standing there empty-handed.

"No, it was the right thing. In the end. Not only could I not locate him—without risking capture—but I fear he was taken hostage along with others from the West, the good Sisters included."

"So, wait," Ruby says, "Bud Downs never had HJ or… his father in custody?" She thinks back to the banks of the York River and Downs's threats—his lies—called over the water.

"No. Or at least not at first." He looks at HJ who gives a small nod. "The Shepherds found Harold at some point. They moved him to the prison camp where they'd taken the adrift. We found him somewhat by accident."

The prison camp. So it was real. She looks at Tyrell and Mary and sees them again in the back of the lorry. Their expressions now are the kind of blank that comes when there's too much hurt to remember.

It's then that Ruby realizes something that unsettles her: she feels no tug of the binding. It's not that she's trying to fight it, it just isn't there.

Brother Q's eyes fill with sympathy as his gaze lingers on Tyrell and Mary. "It was a horrific place on the far side of Denton. A place that should never exist. I do not like to think of what has happened to most of those poor people. But know this: the documents tell of the ASA's plans, all acts of war. Change will come. It won't be easy. But it's coming."

They all jump when outside a raven croaks a sudden loud call of protest, or at least so it sounds. She's not heard many of the big birds, a thing that someday she'll wonder at. But for now, the sound raises the hair on the back of her neck. It feels portentous. She tries to pick out a feeling to bind with some sense of what is happening. But there's nothing *beyond* her own worries and the known fears hovering with all of them. She doesn't have time to think about it though, for Mary takes over the story.

"We was in that camp. Pops and me. Been there since they took us from the shantytown. Every day, more folks got sorted. They told us we were being sent off to better jobs, places with real houses and such, but I ain't so sure. Pops, tell Ruby how you helped Brother Q get us all out of the camp and away."

Tyrell blushes. "Nah. It weren't nothing."

"Without your help, Tyrell," Brother Q says, "I fear I would not have succeeded." He swallows.

"It was so scary, Roobs," HJ says.

"Yes. That it was. I bribed a worker at the Shepherd station for news of Harold. Then HJ and I hid at an abandoned house near the camp. By then, I was able to remove some supplies and money from the wreckage of the burned Outreach. Denton, you see, was still in great disorder. I changed my look as much as possible—removing the monastic garb provided a surprising transformation—and bribed my way into the camp, saying I was a relative of one of the detained."

"I recognized Harry's dad right away," Mary says in a small voice. "I seen him with Harry bunches of times, when I was living in the shantytown. I told Pops we had to help him, didn't I, Pops?"

"Yup. True enough," Tyrell says. He's looking at his feet, stretched out before him on the quilts of his bed pallet. Ruby wonders if he's regretting the loss of his spare shoes to her feet.

"And we tried. We really did, Harry."

"I know you did. I know." HJ lifts his chin. "Brother Q found Daddy too. But it… But it was… too late. But he gave him some medicine, didn't you, Brother Q?" HJ's voice quivers, but he speaks with a strength that hurts Ruby's heart.

"I did. I did that. And then Mary found me with him and saw right through, or around, my clever disguise."

"I thought," HJ says, "for a while, Brother Q wasn't coming back. I was fixing to go looking for him and my dad when…"

"I arrived to where HJ was still hiding with Tyrell and Mary. We left the camp through the same small tear in the fencing. I still don't know how it was that easy, but it was."

As Ruby pictures the escape, the heartbreaking impossibility of helping Harold Sr. leave with them, she happens to glance at Tyrell. There's something in the way his eyes dart to the floor that raises an alarm in Ruby. Before she can try to parse it out, Brother Q continues.

"From there our luck held. We made our way to the rail yards south of Washington and found a freight train heading away. It took days, with many changes and some close calls, but at last we made it here. I remembered this place, you see. But it was HJ who insisted we would find you here also."

"I dreamed it!" HJ pipes. His dreams. HJ and his dreams. How had she forgotten about them? The young girl. The bad men. And now finding her. She stares at this boy she's known since birth. He's a miracle, she thinks.

Now, all they need is one more.

26
Kaileh

The Plan

It's all Kaileh can do to not march into the commander's office and tell xem she's heading east on her own. It's been three days since they began gathering the reconnaissance and intel needed for planning the mission. Kaileh stews and fumes, frets and hopes, despairs and elates. Every second wasted is another kilometer Ruby Roth could be slipping from their grasp. Another kilometer stealing the truth away. Her heart is ready to explode from the possibility that her brother lives. The possibility of another chance—after she gives him a piece of her mind for putting her through this, that is.

Over the days of waiting, her own skills rarely needed, she runs the trails, researches everything she can on the Atlantic States in the enclave's library, and spends what, for her, is an inordinate amount of time on her keitai and the library's noto.

She sees Onas and Mateo often, usually from a distance, walking together or heads bent in conversation in some secluded corner. Her curiosity almost pulls her to them; answers would bring some sense of satisfaction, of closure. But her feet never respond to the orders from her brain.

At last, they reconvene in one of the small sortie rooms. A large clear-board has been set up and displays tiled boards planning the mission. She steps to the seat farthest from Mateo, but hesitates, then moves to sit across from him and settles beside Halek, who gives her a smile so filled with hope Kaileh cannot help but return it. She has to keep reminding herself of the decades-long loss he's suffered and the hope he must feel at its possible end.

"Ah, my friends," Commander Briento says. "Thank you for your patience. It's been critical we prepare properly for this mission. Now, let us go over the facts." Kaileh hears joy in xyr tone and her heart lifts. Briento taps xyr keitai, and one of the tiled boards expands to fill the clear-board. Xe reads aloud:

"What We Know:

"One: Brother Q, a man matching Tareq's description, gave Ruby Roth the documents and presumably also the pendant once belonging to Tareq.

"Two: The Elohi Monastic headquarters in the West has no record of a Brother Q, other than one, a man in his seventies, serving at an archival library near Mount Takoma Sacred Site Park.

"Three: Officer Bud Downs, suspected of acting alone at the border, has not returned to Denton but has been reassigned to Morgantown, North Carolina, not far from the borderlands.

"Four: There is no record of him having captured or turned over the escaped Denton citizen, Ruby Roth.

"All good?" Xe looks at the faces following along.

Kaileh nods, her fingers stuttering on the table before her. There's a hush of excitement in the room. Ruby Roth is not back in Denton. Close. She could still be close.

Xe taps again and the bullet points fade, the screen animates, a large map fills the screen, and the key players—Downs, Roth, Brother Q, Halek, Onas, and Kaileh—sparkle in as colored dots. It plays twice through slowly, each player moving along known or projected paths, beginning in the summer when Halek was in Denton and ending in real time. Kaileh leans forward; the blue dot designating the Shepherd Downs glimmers not far from the border.

Briento highlights the marker for the Shepherd, walks forward, and taps it with xyr finger. "Right here is where we're focused. We learned Downs's parents left him a small farmhouse here, about twenty kilometers east of the border."

"Ah," Mateo says. "Almost inside the borderlands. Maybe this is where he took her. And it's close enough for a retrieval sortie, correct?"

She scans the map. The last known location of Brother Q is still the Kent Narrows dock. Nothing for months. Her shoulders settle, her body feeling suddenly drained of energy.

"What of my brother? Is this really all we know? No one's seen him since… since June?"

Mateo gives her a side look. "Commander?"

"We're working on that, Officer Kaileh." Xyr tone shushes her, but she sends Mateo a glare.

Beside her, though, Halek practically vibrates. He sits at the edge of his seat, hands flat on the padded chair, as if ready to spring up, run out the door, and retrieve his possible grandchild.

Briento says, "A retrieval sortie. Precisely. I'm waiting for satellite information on the house. We may even be able to tell if Ruby, or at the minimum, if someone else is there. We have satellite view of a vehicle that comes and goes. It matches the one registered to Bud Downs."

Mateo's keitai pings. He glances at it. Smiles.

"Mateo?" Commander Briento says.

"The commander"—Mateo glances at Kaileh—"encouraged me to reach out to a source. I've just heard back. Kai, to get right to it, we may, just may, have some unverified sightings of a man matching this Brother Q's description."

Her heart is suddenly in her throat and she can't stop the hot burn filling her eyes.

"The man matching Tareq's description is, or was, on the move and working his way east—which we have to assume is exactly what Tareq would do faced with what happened in Denton. This man, though, is reportedly traveling with a small group. Which I suppose is not surprising, right?"

"Mateo, please, just tell us," Kaileh says, her voice blasting into the room.

"Yup. All right. So, our sources say he's traveling with two children and another adult. Whether by intent or truth, they appear adrift. Blending in, is what I think they're trying to do."

Kaileh frowns, not wanting her hopes to rise too high. "That could be anyone."

"Right you are," Mateo says. "But my source said the sighting came from someone who once met Brother Q. I know, I know, it's not granite, but it's something."

"All right, where?" Briento says. "And"—xe takes a deep breath—"as much as I want to, I'm not going to ask about these sources, got it?"

Mateo and Onas nod with vigor.

Mateo's keitai draws his attention again. He scrolls through what Kaileh guesses to be a script. "Listen to this: the last sighting came from a rail yard outside of Washington, on the south side. They appeared to be trying to board a freight train."

"Officer Kaileh, work with Mateo," Briento says. "Get on the maps and datafiles and find out what we have on this rail yard. Coordinate the date and time of the sighting with that of trains leaving, particularly those heading either south or east. Find their connections, and so on."

An hour later, they've narrowed it to three possibilities. One terminal line is farther south, closer to the Port of Tomochichi, one is near Lynchburg, Virginia, and the last is at Charlotte, North Carolina, not that far from Morgantown. Not that far from where the Downs farmhouse lies.

Back in the sortie room, Briento says, "All right, you all know him better than I do, assuming this is our man." Xe clicks xyr pen rapidly. "Where would he head once he made it to this point?" Xe taps Morgantown on the clear-board.

There is a short pause, and Kaileh tries to picture where he might cross the border. But Onas doesn't hesitate. "Here," he says, pointing to a location not far from where they tried to bring Ruby across. "I, uh… This is where we would… bring travelers over…"

"I see," Briento says, xyr eyebrows raised. "All right," xe says. "All right."

The commander is on xyr keitai moments later. "Right, yes. That's in addition to the surveillance on the Downs farmstead… Yes. Look for small and large camps of unhomed, or any other remote locations where a small group of people could hold camp. Water, shelter, that sort of thing, will likely be nearby."

Briento hangs up. "It will take another hour or two until the next satellite pass. Don't look at me like that, Officer Kaileh, we're lucky it won't be another twelve." Xyr voice is stern, but not unkind.

"But, Commander—"

"Officer." Briento says it as a statement. A reminder. Kaileh clamps her lips tight.

"Let's see, it's midday now. While we wait, why don't you three younger people go and prepare for a quick trip east once darkness nears."

A few hours; it feels like an eternity to Kaileh, an impossible length of time, as if all the potential, all the hope and happiness of finding her brother alive, is being dangled just out of reach.

27
Ruby

The Last Stretch

The ragtag group marches into the night. Ruby trusts Brother Q, as her own senses seem to turn her in circles. They follow no real pathway, at least as far as Ruby can tell, Brother Q in the lead, her next, with HJ, Mary, and Tyrell bringing up the rear. Often the brush is thick, clutching at them from both sides even as they move in single file. Soon, she grows accustomed to the swipe and snap of brambles and branches. Her knees lift. Her numbing feet slap the ground. Over and over. Nothing matters now except continued forward movement.

It's a dark night. Even starlight seems stingy. She remembers the night spent fleeing with Rafe and Betsey and Booboo. Of how the moon came out to help them. Of the mysterious mist that enveloped them on the deep waters of the York River. It feels so long ago.

Her body tires all too quickly, worn and frail from her captivity. As the hours go on, she stumbles with increasing frequency, feeling as if she's an elder, not a woman who should be at her peak. Behind her the young people, and even Tyrell, seem strong and fit by comparison. She feels a kind of shame for her weakness, despite the unspoken logic of it.

"Not much farther," Brother Q says, helping her up. "Not much farther," he repeats, but she wonders if it's just to cheer them on. Sometimes she's sure she recognizes something in the landscape from her first attempt at crossing the border. Is that the tree where Onas had leaned? Is his blood there on the dusty path? Is that where the woman dragged Ruby's satchel away as Downs fired his first shots?

And Bud Downs. Where is he now?

Occasionally, they hear sounds other than their own plodding steps and chuffing breath. They pause. They listen. Then they walk on.

Soon, the path that is no path grows steeper. Surely this is a good sign, she thinks, for isn't the actual Proclamation Line along the mountain's crest?

Her own breath coming in gasps, they pause for a short rest, for sips of water, for the adjustment of the chaffing straps from their packs.

"Oh no," says Mary from behind. "I hear something."

"I don't. I swear, my hearing's going," Tyrell says.

Ruby tips her head each way, trying to pick up what the girl has heard, certain it will just be another false alarm. Certain in the way one is when they know they're fooling themselves. Her skin prickles. Suddenly, Ruby's sure she smells the smoke from a smallcig. He can't be that close, can he? And certainly, he wouldn't give himself away by smoking. Or would he? Her heart thuds loud, rattling her head with each beat.

"Move. Move out, now," Brother Q says.

They do. Her muscles scream. A moment later, they all hear it. It's not the sound of one though, it's the sound of many. Suddenly, whirring from above, a surveiller seems to come from nowhere. It hovers above, its prey sighted. It lights them up, revealing the open glade where they've been caught. There's no cover, no place to hide, nothing but to keep moving forward.

"There!" Brother Q calls. "Just ahead. I can see the marker for the border." His voice fights the hum of the surveiller.

Ruby blinks and squints in the intense brilliance. She almost goes down, mistaking a shadow at her feet for what is actually a small boulder. Then, at the rear of their group, Tyrell calls out. "Oomph! Oh, my leg, I think I've broken my leg!"

"Pops! Get up, you gotta get up!"

Ruby falters. HJ stumbles into her. They grip each other, staying upright. Yards behind them, Tyrell moans, Mary pleads. "Pops, come on! We gotta go."

Ahead, Brother Q pivots, trots back. "Keep going," he says to HJ and Ruby. "I will go."

She does as he says, but something in her heart sinks. She wants to tell him no, to not go back, for suddenly, with a clarity whose source she does not know, Ruby knows it's a trap.

28
Kaileh

The Sortie

Kaileh, Onas, and Mateo move through the night, marching, pushing, toward the Proclamation Line. It's all Kaileh can do to hold back the muscles of her legs from breaking into a sprint. Her mind thinks of nothing but the last report from the satellite pass. It revealed not just a small cabin, recently inhabited and only twelve kilometers from the border, but something else: an apparent scouting force of Shepherds traversing the same area. They set out with orders to avoid confrontation with the Shepherds, if at all possible.

A bone in the fish, she thinks as she moves along the path; there's always something you have to chew carefully around rather than just getting the job done.

They move swiftly, their nightseers showing the way. Kaileh clutches her keitai, monitoring the screen every few strides. As the only one still legitimately in the Warrior service, she is tasked with receiving any updates. She's in charge, but somehow it feels less important than she expected.

Ahead and above them fly all the surveillers Briento could muster in the short time allowed. They sweep the sky, night birds of prey, sharing their discoveries on her screen. In one tiled window she sees themselves, three red dots moving toward the gold line of the border. And beyond that, making what will be called, if need be, an accidental crossing of the Proclamation Line, fly several of the reconnaissance aircraft.

From the east, two other groups of red dots move toward the border, one group, presumably the Shepherds, closing in on the other smaller group. Red specks, anonymous, but Kaileh is certain one is her brother.

The team is close now. The border itself only a kilometer away. Briento's earlier command sits heavy in her gut. "Do not engage the Shepherds. Do not. Get our quarry *if you can*, but do not start a war." She tells herself she won't. *She* won't be the one to start it.

They're half a kilometer away when her screen lights up. Just meters from the border, on the eastern side, something big is happening.

"Faster," she shouts. She can't make out just what's going on, not while keeping her pace, but her instincts scream of disaster.

Mateo and Onas, even with his still-healing arm, pull ahead of her. She scowls, breathes through her mouth, and pushes harder, ignoring her screen, trusting her instincts, and catches up.

A few seconds later, they see a flood of light. A surveiller, theirs, it must be, illuminating the ground below. She should look at her screen, study the situation, figure out the best strategy, but instead, she begins to pass the men. Onas or Mateo makes a growling sound and adds speed. They reach the perimeter of the light, too bright, blinding. She yanks off her nightseers and squints to take in the scene before her.

A strange, lurching silhouette moves toward her. Her eyes adjust. It's not a person, it's two, limping toward them. Neither are her brother. Where is he? Then she sees a tall figure moving away. Toward a shape on the ground, another standing above it, apparently pulling on an arm of the downed figure.

Then she sees the Shepherds. They step from the trees, three, no four, five of them, zap-crooks drawn. One with a handgun held, but not yet raised.

The light from above dances and shifts. The shadows moving as if they too are alive. Everything slows. Everything blurs. Everything sharpens. The tall figure is one moment foreign, the next her brother, she's almost certain. It's nothing specific, more as if myriad intangible traits materialize in the figure. A shape. A way of moving. An essence of some kind.

"Tareq?" she screams. He doesn't turn. He's trying to pull the smallest figure from the one on the ground. Gesturing, yelling his own commands. Her voice drowned in the melee.

Onas adds his voice. "Tareq! Run. Please. Please. Please!"

She, Mateo, and Onas reach the two figures moving toward them. One is the woman Ruby Roth, but greatly changed. She looks as if she's lost a fight. The other is a young boy.

Mateo waves them past. "Keep going!" They nod.

"Tareq?" she screams as they run. "Tareq."

Ahead, the five Shepherds are closing in on the three other figures. Then the small figure moves away from the tall man, hesitates, and then runs toward them. The tall man she's sure is Tareq still does not look back. He keeps his attention on the Shepherds, talking, telling them something she can't hear, but seemingly giving the small figure time to flee.

"Tareq!" she yells again. Then, ignoring the voice of Commander Briento in her head, she plants her feet to run to her brother. The small figure, a young girl, runs past them sobbing. The other refugees call, "Come on, Mary, you can do it!"

They call for Tareq. The Shepherds close in.

The Warriors are unarmed. *Do not start a war*, rings in her ears. But she cannot, will not, leave behind the thing she came for. Beside her stand Mateo and Onas. They move closer. They're only twenty meters away. The tall man is still pleading with the Shepherds. The man on the ground whimpers and begs for something.

"Let him go!" Kaileh calls, not bothering to specify which "him" she means.

"One is a citizen of the West," Onas yells. "Let him go."

"You're out of your jurisdiction, Warriors," the armed Shepherd says with a mocking laugh, his weapon lifting.

"Tareq!" she pleads. "Please, Tareq. Brother." Her voice wavers. She lets her emotions bleed into the night.

Then the tall figure turns. There! His profile, that nose she used to make fun of when they were little, calling him pharaoh-face, not even knowing pharaohs were kings.

She knows it. It's him. It's him. Beside her, a sob escapes Onas. He's seen it too.

Then several things happen at once. The Shepherd clicks off the gun's safety and takes aim. Fingers grip her arm, Mateo trying to pull her back, his other hand on Onas. "We can't. We can't," he hisses. And suddenly, someone else is at Kaileh's side: the woman, Ruby Roth, with something in her hand.

The armed Shepherd shifts his aim to Tareq and the man on the ground. "You are both under arrest for smuggling stolen property out of the sovereign nation of the Atlantic States of America. Get down! Now!"

The man who is already down whimpers and cries. "You promised me. You promised if I did this, me and my girl'd be let go! Mary! Oh, Mary."

Another Shepherd extends his zap-crook. The man screams. Behind her, Kaileh hears a faint wail. Mary, she supposes.

Then, beside her, almost forgotten until now, Ruby Roth is raising her arm. It's then that Kaileh sees the knife. Small and silver and shimmering in the illumination from above. The fugitive throws. The blade flies fast. Faster than Kaileh would have thought such a scrawny, beat-up body could muster. And for a moment, just one beautiful moment, she thinks it will find its target. But it skims just past the upper arm of the Shepherd holding the gun and falls with a too-loud thunk to the ground.

He spins his aim toward them, fury twisting his face. Tareq looks back, shakes his head at them, at her, she's certain. *Go back*, he mouths. *Go back*. And then, he lowers himself to the ground.

"No no no!" Kaileh's and Onas's and Ruby's pleas combine as Mateo pulls them back. She tries to shake him off. Hating him more than ever before.

"We can't do this. Not now," Mateo says. "We'll never win. Not this time. Come. We have to go. It's the only way. For now."

Mateo pulls her backwards toward the Proclamation Line. Away from Tareq. She does not turn. She faces the east. The sky is lightening. The horizon gray purple. She watches until she can't see him anymore.

29
Ruby

The Cost

When Brother Q passes Ruby, heading toward Mary and her fallen father, the hair on Ruby's neck prickles and her stomach twists into a knot. Then there's something: she almost connects, almost binds. But it slips from her like a fading dream. Still, she knows Brother Q is in terrible danger. Her arm, now around HJ, sags, wanting to let go, wanting to run back, desperate to keep Brother Q from danger.

Three figures burst from the dark wall ahead. They yank goggles of some kind from their faces. Ruby recognizes Onas first. Her heart lifts. *Warriors.* Surely they will help Brother Q. The new arrivals run past her and HJ, calling toward Brother Q, Tyrell, and Mary, yelling a name she doesn't know: "Tareq."

As they pass, one, a short, wide man, yells at her, "Keep going!" and waves toward the marker.

HJ says something she doesn't hear. He tugs her toward Brother Q. But she shakes her head, suddenly back at the Kent Narrows dock. It's all happening again. But this time… this time, she'll get HJ to safety. She has to. For his sake. For the memory of his father.

The craft overhead still shines its small sun on the scene. Even the night sky seems to want to help, with dawn bleaching the east. Ahead she sees a marker. It looks old, formed of iron with darkened numbers stacked vertically and two letters below that. *PL.* The Proclamation Line. They're almost there. She tightens her grip around HJ, and they move as one.

Ten steps.

Five.

Two.

And they're across. Although it's impossible, the air, sharp and crisp in her nostrils, smells cleaner. The shrubs and small trees seem somehow greener, growing with more vigor. They make it a few more paces, her feet ablaze with broken blisters, tender wounds. She moves them past the border marker, into the line of small trees.

"Are we here? Did we make it?" HJ pants.

"Yeah… buddy… we made it."

"But… Brother Q… Mary… her pops." His voice is small, almost lost to the commotion behind them.

In the growing light, they see the small figure of Mary has broken free. She's moving past the officers from the West and toward Ruby and HJ. It's something at least.

Beside her, HJ cries, "Come on, Mary! You can do it!"

The Warriors have come to a halt. They're still many yards from Brother Q and the trap. Why aren't they helping him? Ruby's arms twitch. Her hand itches.

Mary reaches them, her sobs blurring with her gasps.

"Stay here," Ruby orders.

HJ tries to rise. "But Brother—"

"No, buddy, stay here. Do it for your dad. He would have wanted it."

Then she runs, freeing the knife Brother Q lent her from its makeshift sheath. It's not her old pig sticker; the weight feels wrong in her hand. She sends a prayer to whatever powers are out there. *Let me help make this right. Please, help me.*

She reaches the Warriors, the two men and the woman officer who took her satchelpack at the border. Onas seems healed. A small weight falls from Ruby's shoulders.

But why aren't they helping Brother Q? Why aren't they drawing their weapons? They only call for Brother Q using the strange name, their voices echoing with anguish and love and fear. They know him. They know him from before.

When the unfamiliar knife leaves Ruby's hand, she knows her throw is off. In the short second it takes to reach its target, she hopes, she prays, she begs for a miracle as with the wild sow. But it doesn't come.

And then it's too late.

"No. No," is all she can manage. Beside her the woman screams threats in a language that needs no translation. Onas cries something too. It sounds like, "We'll find you. I love you. I love you." And then the short, stocky man is pulling the other Warriors away. Away from Brother Q and toward the iron marker in the earth and the safety of the West.

30
Ruby

The Infirmary

Ruby won't remember much of the journey from the marker to the enclave's infirmary. The sight of Brother Q being arrested, of Tyrell lying there, somehow having betrayed them, plays over and over in her head, wiping away all but a faint awareness of the walk, of the trees growing ever taller as they progressed, of Mary, weeping quietly, her head bent forward, trudging at their heels. HJ trying to console her, but to no effect. Even without the binding, Ruby knows Mary's guilt and sadness, knows she'll bear it for the rest of her life. The girl's lost her father two ways.

The woman officer, Kaileh, Ruby hears her called, is rigid with anger and grief. The two men, Onas and the stout man who held the woman back, leave her be, focusing on helping Ruby and HJ navigate the last portion of their journey.

The officers say little during the march, other than tossing an occasional encouragement to the refugees. "We're almost there," and, "You can do it." There's also a brief conversation over a device Ruby has heard of but never seen, a keitai. The woman Kaileh speaks into it, her voice as sharp as a newly whetted blade. "We have them. We lost Tareq. Can you… No? But Commander… But…" She disconnects, her rage a white-hot color almost visible around her.

At some point they reach a wider path and are met by vehicles. They ride the rest of the way, jostling and bumping, too tired, too despondent, to rejoice.

They arrive at a sprawling complex of compact buildings. The sun is well above the horizon, though scattered clouds block part of the sky, Ruby stares at the blue of it. There's still a grey haze from the east, but it's so close to the blue of Sister O's ring. Oh Sister O, Ruby thinks, and stares back toward the sunrise. Back toward the Atlantic States. Denton. Bud Downs. Sisters O and M. And Brother Q. Tareq, the others call him. But still, she cannot believe she's here.

An older man, tall with silver streaks at his temples meets them. His face is shining, eager and happy and filled with a joy that, at the present, seems disproportionate. There's another person too, more middle-aged. It's a person she thinks is male, but there's something not-masculine about them. The others call them "Commander."

The man with the silver-streaked hair stares at Ruby with eyes so wet and glistening, it gives her a dizzy feeling. "Do I know you?" she says.

"Hello Ruby. We've waited so long to find you."

Ruby's tongue is tied by a rope of confusion and exhaustion. She wants to sleep. She never wants to sleep again. She wants Brother Q here. Here to explain. Here to celebrate.

Why? Why did Tyrell do what he did? They would have made it, all of them, if he hadn't gone down. She finds herself avoiding Mary.

They're taken to rooms. They're cared for by healers, some for their bodies and wounds, some for their souls and minds. Days pass. She visits HJ's room across the hall from hers. It looks out to a beautiful meadow with fluffy, brown-wooled sheep grazing. Sometimes the both of them sit and stare at the animals. Ruby thinks of Betsey and wonders if somewhere nearby there might also be goats.

A day after they arrive, while Ruby and he are watching the flock of sheep outside his window, wooly blobs in whites and beiges and grays, nibbling on grasses frost-tipped by the early-morning chill, HJ at last speaks of his father. "I miss him, Roobs. I miss him like someone chopped off my arm." Ruby holds her breath but reaches out and places a hand on the boy. "Brother Q, I mean Tareq," HJ continues, "he doesn't say—and I'm not fixin' to work it out of him—but I know one thing. He gave Pops some pills, there in the camp. I'm pretty sure those pills, they weren't just for pain."

Ruby shivers as if the chill morning air has just filled the room. She doesn't argue with the boy. Her own recent possession of a dark amber bottle still fresh in her mind. "I'm sorry, HJ. I'm so sorry."

There's a long pause. They watch as a big cream-colored dog, almost as fluffy and round as the sheep, works its way through the flock, seeming to inspect each one. The flock ranges in and out from beneath the tall stalks of what Ruby has been told is called a solar energy forest. Though the flat blades of the panels look nothing like trees, she sees now how the sheep use them for shelter and cover from the elements. Moments later, HJ speaks, his words tumbling out like spilled treasures from his long-ago mudlarking.

"At least he found out, you know. At least he got to learn that you got away and he knew I was going on with Brother Q. Tareq I mean. That'd make him happy, wouldn't it, Roobs?"

"I know it would. I know it did, buddy. It did."

The older man who met them on arrival visits her often. He tells her his name is Halek Tuskenugee. At first, she wonders if he's someone tasked with screening her. Maybe they'll find her unfit for asylum? Maybe they'll send her back. But soon, his visits turn to talk of Sister O and what happened that day in Denton. The pieces click into place as the figure of the man sitting beside her meshes with that of the man at the Kent Narrows dock. The man with the badge. The man who helped her get away. It seems so long ago, yet like a freshly opened wound. A sharp pain stabs her upon remembering the sight of the Sisters being loaded into the livestock lorry.

"Do you think they, your people, I mean the Warriors or whoever does that kind of thing, will find them?"

"I do," he says. "They found and freed me very quickly. If she had not just been moved, well, she might be here with us now. These things, though, are often, sadly, a matter of political nuances, of balancing knowing where they are with the safety of the monastics and other prisoners. I was fortunate. So fortunate." He pauses. Ruby feels a volume of words behind the few he now speaks: where would she be now if he hadn't told the West about the documents, about Brother Q, about her and HJ?

"Ruby, there's something I need to talk to you about."

She waits. They're sitting in an atrium overlooking a clear running river. Much of the area is open meadow, but swaths of trees paint the landscape. Some are bare of leaves, but many still cling to foliage so filled with color, it almost hurts her eyes. A large map hanging on one wall entrances her. It draws her to it, even when she has no one to converse with. Her location now, the long path leading from Denton to here, seem like impossibilities.

"There is no easy way for me to tell you this," Halek begins just as the atrium door opens.

"There you are, Ruby. Sorry to intrude," a medic says, walking in, her face shining with kindness and a glow of health Ruby's only just becoming accustomed to thinking of as "normal."

"Again," the medic says, "apologies for interrupting, but it's time for Ruby to say farewell to the micro-ID in her arm."

With all the other diagnostics, from bloodwork to scans to something called a DNA test, Ruby had almost forgotten about the artifact in her arm.

"Yes yes, by all means," Halek says as he stands. "I will see you again. Soon, Ruby." He looks at her with an intensity that's almost too bright, like she's staring at the sun. It's unsettling, but she has no time to ponder it, the little rice-sized mircroID in her arm suddenly itching like it's on fire.

"I'm ready," she says, and follows the medic out.

Onas visits too. They don't relive her first attempt at crossing the border, or speak of the loss of Brother Q—of Tareq. Instead, Onas tells her how he and Tareq met. How they fell in love. How they came to be part of the Path.

"Did he ever tell you how he ended up in Denton? Or maybe before that how he became involved with the monastics?" Onas's brown braid lies over his shoulder, its plait fuzzed as if he's neglected its care. Dark circles under his eyes highlight the tired lines across his forehead. She's never been in love. Whether from lack of opportunity or something else, she doesn't know. Now, looking at the pain it can cause, she wonders if it's a mistake anyway, this adding of more things to your life that can bring such loss.

They talk about Tareq for hours. Ruby tells him what little she knows: of the two women who rescued Tareq, of his head injury, of memory loss, of the Brethren, of the likelihood of them making the connections and helping Tareq make his way to Sister O and Sister M. She can see on his face a kind of confusion and disappointment, as if he, as if their relationship, perhaps, wasn't strong enough.

"Do you think," Ruby finally braves asking, "he's… he's safe?"

Onas's eyes fill with tears. Ruby bites her tongue, regrets her words.

"It is all right. You say nothing I have not obsessively discussed with myself." He wipes his nose on his sleeve. "I do not know. I want to say yes, that I can sense such a thing. But love, it changes your perceptions. I seem unable to tell the difference between my intuition and my hopes."

During one visit, he walks with her on one of the many paths on the grounds. Despite the growing cold, the healers say she should spend at least an hour a day being outside, drinking in the fresh air, the land, the seasons.

After a deep breath, she at last asks a question that's plagued her since that night of the border crossing. "Have you talked to Mary about what her father did?"

"Yes, and so have our people." Onas sighs, shakes his head. "She didn't know her father had made a deal with the Shepherds back at the internment camp. It's how the three of them escaped so easily. I'm not sure, she isn't either, how the Shepherds knew of Tareq and his presence there. Maybe Tyrell told them. We are likely to never know. But in the end, Tyrell allowed the Shepherds to put a tracker on him, being promised that if he helped them catch a smuggler in the act, he and his daughter would be allowed to go free."

"But they could have caught them much sooner. Why wait?"

"If you think about it, the closer they were to the border, the better the case against Tareq."

Ruby shivers, thinking of how all that time crossing the East, HJ and Tareq were being tracked. It was like Tareq was a golden prize, his value increasing the closer to the border they got. What will they do with him now? It's a question she has not the courage to ask.

As if Onas partly reads her mind, he says, "Some of us have theories as to why they did it and what it means for our two countries."

He rubs his hand across his tired eyes as if wiping away the contemplation of it all. "Mary begged me to believe her." Onas shakes his head. "Of course I do. There is no doubt the child had no knowledge of her father's duplicity."

There's a long pause. "I fear for him, Ruby. I fear for him. But I fear for Mary, too."

They walk in silence for some time. Ruby's nose drips from the cold. But her body thrums with energy. She thinks of Mary and the burden, right or wrong, she'll carry for the rest of her life. Ruby's own shoulders, stooped with her own choices and errors, feel as though they may never again straighten.

Kaileh comes to Ruby's room only once. On a morning after the first hard frost, when the blades of grass are tipped in white and a flock of emerald green birds, the staff has told her are called puzzi-la-nee parrots, has descended upon the lawns, their colors brilliant against the icy expanse. In only a few days, Ruby will be released from the infirmary. A future she has no idea how to start lies only hours ahead. When Kaileh walks in, Ruby notices there's something's different about the officer. It takes Ruby a moment to realize she's cut her hair. It's short and sleek and somehow suits her perfectly.

"I need to know," the tall straight-backed woman says, "about my brother."

By now, Ruby's told her story many times. To officials she doesn't know. To Halek. And of course, to Onas. She's sure Kaileh has read the reports the officials recorded of the facts. Ruby told it without omissions. But now she suspects Kaileh wants something more. Ruby tries to compose herself, to make her tongue work around this woman whose confidence and bearing make Ruby's pulse stutter.

"I… ummm… think he… he knew," Ruby says.

"What do you mean, *he knew*?" Kaileh interrupts as Ruby tries to find the best way to phrase what she hopes to convey.

"I think," she says, making her voice stronger than she feels, "somewhere inside him, he knew you were there, here, I mean." Ruby is sitting at a small desk in her room reading a book on cultural etiquette for citizens of the West. It's one of many books she's been tasked with studying: from the Border Wars to the long, violent history of the unification of the cultures; from a diet that "honors the body and the planet", to the basics of job rotation, described as every citizen taking a turn at even the most mundane of tasks. When she first read this, a part of her panicked; she couldn't work in a hatchery again, she just couldn't. But so far, she's seen no signs of anyone here eating chicken. In fact, the diet is mostly comprised of plants and nuts and beans and fruits, things so rare in the East, Ruby finds every meal a luxury.

"Explain," Kaileh says, her brows pinched.

"Well, there was just something. I couldn't read it exactly. But when he gave me the pendant, I think he knew. Maybe he even knew we'd meet." In her old life, such a statement would have been demeaned, laughed out of possibility. But here?

Kaileh's hand is at her throat. She runs her fingers down a black cord peeking from her neckline.

"Is that it?" Ruby asks.

"No, but it's almost a twin." Ruby waits for more. But the officer rises. Just as she's leaving, she tosses a small packet at Ruby. Then, as her door closes, Kaileh says something Ruby doesn't understand. "Maybe you're lucky to not know where your own brother is."

The odd statement tumbles around, making no sense. After a few minutes, Ruby looks down at the packet. At last, she unfolds the crisp paper wrapping. The pendant is there. Ruby turns it in her hands before slipping it over her head. Then she caresses the other object, the smooth, mahogany-colored section of wood from the beautiful table. How had she forgotten it? It's warm in her hands, the heat of Kaileh's body still held in the tight grain of the wood. Ruby already knows what she'll do with it, someday, but for now, it will remain like this.

There's something else in, or rather, that is a part of, the small bundle: a note written on the inside of the paper. It's scribbled, almost like an afterthought.

She reads the words. Are they even intended for Ruby? Did Kaileh mean to share them or was it happenstance?

She startles when Halek raps gently on the doorframe. "May I come in?"

"Of course." She's glad to see him, but something makes her tuck the note under the book she's been reading.

Halek doesn't move in the doorway. He clears his throat. "Um, I am not alone."

He steps to one side and a woman, younger than him, maybe in her late thirties, moves into view. She's petite, with long wavy hair the dark brown of tree bark after a rain. She's beautiful, this woman, but Ruby knows without any use of the binding that something haunts the woman.

"Hello," Ruby says.

The woman looks at Halek, then back at Ruby.

"Ruby, this is my daughter. This is Hahsi." The woman shifts back and forth as if trying to stop herself from fleeing. Yet her shoulders lean toward Ruby, the conflict of two battling energies is strong.

Halek says, "I wanted to tell you sooner, Ruby, but there has not been the right moment. And, I must confess, I have been rather timid."

Ruby frowns. What is he worried about? She stares at the woman. There's something about her. Something familiar.

"Ruby…" Halek clears his throat. "Ruby, I'd like you to meet your mother."

The Note

Later, alone and in a daze, Ruby slips Kaileh's note from under the book on her writing desk. She doesn't open it again, not yet. Outside, the day is coming to an end. Another day with a piebald sky of blue and white and rain-heavy gray. Another day in the West.

They're going to give Ruby time. Time to decide where she wants to live, who she wants to be. There's even an offer for her to go to school, to learn for the sake of learning, or to gain a skill, or knowledge, then share her expertise through work or research. It's too much, these myriad offers, this unlimited potential, an empty vessel, impossibly big to fill.

So for now, she just thinks.

A loss, small in comparison to that of Tareq and Harold Sr., torments her. The healers say her empathic abilities might or might not ever return. They tell her this with sadness in their voices, as if an essential part of her has died. But Ruby's not so sure she misses it. At least for now, it's a comfort to not feel.

But a new gift has replaced it, perhaps. A gift resurrected from the mist of dreams and hopes: a mother. Her mother. As much as she imagined it, the reality is surreal. It will take time. But that's something she now has. Her life now, she sees, is still filled with questions, more links in the chain. But now, it pulls her forward, an anchor and a guide.

Ruby caresses the soft surface of the paper. It's a message. A plan. A hope. Written in the messy hand that Ruby will come to know one day as the writing of her best friend.

I will get him back. I will find him. To this, I am bound.

Let's Connect

For discounts, news of new books, book club info, or just to connect, find me at the following:

 Subscribe to newsletter

 https://gianacliscaldwell.com

 gianaclis@gmail.com

 @gianaclis.bsky.social

 https://linktr.ee/gianaclis

If you liked *The Binding*, please consider **writing a review or rating** the book on the platform of your choice.
Thanks, i really helps!

About the Map

I've always loved maps. Maybe studying one makes me feel like I'm flying, viewing the land from above. In creating the map for Ruby and Kaileh's America, I turned to multiple sources. Historical maps showing the real Proclamation Line, a basic continental map showing rivers and mountain ranges, maps from Tribal Nations Maps, and the fantastic app Native Lands were my primary sources. If you don't have the app Native Lands, I highly recommend it. Wherever you travel, you can open the app and see who's land you are standing on. Although we cannot change the past, we can appreciate it. The phone app can be found in your phone's store. The web app is at: https://native-land.ca/

If you'd like print versions of native lands, you can find a free, downloadable map at: https://indigamerica.blogspot.com/p/downloads.html . Another source, although not free, (I've purchase several beautiful maps from this company) is Tribal Nations Maps: https://www.tribalnationsmaps.com .

Regarding my version, I used both colonial versions of Indigenous names and transliterations of the "real" names. This book is speculative and I had to try to imagine where some of the cultures might be at the time the book takes place. I did my best to honor history too. Please feel free to reach out with suggestions.

Understand this: at the time of colonization there are believed to have been between 900,000 to 18,000,000 native people living in North America speaking 300-500 different languages, and identifying with perhaps 1,000 cultures (or tribes as they are often still called.) Many were wiped out before direct contact with colonists—as diseases travelled rapidly ahead of colonization settlements. Anyway, the takeaway is that who knows how these cultures would have meshed and merged and even remerged had interference not been so extreme.

Please, let us all honor that truth.

Fact and Fiction List

Agiqua River. Fact: Cherokee name for the French Broad River in North Carolina.

Apserkahar. Fact: Takelma leader (died 1854) known by Whites as Chief Jo and other names. Had close ties to the Shastas and Athapaskans. Along with his brother, Toquahear, and his wife tried to navigate the growing incursions of colonists and gold seekers into Oregon's Rogue Valley. His children were kidnapped by Territorial Governor Joseph Land in 1853 and were used to force the signing of the Table Rock Treaty. (Which included the land the author was raised and now lives on.) A final battle in 1855 lead to the survivors forced removal far from their native lands. Fiction: That battle was won by Apserkahar.

Apserkahar Creek. Fiction: My name for what is known as Evans Creek, a 35-mile-long tributary to the Rogue River (Takel River in the book). Davis (Coyote) Evans established the first ferry near the mouth of Evans Creek in 1851.

Black Brethren. Fact. Early Mennonite community in Junaluska (part of the town of Boone), North Carolina settled in the 1800s by African American practitioners.

Chalagawtha. Fact: From the Shawnee people's name for their original settlement cha-la-gaw-tha, meaning principal town. Now called Chillicothe, Ohio. It was the birthplace of Tenskawata, a prophet and younger brother of the great Shawnee leader, Tecumseh. Chillicothe was also an important stop along the underground railroad. It is the location of a tremendous number of Hopewell and Adena earthworks that still survive today.

Chota (also EChota). Fact: Was a long established Native American (Cherokee) town south of present-day Knoxville, Tennessee. Site was flooded by the building of the contentious Tellico Dam in 1979. The dam also flooded other communities such as Toqua and Tanasi. In this same area, the great creator of the Cherokee syllabary, Sequoyah, was born.

Elohi Monastics. Fiction: I combined the Cherokee word for "earth" and Hebrew word for "divine" for this fictitious order of service.

Warrior Service. Fiction: Inspired by the Redstick warriors, a large group of traditionalist Creek (Muscogee) that supported the great leader Tecumseh's desire to keep their cultures intact.

Fort Pitt. Fact: British stronghold built between 1759 and 1761 to oppose the French and native forces during the "French and Indian War" also known in Europe as the "Seven Years War"

Gap Creek. Fact: Really Flaugherty creek in Somerset County, Pennsylvania

Giiwas, *jhee-u-wos*. Fact: native name for the mountain that formed Crater Lake, in southern Oregon. The often-heard name, Mount Mazama, is not native, but given by a white explorer in the 1800's who wanted to name it after his own group of explorers.

Great Gathering. Fictional name for The Newark Earthworks, most of which have been destroyed for development, but are still worth visiting!

Headwaters Island. Fictional name for Brunot Island, located just downriver from Pittsburgh, Pennsylvania

Headwaters Mound. Fictional name for McKees Rock Mound, the site, now a construction/industrial site, has been mostly destroyed and decimated. As of writing, the remains of at least 33 Hopewell and Adena ancestors are *somewhere* in storage under the control of the Carnegie Museum.

Jah'gowa. Fact: Onöndowa'ga (Seneca) name for what the Europeans called the Passenger Pigeon. Species went from numbering in the millions (the most abundant bird in North America) to extinct. The last one died in 1914 in captivity. Was an important and purposefully maintained food source for indigenous peoples, particularly in the Northern and Southern Woodland regions.

Junaluska. Fact: For place, see Black Brethren. Actual Cherokee leader (1775-1868). Initially supported the war efforts of Andrew Jackson, even saving his life in the War of 1812. Later in life regretted his part in assisting the whites.

Ki-He-Kah-Stah-Tsa, Elizabeth *kee-hay-kah-stah-tsa* . Fact: Osage family name of Elizabeth Marie (Maria) Tallchief, 1925-2013. She is considered by many to be the US's first prima ballerina for the newly founded New York City Ballet and George Balanchine.

Klamath. Fact: Indigenous people of Oregon and Northern California. Tribal group now includes other local peoples including the Modoc, and Yahooskin.

Klikitat, *klick-**ih**-tet*. Fact: Native culture of the Pacific Northwest. Some Klikitats were used by General Joseph Lane (Oregon's Territorial Governor) to fight the Takelma under Leader

Apsekahar. Fiction: In this story, the Takelma and Klikitat were allies.

Kudzu. Fact: Native to East Asia and brought to the US in 1878 and later used to stop soil erosion. Has multiple potential uses as animal feed and human food. Considered highly invasive.

Lappites. Fiction: A branch of anabaptists founded by Marvin Lapp that espoused defensive violence.

Lenape, *leh-nuh-pee*. Fact: Lenni Lenape. Native American people referred to as Delawares by the colonists. Completely displaced early during colonization. Fiction: City in the Northern Woodlands region, the United West, so named to honor the people who lost their homelands and lives to the colonists.

Little Yok-i-gay-nee. Fact: Really Casselman Creek, Somerset County, Pennsylvania

Marlburg Tobacco. Fact: Marlburg Brothers Tobacco Co. operated out of Baltimore Maryland in the late 1800s.

Mexica. Fact: Indigenous people of Mexico who ruled the Aztec Empire.

Mexico's borders on map. Fact: The land held by Mexico in this story was originally within the Republic of Mexico's borders.

Monongahela River.   Fact: Lenape for "falling-in-banks"

Nemisis Peak. Fiction: Really mount Steeprock, but there was a black man known as Nemisis who died in battle there, so I renamed it.

Neolin. Fact: A prophet of the Lenni Lenape (Delaware Indians) who was inspired by a vision in 1761 and preached returning to traditional values.

Nippon. Fact: Or Nihon, Japanese name for their country. The word "Japan" is based on Chinese pronunciations and came into use with European trade.

Noto. Fact: Japanese word for "note" also short for notebook. In this book, used instead of laptops and personal computers.

Nuevo Tenochtitlan, *tuh-nowch-teet-laan.* Fictional: Based on fact: The rebuilt canal city of Tenochtitlan, at its peak the largest city in the Americas, which was destroyed by the Spanish invader Cortes in the early 1500's in order to build the Spanish Capital of Mexico City.

Ohi-yo River, *oh-hee-yo.* Fact: Haudenosaunee (Iroquois), Ohi:yo', name, meaning Good River, for the Ohio River.

Pontiac, Chief . Fact: Odawa (Ottawa) leader (1714/20 – 1769) war leader who tried to unite the cultures against the British during the Seven Years war (also known as the French Indian war).

Proclamation Line. Fact: Created as described in book and in the Treaty of Paris. Fiction: Continues to exist as the border between the New England States (NES) and the United First Nations (UFN)

Puzzi-la-nee parrots. Fact: puzzi la née ("head of yellow") also known as *pot pot chee* by the Seminole and *kelinky* in Chickasaw. Known by the colonists as the Carolina parakeet or conure. Now an extinct species formally indigenous to North America. Last bird died in 1918 (almost the same year as the last passenger, jah'gowa, pigeon). Extinction due to human encroachment on habitat, hunting, and destruction by farmers due to crop losses.

Reo Cars. Fact: REO motor company was based in Lansing, Michigan and produced cars and trucks from 1905 to 1975. Founded by Ransom E. Olds (of Oldsmobile fame.) In this story, it was located instead in New York.

Royal Proclamation of 1763. Fact

Salish Sea, *say-lish*. Fact: Current name for the body of water most recently known in our world as the Puget Sound, Strait of Georgia, and the Strait of Juan de Fuca. Honors the native people of the vast area rather than European explorers.

Serpent Mound. Fact: Largest (at 1,348 ft/411m) existing effigy mound in the world. In Ohio. Built by the Adena (a European coined term) around 320 BCE. Repaired or augmented by the Fort Ancient (another non-native term) people around 1100 CE.

Shelter Rocks. Fact: Ancient shelters once located near the town of Myersdale, in Somerset County, Pennsylvania (where I placed the Enclave). They were destroyed for highway construction.

Takel, t*uh-kel.* Fact: Native American name for the Rogue River, located in southern Oregon.

Takelma. Fact: Native American people (also Dagelma) living in what is now called Oregon. The last of this culture was marched to a distant reservation during the winter of 1856.

Tanasi. Fact: Cherokee word that colonist translated to Tennessee

Tenskwatawa *tenz-kwu-·**ta**-wuh*. Fact: Also known as the Prophet or the Shawnee Prophet (1775-1836) A younger brother of the leader, Tecumseh. In the early 1800s he encouraged avoiding alcohol and traditional ways similar to the Prophet Neolin (see listing) in the previous century.

Tomochichi, *to-mo-**chee**-chee,* Fiction: Port and city where present day Savanah, Georgia exists. Real name of former Muskogee leader who founded a separate, British supporting, culture called the Yamacraw. Lived in the early/mid 1700's.

Trabajadoras. Fiction: Spanish for worker. My term for worker bee "drones".

Waccamaw, *waah-cuh-maw.* Fact: Native people living and farming in what became South Carolina. Fiction: A border outpost in the book, located where present-day Asheville, North Carolina is.

Werowocomoco, *wehro-woco-**mo**-co.* Fact: Village that served as the headquarters for Chief Powhatan and the Powhatan confederacy.

Yok-i-gay-nee river *yok-ə-**gay**-nee.* Fact: My phonetic spelling of the Youghiogheny River in Pennsylvania. Algonquin word translates "contrary river" for the fact that it flows north before joining the Ohio River and heading south.

Zhongguo. Fact: Mandarin word for China. In this book, China is a powerful ally of the United West.

Acknowledgments

When I started this book in 2018 (for the now mostly defunct, but trying to rise from the ashes, NaNoWriMo: National Novel Writing Month) I had no idea how many people would help bring me forward in craft and in confidence—and not just individuals, but uncounted online courses, websites, blogs, books, videos, and on and on.

From the beginning, I have been nervous about my "right" to tell a story that is, in great part, not my own—despite that being what writers, for the most part, do. Yet I absolutely couldn't live with NOT at least trying to bring this "world that could have been" to life. To that end, I researched as if for historical fiction; read and watched courses on the thoughtful, sensitive, respectful telling of other cultures stories; and reached out to a diverse set of readers (names also included below) including Matt Patterson-Muir, Stacey Parshall Jensen, Virginia Johnson, and Elizabeth Bryant. Thanks to this feedback, over the six years I wrote at least 15 versions of this book. Whether the one in your hands now is the best, who knows?

Now for the complete (I hope!) list:

Early readers: Tami Parr, Maud Powell, Rachael Shinn, Jonathan Koven, Matt Patterson-Muir, Jessca Posey, Stacey Parshall Jensen (Mandan, Hidatsa, and Black), Virginia Johnson (Lakota), and Susan Defreitas.

Midpoint readers: Blackstone Publishing, Danna Gibson, Amelia Caldwell (dear daughter),Tami Parr (again), Gabrielle Hahn, Meridith Leigh, Kirsten Shockey, Christopher Shockey, Sandra Phoenix, and Cara (Carol) Stevenson.

Later readers: Gabrielle Hahn (again, bless her), Patricia Florin, Joe Hall, Amy Collins, Allison Martine Hubbard, and Kenneth Zink (my amazing editor).

Other valuable insights: Julie Kingsley (Manuscript Academy), Amy McAnlis, the Talent Writers Group (including Dorothy Vogel, Patricia Florin, Francis Xavier McCarthy, Ellen Gardner, Sandra Phoenix, Deborah Rothschild, and Marilyn Joy).

A special thanks to Elizabeth Bryant of the Cow Creek Band of Indians, and a teacher of the all-but-lost language of the Takelma, for both reading the manuscript and providing a pronunciation guide to the Takelma words and phrases included in the book. Other assistance came from Noah Martin Shadlow, language teacher, Osage Nation.

I'm so lucky to have found the amazingly gifted and talented D'ella Rayne to perform/narrate the audio version of the book. As a big consumer of audiobooks myself, finding the right voice was critical. I also wanted a human that represented cultural and racial diversity, simply because it's important to me and the message of this novel. I hope you all enjoy D'ella's performance!

I also want to thank the large group of writers with whom I've found an online community. Whether through a private Discord group I started or Bluesky Social or my regional chapter of Willamette Writers, the support and comradery of such groups is irreplaceable. If you're just getting started on your writing journey, find your people!

When, after about 40 rejections and two years of trying, I got an agent in 2023 I was over the moon. But a year later, I made the decision to pull the plug. My mom, my biggest cheerleader, who broke my heart by leaving this plane in the summer of 2023, always said I was born feet first (I was breach) and running from the start. She also said I was a know-it-all! Being in the agent/client position put me in a frustratingly blind-spot. Taking on the indie approach, keeps my feet on the ground and moving forward.

About the Author

Gianaclis (gee-on-a-klees) is a multi-award-winning author raised in the wilds of Oregon believing trees were spirits and failing at picking string beans. She writes cheesy (no really) non-fiction on cheesemaking and goats, and hopeful speculative fiction. In her spare time, she guides other old ladies in plies, ronde jambes, and the occasional pirouette. She still talks to trees; sometimes, they answer.

www.ingramcontent.com/pod-product-compliance
Lightning Source LLC
Chambersburg PA
CBHW030514120726
47904CB00005B/1461